ABOUT THE AUTHOR

At home in Surrey, JULIET ASHTON writes all day in her small study while her two dogs stare at her. The rest of her house, which is full of music and books and comfy places to sit, she shares with her thirteen-year-old daughter and her husband, who's a composer (hence the music). She believes wholeheartedly in the power of books to improve lives, increase understanding and [illegible] happy hours.

Praise for Juliet Ash[illegible]

'Funny, original and wise' **K**[illegible]**de**

'Gloriously and irresistibly romantic . . . It's like *One Day* with all the additional trials and tribulations of female friendship' **Hannah Beckerman**

'Warm, witty and surprising' **Louise Candlish**

'This brilliantly written and captivating story instantly drew us in and refused to let go. Fresh, funny and utterly fabulous, it's the perfect holiday read' ***Heat***

'Cecelia Ahern fans will love this poignant yet witty romance' ***Sunday Mirror***

'You'll laugh and cry your way through this original and touching love story' ***Closer***

Also by Juliet Ashton

The Valentine's Card
These Days of Ours
The Woman at Number 24
The Sunday Lunch Club

THE FALL AND RISE OF SADIE McQUEEN

JULIET ASHTON

SIMON & SCHUSTER

London · New York · Sydney · Toronto · New Delhi

A CBS COMPANY

First published in Great Britain by Simon & Schuster UK Ltd, 2019
A CBS COMPANY

1 3 5 7 9 10 8 6 4 2

Simon & Schuster UK Ltd
1st Floor
222 Gray's Inn Road
London WC1X 8HB

Simon & Schuster Australia, Sydney
Simon & Schuster India, New Delhi

www.simonandschuster.co.uk
www.simonandschuster.com.au
www.simonandschuster.co.in

A CIP catalogue record for this book
is available from the British Library

Paperback ISBN: 978-1-4711-6840-6
eBook ISBN: 978-1-4711-6841-3

Typeset in Bembo by M Rules
Printed and bound by CPI Group (UK) Ltd, Croydon, CR0 4YY

This book is for Claire Conlon

THE FALL AND RISE OF SADIE McQUEEN

WEEK ONE

To	The Bobs <bob@bobscaff.co.uk>, Amber <amber@yummymummymews.net.co.uk>, Michael T. <qwertybookshop@hotmail.com>, Fiona J <filove@aol.com>
From	Sadie <sakuraspa@gmail.com>
Subject	CHERRY BLOSSOM MEWS RESIDENTS' ASSOCIATION MEETING

Hi guys!

It's my turn to host. I made a cake. Sort of.

Date	23.5.18
Time	6.30 p.m.
Location	Sakura reception
Agenda	*Those* new residents . . .

Somebody remind Mary (WHEN will she give in and buy a computer?)

Sadie xxxx

A Londoner to the ends of its wingtips, the sparrow took off from the balcony of a high-rise block of flats. It flew over the crumbling estate, over the roofs of a modest terrace, above a renovated Georgian gem and the blocky outline of a gym. It soared and swooped, its bird's eye view taking in the typical inner-city confusion. A church. A row of shops that offered cold pressed coffee at one end and the Colonel's fried chicken at the other. An office block. A playground.

And a mews.

The shape of a U, filled in with cobbles. A tree spilling out from its centre. The curved wrought-iron gates at the end supplied a vital buffer from the main road, and spelled out its name:

Cherry Blossom Mews.

The sparrow couldn't read. It didn't care what the mews was called. It had had a full dinner and now it had an urge. An urge it gave into as Sadie McQueen crossed the glass frontage of the wellness salon that straddled the end of the mews.

Sadie felt the soft splat on her hair. The sparrow was long

gone by the time she looked up into the cloudless sky and muttered a 'Thank you *very* much'.

A veteran of Cherry Blossom Mews residents' meetings, Sadie knew the order in which the others would arrive. Michael would be first.

Bang on time, there he was. Crumpled, wild of hair, but with a sweet expression behind his round glasses, Michael was more sardonic than his appearance suggested. Sadie liked him a lot; a standing joke in the mews was that Michael liked her rather more than a lot and would someday declare himself.

'Greetings.' This was a very Michael-ish way of saying 'hello'.

'Um, greetings.' Sadie heard a door slam across the cobbles. This was Mary, on her way from the charity shop with Noel, a Cairn terrier of small stature and great hairiness.

'Waste of time,' muttered the elderly lady as she ambled towards them. White curls, nylon dress, she made no attempt to defy old age. Perhaps Mary had always been about eighty. She tutted, as she always did, at the white modular seating that Sadie had splurged on during the refurbishment. 'Whoever designed these,' she said, 'had scant knowledge of the human bottom.'

Sadie had to agree. The chairs looked right, though, setting the tone for the space-age calm of the Sakura Spa's all-white reception area. She had gutted the old stable three years ago, tearing out the old and laying down the new.

Sadie knew the price of each doorknob, tap and tile. She remembered the old carriage doors being wrenched out. Moving halfway across the country to transform Sakura from mouldy cavern to chic salon had been a distraction that had saved her life. She knew how dramatic that sounded, but didn't care. Lives had been lost around Sadie, and for a while it had looked as if she might be next.

Amber teetered over the cobbles in wedges, her floaty boho dress a chic fog about her slender frame. 'Don't you all look *gorgeous*!' Amber scattered compliments like a combine harvester scatters fertiliser. She was a well of positivity, just like the unicorn bunting she sold in her Yummy Mummy Café and Party Emporium. 'Where's this cake, then?' She waved her phone about; it never left her hand.

Sadie pointed at a sponge beret panic-baked that morning.

'Might need a filter . . .' Amber took twenty shots of the sad little confection.

'Might need a miracle.' The Bobs were there, of Bob's Caff. He was small, round, in a once-white vest whose stains were a menu. She was tall, all angles like a fistful of knives. 'Can we get started?' she snapped. Snapping was her default setting. Possibly Mrs Bob had snapped, 'Yes, yes, I bloody *do*,' at the altar. 'What's *she* doing here?'

The 'she' was Fi, sole employee of Sakura, excellent

masseuse, and even better friend. 'You ask that every week, Mrs B. I'm here 'cos I'm here.'

'But you don't *live* here.' Mrs Bob reached out for a slice of cake, then thought better of it.

Mary heaved Noel onto her lap. His perfume overpowered the lavender oil scent of the spa. 'Can we get on?'

Sadie read out their names, made them all say 'present', and called the meeting to order. She ignored Mrs Bob's insistence that it wasn't a 'real meeting' and was glad of Michael's sympathetic raise of his eyebrows.

'First item of business . . .' Sadie referred to her clipboard. 'Yet again, a plea for somebody to take proper minutes of these meetings so we have a record of what's said.'

'Why?' Bob seemed puzzled. 'We never say anything important.'

Mrs Bob was forthright. 'Why don't *you* do the minutes, Sadie, if you're so keen on them?'

'Because I can only type with one finger, because I can't read my own handwriting, because it'd be nice if, for once, the rest of you showed an interest.' Sadie gave up. It was a tradition of sorts: every few weeks she called for somebody to do the minutes and every few weeks they all refused. 'Anyway, thanks, everybody, for putting the word out about the vacancy for a new receptionist.'

'I didn't,' said Mrs Bob. She nudged Bob. 'Did you?'

'Yes,' said Bob.

'Oh shut up, you berk, you didn't.'

When Bob laughed, his narrow shoulders lifted. He found his wife's rudeness hilarious. Even when – *especially* when – it was directed his way. 'She's terrible, isn't she?' he asked fondly.

She really is, thought Sadie. 'I'm interviewing tomorrow, so there'll soon be a new face on Cherry Blossom Mews.' She waved a sheaf of CVs.

'Hang on.' Eyeing them, Mrs Bob scowled. 'That top one . . . is the surname Mogg?'

'Yes. Like the cat in the children's books,' said Sadie.

'Like the crime family, you mean.' Fi snatched the page. For once she agreed with Mrs Bob. 'You never showed me this one. Cancel. Now.'

'Ooh, yes. We can't have a Mogg on the cobbles.' Bob was unusually grave.

They explained, while Fi doggedly ate the cake. Slice after over-cooked slice.

'The Moggs,' said Bob, 'are this neighbourhood's version of the Krays.'

Fi, spitting crumbs, agreed. 'They're identical twins, right down to their fondness for casual violence.'

Even Mary joined in. She was rarely moved to speak in meetings. 'I would proceed with caution, Sadie.'

'Drugs. Burglaries. Mugging.' For once Mrs Bob's scorn was appropriate. 'They live over in India Park Estate. At the top of Orissa House.' She nodded in the direction of the blocks looming over the mews. 'Everybody's terrified of them.'

'I get the message.' Sadie turned over the CV. 'Next on the agenda—'

'Stop pretending there's an agenda,' said Fi. 'You know these meetings are just an excuse to gossip.'

Michael, sitting back, enjoyed the show. 'Same every week,' he said.

Amber lifted her eyes from her phone. 'I'd like to say something.' She turned to Fi, who was chasing the last dry morsels of sponge around the plate with her fingers. 'I really admire you, you know?'

Fi cocked her head.

Sadie braced herself. Amber could be, well, *clumsy*.

'There you are, a large lady, and you're perfectly happy to eat in public. That's, like, so brave.'

Michael closed his eyes. Mrs Bob sat up a little straighter.

'I'm not large, love,' said Fi. 'I'm fat.'

She was. Fi was fat. She had love handles and a tummy and thighs that spread like a blanket when she sat down. She was also gorgeous. Perhaps because she was unashamed, even when magazines and media conspired to convince her otherwise.

'No, no!' Amber was outraged. 'You're *lovely*.'

'I didn't say I wasn't lovely.' Each of Fi's breasts weighed about the same as Amber. 'Eating in public isn't heroic. It's just eating. And if we don't eat, we keel over, so . . .' Fi rooted in her bag and found her emergency Mars Bar.

'Can we move on?' Mary's diction was old-school upper class, nothing like Fi's local glottal stops. 'We've ascertained that Fi is fat and the Moggs are gangsters. What's next?'

'The new residents,' said Sadie. 'They'll move in any minute. Thoughts?'

'I'm frightened,' said Amber, eyes wide like a fawn. Or a thirty-year-old trying to look like a fawn. 'I mean, alcoholics. That's not nice, not on our mews.'

'The online description is . . .' Sadie referred to her beloved clipboard. '"U-Turn: respectful, client-centred, community addiction services. We offer free confidential one-to-one therapy, comprehensive recovery service and relapse prevention. We are committed to improving the lives of vulnerable people."' She raised her head. 'Sounds rather lovely.'

'Lovely?' The mission statement didn't impress Mrs Bob. 'Pissheads watching me dish up my mixed grills?'

'Maybe,' suggested Fi, 'the pissheads will *buy* your food. You could offer a hangover special.'

'I'm with the lovely Mrs Bob,' said Amber, prettily earnest. 'I can't expect my yummy mummies and daddies to push through a gang of drunks.'

'U-Turn's not a pub,' said Sadie. 'It's a clinic. People won't be drunk, that's the point. They'll be sober.'

'We could write to the landlord, ask him to address our concerns.' Michael took the middle way, as ever.

'Yeah, right.' Mrs Bob was not at home to such liberal nonsense. 'When has he ever addressed our sodding concerns? I've been complaining about our roof for months. No response. I can't get up a ladder 'cos of me sinuses and you all know how useless my stupid husband is.'

Bob rolled his eyes. 'She loves me really.'

'Oh no I don't.'

'We have it pretty good,' said Sadie. 'The rents are in a time warp.' Fleeing her old life, Sadie had been astonished to find she could afford a bolthole in the middle of the big bad city.

Mary said, 'I for one never ask the landlord for help. I'm perfectly happy falling apart alongside the mews.'

Mary wasn't the sort to catch your eye, so Sadie didn't try. The two women were, despite their differences, kindred spirits: both were in hiding. No family ever came calling for Mary, either. 'I like the idea of the addiction centre,' said Sadie, accepting the sighs. 'It feels like giving something back.'

'Back to what?' asked Amber. 'If we didn't have those gates, we'd be burgled every night. This area's dangerous.'

'Not according to your Instagram,' said Fi.

@ambermagiclondon made the flyblown neighbourhood look like the riviera.

'The impact on a lifestyle business like mine,' said Amber, 'could be enormous. I don't want little tots finding syringes outside Yummy Mummy.'

'This U-Turn place,' said Mrs Bob, 'will attract the wrong sort. I won't serve them.'

'Me neither.' Amber stuck out her delicate chin. She was certainly Yummy, as per the title of her emporium, but Amber was not yet a Mummy. No sticky fingerprints on her velvets and silks.

Amused at the thought of diehard alcoholics wandering into Amber's café to browse the cupcakes and hundred-pound scarves, Sadie said, 'Vulnerable people need somewhere to go. U-Turn has to be *somewhere*, so why not here?'

Mary said, 'Well said,' and Sadie felt as if she'd been awarded a gold star.

As Amber suggested building clinics in the countryside 'so we don't have to look at them', Sadie touted the last slice of cake.

No takers. She almost told them that Jack was the only person who liked her baking, but she didn't. Jack didn't eat any more. Gates clanged shut across her mind, like the iron ones protecting them from Amber's imaginary criminals. The memory fired her up, and she said, a little more passionately than she meant to, 'If you'd lost your family to alcohol, you might think differently about U-Turn.'

Fi squeezed her arm in the silence that followed. Mrs Bob's antennae twitched; a nugget of gossip she had missed? Amber said, 'I didn't mean . . .' and tapered off.

With customary briskness, Mary wound matters up. 'We have no option but to accept U-Turn so I suggest we make the best of it.'

Sadie made sure her tone was lighter when she said, 'I bet the guy who runs it is an ex-addict himself. Probably a battered Keith Richards type.'

From the open glass doors came a voice.

'If I have to be one of the Stones, can't I be Jagger?'

They all turned.

A man sauntered into the room. 'I'm Hero,' he said.

'You're kidding,' said Fi.

'Nope. I really am Hero,' said Hero, clearly accustomed to her reaction. 'And no, I don't have a white horse tied up outside, and no, I don't know Bonnie Tyler. Hero's my name, not my nature. U-Turn's my baby, for want of a better term. Thought I'd come and introduce myself.' He paused. 'Put your minds at rest.'

An uncomfortable white chair was found. All the women sat up straighter – with the exception of Mary – and both men pulled in their tummies. Hero was tanned, rippling with health. The slow way he settled one foot on his other knee wasn't lost on Sadie. He was, she thought, like the sun. Shining on them. Bestowing goodness.

She pulled herself together and tuned into what this sun king was saying.

'... so the main doors will open onto the street. Only staff will use the door onto the mews. Inevitably, clients – that's what we call our people – will frequent the mews but we won't be doling out syringes or anything like that. We offer recovery services, so there'll be therapy and classes to help rebuild the lives they've shattered. We get really stuck in, so we advise on housing and employment, and, well, everything.'

'I think that's beautiful,' said Sadie. She felt Michael shift in his chair.

'Hmm,' said Mrs Bob. She wasn't about to let a handsome face overturn years of mistrust.

Amber leaned forward, her beads jangling. 'You're really giving something back, aren't you?'

Sadie and Fi shared a look. Later they would agree they'd heard a screech of tyres as Amber executed the swiftest turnabout in history.

'Meeting adjourned at ...' Sadie consulted her watch. It was mannish, with a large square face. Jack's watch, borrowed indefinitely. 'Seven fourteen p.m.' She knew they were laughing at her use of the word adjourned, but that was the proper word.

Hero helped Sadie slide shut the glass doors.

Amber, who usually melted away whenever there was a chore to be done, offered to help clear up. Fi saw her off with a loud, 'Nah, you're all right, love.'

'How did I do?' Up close, Hero was boyish yet weather-beaten. His eyes were a bright flat blue. Like china. 'I expected opposition. Nobody wants an addiction centre in their backyard.'

'I do.' This wasn't flirting; Sadie meant it. Besides, she never flirted.

Hero regarded her. She felt his gaze land and linger. She wished she'd thought to put on some make-up. She wished her hair wasn't cut like a medieval serf's. She wished she'd wiped her nose. 'Where do people go for a cup of something on a soft seat around here?'

It took a moment to realise what he was suggesting. 'You and me, you mean?'

'We're people, aren't we?' That amused look again. As if he'd heard a joke just out of her earshot.

And that's how she came to find herself sitting in a dark basement on a fine May evening, with a Hero.

Like Rapunzel with insufficient hair, Sadie stood at her bedroom window watching the activity around U-Turn. Men with tools. Hammering. Shouting. A removal van disgorging a spectacular brass bed. And Hero, emerging with dust on his shoulders. He looked up; he'd seen her.

Sadie stepped back into the shadows. Last night he'd asked, among the polite getting-to-know-you chit-chat, if there was 'a mister Sadie'.

She'd wanted to be honest so she'd said yes. 'But it's complicated.' She'd been grateful when Hero left it at that.

Avoiding the window, she righted the bedclothes and her mind strayed – no, *leapt* – to another bedroom. Larger, more lush and better appointed than this monk-ish cell. She'd lain beside Jack there, and then she'd lain alone, drenched in guilt, saying her sorries out loud to an empty house.

Like a deer running from a huntsman, Sadie dashed downstairs, past the bare spare room and the featureless sitting room, through the swing door into Sakura.

There she found life. Flowers on the marble reception desk. Radio playing. Fi faffing in the kitchenette which was out of bounds to customers and therefore somewhat less swish.

'There was something on the mat for you,' called Fi, swilling out white mugs and white plates and white trays; Sakura was a chic tundra.

A 'Qwerty Bookshop' bag sat by the computer. Sadie drew out a paperback with tattered corners. On its cover, a buck watched a ringleted lady in Regency dress stroll by. Sadie read its title aloud: '*Admired from Afar.*'

'Told you.' Fi was triumphant as she dried her hands and brought the virtual diary to life with a keystroke. 'That Michael's nuts about you.'

A remembered conversation. Sadie had run her finger along the colourful spines of a row of second-hand paperbacks. 'You have the complete set,' she had marvelled.

Michael was proud. 'Took me years to collect them all. Are you a Dorothy Ball fan?'

'More like an addict.' Some covers Sadie remembered from her teenage shelves. With over a hundred titles to her name, the deceased Ms Ball could be forgiven the formulaic plots, but the heroines were as dashing as the dandies who pursued them; always adventuresses, never simpering misses. 'I remember this one! It's the exact one I had when I was sixteen!'

Michael had said he would sell only to good homes, and Sadie had promised to hotfoot it back with her purse. She'd forgotten, yet here it was in her hands.

Sadie looked out and, as if by magic, there was Michael setting out his trestle tables. He looked sheepish as she raised the book and smiled her thanks.

'You've scared him,' laughed Fi. 'Right.' She squinted at the screen. 'First applicant is due round about . . . *now*.'

A knock on the glass. A sensibly dressed woman. They were off.

*

By the end of the day, Sadie knew a great deal about eight strangers' ambitions, weak points, special skills. She knew that interviewee number two was a people person, interviewee four was *too* punctual, and interviewee five was scary.

'I'd knock this place into shape!' said interviewee five, as if the tranquil reception area was in uproar.

Number seven had a phobia about cats. She left before Sadie had finished her first question because she could 'sense a cat'.

Fi showed her out, warning her to be on the lookout for pussies. She sat in on each interview, uninvited. Fi never waited for an invitation, a fact Sadie had reason to be grateful for. When she first hired Fi, the job description had covered massage and facials; it hadn't included propping up Sadie with unconditional approval and affection.

'Shit, it's the Mogg girl.' Fi's merry face became a grim mask. The young woman coming over the mews, slight as a child, was a tick list of trends: jet black hair extensions, stripper heels, ripped jeans.

Cher Mogg asked more questions than she answered, mainly about time off and holiday pay. 'Do I get a discount on treatments?'

'The successful applicant will enjoy lower rates,' said Sadie cautiously.

'Any experience?' asked Fi loudly, as she led a client through to Treatment Room 1.

Cher wrinkled her nose. 'Never had a job before.'

'But it says on your CV you work for the family firm.' Sadie flicked through her notes.

Fi's snort could be heard as the treatment room door closed.

'That's, you know, casual.'

'The family business is . . . ?'

'Breaking legs!' came through the door.

'Import and export,' said Cher with a face that dared Sadie to say any different. 'Do you own this place?'

'Yes.' All Cher's questions, even innocuous ones, felt like a slap in the face.

'So you're like a boss lady?'

'I *am* a boss lady. Well, a boss. The lady bit's incidental.'

'Respect,' said Cher.

'Thanks,' said Sadie. The girl – no, hang on, this was a woman in her early twenties – the *woman* was unexplored territory. She didn't give the usual responses. Manners? Irrelevant apparently. 'You haven't asked about salary.'

'The money doesn't matter.' Cher stood up. 'That it, then? Do you want to ask me one of them trick questions like what's my main fault and I say "oooh, I'm a perfectionist"?'

Sadie laughed. Interviewee number three had said exactly that. An empty nester with time on her hands and a solid background in the beauty industry, three was currently the front runner.

'I do have a question, actually,' said Cher. 'Sakura. What's it mean?'

'It's Japanese. It means cherry blossom.' Sadie gestured through the glass. 'After the tree.'

'That one?' Cher scowled. 'It's bare.'

'Back in April it was a riot.' The mews' cherry tree bore no fruit; it saved all its energy for the profusion of pinkish double flowers that burst like supernovas once a year. 'It's still lovely when it's bare. You just wait; in autumn the leaves turn orange like flames. The cherry tree's a symbol of spring. Renewal.' Sadie had named the salon with care. 'Tell me why you want the job.' She walked Cher the short distance to the doors, propped open to make the most of the late May sun.

'I don't want the job,' said Cher. 'I need it.' She pointed at the price list hanging by the desk. 'That should be on the door. In case a shy person can't make their mind up whether or not to come in, and worry they'll be embarrassed if it's too pricey. That's a customer you've lost.' Cher turned. No goodbyes for her. 'People can be right muppets.'

By Friday, U-Turn's sign was up. Hero was in several places at once, painting window frames, shouting instructions, carrying boxes, boxes, endless boxes.

Popping out to buy towels – Sakura's washing machine was a temperamental creature and had let them down yet again – Sadie stopped awkwardly to say good morning and ask how it was going. She wondered why he made her feel awkward; she'd met many a good-looking man in her life but there was something different about Hero: a vitality that buzzed off his warm skin. A promise of something.

While she was wondering she forgot to pay attention and he had to repeat himself. 'How's the mutiny going? Mrs Bob still gunning for me?'

''fraid so. I did point out that all these workmen are good for the bacon sarnie business, but she thinks you'll lower the tone of the mews.'

'Doesn't Bob's vest do that all on its own?'

Sadie laughed. Maybe a little too much. She coughed and ended the laugh abruptly. 'Well, anyway . . .' She backed away from Hero.

'Yes, anyway,' he echoed. Amused again. As if he knew the effect he had on her.

When she returned with a bale of white towels, Fi said, 'You took your time! I should be in with Mrs Lightfoot and her enlarged pores.'

'Sorry, sorry. I ran all the way down the high street.' Sadie dumped her towels and Fi snatched one.

Fi frowned. 'The high street? Why didn't you cut through the estate, past the church? Much quicker and—'

'I just didn't, Fi, okay?'

Fi looked at her. Really looked. Dialled down her attitude. Filled the kettle and said that Mrs Lightfoot's pores had been waiting forty years, they could wait a minute more. 'There.' She put Sadie's favourite mug in front of her. She didn't ask; she knew better. 'We need a receptionist, like, *now*,' she warned as she sashayed away.

Cherry Blossom Mews was good at Sundays.

The businesses were all closed, as befits the day of rest, but their cheerful fronts, each so different, detracted from the loneliness that Sundays can bring. Amber's pea-green painted window crammed with *How-much?!*-priced soft toys sat chummily beside the only vacant shop. Opposite them, Qwerty's books were piled in enticing columns alongside Bob's banner of those three little words: FULL ENGLISH BREAKFAST.

Traffic coughed hoarsely beyond the gates. The grand houses opposite, long since chopped into bedsits, oozed radio programmes and squeaking babies. Sadie, her arms full of flowers, dragged the gates open. The drawbridge was down; she stepped into the morning.

'Off somewhere?' Hero was there, wearing a tee spattered with paint. 'Time for a coffee first?'

'Coffee?' Sadie responded as if coffee was some exotic substance she'd once heard of. She shook herself. 'Sorry. I mean, no, not really.'

'Right.' He pursed his lips slightly. He'd wanted – expected? – her to say yes. 'Lunch with a friend?' He nodded at the flowers.

'He's more than a friend.'

Two and half hours later, Sadie pulled up alongside a high wall. Old and venerable, as befitted its purpose. Trees nodded over it, shedding a leaf or two on her faithful old Saab. It was, she thought, a long way to drive for a picnic.

First, there was a chore to do. *Get the rejections out of the way first*, she decided, dialling Cher's number.

'Hi, Cher? This is Sadie McQueen from Sakura. Just calling to say—'

'I didn't get the job. My name. S'okay.'

'Well, no, I – don't hang up!'

'What?'

'Can you start tomorrow?'

Cross-legged on grass, Sadie picked at her tuna sandwich. She hadn't put enough cucumber in it.

I should have let Bob do it.

She said, 'She screamed, this Cher girl. Thing is, I went with my gut. I can't give you one solid reason, except for the crushing disappointment in her voice. And that idea about moving the price list . . . She was right. I can polish her rough edges, I hope.'

Sadie laughed at her confidence, but she laughed alone. Standing up, her knees clicked like a firing squad. From a large bag she took out a cloth, some polish and a stack of wet wipes.

'Soon get you nice and smart.' Sadie took pains to polish the granite headstone, tracing around the etched writing. JACK MCQUEEN, it said, beside that pitifully short timespan: 11TH DECEMBER 1976–4TH OCTOBER 2015

Around the edge of his grave, Sadie had planted low-growing alyssum. The mass of small white flowers, so modest but so happy, seemed right for this cemetery by the sea. She'd learned that high growing blooms were chopped down by the wind.

I know how they feel.

Memories queued, as they always did. Sometimes, if the East Anglian sky glowered, the memories were oppressive. Today, in the promising weather, they felt gently nostalgic.

Jack.

Jack telling her she looked gorgeous when she stepped out of the shower, grabbing her wet body, kissing her and getting his shirt damp.

Jack telling her she looked gorgeous when she came in out of the rain with a Sainsbury's bag in each hand, her nose radioactive red.

Jack telling her she looked gorgeous when she lost seven pounds. When she put on seven pounds.

Sadie stroked the headstone. 'You thought all your geese were swans.' It was hard living without Jack's berserk bias. She recalled his arms, the weight of them around her. It was challenging, still, to accept that Jack McQueen, solver of crosswords, drinker of beer, teller of jokes, was silent beneath her feet. He'd built boats with his bare hands, designed ocean-going yachts that traversed the globe; how could all that be snuffed out?

'Talking of gut feelings, I have something to confess, darling. Well, not confess. Something to *tell* you. Or maybe confess. You decide.' Sadie knelt. Put her cheek to the stone. It was warm from the sun. 'Desire, Jack. I thought it died with you. Turns out it didn't. What do I do with it? He's not you. Nobody's you.'

Jack didn't answer. Sadie searched for his voice in the rustling of leaves, or the pulsing of her own blood. Sometimes she found it. Sometimes she heard him. But not today.

WEEK TWO

To The Bobs <bob@bobscaff.co.uk>, Michael T. <qwertybookshop@hotmail.com>, Sadie <sakuraspa@gmail.com, Hero <hero.smith@u-turn.net>, Fiona J <filove@aol.com>

From Amber <amber@yummymummymews.net.co.uk>

Subject CHERRY BLOSSOM MEWS RESIDENTS' ASSOCIATION MEETING

Hello!!!!!

Can't wait to see your lovely faces. There'll be cronuts and speciality teas and superfood salad – all locally sourced OF COURSE!!!!!

Date 30.5.18
Time 6.30 p.m.
Location Yummy Mummy café & party emporium
Agenda Summertime loveliness!

(Please tell Mary)

Amber xxxxx

A morning routine of pulling a flannel over your face and aiming antiperspirant at your armpits is quickly achieved.

Sadie tugged on her crisp white uniform. Time was of the essence; she felt the salon calling her, and the small bare rooms above it offered nothing to make her stay. Tucking her hair behind her ears, she peeked around the door of the box room.

I should get rid of that bed.

A child's bed in a house with no child was a joke without a punchline.

Down. Out. Across the cobbles. Around the tree. Towards the charity shop. Sadie had an urge to check up on Mary.

That's not how I'll describe my mission to her face, unless I want to feel her wrath.

She passed Yummy Mummy, which wouldn't open for another three hours or so; Amber wasn't a morning person. She hoped there was no children's party planned for that day. It was ironic that Amber fretted about U-Turn's clients being noisy and disruptive, when her own short-arse clients were exactly that.

The flat above the MOBuk charity shop was only marginally less cluttered than the ground floor. Mary was dwarfed by hoarded furniture and books and art and whatnots. Noel greeted Sadie with a gruff noise before trotting off to widdle on an antique something or other.

'You left your front door open.' Sadie cleared a space at a mahogany table invisible beneath 1950s copies of *Vanity Fair*. 'Again.'

Mary was impervious to nagging, even if – especially if – it was for her own benefit. She'd warned Sadie early on in their friendship that she was allergic to do-gooders. 'Have you come to scold or have a croissant?'

'Both.' Sadie gave half the croissant to Noel, who was an experienced and skilful beggar.

'Stop that. He's too fat as it is.'

'How many Noels have you had?' Sadie knew the hairy little chancer was the latest in a long line. Always small, always greedy, always called Noel.

'He's Noel the sixth.'

'Has a ring to it. Like Henry the eighth.' Sadie noticed a rectangle of wallpaper lighter than the rest of the room. 'Wasn't there a big oil painting there?'

'So nosy,' muttered Mary.

'There was, though. It had a deer in it.'

'Hmm?' When Mary wanted to, she amped up the old-dearness.

It was clear that Mary got by financially by selling off heirlooms. She wore it lightly but her family were a noble clan. A family crest that used to hang over the loo before it, too, was hocked, had sported a motto: *Absque labore nihil.* 'Don't sell Noel, will you?' she said as she left.

Jogging back over the cobbles, sensing rather than seeing Michael rearranging Qwerty's windows, Sadie stopped to fish her buzzing phone out of her tunic pocket.

'Hi, Fi.'

A gassy hissing seeped from her phone. Then a honk. A rustle.

'Fi!' she yelled. 'You're pocket-dialling me again!'

Hero materialised, gritty-eyed like a cat that's been prodded awake. 'Does she do that often?'

'Yup.' Sadie switched off her phone.

'I'm off to Bob's for something caffeine-y. Maybe a sausage will be involved.'

There was an invitation in his remark. Sadie hesitated.

Jack, is this okay?

'Look, I'm not suggesting a hot date. Just a cup of Bob's surprisingly good coffee.'

'Sounds good.'

They both tried to go through the door at the same time. They were out of kilter. They both felt it. For Sadie's part, it didn't feel clumsy, it felt intriguing.

I make him nervous.

A surge of power, a feeling almost forgotten, rushed through her beneath the crackling white cotton.

Hero was barely inside before Mrs Bob looked up from a couple she was telling off to tell *him* off.

'Oi! You! Posh pisshead fella! I've got me eye on you, matey. One wrong move and you're barred for life!'

'Be nice, love!' called Bob through a hatch, happily grilling economy meats.

Sadie wiped the table with a tissue. Partly to annoy Mrs Bob and partly because it needed a wipe. The caff – definitely not a *café* with its effete accent – was traditional right down to its grubbiness, but somehow the terrible ingredients achieved perfection in Bob's genius, if unwashed, hands. His bacon sandwich could turn a vegetarian at ten paces. 'Mrs Bob loves barring people for life.'

'Does life mean life?'

'It means until she forgets she's barred you. Usually about a fortnight.'

Scanning the menu, Hero said, 'This place was the clincher for me when I was property hunting. Everybody mingles in a proper caff. That Yummy Mummy place is full of, well, yummy mummies.'

'The ridiculously low rent can't have hurt.'

'That too,' conceded Hero.

A roar went up in the kitchen. 'Ketchup, not brown

sauce!' Mrs Bob threw a tea towel at her husband. 'I could have married a millionaire, and here I am with you in this dump! My mother was right about you.'

'And my mother was right about *you*.' Bob dodged the towel with practised ease. 'She told me I should hang onto you and I did.'

Hero, entertained by the marital circus, looked at Sadie and his expression changed. 'What?' His brows met.

'You asked about a mister Sadie.' Time to come clean. 'I do have a husband, but he's dead.' She was aware how daft that sounded, and decided to use the proper term, one she hated. 'I'm a widow, Hero.'

One day she might get used to using his unusual name. *Not yet though.*

He was quiet. He looked at her. Looked *into* her, was how she recalled it later. Sadie was grateful for his reaction. She was bad at telling people about Jack; three years practice and she still couldn't quite believe it herself. People said she looked too young to be a widow, or put their head on one side, or went red, or said nothing.

Hero took his time to speak. 'That's hard, Sadie. How are things, now?'

His empathy infused the simple words. 'Up and down. Still!' She managed to laugh.

'How did he die? Sudden, or was it expected?'

She almost blurted out, *'I did it.'* Sadie shut her eyes,

only to find Jack's last words to her printed on the backs of her eyelids.

Love, watch out!

When she said nothing, Hero didn't press her. 'We all lose people we love, but that doesn't make it any easier. It's normal and devastating.'

'An ordinary heartbreak.'

Hero seemed to like that. The sides of his mouth lifted. Sadly. 'Exactly.'

They were having a moment.

She hardly knew him and she rarely talked about this subject – the last conversation had been with Fi years ago and involved much hugging and crying and being called 'babes' – yet here they were, having a moment.

Maybe I can tell this man the whole story.

She couldn't. That was the Everest of emotional truth; Sadie was ill-equipped to climb just yet. Instead, she said, 'We're getting a bit deep for this time of day. Fancy a bite later?' Jack had encouraged her to be impulsive; this haircut was his fault. 'I could show you the swanky new place over by . . .' She stopped. The surprise was there, beneath the politeness. 'Sorry. Forget it. You've got loads to do. Where *is* that sandwich?' She glanced at Bob's combover for comfort.

'I'd love to. After the residents' meeting?' Hero tapped her forearm, brought her back to him. The hairs on her arm lifted slightly. As if danger was near.

She was practising what Jack preached. Going with the flow. Saying 'yes' after three years of saying 'no'.

As they parted out on the cobbles that had twisted many an ankle, she said, 'Will U-Turn change Cherry Blossom Mews, Hero?'

He considered his answer. 'For the better, I hope. If you're worried about it making the mews ugly . . .' He raised a hand as she opened her mouth to protest. 'Sorry. Poor choice of word. I don't mean ugly in the literal sense. It's not your pots of geraniums I'm talking about. It's the feel of the place.'

'Yes.' Oh, it felt good to be understood.

'I'll do my best to make sure we're part of the landscape, not dominating it. My clients are just people, like you and me.'

More like me than you.

As Sadie turned away, she was a carbonated bottle of secrets. A breeze, warm with early summer sensuality but with the ever-present urban base note of bins, slithered by. Change was coming. There was potential for hurt in that change.

Isn't there always?

Sadie had wrapped the mews about her to protect her from that cheeky, treacherous wind. So many years she had lived with Jack, her sister, Tish nearby, believing herself secure. Now the residents were the nearest thing she had to a family. A typical one, insofar as they didn't all get on but had no option but to rub along together. Sadie appreciated them and forgave them, and she knew first-hand how fragile a family's eco-system can be. Sadie didn't have to catastrophise; she'd been through what many people would consider to be the worst of times.

The mews was a coat. A little tight at times, not the style she'd choose and not at all trendy, but it was comforting to pull up the collar and snuggle down into it when the nights bit.

Through the gates nosed a sports car, low and sleek. Fi got out of it, after kissing the driver and beeping the horn. A plate smashed in Bob's Caff.

'Isn't he fabulous?' Fi's question was rhetorical as the car backed out into what Sadie thought of as the real world. 'Ten out of ten boyfriend behaviour.' She took Sadie's arm, the bulk of her solid and warming. 'He goes, "No babes, can't have my princess walking to work," and gives me a lift in the shagmobile.'

'It's actually a Mazda MX5, but we'll let that pass.' Sadie opened up Sakura. Felt Fi fill it with life and potential and cheer simply by being there. 'He's a step up from He Who Cannot Be Named.'

'Tell me about it.' Fi pulled on a white tunic whose buttons strained at the job expected of them. 'Cheating. Lying. Stealing.' She paused, nostalgic for her infamous ex, Emanuel. 'Handsome, though.'

'Cole's handsome!' Sadie didn't mean this; Cole was a bit too nicely put together for her liking. He was Fi's attempt at respectability, after a romantic history that doubled as a police line-up. She liked, she claimed, a bad boy; Sadie had asked, 'But do they have to be *that* bad?'

So far the attempt at respectability was going well. Fi was amazed by any display of boyfriend/girlfriend behaviour, like a starving woman confronted with a buffet.

'You pocket-dialled me again by the way.'

'Soz. Cher's late.' Fi lifted her eyebrows.

'Not quite.' As the clock's hand juddered to the half hour, a blinged-up jeep tore into the mews, startling Noel VI as he contemplated his morning toilette.

'She's trouble, Sadie.' Fi was dark as she refilled lotion bottles from a pump. 'When the time comes, I'll shout "I told you so" from the roof of Sakura.'

Sadie endured this comment, as she had endured dozens of others. Fi was a battering ram. She also had a point. Cher was rude. She was just about punctual, yet she left on the dot. Outside, she was mincing in her stilt heels to open the passenger door of a car that was, surely, way beyond her pay grade.

Her passenger came in with her.

'This is me nan.'

Nan's wrinkles were beyond the help of the spa's various treatments. Her dentures clacked when she said hello. She looked at Cher as if her granddaughter was the sun; Sadie liked her for that.

'She's your first client of the day.' Cher led the lady to Treatment Room 2. 'I booked her in for a massage. Her feet hurt, so you could concentrate on them a bit.'

'Reminds me of training,' said Sadie. 'We never get older people in here.'

''xactly.' Cher closed the door on her grandmother. 'I hear you pow-wowing about expanding your client base and all that bollocks, but you're not tapping into the old girls. They've lived round here forever, long before these middle-class types came in and started gentri-bleedin'-fying all the damp old houses. The oldies deserve a bit of pampering, and their money's as good as anyone's.'

'Of course,' said Sadie, who didn't like the prejudice Cher was sort of implying.

'You should offer an OAP discount on Thursday mornings. That's our slump time, innit?'

'Good idea.' Sadie had the sensation she was sleepwalking. Cher was so certain of herself.

Never a sleepwalker, Fi said, 'Fancy tackling world hunger while you're at it, Ms Mogg?'

Ignoring her, Cher tweaked her extensions. 'Me nan's a freebie, though. You'll get your money back when she tells all her bingo buddies.'

*

Once in a while Sadie liked to walk Mary, like a pet, to stop the old lady becoming a hermit.

'Can we turn back now?' Mary was stoic for the first fifteen minutes, before she began to behave much like her little dog. Constantly turning her head, huffing, pining for Cherry Blossom Mews.

'Sure.' Sadie enjoyed walking with Mary. The enforced slow pace. The noticing of things. 'Not down there,' she said, a little sharply as Mary turned a corner.

'It's the quickest way. Do shush and come on.' Mary ploughed ahead, Noel straining at his lead.

'But . . .' Sadie's feet slowed. She never took this route.

She glanced at her watch. Jack's watch. They might just get away with it. Surreptitiously, she sped up, but Mary's octogenarian feet in their wider fit sandals didn't match her stride.

Not only did they not get away with it, but the timing was the worst it could have been. As they passed, the wide wooden gates set in a new brick wall slid open and released a torrent of schoolchildren.

It was a girls' school. Mary laughed as they were surrounded on all sides, Noel getting stroked as he had never been stroked before. Sadie clung onto her arm; for once it wasn't for Mary's benefit.

It was too much. She could barely breathe. The loveliness of them all. The quirkiness. Schoolgirls *en masse*, a joyous clump of energy and falling down socks and hair.

So much hair. The waves, the cowlicks, the shimmering colours in each plait. There were chums. Loners. Best mates. A gang bent over a phone.

They smelled of perfume from Boots, of talc, of crisps. A gentle undertow of body odour. And in the middle of it, her heat-seeking brain found a girl just like her own long-gone girl. A face with a pointed little chin, disgruntled expression exploding into laughter. But the height was wrong. And the body language was wrong.

It was just another kid.

One look told Fi. 'You all right, babes?' She left her client with a brochure and moved nearer. Her voice was low and intimate. 'Where've you been?'

'Is she crying?' called Cher from the reception desk like a foghorn. Amber, sitting awaiting a pedicure, looked up from her iPad. Interested.

'OhmyGod!' Cher pronounced this as one word. 'What's going on?'

'Nothing.' Fi's teeth bit the word. 'Get the kettle on, Cher, and before you say it, tea making *is* in your job description.' Turning a professional face to Amber she cooed, 'Be with you in one minute,' and led Sadie like a child into the stock-room where she could cry the way she needed to with Fi's warm arms wrapped around her.

A crack is a crack, no matter how cautiously you handle the china after it's been repaired.

A Nan anecdote broke the ice.

Post-residents' meeting, Sadie sat opposite Hero at a copper table barely larger than a dinner plate. His elbows were on its surface. His face was near. Tonight his hair was flattened. Hero was tired.

But he's happy.

Hero was happy by nature, but he was specifically happy to be there, that close to Sadie. Which made Sadie happy.

Happiness is as infectious as the Black Death, and much easier to clear up after.

'So we found her dentures and sent her on her way,' said Sadie, wondering why she was telling a dentures-related story to such a man.

'How's Cher working out?'

'I'm not entirely sure.' Sadie's fringe fell in her eye. Her hair was unwashed, and her dress, a stripey thing that had been insouciant once but was now too old to be anything other than knackered, rode up her thigh. She hadn't shaved her legs.

I am a walking talking example of how not to impress a man.

'Do you regret employing her?'

'Not yet,' laughed Sadie. 'She's rude, like *really* rude. The insults fall like rain. She's nosy. She swears if she's asked to wash a mug. But all the clients turn up on time and the appointment book's full. Seems like Nan spread the word at bingo. I had three pensioners today.' Sadie remembered them. Their tortoise movements. Their appreciation. 'They aren't touched very often.'

We have that in common.

Hero's knuckles had grazed Sadie's arm as they squeezed into the dark alcove, and her skin had erupted. The walls closed in around them; a cool spot in the heatwave.

'Did I miss anything?' Hero had been twenty minutes late for the residents' meeting. 'A group therapy session ran over, then I couldn't get my little sis off the phone.' He frowned. 'I should stop calling her that. Effie's a grown-ass woman, but she relies on me, you know? Especially since she lost her boyfriend.' He heard himself, and looked hastily at Sadie. 'He died. She's finding it hard.'

'It *is* hard,' she said. 'Were they serious?'

'She loved him.'

'Can't get more serious than that.' Sadie coughed, changed the tone. 'You missed nothing, although tonight's meeting was productive by our standards. Nobody actually fell asleep. Bob once dozed off while Michael was talking about a communal watering system for the flowerpots.'

'Amber took being chairperson very seriously.'

There had been an array of wholesome food. Cushions of many colours scattered on artfully distressed wooden chairs.

They drank their tea from Moroccan glasses and chimes tinkled above their heads. 'Amber's an influencer, you know. On Instagram. She tinkers with Yummy Mummy all the time, making sure it stays current.'

'Exhausting,' said Hero. 'I'm glad she's pro U-Turn, though.'

Sadie smiled at his naivety. Amber was pro *Hero*; he hadn't noticed the whimper of irritation when Amber had realised that Hero and Sadie were heading off somewhere together after the meeting.

'Mrs Bob, however,' said Hero, 'will never be a fan.' He rubbed his jaw, as if Mrs Bob had physically punched him.

'Did you see how Michael shut her up?' Sadie had almost high-fived her admirer. 'When she was going on about drug addicts roaming the mews, and he reminded her of when our window boxes were all nicked and she insisted it was kids from the India Park estate. Turned out to be one of Amber's Boden-wearing customers.'

'Michael's a good egg. We're putting together a library for U-Turn. You know, positive thinking books. He's pulling out all the stops to set it up before we open next Wednesday.'

The conversation roamed from favourite smell to respective opinions of the prime minister. Then he asked, 'How long have you been on your own?'

'Three years.' Sadie sat back, suffering emotional whiplash from the abrupt change of direction. 'We were married for fifteen. His death was an accident,' she said, without waiting for him to ask. 'One of those treacherous bendy country roads.' She made her arm into a snake to illustrate. 'Jack . . . There was . . .' Her mouth dried up.

'It's okay, we don't have to.'

But I want to.

'There was booze involved. So, you see, I was *always* going to be sympathetic to U-Turn.'

'Shit. I'm sorry.' Hero kept his eyes on her. As if Sadie was walking a tightrope and he was guiding her to him. 'Come on.' He stood up. Threw down his napkin. 'Home.'

The gates were closed. As Hero pushed them open, their joints creaking, Sadie felt that breeze again, saturated with diesel fumes this time.

'My sister,' began Hero, as the gates groaned shut behind them. 'She lost her boyfriend in a car crash, too. Effie holds herself apart. It's hard to watch.' Hero put his hands in his pockets, rocked on his heels. 'I didn't mean to dredge up your pain, Sadie. Next time tell me to shut up.'

'I liked you asking.' Sadie was glad of the few feet of clear space between them.

I want to kiss him.

If Sadie kissed him, she'd feel guilty. The lack of logic made no difference. She was weary of guilt; it's thin gruel for a woman to live on.

Indoors, alone, Sadie did something she rarely did.

She went into the tiny room across the small landing from her own chamber. She lay on the narrow bed. It was always neat, that bed, never ruffled. Sadie permitted herself to *feel*, instead of stoppering up her grief in case it flooded her house, the mews, London.

A framed photo sat on the bedside table. A girl, four years old, looked out at her. The big knot of a school tie sat under the pointed chin. Only Sadie or Jack would have recognised the slight anxiety in the wide-open eyes. The child was smiling, saying 'cheese', but Sadie knew her daughter was ever so slightly nervous and desperate not to show it.

She knew her. Really knew her.

'I told him about Dad, darling. But I couldn't tell him about you, Teddy. I just couldn't.'

WEEK THREE

To The Bobs <bob@bobscaff.co.uk>, Amber <amber@yummymummymews.net.co.uk>, Sadie <sakuraspa@gmail.com>, Hero <hero.smith@u-turn.net>,Fiona J <filove@aol.com>

From Michael T. <qwertybookshop@hotmail.com>

Subject CHERRY BLOSSOM MEWS RESIDENTS' ASSOCIATION MEETING

Dear All

I will provide basic nibbles.

Date 6.6.18
Time 6.30 p.m.
Location Qwerty Books
Agenda The tree

I have informed Mary. She and Noel will attend.

With all best wishes

Michael

'I'm only saying, you can't vote on the bins because you're not a resident, Fifi. You have no right to be here.'

'I've known you for three years and you still haven't learned my name. If I've no right to be here, Mrs Bob, how come I'm on the email list?'

A suggestion that residents should club together to buy a storage shed had deteriorated into a 'Fi vs. Mrs Bob' catfight. Michael was pulled into it, and he shrank in his chair as Mrs Bob turned on him.

'Traitor,' she spat.

'Fi's part of the furniture,' offered Michael by way of an excuse.

'Thank you, I think,' said Fi. 'By the way, Michael, these nibbles are beyond basic if you don't mind my saying so.'

'And if he did mind?' asked Sadie. 'Would that stop you?'

'He can take it.' Fi leaned over and chucked Michael's cheek. 'I used to come in here long before I worked in Sakura.'

'One of my best customers. Well, that's to say she didn't buy much but she liked sitting here out of the rain.'

It was that sort of place, Qwerty Books. Nothing modern.

Everything cared for. Wooden shelves. Leather seats. Low lights that showed the ageing spines off to their best advantage. Qwerty smelled slightly of mould, but that added to rather than detracted from its charm.

Sadie had chosen to sit beside the shelves dedicated to Dorothy Ball. Michael had noticed, she knew.

'Whenever Fi left the shop,' said Michael, 'I used to find pages with the rude bits turned down.'

Amber snorted with laughter. In good form, she had already posted a picture on @ambermagiclondon of Mary pretending to read *Fifty Shades of Grey*. 'Forty-eight likes, Mary!'

'From forty-eight people I will never meet,' said Mary. 'Thank heavens.'

The street door opened with a bang, setting off the trembling bell above it.

'Sorry, sorry, I'm late, sorry.' Hero's eyes flashed with excitement. 'But you'll forgive me because I brought *these*!' From behind his back he produced two huge bottles of champagne.

'Ooh!' Amber jumped up and clapped. Actually clapped. Sadie somehow found the strength not to lock eyes with Fi.

'That's more like it.' Mrs Bob nudged her husband. 'See? That's what a real man does.'

The popping of a cork always gets a party started. Mary held out a paper cup and poured some into a saucer for Noel.

'This is a thank you.' Hero did the rounds with the foaming bottle. 'For putting up with the building works, and the noise and the aggro. It's a bit inappropriate for an addiction counsellor to bring champagne, but . . .' He stepped back, spilling a drop or two as Sadie put her hand over her beaker.

'None for me. Gives me a headache.'

Amber said, 'Don't be a party pooper! One drop won't hurt! It's *fizz*, Sadie!'

'She knows what it is,' said Fi. 'I'll have her share,' she whispered to Hero with a wink that had felled many a lesser man. As the others whooped and giggled, she leaned into Sadie. 'What's the latest on you and him, eh? It *is* going somewhere, right? You and Mr Posh Bollocks?'

'Such poetry.' Sadie tried not to answer but the laser stare was impossible to ignore. 'Dunno. We only spend time together after residents' meetings. It's a new tradition.' Sadie's life was short on tradition, unless you counted bin day and she'd rather not. Since Sadie had told him about Jack, Hero had been warm but wary; the widow word does not bring all the boys to the yard. Pleasantries were all they exchanged. Sadie shuddered at that least erotic of words: *pleasantries*. She wanted to tear off Hero's shirt. Nuzzle his neck. 'It's as if he's waiting to be activated.'

'So *you're* in the driving seat?' Fi threw downed her drink in one. 'We're doomed! Doomed!'

'Mr Chairman,' said Amber, raising her hand.

'You don't have to . . .' Michael gave in. They'd been through this; Amber liked putting up her hand. 'Go ahead.'

'Swearing,' said Amber, with a quelling look around the circle. 'Could you not? All the tots going in and out of my party emporium don't need to hear bad words.'

'Then they'd better move to a desert island,' suggested Fi.

Hero took a seat. 'I don't think you can ask people not to swear, Amber.'

Amber pouted. Actually pouted. Like a Kardashian. Or a carp. 'But their poor little ears.'

'I tell you who swears a lot,' said Mrs Bob, with the air of one sharpening an arrow. 'Drunks, that's who.'

'Oh, not Hero's drunks,' said Amber.

'They're not *my* drunks, per se,' said Hero.

'I'll take it up with the landlord,' said Amber, typing a note in one of her three phones.

Bob snorted. It turned into a protracted cough, during which Fi thumped him on the back and Mrs Bob rolled her eyes. 'You won't get far,' he managed eventually. 'Christmas Properties is just a name on a direct debit.'

'Don't bug Christmas Properties, whoever he is,' said Michael. 'He might realise how low the rents are. If he puts them up to market rates Qwerty will have to move elsewhere.' He looked at Sadie, just as her face clenched in panic.

So I'm not the only one who fears the outside world.

'Can we get a move on?' Fi looked ostentatiously at her watch. 'My boyfriend's picking me up in ten minutes.'

This banal statement was a boast; none of Fi's other men had ever picked her up. Cole, she'd told Sadie in disbelief, *sometimes even paid for dinner.*

Sadie spoke up. 'Michael, the agenda is just "tree". What do you mean?'

'Ah.' Michael looked shifty. He pushed at his glasses. 'That was Mrs Bob's idea.'

'It has to go,' said Mrs Bob, with her customary charm.

Sadie gasped. An audible gasp, like a shocked duchess. 'Never,' she said.

'The tree's pretty,' said Amber, 'but . . .'

'But all the delivery men complain about manoeuvring round it,' said Mrs Bob. She reeled off her grievances with gusto. 'It makes parking difficult. Those stupid blossoms are a health hazard in the wet. Nobody ever sweeps them up except me.'

'It only blooms in spring,' protested Sadie, looking around for backup.

'And the rest of the time,' squawked Mrs Bob, 'it stands there like a bone.'

The tree's silvery bark with its horizontal dashes could, in the wrong light, look like bone. In the right light it looked magical, other worldly. 'Surely its beauty counts for something?' Sadie needed the tree to be treasured; she needed to feel there was a place for goodness in the mews.

'The tree stays,' said Mary. She was complacent, as if Mrs Bob was a gnat to be splatted. 'Various appeals have been made to Christmas Properties over the years. The tree is very old, apparently.' She side-eyed Mrs Bob. 'Some people appreciate old things.'

'Some people *are* old things,' said Mrs Bob.

'Wouldn't be the same,' said Michael, 'without our lovely sakura.' He smiled at Sadie.

Sweet, thought Sadie. If a trifle late. The tree was safe. For now. She wouldn't put it past Mrs Bob to tiptoe out in the dead of night with a chainsaw. 'I've heard that trees can be protected by law, like a building being listed.'

'I'll look into that,' said Hero.

'Any other business?' asked Michael meekly. Before he'd even finished the short sentence, Mrs Bob leaned over him to say, 'Met the famous Mogg twins yet, Sadie?'

'Yes.'

Amber pulled her feathered boa round her shoulders. She was the only adult Sadie had ever met who owned one. 'What are they like?'

Fi got there first. 'I don't understand what Mother Nature was playing at. She makes one violent git and then decides to make another one, exactly the same.'

'They're . . .' Sadie searched for the right word. 'They're horrible.'

With the bulk of gym aficionados and the swagger of medieval kings, the Moggs had sauntered around Sakura as if they owned the place. They'd looked Sadie up and down, misogyny wafting off their bodies along with the lively aftershave they wore. She'd answered yes, of course she was 'looking after' their little sister, whatever that meant, and was keenly relieved when they left. The air around them was sour.

'Those boys are dangerous.' Mary held Noel while he hiccupped. Champagne and small dogs do not mix. 'Never forget that.'

Something about Mary's certainty suggested a story, but before Mrs Bob or Amber could blunder in with a question, Hero stood up and said, 'I don't like making speeches.'

'In that case, sit down,' said Mary.

Hero paused. Closed his eyes. Opened them. Started again. 'Despite the heckling, I need to say a few words.' He paused. Bit his lip. Whatever these few words were, they seemed to matter. 'I have big ambitions for U-Turn. Not in a business sense. Nobody gets rich helping broken people. I want it to be a vital part of this community. If we do it right, U-Turn will be a shining light, a beacon in the dark. I need your help to do that. I need your goodwill. Then me and my staff can pick people up when they falter.'

'Beautiful,' murmured Amber.

'Sounds ace,' said Fi.

Sadie was impressed. And moved. She could tell he meant every word.

'That's all very well,' said Mrs Bob. 'But what about when one of your alkies vomits on my doorstep?'

Hero took a deep breath. 'I promise to personally clear it up. It's not likely, though. My clients are just like you and me. Ordinary. Calm.'

As he spoke a shout fractured the early evening outside Qwerty.

'BASTARD!' Something heavy clattered and fell on the cobbles.

Sadie joined the gallop to the bookshop windows. A large man waved his arms around, his shirt torn, dark blanks where his front teeth should sit.

'I know you're there, Smith!'

Hero passed a hand over his face. 'Great timing,' he muttered.

'Who *is* that?' Amber clasped Hero's arm. Gave the muscle, Sadie noted, a surreptitious feel.

'One of Hero's calm customers.' Mrs Bob ignored her husband's 'shush'.

'I'll deal with him. He's a troublemaker.' Hero was through the shop door before Sadie could ask if that was a good idea.

'Should we call the police?' she asked.

'Nah.' Fi was sanguine. 'I reckon Hero's got this.'

A smaller, wiry guy, with dark curls and a face that bore the stamp of a life colourfully lived, was reasoning with the hooligan.

'Jez, let me handle him.' Hero rolled up his sleeves.

Marie Antoinette-like, Amber poured more champagne. From their front row seat in the window, the residents couldn't hear what Hero said, just the roars of his adversary trotting out his repertoire of cuss words.

Fi put her hands over Mary's ears. When Mary said, 'I've heard worse, I assure you,' Fi put her hands over Noel's ears instead.

'I can smell him from here,' gloated Mrs Bob. 'Ooh! He's going to hit Hero!'

Michael covered his eyes.

Sadie flinched.

Noel yapped.

Amber squeaked, 'God, this is sexy!'

The threatened punch didn't land. The noisy man lowered his fist, and allowed Hero to lead him like a lamb out through the gates.

Amber was disappointed. Sadie's relief surprised her. She was averse to violence – natural in somebody who woke from nightmares of crunching bones – but this wasn't about violence. It was about Hero.

I don't want to see him crumple.

Part of Sadie felt it was better that she and Hero barely interacted; if nothing happened with Hero, there'd be nothing to awkwardly confess to Jack.

That wasn't the part that watched Hero as he returned to the bookshop.

'I thought, as we usually go out after a meeting . . .' Hero seemed uncertain.

'Yeah. Nice. Um, yeah.' Sadie was out of practice. Pre-Jack, her love life had been chaotic, the emotional equivalent of a supermarket trolley with a wonky wheel. With Jack it had been beautifully straightforward, like trained dancers gliding into position. Now she was back in the shopping trolley. A joke might help. 'Your shouty friend robbed me of my weekly opportunity to say "adjourned".'

He didn't get the joke, so it didn't help.

'Take this.' Amber burrowed between them, holding out the second, unopened bottle to Hero. When he demurred, she foisted it on Sadie.

When Sadie stepped back, Amber, all a-bustle, insisted, slipping it into Sadie's bag. She was prolonging the moment, Sadie knew. Trying to hang on to them, trying to lasso Hero.

Love is a game of winners and losers. Sadie had lost often enough to know how Amber felt.

Strolling through a scrubby park, they shared chips from a bag.

'You can keep your Michelin stars.' Sadie licked her fingers. 'Fish and chips are the height of British cuisine.' Now that she'd grown accustomed to his face, she noticed the imperfections. They endeared him to her. Beauty is not enough on its own; there has to be vulnerability. 'Bet you don't eat chips that often.'

'How do you know I'm not built entirely on cod and chips?'

'Because you're posh.'

'I am *not*.'

'Hero, no posh person ever admits to it. I don't know why. It's not like I'm accusing you of murder.'

'I'm really not posh, Sadie.'

'Your name. Your accent, however much you rough it up. Your hair.' She pointed to his thick, quiffy waves. Almost touched it. Didn't dare. 'I don't expect you to own up to it. Even the Queen thinks she's "street".'

He gave in. 'I am a bit posh, I suppose.' He eyed her, weighing her up. 'Too posh?'

'Just the right amount.'

They walked in that stumbly way couples do, shoulders touching, getting in each other's way. 'Yuk.' She sidestepped a used condom on the tarmac.

'Nice touch,' said Hero. 'Gentrification hasn't quite reached this park.'

'Just two streets away, there's a chichi little green with a bandstand and pretty flowerbeds. Inner London has a split personality.'

They sat, or perched, on an abused-looking bench. The chips were finished, but neither seemed ready to go home.

'Full disclosure,' said Hero suddenly. 'As you were so honest last time, I feel I should tell you about me. My past.'

Something went taut inside Sadie. He was behaving as if this was a date. And not their first. A sudden fear that she wouldn't be up to what was expected of her made her miss Hero's first few words.

'... married. We've been divorced for, ooh, feels like a hundred years. We were too young. Things didn't work out. There's no yearning.'

'Right.' Sadie tried frantically to translate; he was talking not English but Mannish. Could he be letting her know that he was ready for a relationship?

That makes one of us.

'Me and Zizzi, we should never have got together.'

'Zizzi? Like that social media personali— oh God, you were married to *that* Zizzi?'

Hero nodded.

'She's famous.'

'I know.' Hero looked thoughtful; as if fame was a disease. 'It's all she ever wanted.'

The story came out in unembroidered dribs and drabs. Zizzi had been 'the girl next door', he said.

Sadie imagined two very upper-class doors.

'We thought we fell in love, but now I realise I just fancied the pants off her. She was the only girl I really knew, apart from Effie, my sister. Getting married was expected.' He huffed a little laugh. 'Zizzi posts her whole life online but you'll never see that wedding dress. It was a meringue. A pageboy got lost in it. This was before she discovered style.'

'My mother-in-law wanted us to have a big wedding,' said Sadie. She rarely thought of Merle; it hurt too much. 'We sneaked off and had a registry office do. I was in jeans.' The new silk shirt was blue, and borrowed, two superstitions ticked at once. She'd felt beautiful, because that's how women who are loved feel.

'What did your folks want?'

'They were out of the picture by then.' Thinking of Sadie's parents hurt even more.

'After the honeymoon, I started my studies.' All Hero ever wanted to do was counselling. Zizzi, though, lobbied for a move. To London.

'You're not a Londoner?'

'God no. I'm a country boy.'

'Me too. Well, a country girl.' They laughed the relieved laugh of people who fancy each other realising there may be some rational basis to the lust. 'I came to London on a whim.' Half true; Sadie had come to London because of the sheer irrationality of it. She'd always railed against the capital's self-satisfaction, which meant that nobody would ever think of looking for her there.

'That's when Zizzi got interested in surfaces, in how things look.' Hero looked sad, as if remembering a terrible loss. 'She'd dress up just to pop out for milk. Our flat was full of possessions that meant nothing to me. Whimsical antiques and ironically bad paintings.' The newlyweds began to squabble. 'I was expected to make a ton of money. Zizzi obviously hadn't been listening when I talked about my goals.'

The gulf widened. Hero wanted to make a difference to society, whereas Zizzi wanted to be a size 6. She built an online presence while he sat his exams. Children, they'd decided, should wait until they were more settled.

'Besides, Zizzi was too obsessed with her waist to get pregnant. Bo was an accident.'

'Bo?' Sadie was startled. 'You have a . . . you're a dad?'

'Don't I look like one?'

'Yes. No. It's just . . . Go on.' The topic was incendiary for Sadie.

'He's twelve. He's great. Everybody thinks their kid is great. But, actually, Bo *is* great.' Hero smiled. An inward smile. Personal.

True love.

Knowing envy isn't a good colour on anybody, Sadie fought it. She tried to be glad for Hero; she knew how that inward smile felt. She missed it.

'Zizzi got into reality TV. One of those "rich women behaving badly" programmes.'

'I remember.' It had been a guilty pleasure for Sadie and Jack. '*Belgravia Badasses.*'

'She got modelling jobs and became a brand ambassador. I'd never heard of a brand ambassador before that. I was, you know, disappointed in her.' Hero dipped his head, checking out Sadie's reaction from beneath his brows. 'That makes me sound like a Victorian papa.'

'No, I get it. Zizzi was interested in how things look and you were interested in how things are.'

'See, put it that way and I don't sound like such a humourless sod!' Hero described how he opened the first U-Turn in an old warehouse in Bermondsey with next to no money. 'Bo cut the ribbon. With child-safe scissors, of course.'

'What broke you up?' Sadie wasn't proud of wanting to get to this bit, the bit where Hero parted from the noted beauty.

'Everything. Nothing.' Hero dropped his head back. Closed his eyes. 'Divorce was worse than I'd imagined. I had to start over.'

'And Bo?'

'He lives with his mum.' Hero swallowed. 'In LA.'

'Why didn't you—' Sadie stopped short. She saw a flicker cross Hero's face.

'Why didn't I stop her?' Hero stood. Abruptly, as if shaking off an itchy thought. 'I gave in.'

'But you're not a giver-in.' Sadie put up her hands in mock apology. 'Ignore. Ignore. It's none of my business.' Another flicker. Another bruise. Truth was, Hero disappointed her. He'd let this Bo be whisked away by a reckless woman who roped him into her social media adventures. Staging shots. Monetising even her child.

It's dangerous to build up a man you've only just met into, well, a hero.

He took her hands. Tugged her upwards from the bench. She pulled away and sped ahead of him. He caught up as she said, 'Full disclosure part two.' Her mouth was dry. 'I have a daughter.' She said it so rarely she used the wrong tense. 'No, Jesus, I had a daughter.'

Hero stopped dead.

She stopped too. 'Teddy. Not her real name, of course, but she never looked like an Amelia.'

She hoped he'd read between the lines. She didn't want to say the next bit – the last bit – out loud.

He seemed to. There was a weight of dire knowledge in Hero's voice when he said, 'I'm sorry, Sadie.' He reached out and took her hand. Carefully this time.

She liked the feel of his fingers. They were so much stronger than hers. With a slight calloused edge. Sadie yanked her hand away. 'We should get back.' Her voice was brittle.

They walked in silence. As he pushed at the gates she turned and sped away from him. Instinct told her he might kiss her; that must not happen.

I'm untouchable.

Sadie had sealed her own fate the day of the crash; now she wandered the earth like a leper, ringing a little bell and shouting, 'Unclean! Unclean!'

The flat was cold and unresponsive. The rooms, even emptier than usual, mocked her with their blankness. She hadn't even said goodnight to Hero, just ditched him on the street in her impatience to be alone.

A metaphorical lightbulb lit up – *ping!* – above her head. It threw the shadows of her few sticks of furniture into frigid relief. Sadie fished out the champagne from her bag and stood it on the table.

Standing back, she regarded it as if it were an art exhibit. She walked around it. She put a hand on it.

Memories jostled.

The day after the accident. The Big Bang that blotted out the only two faces she would never tire of.

She had hurt all over. Every limb affected. Unable to face facts. *Where are they?* her deluded brain asked over and over.

Action helped.

Sadie had somehow pulled her broken body together and hauled herself to her sister's door. The only member of her immediate family still speaking to her, the woman she and

Jack had nursed through a divorce, whose baby son played at Teddy's feet.

She remembered the staggering run in her slippers through the broad sleepy streets in a market town on the edge of the eastern hump of England.

Tish would help. Tish would feel her pain, and join her in it.

But Tish already knew. 'Don't come here with your grief,' she had said, slamming the front door and leaving her sister on the step.

Now, the champagne bottle seemed to swell to twice its size. It pulsed, as if it might pop its cork without any help from Sadie.

She fled upstairs, and brushed her teeth so violently her gums bled. She crept to her bedroom. She was breathing hard. She was the opposite of the calm she had cultivated since arriving in Cherry Blossom Mews.

The boat.

Sadie reached out and took down the perfect 1.33 model of an elegant racing yacht from the chest of drawers. She cradled it like a child. She traced the name painted on the bow. *Lady Sadie*. Made of light wood, carved by Jack, it held something of him.

She tried desperately to believe this.

Every yacht designer has their dream project; the *Lady Sadie* was to be Jack's retirement present to himself. He would build it with precision and love, he'd vowed, and he would whisk her away beneath its sails. Teddy would be grown and happy and they could be a crazy old couple on the high seas.

Bitterness flooded Sadie's mouth. All that time working, building up his business, chasing commissions that took him away for weeks at a time, and for what? She admitted to herself a ravenous greed for all the time they'd been cheated out of.

The bed seemed lumpy. She turned. She tutted. She leapt up, down the stairs, to that bottle which seemed to be singing her name.

Out into the mews she ran. The cobbles were slick and treacherous beneath her bare feet. Overarm, she slung the champagne bottle into the skip that stood outside U-Turn.

A breeze curled around her legs, like a cat. It brought her back to her senses. Reminded her that her feet were cold. Wind meant change, the approach of the new.

Sadie had learned that change was bad. Could this wind be bringing something positive for a change?

She wasn't alone.

Hero stood outside U-Turn, silhouetted in the door, a full bin bag in each paw. He dropped them both. 'You and me,' he said, 'have unfinished business.'

The speech about Jack, about loyalty, about guilt, sprang fully formed and grammatically correct to Sadie's lips. She didn't say it. Instead she took one step, then another, half afraid that she was stepping off a cliff and might end up dashed against the rocks below.

But no. Her feet found the cobbles, and she ran to him.

Sadie kissed him. Fierce and gentle, like her fantasies.

She stepped back. She breathed hard.

Hero said, 'I actually meant we had unfinished business about checking out the listed status of the cherry tree.' He laughed, reaching out to grab Sadie as she made to bolt. 'Whoa!' He put his finger under her chin to tilt her face, with its blazing embarrassed cheeks, towards his. 'I much prefer your version of unfinished business.'

He kissed her. She let him. She kissed him back.

The tree whispered behind them.

WEEK FOUR

To	The Bobs <bob@bobscaff.co.uk>, Amber <amber@yummymummymews.net.co.uk>, Sadie <sakuraspa@gmail.com>, Michael T. <qwertybookshop@hotmail.com>, Fiona J <filove@aol.com>, Cher Mogg <whatulookingatcher@gmail.co.uk>
From	Hero <hero.smith@u-turn.net>
Subject	CHERRY BLOSSOM MEWS RESIDENTS' ASSOCIATION MEETING

Dear Mewsites

Chuffed you're letting the newbie host a meeting. Expect sausage rolls.

Date	Wednesday 13.6.18
Time	6.30 p.m.
Location	U-Turn therapy suite
Agenda	Community Spirit

Could somebody tell Mary? Thanks.

H x

Not a soul was about, except for a woman tiptoeing across the sun-washed mews like a cartoon burglar. The woman let herself into Sakura with exaggerated care, sliding the door behind her silently.

An hour later, Sadie came back down the same stairs. She was showered. She was humming.

The tumble dryer grumbled from the utility nook.

'I got in early.' Fi stretched out on the uncomfortable white seating, studying her phone. 'Put on a towel wash.'

Sadie woke the computer and faffed at the desk.

'Bob opened up the caff especially.' Fi carried on in a bored voice, eyes still on her phone. 'Cooked me breakfast.'

'Nice.' Sadie was only half listening.

'We both saw the strangest thing.' Fi sat up, supporting herself on one elbow. 'This woman came out of a door that wasn't her own and skulked past the cherry tree. A bit dishevelled, as if she'd spent all night making crazy, passionate, tie-me-up–tie-me-down love.' She was staring now at Sadie, whose head was emphatically down. 'What d'you think was going on, eh?' She threw a copy of *World*

Spa & Wellness. 'When were you going to tell me, you dirty little stop-out?'

'There's nothing to tell.' Sadie's smile said different.

'Don't make me come over there,' threatened Fi, hauling herself up.

'Did Bob really see me?'

'We high-fived each other. There's nothing to be embarrassed about.'

'It's just . . . well . . . I'm married.'

Fi looked as if she could say a great deal but she contented herself with, 'We've been through this, babes. Jack'd approve. And if he didn't . . .' She spread her hands wide. 'You've got to live your life, Sadie McQueen.'

Fi wanted details. And she wanted them before Cher arrived. The girl's timekeeping had improved. A little.

'The first time was after last week's meeting.' Sadie was reticent: shining daylight on the details might make them fade. Other people's opinions and judgement – well, Sadie had had enough of those. In answer to Fi's interrogation she admitted that, yes, she'd slept in Hero's big, tousled bed every night since.

'Four nights? My information gathering techniques need an overhaul.' Fi paced, energised by this big news. 'What's he like?' she asked suddenly. ''Cos Hero looks like a sex beast if you ask me.'

Sadie was tight lipped.

'Is he kinky? Is he all masterful?' Fi closed her eyes, groaned a little. 'Mm, bet he is. Can he go all night or is he one of those—'

'Fi, shut up,' begged Sadie. 'We haven't . . . I didn't . . . you know. Not yet.'

Fi was aghast. 'That's like being offered Viennetta and saying you don't do dairy. Why, Sades? You're not a virgin, for God's sake.'

'It's personal. I don't quiz you about your sex life.'

'You can if you want.'

'I do *not* want.' Sadie held up a warning hand in case Fi delivered an impromptu Ted Talk on Cole's erogenous zones. 'We're close; there's kissing. A lot of kissing. But no actual hanky-panky.'

'You can't even say the word,' marvelled Fi. 'SEX!' she screeched just as the first customer of the day arrived.

Out in the mews, the day revved up and the cast of Sadie's life criss-crossed the courtyard. The Bobs plonked down cracked mugs of tea on outdoor tables they'd bought in a hasty job lot as the summer hotted up. Amber was taking down bunting and putting up more bunting in a photo-shoot-ready ensemble that encompassed broderie anglaise, pompoms, and a peony in her up-do.

On her, it works.

Sadie knew full well she'd look deranged if she put a flower in her own hair.

Cher turned up. The phone rang. The computer chirruped. Customers came in looking wan and left looking brighter. Somebody complained about the tinkly music. Somebody else warned they were allergic to massage oil. Cher said she was allergic to wanky customers, but only after the woman had left.

Which was, in a way, progress.

Michael and Hero stood deep in conversation under the tree, at the epicentre of the mews. Michael looked up into Hero's face, nodding, eager.

So that charisma works on men, too.

Michael held a bundle of books; he *always* held a bundle of books.

Another Dorothy Ball had arrived the day after last week's meeting. Fi had picked it up from the doormat to read the title with a leer. *You Should Be Mine* by Dorothy Ball. Pulling in her chin, she had given Sadie a meaningful look. 'Michael's making a move on you right under Hero's nose. Never knew he had it in him.'

'It's a very Michael-ish move to woo a woman with novels.'

He saw me kiss Hero by the cherry blossom tree.

Now, Sadie took up the book, its cover colourful and dated amidst Sakura's millennial minimalism.

She would have liked to sit with it, the way she used to in her teenage bedroom: cross-legged, the world shut out except for the reassuringly samey style of Ms Ball and her exclamation marks. She saw Michael's offerings for what they were; she would be gentle with him. He'd entrusted his feelings to her and she took that responsibility seriously.

Mary often 'forgot' about the meetings.

'Come on, old woman,' laughed Sadie, in Mary's disordered sitting room. 'Get yourself together.'

From her dark bedroom across the hall, Mary tutted.

'Who's the woman in the oil painting?' called Sadie. She read out the name on the small plaque attached to the frame. 'Augusta Madeleine Lockridge.'

'Mother,' said Mary, with a breathlessness that suggested she was changing her clothes. 'She used to say I was sent from heaven.'

'My mother never said that about me.' The last thing Sadie's mother had said was 'I'm ashamed of you'. 'Must be nice to have a parent who admires you.'

'Ha!' Mary tottered out of her bedroom. 'She meant I was sent from heaven to look after her when Father died. To be a skivvy with no needs of my own. Mother was a queen bee and I was a little drone buzzing around her day and night.' With her strange, lurching gait, Mary approached the painting. She looked at the austere face, nothing like her own. 'It wasn't admiration, Sadie; it was tyranny.' She jangled Noel's lead and he appeared from beneath a stool. 'Well?' she said impatiently to Sadie. 'Are we going or not?'

U-Turn's therapy suite turned out to be a plain room, with a pot plant and a small sofa. It smelled, like the rest of the revived building, of fresh paint. Hero lugged chairs in. He was nervous, bright eyed, like a debutante worried about the impression she was making.

The last to arrive, Cher had laid a false trail all afternoon, prophesying she 'probably coudn't be arsed' to attend.

'Look what the cat dragged in,' said Fi.

'It'd have to be a brave cat.' Mrs Bob's hair smelled of Welsh Rarebit. 'What's she doing here, Hero?'

'I invited Cher.' Hero was calm but repressive, as if Mrs Bob was a skittish Yorkshire terrier who needed a firm hand. Before she could launch into a characteristic rant, he said, 'We're a community here, Mrs Bob. We're inclusive. Either everybody's welcome or nobody is.'

Sadie waited for an explosion. None came. The Yorkshire terrier responded well to training, and got on with inspecting the sausage rolls and finding them wanting.

'Welcome, Cher,' said Amber, who'd never previously

addressed one word to the girl. She threw a glance at Hero to see if he'd witnessed her broad mind at work.

Ostensibly bored, legs crossed, Cher sighed, 'I had nothing better to do. Thought I'd have a laugh at your poncey little meety-weety.'

Somewhere in the innards of U-Turn somebody coughed meatily. There was laughter. A slammed door. The place felt alive. Sadie remembered the shell it had been, propped up on mouldering beams.

Everything evolves.

'Right, so, um, what happens now?' Hero faced the semicircle of his neighbours.

'We all talk at the same time,' said Fi. 'Mrs Bob moans. Bob apologises for her. Sadie says something ever so sincere about something nobody's interested in. Mary falls asleep. Amber takes a photo. Sadie asks for a volunteer to do proper minutes. We all snigger. Noel has a widdle. We go home.'

'So, we never actually achieve anything?'

'Christ, no,' said Mrs Bob.

It was that time of day. Between three and four p.m. The afternoon petering out, early evening getting its boots on.

Sadie was feeding her addiction. Perhaps the wind of change had signalled a return to bad habits. Not just bad. Ruinous.

She had fobbed off Fi, who had looked at the clock and said, 'What? *Another* errand at this time?'

Sniffing the air, Cher had realised her elders were having an unspoken conversation. 'What's going on? What's she up to?'

'None of your business!' Fi's temper had given Sadie cover to slip away.

She took a right and another right, passing the infamous India Park estate. It looked neat and appealing in the sun, its many windows winking like golden eyes. The deep shadow between the towers hinted at menace, but Sadie refused to demonise the estate. It was a neighbourhood like any other, only vertical.

Opposite it, India House, the grand old mansion which had spawned Cherry Blossom Mews was now a prestigious apartment block. A stretch of tarmac was all that divided the two sets of flats, one hated, the other an object of desire.

Sadie hurried on. Past the roundabout. A right turn by the Lidl which stared across the street at a Waitrose. Along a green garden square. As she got closer her symptoms escalated.

They were horribly familiar. Her heart knocked at her ribs. Her palms dripped. Excitement. Dread. She had avoided just such a buzz for years but now she sought it out.

Her timing was perfect. As Sadie turned the corner, the school gates burst open. Out they gushed, girls in their navy-blue uniforms.

Smells of poster paint and sweets. Wild laughter. Outrage. Singing.

Sadie stood still as they parted around her and ran to the adults, whose arms were outstretched to greet them. For three, four, maybe five seconds she could believe she was here to pick up Teddy. Just a mum, looking out for her girl.

It was a rush. Then it was over. That's the nature of a rush; the acute joy is only possible because of the crushing comedown.

It was worth it.

Sadie scurried home, her legs hollow.

Fi leaned on the reception desk, taking advantage of Cher's visit to what Mary called the little girls' room. The newcomer guarded her turf like a lioness and discouraged any pottering near the desk, or looking over her shoulder. Leaning was also forbidden.

'Careful,' she said, as Sadie scrolled through her bank statement on the laptop screen. 'Madam Mogg won't like you messing with her computer.'

'Strictly speaking, it's my computer.' Sadie talked a good fight but her eyes flicked neurotically to the loo door.

'Have a word with her about her clothes.'

'She wears a Sakura tunic, just like you and me.'

They talked in hushed tones, as if the junior employee had bugged the bonsai tree.

'True,' said Fi, 'but then she steps out from behind the desk and suddenly she's a hooker.'

Cher's bottom half was out of synch with her starched top half. A bum-grazing skirt displayed spray-tanned legs that inevitably ended in six-inch heels.

'And her make-up.' Fi was on a roll. 'You and me, we wear our hair back, we keep our look natural. Meanwhile, the receptionist has a face full of slap. Badly applied slap, at that. It's bad for our image.'

'Didn't know we had one.'

'Of course we do!' whispered Fi. 'In here it's all clean and calm and serene. That girl' – Fi stabbed a finger at the loo door – 'is *not* serene. She called me a whore's handbag this morning. Do *not* laugh,' admonished Fi, springing away at the sound of the toilet flush.

'What you doing at my desk?' Cher was suspicious. 'Checking up on me?' She tried to elbow Sadie out of the way.

Sadie resisted. There was a tussle. She won. 'I'm viewing my bank statement, Cher. Give me room.'

Grudgingly, Cher gave her room. She stared, unabashed, at Sadie's personal details. 'Who are Christmas Properties?'

'The landlord.' Sadie frowned. 'This is private, okay?'

'You spend a lot at Marks and Spencers. Knickers, is it?'

Sadie cleared the screen. 'We need a chat about boundaries, Cher.'

The glass door slid open and a small man, lean, sooty with stubble, leaned in.

'Jez, isn't it?' Sadie recognised Hero's right-hand man from U-Turn. 'You saw off that gorilla the other day.'

'He's harmless,' said Jez. His voice was a rasp. A soft rasp, if such a thing is possible. 'I was wondering . . .'

'Wonder away.' Sadie was prepared to like him. He had a raffish, Romany air, and his shortness was deceptive. Jez looked resilient, as if he could survive anything.

'The next meeting. Can I come? I mean, I work on the mews, so . . .'

Fi tee-hee'd. 'Don't you have better things to do?'

Eyes tell tales. Jez's eyes were on Cher. Cher's eyes were on the floor. A penny dropped. A pretty penny; Sadie liked the *clang!* it made. 'Everybody's welcome, Jez.'

'Ta.' Jez coughed and in Cher's general direction said, 'You going to the meeting?'

Cher concentrated on the floor as if the secret of life was carved into it. 'Maybe.'

'Might see you there, then.'

'Whatever.'

While Sadie kneaded the feet of her next customer, she

re-evaluated Cher. The violent blush was that of a virgin, not a moll. For all the streetwise smarts, the wall-to-wall swearing, the belligerence, Cher was younger than her years.

The Moggs had protected her, reared her like a hot-house flower. Perhaps Jez was her first taste of adult sexual attraction; Sadie had seen how Cher watched him walk away. The make-up was a mask; the outfits a defiant two fingers at a world she didn't feel quite ready for.

Later, out on the mews, Fi's eyebrows disappeared into her fringe at this analysis. 'Cher's just mardy. You're overthinking it. Just like you're overthinking *that*.' She flicked her eyes to where Hero stood outside U-Turn, talking with his trademark intensity to an older man whose shoulders sagged with invisible burdens. 'Get on with it.'

Earlier, Sadie had envied Cher and Jez their youth. A blank page not yet scrawled on. 'It's not easy,' she began.

'Nothing is.' Fi shrugged. 'I get it, babes. Jack. Teddy.' She wavered but went ahead. 'The guilt about . . . you've got to let it fall away at some point, so why not now?' As if sensing she'd brought Sadie to the edge of her capability, she changed gear. 'Here he is! My lover boy!'

Cole beeped the horn as he parked a millimetre from the tree. It seemed to bristle at his cheek. 'Netflix and chill, yeah?' he beamed.

'Perfect,' said Fi, settling herself in the passenger seat.

She'd boasted earlier about Cole's 'lovely house'. She and Sadie had watched the small mews development being built just a year ago and there had been loud scoffing from Fi about the dainty monotony of the redbrick boxes. Now, apparently, the banality was balm after her ex-boyfriend's dingy flat on a busy road.

Emanuel had been devastatingly handsome, catnip to women, but with the morals of, well, *not an alley cat*, thought Sadie, since there was no evidence that alley cats stole from their girlfriend's purses or knocked them about after one spliff too many. Their nightly rows had been punctuated by the beep-beep of the zebra crossing signal right outside his window. Even now, Fi would jump if she heard that innocent little noise.

The car reversed. Fi whooped. Mrs Bob shouted, 'Shut up out there!'

Wednesdays could be slow but this was unusual. Sadie had no bookings at all. Pressing random keys, she panicked. 'Something's up with the online diary.'

A glance passed between Fi and Cher. A sixth sense made Sadie turn and intercept it. 'What's going on?' This was an unholy alliance; Fi and Cher never cooperated.

'You've got the day off.' Fi's broad face fought a smile and lost.

'But my clients . . .'

'I rearranged everything.' Cher was smug.

'She was magic, actually.' Fi forced out the compliment. 'I'm working late to keep everybody happy. My Cole's not pleased, I can tell you.'

'All right, all right.' Cher was unimpressed by Fi's sacrifice. 'It's not like it's real work. You're just rubbing primrose oil into people's legs and stuff.'

Sadie was firm. 'Put the diary back the way it was, Cher, and don't do stuff like that without asking me.'

'If we asked you,' said Cher slowly, as if explaining quantum physics to a cat, 'it wouldn't be a surprise.'

I have nothing to do.

Spare time horrified Sadie. She got through Sundays somehow, but the thought of being incarcerated in her barren rooms while Cherry Blossom Mews motored on without her was unbearable. 'I don't want a day off.' She was surprised at how shaky her voice was.

Fi whispered, 'You might be about to change your mind,' as a figure crossed the cobbles.

Hero had a holdall in one hand and car keys in the other. 'Come on, McQueen,' he called. 'Get a move on.'

Sadie didn't move.

He put an arm around her, pulled her into his side and planted a kiss on the top of her head. In front of Fi and Cher. Just like that.

'Your hair smells nice. Come on. We're going on a

minibreak.' Hero checked with Fi. 'That's what you called it, yeah?'

'Yeah.' Fi spirited a packed overnight bag into Sadie's hand. Cher put a linen jacket over Sadie's shoulders. The merest of pushes in the small of her back and Sadie set off, dazed and obedient.

At the car she turned to Hero.

'This is too weird for me,' she whispered.

'It's a minibreak, not a satanic orgy.'

'I mean *this*.' Sadie splayed her hands. 'Us. You. This.'

'I thought this, us, you, was nice.'

'It's too soon,' said Sadie.

'Three years isn't soon.' Hero was gentle, certain, an authoritative mix of friend and lover.

'It's not like me and Jack broke up.' Sadie wheeled about and he took a step back to avoid being swiped by her bag. 'Us not having sex . . .' She swallowed. 'Us not having sex isn't about me worrying that you won't respect me in the morning. I'm not a virgin and I don't want to make you *wait*, whatever that means. Hero, you're an attractive man. An unusual man.'

'I hear a but on its way.'

'I can't be your girlfriend. Or anybody else's. I'm a wife, Hero. I'm a phantom limb. When I imagine myself doing normal girlfriend-y stuff it feels like I'm a bad actress trying out for a role.' She almost laughed. 'I can't help you choose clothes or nag you about eating toast in bed or have a point of view about how your hair should be. So let's draw a line under it.'

He was thoughtful, looking her over as if he'd never seen her before. 'Look,' he began, 'sex can wait. I've had tons of it already. So have you. It's nice, it's great, but we can work up to it. You and me – we don't have to be *normal*, Sadie. A normal girlfriend sounds boring. I haven't had a girlfriend of any description for about a hundred years. Too busy, plus I wouldn't have a clue what to do with one. So, see? You're perfect. This weekend is for us to dip our toes in the water with mildly normal girlfriend-y activity. A minibreak in the English countryside. Comfy beds – two of them. Breakfast on a tray. Walking pointlessly in nature. A long car journey where you discover I know all the words to the Abba *oeuvre*. So. What do you say? I advise you don't think. Just say yes.'

He waited. He blinked.

She said, 'Yes.'

Later she wouldn't remember climbing into the low-slung sporty car or buckling herself in. She only came out of her reverie when she saw Michael standing in the open doorway of Qwerty, a mug in his hand which he raised in salute.

On the dashboard was a hardback. Another Dorothy

Ball. Sadie took it, stroked the cover. '*Rivals in Love*,' she read aloud.

Michael ambled to the car and leaned in through the window, like an inquisitive monkey at a safari park. He gestured to the book. 'Not getting me anywhere, are they?'

Disconcerted by such bluntness, Sadie stammered out, 'They're beautiful, Michael.'

'Look at the pair of you, though.' Michael stood back as Hero slammed the bags into the boot. 'Off somewhere lovely, I bet. I'm doomed,' he said quietly as he turned away.

As Hero swung into the driver's seat, winked at her and thrust the car into throaty life, she knew that any other man was doomed in comparison to Hero.

He's not Jack, she found herself thinking, twinning the men as she hated to do, *but he's wonderful.*

After the accident, it had taken months for Sadie to sit in a car. They were purveyors of death, their curves transformed into mangled metal. She heard over and over again, 'Love, watch out!'

That had passed. She drove again. She pushed back when memory thrust her into a corner.

And today, as the car nosed through London, Sadie took Hero's advice.

She didn't think. She felt, instead.

Being driven by a man was mildly sexy. One of the things Sadie was trying not to think about was whether this minibreak was a dirty weekend by another name. When something excites you that much, and at the same time tests the notions of loyalty you've built your life upon, it's best not to dwell on it.

So she felt instead. She felt the simmer of faint desire when she saw his forearm on the wheel. Hero drove efficiently, each movement succinct and sure. There was a daring to it, too.

At roundabouts she watched him concentrate. His expression told her he knew he was being watched. The slight tightening of his jaw was a uniquely male twitch that almost brought on the vapours.

Possibly, I'm feeling a little too much.

Perhaps normality was creeping up on her. Grief is a strong chastity belt, and it chafed. Another bonus to this mini thingy was the fact that it kept her away from her new obsession. She wouldn't have to withstand the compulsion to pass a school today. It would be a relief not to lie to Fi's open, honest face.

'Sadie,' said Hero, turning down the radio. 'Are you an alcoholic?'

'Yes.'

The unexpected question shocked her into honesty; Sadie had been tipped over a cliff, but instead of drowning she found the sea refreshing. 'I haven't had a drink in years. As you know, it's a full-time job being in recovery but yes, Hero, I'm an alcoholic.'

'I saw how you were around the champagne. You didn't take any, but you kept your eye on the bottle as it did the rounds.' Hero smiled, buildings flashing by. 'As if it might ambush you.'

'That's exactly how I felt.'

'The night we kissed, and this allegedly weird relationship started, that crash I heard was you chucking a full bottle in the skip, yes?'

'I can't keep booze in the flat. Too risky.' Sadie felt exposed. As if she were sitting in her underwear. 'You know how that goes. You see it in your work every day.'

'I know how it goes because I'm an alcoholic too.' Hero let her absorb that; it took a second or two. 'Most counsellors are. I had my last drink eighteen years ago, but I take it one day at a time. Just like you.'

Like me.

Accustomed to feeling different, Sadie would have wagged her tail if she'd had one. She was a dog seeing another dog across the park; recognising their shared attributes. 'You don't look like an alcoholic, Hero.'

'What does an alcoholic look like? I'm a person. One of the things about me is that I'm an alcoholic. I'm also a bad dancer and a good cook.'

The tick tick tick of the indicator filled the silence until he said, 'I never drank like other people.'

She knew what he was up to. He was giving her a gentle push. 'Me neither,' she said. 'I always took it too far. It was Jack who noticed I wasn't "partying".' She sketched quote marks around the ironic phrase. She told him how meeting Jack shone a light onto a life littered with destroyed friendships. 'I jettisoned people who dared to ask me what was wrong. I was up to my neck in denial.' Her parents had opted out of her life. 'I don't blame them. I turned up late or not at all to all family get-togethers. I ruined Christmases. They prophesied I'd end up dead. We're still estranged.'

Each morning after had been filled with phone calls to find out what she'd got up to. She didn't recognise the woman in the anecdotes, a harpy who propositioned strangers and picked fights with mates.

'When I lost my job, I cut back.'

Hero let out a sigh. 'Trouble is, you weren't drinking to have fun.'

'I was drinking to blot myself out. I was fighting it alone, and I didn't even know what "it" was. Then . . . Jack.' Sadie ran her fingers along the plaited gold strap of Jack's watch. It grounded her, as it always did. The watch had sat on his skin day in, day out. Now it never left her wrist. 'I was on my best behaviour.'

'How long did that last?'

Sadie made a derisive noise. A flashback hit her hard.

The terrace of a Spanish villa. Scented jasmine. Lit candles. A bay sparkling in the distance. 'Jack's mum, Merle, had a holiday home in Spain. First time I ever met her was when we flew over for some big family do. Merle liked to do things properly. She was, you know, formal. I was shit-scared of her.'

'I think I know what's coming next.'

'I self-medicated, as they say. I desperately needed Merle's approval, yet there I was, downing the local wine as fast as the waiters could pour it.' Sadie took a breather. The memory required a run-up. 'Over dessert, when I'd already taken my shoes off and spilled wine down my new dress, I stood up and went round the table telling Jack's relatives what I thought of them.'

Some of the quotes were lodged in her brain, but Sadie couldn't share them with Hero or, as the saying goes, she'd have to kill him. To a mild-mannered uncle she'd slurred that only perverts had moustaches like his.

'On the plane home, Jack made it clear. Either I went to rehab or we were over.' Sadie recalled her astonishment that he was willing to give her a chance. Only real love, strong and tough, could be so elastic. 'I went straightaway. Like a kid going to boarding school.'

'Rehab's hard.'

'It's like nothing else I've ever experienced.' Sadie guessed that Hero had been through the same self-scrutiny. The emotional honesty. The digging up of ugly truths. 'Something clicked. I *got* it. Jack picked me up on the last day and proposed before we were out of the drive.'

Hero raised his eyebrows. 'Not what therapists advise.' He smiled. 'But it obviously worked.'

'Jack believed in me.' Sadie found a stubborn lump in her throat as she said that. 'He helped me imagine a life worth living. He took away the shame and replaced it with hope.'

'Hang on, *Jack* did that? Surely that was you who did that?'

'He did it,' insisted Sadie. 'Merle never changed her opinion of me.' To her mother-in-law, Sadie was just a lush, no matter how many years went by without a drink. 'We weren't close. To say the least.'

'Not all relationships can be repaired. You have to let go.'

'It's so odd that we never talk now. I mean, Jack was her son. Teddy was her granddaughter. We're the only two people who understand the other's loss.'

'Let go, remember?' Hero chided her gently.

'That promise to Jack saved me.'

'We steer clear of promises in therapy.' Hero was grave. This was his subject. 'One day at a time is the mantra I live by. You did it for yourself, Sadie. It's not something you can do for somebody else. I mean, look at you now.'

'Yeah, look at me now.' Sadie saw a woman fending off sadness, one foot in the happy past, one eye out for trauma that might set her drinking again.

More than anything, she saw a woman who had been the designated driver the night her family were wiped out.

'You turned yourself around. You, Sadie, are a success story.'

Something in his voice made Sadie turn to him. He watched the road ahead as she took in his eyes. His eccentric nose. A face full of feeling.

'I can't stop thinking about you,' whispered Hero. It was a confession. Sacred, almost. Sadie noticed the bow of his top lip as he pursed it. 'You make me nervous. I'm not used to being nervous.'

Not knowing what to say, Sadie said nothing.

They turned to more trivial matters. Hero really did know all the words to 'Super Trouper' and 'Dancing Queen'.

A signpost read WITHAM. 'Is this the A12?' Sadie sat up. They were headed for that hump on England's right coast. 'We're going to Suffolk?'

'Southwold, to be precise. Well, just outside it. I grew up there.'

Sadie's surprise muted her. Then she said, 'Hero, I grew up in Southwold.'

'Seriously?' The car swerved. 'I grew up in Aldeburgh.'

Only a winding flat road, rumoured to be haunted, separated the two towns.

'How come we never met?' Hero was dumbfounded.

She could have said, 'Because you are oh so very posh and I am most definitely not,' but she didn't. 'Small world!'

'I got out very young. Itchy feet.'

'I only left after the accident. I always swore I wouldn't get drawn in by London. It's like a giant magnet, isn't it?'

'I was happy to be an iron filing.'

One of the few topics Sadie and Merle had agreed on was their hatred for the capital. Smokey, they said. Teeming. Dangerous. Stand those defects on their heads, however, and they become advantages if you need to lose yourself. When Sadie dived into London, she'd enjoyed the filthy waters closing over her head. It was dumb luck that she'd washed up on the shore of Cherry Blossom Mews.

'I live so differently in London.' Sadie passed turnings she recognised, relieved when they sped past the corner that would take them to her old house. 'No lawn to mow. No sunsets.'

No Tish.

She always thought of her sister at this stage of the route, when she drove to the cemetery. As usual, she sighed. That betrayal was deep.

'Hero,' she said, so quietly she couldn't be sure that he'd heard, 'you make me nervous, too.'

Hemmed in by hedgerow, the car turned through an almost invisible opening, the tyres scrunching on stones. 'We're here,' said Hero, with a tinge of *ta-dah!*

A pebbly lane widened out into a driveway that wandered through grounds growing more and more tended. Brambles morphed into topiary. Scrubby wildflowers petered out into striped lawn.

'This is the best spot to stop.' The car idled and Hero leaned forward on the steering wheel.

In the middle distance glittered a white-fronted hotel of quintessentially English beauty. A bell tower rose from one corner, eccentric and austere in equal measure. 'It's perfect,' whispered Sadie.

'That's the idea.' Hero put the car in gear and the house grew larger by the second.

'What's it called? I thought I knew all the fancy hotels around here.'

'Hotel?' Hero's brows descended. 'It's my parents' place.'

'Eh?' Sadie made a gormless noise.

'Sorry.' Hero didn't look sorry. 'The other girlfriend-y aspect of this weekend is you're about to meet my folks.'

Dinner that evening was in the orangery.

The mistress of the house, Elizabeth, mother to Hero and

still in possession of her auburn beauty albeit a little faded, decided it was 'too darn warm' to eat on the terrace.

Ribs of white painted steel soared above Sadie's head as she took her seat. Thanks to Fi's packing skills, she wore a thin cami over jeans she had put aside for Oxfam.

Exotic fruit trees stood to attention in tubs. Sadie thought of Tish, probably sitting down to dinner just four miles away as the crow flies.

Tish was so proud of her double-glazed conservatory . . .

'You don't partake?' Gerald Smith, bald, obese, so unlike his son as to seem like a different species, held up a bottle of Riesling.

'Um, no.' Sadie saw the beads of icy sweat on the bottle's neck.

She felt her hand being squeezed beneath the table. She squeezed back. It was good to have an ally. Hero's hand was dry, warm. Reliable.

'Where's that girl?' Gerald waved a fork over his salad. 'Effie always holds us up, Sadie.'

'I'm looking forward to meeting her.' Around Hero's parents, Sadie spoke like a twee child at a Buckingham Palace garden party. Gerald's irascibility made him human, down to earth, yet her awkwardness remained. He was so at home with his privilege, but the house Sadie grew up in would fit inside this orangery.

'Effie has a lot on her mind,' said Elizabeth. Hero's mother was all alertness, all eyes, despite the studied languor that Sadie suspected had been fashionable in the social circles of the woman's youth. Sadie was being scrutinised, no doubt about it. 'She's a sensitive girl.'

The slightest of harrumphs from Hero, but his mother heard it and her lips tightened.

'Ma, you talk about Effie like she's a child.' He threw his arm over the back of his bentwood chair, a habit Sadie had noticed before. 'She's in her twenties.'

'Shush, darling. Here she comes.'

The patter of tiny feet. Effie was tiny all over, a doll-woman. The feet were bare. Her legs were in shorts. Her face was a face to fall in love with. Elfin. Translucent. A smile erupted through her freckles. '*You're* Sadie!'

The attention was head-turning. Sadie was kissed, asked to stand up 'so I can get a good look at you!' She was shown off – 'Isn't she lovely, Pa?' – and then moved so that Effie could sit alongside her.

Effie picked at her plate of cold bits and pieces, keeping up a stream of consciousness chatter that was charming and exhausting at the same time.

'Let her eat, sis, for Christ's sake,' begged Hero. They had the irritable shorthand that Sadie had lost with Tish.

'Sorry. I do go on.' Effie pulled apart a piece of bread, her knees under her chin, her toes curled around the edge of the chair. 'Hero told me you know Amber. She's huge on Instagram. What's she like in real life? He's no use. Men can't describe people, did you ever notice that?'

From the far end of the table, Gerald lifted his shining head. 'Effie, put away your phone, girl. I despair of this generation. Imagine if I'd had a telephone at the lunch table. Your grannie would have shot me.'

'To be fair,' said Hero, 'there was no such thing as a mobile back then.'

'I don't have to be fair,' said Gerald. 'I'm old.' He looked at Sadie. 'Are you a do-gooder too? One of Hero's lot?'

Explaining about Sakura, Sadie noted how Hero's head had drooped at 'do-gooder'. 'I'm not as useful as Hero. He lives up to his name.'

'Good God!' shrieked Effie. 'It must be love!'

Sadie didn't know if Hero went the same tomato colour as her, as she was too afraid to peek at him.

'All that messing about with drunks.' Gerald ignored the reproaching glare on his wife's face, skating on regardless. 'What's the point? If chaps want to drink, let 'em.'

Hero said nothing. It was a loud nothing. Sadie wondered if Gerald knew about his son's alcoholism; clearly he had no idea what it took to beat such a foe.

'Any second now,' said Effie conspiratorially, 'Daddy'll start moaning about Hero letting down the family firm.'

'Most sons'd be only too pleased to take over the family firm but not my Hero.' Gerald enlightened Sadie. 'Smith and Smith are brokers, my dear. Internationally renowned. Some incomer runs it now.' The look he gave Hero was not unkind. It spoke of miscommunication rather than distrust. 'In the end, you have to let your children do what they want.'

That was a conversational cue. Sadie froze as Elizabeth began to speak.

'How about you, Sadie? Do you have—'

'Any more of this quiche thing, Ma?' Hero stepped in. Like a … well … like a hero. As more quiche was found, he changed the subject. 'Bo's coming over in seven weeks.'

The table lit up. Promises were extracted to bring him to visit. Effie was tearful. Gerald suggested a toast. Bo was precious to the Smiths.

Not so his mother.

'Can't we kidnap the little blighter?' Gerald sat back. His tum was as big as Bob's, but covered in pricier cloth. 'Get him away from that monster, Zazou.'

'Zizzi,' said Hero automatically. 'Don't talk like that when Bo's here, Dad.'

'He's still being *homeschooled*, I daresay.' Gerald seemed to distrust the concept. 'The boy spends more time on photo shoots than he does at a desk.'

Elizabeth lit a cigarette. It was a strangely dated thing to do: Sadie remembered her grandparents smoking at the table. It had died out, except, apparently, among the wildly self-confident upper classes. 'It makes my blood boil when darling Bo starts chattering about his latest "uncle". Zizzi always did put herself first.'

'And second,' said Effie. 'And third.' She bumped shoulders with Sadie. 'We're not usually this mean, but Zizzi deserves it.'

'Whether she does or not, could we just, you know . . .'

Sadie had never heard Hero run out of words before. She had a question that she might never find the courage to ask.

If Zizzi's so vile why do you allow your son to live with her?

A court battle would be ugly, but with Zizzi's well-documented vices there was little doubt that Hero, Smith wealth behind him, would win.

Sadie couldn't imagine an answer to her question that would absolve Hero.

'I've never walked around an ornamental lake with somebody who bloody well owns the ornamental lake,' said Sadie.

An irregular oval carved from the flat land, the lake was fringed with reeds and populated with fancy-looking ducks, all of them better dressed than Sadie. An island in the middle sprouted a fairy tale hut. Circular. Thatched.

Hero took her hand.

Mildly transgressive. Absolutely natural. There were no rules on this minibreak.

'It bothers you.' He said it as a statement.

'No, it just—'

'It bothers me,' said Hero. 'This much property in the hands of one family. It's not fair.'

Sadie looked up at him. It still excited her, that she had to look up. A card-carrying feminist, she saw no contradiction in this.

Biology is biology, after all.

'You're an uneasy fit with your family.'

'I am,' said Hero. 'The whole inheritance thing.' He swept an arm around the sleepy, ticketty boo grounds. 'It's as much a burden as an asset.'

Sadie imagined the heated conversations with Gerald and Elizabeth about Hero's refusal to join the family firm. He'd stood his ground. Rarely did respect come with a side order of lust but now it did. She stopped. Reached up. Her kiss was more than a peck, less than a smooch.

It froze Hero. Then he smiled. That smile he only rarely treated her to, the one that created dimples like parentheses. 'You wild reckless harlot, you.'

'The sex thing . . .' began Sadie. As soon as she said it she regretted it.

'The *sex thing*?'

'Are you laughing at me or with me?' Sadie dropped his hand, stood back.

'Bit of both.' Hero wouldn't let her open up any space

between them. He put his arms about her and pulled her against him. 'If we call it the sex thing it sounds about as sexy as stew. This isn't a hit and run, Sadie. I understand that getting close to me, to any man, is a big move. If we rush, it might damage something that might just be important.' Hero looked at her mouth.

The hesitation between this and the actual kiss almost undid Sadie.

'It's not that I don't want to . . .' Sadie put her head on his chest. She liked the fit. She'd discovered how well their bodies worked together when they'd lain together in Hero's bed. A large bed, never properly made. 'It's just that . . .' She was a teenager again, scared of adult words.

'Making love is a step away from the past.'

Sadie heard how he almost said 'Jack' instead of 'the past'. She felt him deflate slightly in her arms and she pressed herself harder against the expanse of chest that was beginning – dangerously – to feel like home.

Jack tailed them wherever they went.

A housekeeper stood in Sadie's room. Sadie wasn't sure how to 'be' around a housekeeper, but the slender woman in jeans just threw her a 'Hello there' and left her to it.

The bedroom was a bridge between eras. The duvet was a fluffy cloud on the mahogany bed. Faded wallpaper gave way to crisp linen blinds. Decorating a house of this size was,

Sadie assumed, a never-ending task. This spare bedroom – one of eight, apparently – was only part-way through its modernisation.

She liked this in-between decor. It suited her mood. It hovered between a future that smelled of Hero, and a past that, although it contained treasures, had become a vault.

A knock at the door and Elizabeth entered, not waiting for an invitation. 'There you are,' she said, as if Sadie had been hiding under tables. 'Settling in?' She looked around, those blue eyes checking, checking, checking. 'Shall I send up some water? It's so nice to have water in the room.'

Sadie held up her plastic bottle.

'Ah.' Elizabeth looked wry. 'You young people and your bottles of water.'

'Young?' Sadie was glad of the description but didn't feel she warranted it, hurtling as she was towards forty as if her shoes were greased.

'Once you get past sixty everyone's a greenhorn.' Elizabeth ventured further in. 'Hero never brings anyone home. For all I know, my son lives the life of a monk.'

'He's very committed to his work.' Sadie felt dull in front of this woman. There was adventure in her past, that much was sure. Nobody was born with eyes like that; the twinkle was earned.

'He couldn't wait to leave home.' Elizabeth sounded bereft, and Sadie saw how she corrected that with brightness when she said, 'Whereas I doubt dear Effie will ever fly the coop!'

'It's a comfortable coop.'

'Too comfortable, perhaps.'

A glimpse into family dynamics. On the whole, Sadie steered clear of families. They reminded her of losing not only her own pair of turtle doves, but of being disowned by her own parents. 'I wish I had somewhere like this to come home to,' said Sadie, meaning it. Meaning it *hard*.

'Well, now you do, dear.' Elizabeth's kindness was automatic, but felt real all the same. 'Dinner at eight. Don't dress up.'

As if I was planning to.

The evening was long, in that way summer evenings are, finding an extra hour or two and painting them pink.

It was a time to stroll. Possibly around an ornamental lake with a man with a silly name. Sadie slipped a borrowed gauzy shawl around her shoulders and set off to find the man, down a path overhung with branches.

Effie foiled the plan.

'Sadie, Sadie, Sadie!' Effie put her arm through Sadie's and propelled her along. The lacey top that Effie wore was ethereal in the pastel dusk. 'Hero told me about your husband.' She leaned in. Her little body gave off a surprising amount of heat. 'I'm so sorry.'

'It's . . .' Sadie felt ambushed.

'I know how you feel. I really do. People say that but I actually know how you feel.' Effie's excitement made her gabble. 'My Steve, he was taken in a crash too. Which was horribly ironic because we used to joke that he'd die on his motorbike. Seems ghoulish now. It's so sudden, isn't it? No time to get used to the idea; just bam, they're gone.'

'Bam,' echoed Sadie.

'I can't, like, *recover.*' They were at the edge of the lake. Two punts, long slipper-shaped boats, trembled in the water. 'I don't think I ever will.'

'Don't say that.' Hearing her own thoughts echoed revealed a deep pessimism Sadie had never tackled. 'You have a life to live, Effie.'

Effie didn't seem interested in that; she dragged them both back to the past, where even the pain was preferable to the emptiness of the present. 'When I heard I went numb. Was it like that for you?'

The numbness had arrived courtesy of Threshers. 'Yup.'

'I woke up last night, panicking, thinking the phone was ringing and it was Steve.' Effie put her head on Sadie's shoulder as they followed the shape of the lake. 'If he'd lived, we'd be married now. I know it.'

You don't know any such thing.

Sadie couldn't burst such a beautiful bubble, even if that daydream was a boulder in Effie's way. 'He didn't live, though, Effie, and neither did my husband. We have to deal with how things are, not how we'd like them to be.'

Do I have this effect on people? Do I make them feel bogged down in the past with me?

'You're saying that 'cos you've met Hero.' Effie winked. She had the same wink as her brother. 'You're going red! Hero would *love* that. Be nice to him, won't you? He had such a shit time with bloody Zizzi.'

Conversation with Effie involved a lot of listening. Sadie didn't feel put upon; the younger woman was engaging, funny, albeit self-involved. She learned a lot about Hero.

'There's ten years, bit more actually, between me and him, so by the time I was a person he was leaving home. My friends are all in love with him. It's the looks, you see. He gets that glamour from Ma. Funny thing is, Hero behaves as if he was plain. He's never been a heartbreaker. Dad despairs. Ma just nags. *When are you coming to see us?* Hero has a huge life outside this house but I can't break away. Ma studies me when she thinks I can't see her. I can hear her thinking that she'd never waste her life crying over some man.'

'You're not sad tonight. That's a start.' Sadie, an outsider, saw the Smiths in vivid 3D. The misunderstood boy who wanted to change the world. The cosseted girl whose feelings were a problem to be solved.

After the long meal, with a different wine for each course, and *fish knives* for heaven's sake, Elizabeth had handed Hero a small box.

'For you,' she'd said. 'I saw it in the jeweller's window and simply couldn't resist.'

Only Sadie noticed the slight hesitation as Hero took the box. Inside was a watch, fifty years old, still ticking gamely. A blue face with gold hands, on a blue leather strap. Unusual. A collector's item. 'It's lovely, Ma,' he'd said, but Sadie saw how the transaction bothered him.

He rejects the value the Smiths put on material items.

Now, by the lake, Effie nudged Sadie. 'Me and Ma had a little conference about you earlier.'

With a groan, Sadie said, 'I really don't want to know what was said.'

'Don't be silly! Ma said something like, "Oh I do hope she looks after him." Because she has this theory about Hero, that he always looks after other people, but nobody looks after him.'

Sadie was grateful for Effie's tendency to ramble. The notion of taking care of Hero hadn't occurred to her.

I cast myself as the damsel in distress; that forces Hero to be a white knight.

Until Teddy and Jack died, Sadie had been the McQueen's anchor. She'd been strong. Capable. Not a damsel.

I was loved.

It was her fuel; Sadie had been running on empty since the accident. She walked a little faster.

What if I'm not capable of looking after somebody else anymore?

What if her strength had trickled out into the ground?

A noise behind them. A soft sweep, like fabric rustling. She turned her head. A punt glided through the water.

'You'd have loved Steve.' Effie sat on a bench carved from a fallen tree, pulling Sadie down with her. 'He was funny. Kind. Sweet. His breath never smelt! Imagine that!'

'I can't,' smiled Sadie.

'He treated me like a woman, not like a kid, the way Ma and Pa, and yes, even Hero, do. He made me feel as if what I said mattered. But he looked after me, too. I'm making him sound perfect,' said Effie, 'because he was.'

'Jack was perfect too.' Sadie qualified it; her rose-tinted glasses weren't as powerful as Effie's. 'Perfect for me, that is.'

The boat stopped at the island, bumping submerged tree roots with a tiny sound that just about reached their ears.

'It was love, Sadie, and love doesn't come along that often. Hero wants me to start reaching out, but . . .' Effie scuffed her sandal in the dirt. 'I'd be letting Steve down.'

Hearing somebody else say it exposed that statement in all its wrong-headed, romantic glory. 'If it was love,' said Sadie, 'wouldn't Steve want you to be happy?'

'Not was, *is*.' Effie was emphatic. 'He was a tiny bit like my bro, I guess. Adventurous but grounded.' She leaned in close, giggling, complicit. 'But he never told me off. Hero has a habit of putting me right, when I really don't need it. Does he do that to you?'

'Not yet.'

'He will,' said Effie.

Sadie rather hoped he would. She'd enjoy the to and fro. Arguing with Jack had been one of life's keenest pleasures.

The Smiths loved Hero, that was clear, but did they value him? Did they *see* him? Did they understand his alcoholism? She imagined him struggling alone, and something shifted deep inside her. An unnameable part of her moved towards him.

'Tell me about your Jack, Sadie. Describe him.'

It didn't come easy. Unlike over-sharing Effie, Sadie kept it all inside. Airing her memories of Jack might render them ordinary. 'He was fun. Reliable. A bit of a know-it-all at times. Always rescued me when I needed it.' Before Effie could gush about that, Sadie said, 'I rescued him, too.' She recalled the dark moods after time spent with Merle, when Jack would be exhausted from meeting his mother's myriad needs. 'That's the deal we strike when we fall in love.'

'I never had time to rescue Steve.' Effie sat forward, chin on her hands. 'We were only together a year. Not even that.' As if she'd heard the workings of Sadie's mind, she said, with a touch of defensiveness, 'We'd have definitely stayed together. I'm not, like, *nursing* these emotions. It was real, me and Steve. We were in it for the long haul.'

The sun was giving up. Or giving in. Melting behind the house. The island firmed up into a dark shape. A light sparked in the window of the circular hut.

Sadie wondered. There was another boat tethered. As if daring her. A shadow moved inside the small house.

Effie stood up. 'There's something else.' She knelt suddenly in front of Sadie, her face beseeching. 'Hero doesn't know everything about Steve. He'd hate him if he knew. And me. I couldn't bear for my brother to hate me, Sadie!'

It was all so urgent. Sadie scrambled to say something that could live up to the occasion but before she could, Effie was confessing.

'He was a married man. I was his other woman. I was Steve's bit on the side.'

'Aw, no.' Sadie took Effie's hands. They were thin, like birds' claws. 'I'm sure you were more than that.'

'I was. I *was*.' Effie seemed to believe and disbelieve it at the same time.

This is why she's struggling to get over it.

'Did his wife know?'

'God, no.' Effie put her head on Sadie's lap and, perhaps because she seemed to demand it, Sadie stroked Effie's hair. 'Nobody even told me he'd died. I thought he'd dumped me. It was days before I heard. I didn't matter, you see. I didn't exist.'

'You matter,' whispered Sadie. For the first time ever she was glad of her widow's status. There was a conflict here; as a wife, Sadie felt outrage. As a woman she was compassionate.

'He didn't tell me he was married at first. Not until I fell for him.'

'It's often the way.' A dent appeared in Steve's halo.

'He couldn't risk losing me.' That seemed to satisfy Effie; she would never notice the dent. 'I blew him away.' She straightened up, looking into Sadie's face, her peony-petal cheeks glowing with injustice. 'I didn't get to go to his funeral!'

'I didn't go to my husband's either.' Sadie blinked away Effie's request for an explanation.

I lay under the coffee table most of the day.

'Do you hate me?' asked Effie.

'I don't think I could,' said Sadie.

Sadie crept back to the lake alone.

She'd never rowed a boat before. The surface of the water was dark and sparkling, like spilled wine. Below there, there would be slippery weeds, and sharp stones.

She had slipped off her gold watch, left it on the nightstand by her bed. Her naked wrists were pale as she rowed. The noise of the double-ended paddle was loud to her ears, but insignificant to the night.

She was thrown back as the boat grounded. She scrambled over the prow. That light still glimmered. Sadie hurried towards it. All urgency. No doubt.

The door of the quaint little hut creaked open at her touch.

A bed, little more than a pallet on legs, with old throws mussed up all over it. And on top of the throws, Hero. Hands behind his head. Eyes impossible to read. 'I thought it was a ghost,' he said. His voice was very quiet, like dry leaves.

'I'm real.' Sadie pulled off her camisole. It ruffled her hair. 'I'm all in, Hero.'

'You mean I have a normal girlfriend at last?' Hero sat up. He held out his arms.

With no grace, just enthusiasm, Sadie landed on him. Kissed him.

'You keep doing that,' he said. 'And I keep liking it.'

Then he took charge.

WEEK FIVE

Dear Fellow Residents

This week it's my turn to host the irrelevant and time-consuming residents' meeting. It's on Wednesday 20th June as if you didn't know that already. The agenda is whatever witless nonsense we talk about on the day. Oh, and it's at 6pm for a change because I want an early night.

Pass this note around. I have arthritis and cannot be expected to write more than one.

Thank you.

Mary

p.s. No food will be supplied. We all eat far too much.

Any mention of Jack's name was tantamount to a contraceptive device, so Sadie left Hero asleep on the island without a farewell.

It was unthinkable to visit this stretch of the East Anglian coast, as familiar to Sadie as the lines around her eyes, without catching up with Jack. In the minicab she ignored the early morning banter of the cheerful driver, unable to chase the embrace of last night from her mind.

Hero had smothered her, surprised by how noisy she was. Then he'd thought better of it, and let her howl. She'd flipped him on his back, taking him by surprise. She had loved him to sleep, and as he drifted off with his arms around her he'd murmured, 'I love your idea of normal, Sadie.'

Graveyards are sobering places. Her feet found Jack's plot on their own. The stone was glazed with early dew.

A woman crouched over a nearby grave. She was tenderly planting some nodding little flower. When the first crash came she looked over, startled.

'Bastard!' shrieked Sadie as the little pottery vase she'd left there on her last visit broke into countless pieces on the headstone. She pulled up the rosemary. 'For remembrance!

That's a joke!' She ground the alyssum into the mud with her heel.

The woman left in a hurry.

'How could you do this to me?' If Jack hadn't been dead, Sadie would surely have killed him.

In retrospect, she'd seen it coming. An unwelcome sixth sense had tickled her neck. Whispering of coincidental car crashes and an actor famed for his love of motorbikes.

'Let me show you a photo,' Effie had said, in the velvet dark beside the lake.

Like a key turning in a lock, a dozen tiny clicks sounded in Sadie's mind. 'Was Steve a nickname?' she asked, surprised by how calm her voice sounded.

'How'd you know?' Effie had been delighted by her new ally's clairvoyance. She fished a small square photograph out of a crochet bag. 'I called him Steve 'cos—'

'Because of his surname.' Sadie snatched the picture. 'McQueen. Like Steve McQueen.' Her mind raced. 'The motorbike wasn't real.'

'To everybody else, he was Jack,' said Effie. 'But to me he's Steve. My Steve.'

Effie's Steve stared out at Sadie with Jack's eyes.

'I didn't even tell her, Jack.' Sadie was worn out. Her arms hung loosely at her sides as she stood by the grave. 'So many questions. And where are you? Nowhere!' She brought her fist down on the stone, as if Jack was conveniently out of town.

If this was the change borne on the soft wind sneaking past the cherry tree, Sadie wanted none of it. There had been hope in that whiff of change, yet here she was, plummeting into an even deeper pit, where her loss was mixed with fury. Sadie was pressed hard up against a truth so ugly she couldn't look it square in the eye.

'You lied, over and over. All those work trips that year. Oh Jesus, did you take her to Florida?' Sadie had wanted to go along, but there'd been talk of 'all work and no play'. 'You pretended to be sad you couldn't bring me. Instead, muggins here stayed at home looking after our daughter while you fucked somebody a decade younger in a five-star hotel room. Was that it, Jack? A firmer body?'

Just as she had been propelled here, Sadie was now propelled to go. She wondered how she'd withstand the car journey to London with these sadistic ants in her pants. 'Thank you,' she spat as she turned away. 'Thanks for your legacy. Teddy died not knowing her beloved Daddy was a shit but I have to live on, without you or her, with my guilt, and now this pain.'

As ever, Sadie's subconscious supplied Jack's response. She heard his defence, his rationalisation.

'Oh shut up!' she screamed at a dead man.

*

'No need to ask how it went.' Fi, arms folded over her lavish bosom, watched Hero walk away from Sakura. He twirled his keys. Whistled. No one would have been surprised if he'd broken into a tap dance. '*That*, my friend, is a man who got his oats.'

That was true. Sadie's X-rated memory box pulsed in her brain. He'd leaned over to kiss her a dozen times on the drive back. As they'd waited at a roundabout he'd said, 'I figured out that you visited the grave. I hope Jack took the news about us okay.'

Sadie pulled on her tunic. 'Who's my first appointment?'

Cher stuck out her lower lip. 'What? No details? Come on, boss lady. Are you two a thing now or what?'

'Are we here to gossip or work?' Cher's question had been light-hearted, but Sadie's response came from a cellar. Dark and deep.

The girl's reaction was predictably curt. 'Mrs Samuel. Nine-fifteen. Back and head massage.' She began to type as if attempting to dismember the keyboard.

As Fi's mouth opened to butt in – Fi was a veteran butter-in – Sadie escaped to Treatment Room 1, saying as she went, 'Cancel my two forty-five please, and yes, I know it's a nana. Just do it.'

At lunchtime, in the gap between a head massage and a rejuvenating facial, Sadie saw Hero out on the mews. She joined him as he sifted through the odds and ends on the table outside MOBuk.

Holding out a porcelain dish of dolls' house proportions, Hero said to Sadie, 'My granny had a piece that looked like this. Hers was worth a fortune.'

'My granny only had china shepherdesses with chipped noses.'

'The sticky label says fifty pence.' Hero was troubled. He beckoned to Mary, who stopped doing something complicated with a sore on Noel VI's back leg and hobbled out.

'If it says fifty pence,' said Mary, 'it's fifty pence. It's only money, after all. Do you want it?'

'Yes.' Hero's immediate answer surprised Sadie. 'I'll give the bowl back, somehow,' he whispered as Mary toiled back indoors for change.

'You're a hero, Hero.'

'And you're a sadist, Sadie.' He looked alarmed. 'God, no, doesn't really work, does it?'

'No kissing on my premises,' warned Mary, reappearing with a shiny new coin.

'We have an OAP discount day at the spa, Mary.' Sadie raised her eyebrows. 'A little spot of massage? Some relief for your aching bits?'

'I do not consider myself a pensioner.' With an arthritically mangled hand, Mary rearranged the broken lids and dusty DVDs on her sale table. 'My *bits*, aching or otherwise, are between me and my maker.'

'That'll be a no,' said Hero as they strolled back across the cobbles. 'Don't you have a business to run?'

'For some reason I'd rather be out here.' Sadie hugged him, hard and quick, for a smorgasbord of motives: partly because, so tall beside her, he exuded a physical pull that their lovemaking had enhanced; partly because she wanted to match his ardour.

He was Tigger. Bouncy, rejuvenated, his internal lights on full blast.

Sadie was subdued. She was drawn to him. He was special, without a doubt.

But.

Jack was in the way again. For a completely different reason, one that Hero knew nothing about.

'Sorry, I'm a bit low key,' she said. Sooner or later he'd notice the discrepancy in their behaviour.

'Are you?' Hero's head seemed full of that makeshift bed on the island. He bent to her, lowered his voice. 'No promises required. No guarantees. Besides . . .' He attempted a coquettish look. 'You'll soon catch up with me. I go a bit fast. I forgot what I'm like when I'm in—'

They both looked startled.

'When I'm in like,' finished Hero. 'Madly, deeply, in like with a woman.'

*

Three p.m. School gates.

Dismembered by Jack's infidelity, Sadie couldn't resist their tug. Fi had asked, gently, if she was okay as Sadie left the spa.

'Stop fussing,' Sadie had snapped.

Standing in the doorway, Fi had called, 'Just so I know, are you gonna be horrible forever?'

Sadie didn't feel horrible. She felt embattled. She felt barely human.

The children streamed past. Sadie held her bag close to her chest, a protective gesture that was nothing to do with the contents of her purse and everything to do with her fear of flying apart.

She wanted to hold a girl to her. A Teddy. She needed reassurance that her little family – so fragile in the end! – had been real. That it had mattered.

None of the girls was Teddy, of course. Teddy was unique. Even though on the surface Sadie had recovered, stitched herself into a simulacrum of a human, any potential baby she would make with Hero would be wonderful but it wouldn't be Teddy.

'It's good to get out of Cherry Blossom.' Hero wiggled his arms and his legs, as if shaking off his working week.

'It's like those villages in Victorian novels,' said Sadie. She held his hand. 'Where so much happens that they never think about the wider world.'

'I thought the mews would just be a backdrop to U-Turn.' Hero had suggested this saunter through their patch of London. 'Turns out that all human life is there. Love. Death. Laughter.' He threw his companion a sideways glance. 'Best sex of my damn life.'

They had left late, held up by a sudden tsunami of I-Want-You in Sakura's stockroom. Gasping up against a pile of cardboard boxes had been a better start to the day than Sadie's customary granary toast.

The shared memory drew them together, both enjoying how they had to keep it wholesome in public, knowing that later they'd reprise their passion.

It felt holistic. Sex and fun and feelings. It was easy to care about Hero. Everything was easy when they were together. It was only when she lifted her head, looked about her, that she remembered.

Jack.

It was inevitable that Jack would come between them. But Sadie had foreseen only ordinary misgivings, not the agony caused by Effie's confession.

She wondered if Effie had griped to Hero about the rude new girlfriend who'd walked away without saying a word the minute she had opened her heart. Sadie had dodged a formal leave-taking the next morning, too tempted to shout, 'You fool! It wasn't love. You were destroying a family!'

Hero was talking. Sadie had to tune back in. She saw a faint tic of irritation. How long before that grew into exasperation? Except when they made love, Sadie was only half present. She agreed that, yes, this area badly needed a cinema, and he was appeased for the time being.

Ironically, Sadie had been feeling closer to Jack in the days since Effie's revelation than she had since his death. Closer even than the relaxed days of married life.

Relaxed? Ha!

Jack had been anything but. Her laid-back husband was secretly booking hotel rooms behind her back and whispering sweet nothings into another woman's ear.

'When do we announce, well, *this*?' Hero pulled her towards him in a circle made of his arms. He jiggled her. 'When, eh? The mews are gossiping their heads off. How about we go official at the next meeting?'

'I thought men played it cool and women fought for the title "girlfriend",' laughed Sadie.

'Maybe in the Neanderthal circles you're used to, woman.' Hero let her wriggle free. 'We're not announcing an engagement, just telling people we're together.'

That was a nice word. Soft and rounded. Full of potential. And somehow unwelcome. 'Can we not?'

'O-kay.' Hero said it slowly, as if inching along the revelations the word uncovered. 'But why?' He frowned.

'Because it's so new and we're so—'

He interrupted. 'You want to keep it between us for a while.' Hero seemed pleased with this interpretation. 'Yeah, okay, let's be a secret.'

He hadn't divined her real reasons. Or he was ignoring them. Sadie was too torn inside to face even gentle teasing from their neighbours.

'It's just that I want to rediscover the world with you, Sadie.'

This man was impetuous but sure-footed, carrying his emotions tattooed across his forehead. Hero was the answer to many a woman's dream, but Sadie had only nightmares.

'I promise I'll go slow. Best behaviour.' Hero put his hands in a praying posture and executed a respectful bow. 'But not right now.' He grabbed her. He kissed her. For a while she didn't think.

There was an influx of nanas.

Every elderly woman in the vicinity seemed to be taking advantage of Sakura's OAP discount day. There were a Phyllis and a Betty lined up on the modular seating, and two Ethels had broken the Nespresso machine.

Cher serviced them with builder's tea and pink wafer biscuits. 'They won't want your stupid organic multigrain energy bars,' she'd told Sadie with disdain.

'They're so *loud.*' Fi's hangover made her delicate.

Also hungover, although not from alcohol, Sadie was glad to escape into the dim, scented haven of Treatment Room 2. Her client had never had a massage before, she said, as she extricated herself from complicated undergarments.

'Where would you like me to focus on?'

'It all aches, love!'

Sadie was tender. She trusted the rhythm that sprang up between her and the body beneath her fingers. Energy travelled both ways in the little cubicle. Sadie was becalmed by her client, and the first-timer was lulled into a trance.

'You have magic hands, lovey,' she told Sadie.

'And you've reminded me why I do this.' Sadie had changed that woman's day for the better. She had touched her with no judgement for her wrinkles or the soft sag of her skin. They had achieved something together. Sadie was grounded again, cleansed of her regrets about the school gates.

That's the last time I give into myself.

Out in reception, the remaining nanas were in a noisy huddle. The nylon mob parted and there was Jez, with the darting eyes and nervy demeanour of prey.

'Lovely young man like you,' Betty was saying – or was it an Ethel? – 'surely you've got yourself a nice girlfriend?'

'Not really,' stuttered Jez.

Watching, loving it, Fi and Cher were united for once in their glee.

'Wassamatterwivya?' a burly octogenarian wanted to know. 'Get on wivvit!'

'I don't know what you mean.' Jez's wild hair was lank with stress. He looked as if he feared he might die there, amongst the wild and merciless nanas.

Taking pity on him, Sadie asked, 'Annie? Who's Annie? I have Annie next for a head massage.'

'That can wait,' barked a permed lady. She pointed at Cher. 'Look at her, son, she's a nice young woman with no boyfriend. The least you can do,' she said to Jez, 'is take her out for a shandy.'

Cher stopped sniggering. Fi retreated niftily from the spotlight.

'No, no, *no*, I ain't having this.' One of Cher's false eyelashes came adrift.

'Ask her.' A nana jabbed Jez with a forefinger.

He rubbed his arm. 'I should be getting back to work.'

'Ask her!' The nanas took up the cry. 'Ask her! Ask her!'

'Cher!' yelled Jez suddenly, without looking at her. 'Will you come for a drink with me?'

'S'pose.' Cher's look dared Sadie to comment, so Sadie simply pegged down her grin until she and Fi could meet in the stockroom and have a good scream about it.

The Swatch on the bedside table told Sadie she should be asleep. It was a poor substitute for Jack's gold watch, but that was in solitary confinement at the back of a drawer.

'We can't!' had been Sadie's first thought when Hero had suggested booking into a hotel for the night.

'We bloody well can. Jez is on duty at U-Turn and tomorrow's Sunday so you're not needed at the spa.'

A bubble had risen within her. A golden glimmering thing that popped with a delicious tinkle when he threw her on the wide bed.

Now, hanging over the bathroom sink, Sadie communed with her reflection in the mirror. She'd been so careful to create a safe place for herself: a place where emotions were small in scale, and easily managed. Now here was Hero, blasting her queendom.

The wind of change had blown warm in her face after she'd been shivering for so long. Sadie melted, flowed, like that first feel of sand between your toes after a long winter.

Sensuality swamped her. Sadie felt present in her body; she hadn't realised how many sensations were missing until physical desire threw its arms around her. Its whisper was louder than the shouts of her memories.

She crept back to bed.

Hero slept on. Sadie thought of the barren flat awaiting her. The empty child-sized bed. The carved boat sitting in the dark. She wasn't needed at home; even the *Lady Sadie* would float on just fine without her.

A room service tray sat on the carpet. The waiter had hung around a little too long, saying, 'Whoops! Drunk already?' when Sadie tripped on the hem of the towelling dressing gown she had hastily scooped from a hook before answering the door.

Breaking open the sparkling water, Sadie and Hero had shared the countless times they'd heard that phrase so lightly.

'For us, though, it's a slap in the face,' said Hero.

'Makes me feel guilty, as if I really were drunk.'

'Being drunk for me would mean the loss of everything I've built. For that bloke, it just means being merry. I'm glad he doesn't know how deep that expression goes. I wish we didn't either.'

There's never been a 'we' in my addiction until now.

Sadie could look at Hero and see the admirable person beyond the alcoholism. Perhaps Hero could reflect Sadie back to herself, with some of the guilt erased.

Not all of the guilt. That was impossible.

Because the accident was my fault.

She rolled against Hero's back, smothering the rise of bile. His shame wasn't half as dark and ugly as her own.

More than memories of Jack and Teddy, more than the excitement of Hero, the remorse about the crash was her constant companion.

They had touched on it, the two of them, when discussing the waiter's flippant remark.

'My mother-in-law used to say, "*Ooh drunk again!*" every time she saw me.'

'Some people can't believe you ever truly stop drinking.' Hero was sympathetic. Perhaps he had a Merle in his life.

'Whenever anything slightly out of the ordinary occurred, Merle assumed it was down to booze. Every childhood scrape my daughter had. Once, Jack left Teddy outside a shop in her pushchair and Merle insisted he was covering for me.'

'Sounds like a bitch.'

'Ha!' It was cathartic to hear the sainted Merle, beloved mother of the sainted Jack, described so acidly. And so accurately. 'She's *horrible*. We weren't allowed to criticise though.' Sadie put a theatrical hand to her brow and stage-whispered, 'She'd been through so much.'

'We all have.' Hero had disappeared to brush his teeth. As good a way as any to signal his intention to kiss her. A lot.

Rearranging her dressing gown, trying to sprawl seductively on the enormous bed, Sadie had remembered the war with Merle. There had been no truce. Merle had fought the imaginary drinking all the way. Midnight trawls through her daughter-in-law's kitchen cupboards, when she visited from her chilly stone house up in Scotland. Surreptitious sniffing of Sadie's lemonade glass. A raised eyebrow if Sadie hiccupped. 'Merle never let me forget I was a marked woman. A big red A for alcoholic on my forehead.' Sadie drew the letter with a forefinger on her skin.

From the blingy en suite Hero said, his voice clogged with toothpaste, 'Perhaps she *hoped* you'd relapse. That way she'd be proved right *and* get her son back. I don't need my degree in psychology to guess she was a possessive mother.'

'She had awards for it.' Sadie, so accustomed to shouldering all the McQueen guilt, was surprised by Hero's assessment of Merle. 'She did have a point, Hero. Alcoholics do fall off the wagon.'

'Yes, but *you* didn't.' There was a pause while Hero spat and wiped his face. 'This Merle woman wanted you to feel bad about yourself, and she succeeded.' When Sadie didn't respond, he said, 'Maybe it's time to stop letting her win.'

But, Hero, she knows more about me than you do.

There were shaded valleys that Sadie couldn't lead Hero into. She visited them every day, aware that the visions they triggered could lead to relapse.

Snapshots.

One after the other, like Amber's Instagram feed.

Merle visiting that last time.

As usual, Sadie had made nice, preserving the relationship between Teddy and her grandmother. Merle, whatever her faults, was loving and interested in Teddy. The little girl adored her.

That strained Sunday lunch at a restaurant chosen by Merle, and paid for by Merle, of course. The woman exercised whatever power she could, and liked to mention her will.

As if Jack gave a toss.

Teddy – funny, bright little Teddy – gobbled up the Michelin-starred food, giggling, pulling faces, unaware of the ley lines of hatred criss-crossing the starched tablecloth.

Disapproval radiated from Merle, competing with her Dior perfume. A comment. Another comment. Telling the sommelier, 'My daughter-in-law won't have the wine. At least, not in front of us.'

Sadie stood up so quickly that her chair fell backwards. The room fell silent as if a spell had been activated. She felt the other diners watching – none more keenly than her husband – as she shouted, 'Is this what you want, Merle?'

The crystal carafe in her hand. Sadie could still feel the swan-like curve of its handle. She still felt the wine hitting her face like acid. The taste was radioactive. She poisoned herself in public. And she wrote her family's death certificate.

'Happy now?' Sadie had banged down the carafe. 'Happy, Merle?'

Teddy had burst into violent sobs.

My girl spent her last hour on earth in tears.

When Hero emerged from the bathroom, she allowed herself to forget. For an hour or two. She had concentrated on the now, because the now was unexpectedly so very nice.

*

Hero gave a soft grunt. Flung an arm awkwardly. He was sated with sex, worn out by their passion.

You're still grinning. Sadie touched his mouth with her fingertips. That mouth had kissed her body. Each caress had felt like an unbinding, as if Hero was unwrapping the smooth, unmarked woman beneath the worries.

She was re-wrapped now, practically mummified.

As if Hero and Jack were Siamese twins, thoughts of her husband had snuck in the moment she and Hero flung themselves apart. She remembered when she and Jack had been new, and unable to get enough of each other's nakedness.

Stop it!

Sadie had to get past this habit of conflating the two men. Hero was not Jack.

We made love less that last year.

Sadie had wondered why; now she knew that Jack had been depleted by his sexual adventures with Effie.

Sadie punched the hotel pillow. Hard.

WEEK SIX

To Amber <amber@yummymummymews.net.co.uk>, Hero <hero.smith@u-turn.net>, Sadie <sakuraspa@gmail.com>, Michael T. <qwertybookshop@hotmail.com>, Fiona J <filove@aol.com>, Cher Mogg <whatulookingatcher@gmail.co.uk>, Jez <jeremy.gray@u-turn.net>

From The Bobs <bob@bobscaff.co.uk>

Subject ONE-END MEWS RESIDENTS' ASSOCIATION MEETING

Please note that ketchup sachets are NOT toys and are not FREE.

Date Wednesday 27.6.18
Time 6.30 p.m.
Location Bob's Caff
Agenda Who cares?

Somebody tell Mary.

Side by side, Sadie and Cher tramped in a widening circle with Cherry Blossom Mews at its centre. The flyers – colourful, amateur – were pushed through the letterboxes of the down-at-heel houses that had yet to attract the eye of a developer, the Grade II listed stucco beauties, the sharp-angled newbuilds, the newsagents, the estate agents, the delicatessens.

'I'm knackered,' said Cher.

'Just one more drop.'

'What we going in here for?' Cher's voice was a soprano squeak of irritation. 'The health centre?' She pronounced it 'elf centre', and made Sadie smile.

The newly built, award-winning centre was an echoing place. Sterile. Multi-windowed. The receptionist was a long walk away. Sadie left a pile of leaflets with her, for all the new mums and the chronically ill.

I'd need a massage if I had to spend much time in this place.

On a corner as they neared 'home' stood a school. The Victorian variety of red brick and tall windows. The usual tumult could be heard over the high wall. Sadie picked up the pace – 'Come *on*, Cher!' – and felt her breathing grow laboured.

'Hang on.' Cher stumbled behind. She hitched down her stretchy black skirt. 'Me skirt's all caught up.'

'Perhaps if it was longer.' Sadie stopped. 'Listen,' she began, 'the way you dress . . .'

'What about it?'

'It's not really suitable for work. Is it?'

'What you trying to say?'

'I'm not *trying* to say anything.' Sadie stood her ground. Cher was formidable, despite her lack of inches. 'I *am* saying that you need to dress for your job. So, maybe not so much make-up.' She took a step backwards; Cher was volatile. 'Maybe a more sensible shoe. Definitely a skirt that's nearer your knees.'

'You saying I look like a tart?'

'Are you listening? Everybody needs to present themselves in a way that's appropriate for what they're doing.'

'I'm not everybody.'

The phrase. The tone. The curl of Cher's lip. A phrase leapt to Sadie's mind, one she was instantly ashamed of.

Spoken like a true Mogg.

'If you want to be taken seriously, Cher—'

'I'll sue.' Cher stuck out her dainty chin. The bones of her face were delicate and bird-like, at odds with the clownishly overdone make-up. 'You're giving me stress.'

Sadie told herself her surrender was a strategic retreat. 'Come on, let's get back or Fi'll sue us both.'

*

Treatment Room 1 was Sadie's favourite. Small enough for that boxed-in, intimate feel, but not so small that she bashed her stool against the partition walls when moving around her client.

A middle-aged woman lay beneath a white sheet, only her shoulders and face visible. Sadie had cleansed and exfoliated the face, gently wiping it, every movement considered.

The ritual mattered. It brought meaning. There were just the two of them in that dark, scented space. The crinkle of Sadie's tunic. The swish from the wheels of her stool. The discreet clanks and clinks as she decanted lotions.

The woman sighed. A gentle flutter of breath. She was thoroughly in this moment, a moment built just for her.

Some days Sadie rushed through massages and facials. One eye on the clock, keenly aware that they were fully booked, that Cher would scold, that Fi would need the room.

Today she grounded herself. Said to herself over and over until it didn't need to be said that she was right here, right now, and that this was all that was happening in her world.

The woman's skin was damaged. A pockmark by her eye. Ancient sunburn still causing trouble. Red veins like coral on her nose. Sadie slid cooling cream on her brow bone.

You've been overplucking your poor tired brows.

She felt a kinship. Women are encouraged to alter themselves. Not loudly or directly, but subtly.

Which is far more difficult to ignore.

To be acceptable meant to be waxed, stained, chopped about.

In Treatment Room 1, for fifty minutes, this woman was merely herself, perfect as she was, enjoying the attentions of a sympathetic professional who didn't judge or seek to change.

For an almost-hour, they were sisters.

When Sadie emerged, hands smooth with oil and upper arms pleasingly worked out, Hero was waiting.

'Hey,' he said.

'Hey yourself.' Sadie didn't draw near. His presence surprised her. Her nerves jangled.

He winked. He enjoyed her scramble to act normal.

That man sure knows how to wink.

He deployed his power with precision. Nobody else saw.

Stop! thought Sadie, and hoped he wouldn't.

Flirting. It had been so long. Yet she still knew the steps. She felt something rise in her body. Something lusty.

At the reception desk, Cher and Fi were bent over something. Heads together. It was a rarity to see them so close.

'Look at that one!' Cher was happily outraged.

'She'll stay like that if the wind changes!' shrieked Fi.

'Who are you pulling apart, you cats?' Sadie peered over their shoulders at Cher's phone. 'Is that Amber's Instagram?'

Square after square of highly coloured, enviable, hipster London life.

'She's *good*.' Sadie was impressed. Amber looked beautiful, and in her capable hands so did the battered old mews. 'You'd think the mews was in Mayfair.'

Geraniums nodded in a hanging basket over Amber's floppy hat. In the next shot she stood in front of Sakura with a sheaf of roses, the spa framed so the chrome and white interior gleamed but the sofa with its cargo of untidy old bats was cropped out.

'Look at this.' Fi scrolled back to her favourite and read the caption. '"Every gal needs a no make-up day."' She could barely breathe for laughing out, 'Hashtag: breathe!'

Hero had joined them. 'She looks great with no make-up,' he said.

The women pitied him. Cher pulled a disgusted face. 'She's wearing foundation and she's filled in her brows and put nude gloss on her lips.' She added a disparaging, 'Men!'

Sadie was silent. The pictures had a hypnotic effect. They slid past her eyes, neat and gorgeous, and with each one went a tiny chunk of her self-esteem. Each image forced a confession from her.

I don't look like that.

My bedroom doesn't look like that.

My breakfast doesn't look anything *like that.*

'She lives on sodding açai berries,' snorted Fi.

'Imagine how long it takes to light that many tea lights.' Cher jabbed a silicone nail at Amber's bathroom, a soft-focus shrine to beauty.

They were quiet now. No more hooting as they compared their complex, messy, reality to Amber's perfection.

'It's not real,' said Hero. 'It's PR.'

'Yeah,' said Sadie, thinking she'd look like a heffalump in the gossamer harem pants Amber modelled above the hashtag 'keepincool'.

'We'd all look like Amber with decent lighting.' Fi blew her nose vociferously.

'Hmm.' Sadie wasn't sure. She felt Hero's gaze on her face and bent her head. She could claim truthfully 'I woke up like this', but it was no boast.

Cher was the first to break the self-deprecating trance. She waved a printout. 'Lots of take-up for our office workers' lunchtime specials.' That had been her idea. 'I've been doodling designs for the mother and baby massage leaflet.'

'Eh?' Fi snatched the piece of paper, frowned at it. 'Is this, you know, a good idea, Sadie?' Her comment came with a side order of meaning that puzzled Cher.

'It's a brilliant idea,' said Sadie.

'But ... kids all over the place.' Fi's insistence piqued Cher's curiosity.

'So? What's wrong with kids?'

'Nothing.' Sadie was firm. She appreciated Fi's concern,

but she had to kick against the protective cordon her friend had set up around her.

I'm coming back to life.

She returned Hero's stare. She even winked.

The spa had visitors on Tuesday afternoon. The Mogg twins were displeased that their 'little sis' wasn't at the desk.

One twin displayed his irritation with straightforward bad manners. The other sent a chill all the way down Sadie's back with his broad smile and the lazy blinking of his eyes.

'Aw, that's a shame. Tell Cher we were here.' He added a slight bow.

'Sure.' His synthetic charm made Sadie queasy. The twins' differing attitudes were the only way to tell them apart. She had never seen grown men dress identically; the effect was alarming.

Presumably that's the point.

Two bald heads. Two sharp suits. Two pairs of dark glasses. They were a parody of screen gangsters, but the menace was real. Sadie could taste it.

'Hope you're looking after her,' said the surly one. Joe.

Or is he James?

'We're very fond of Cher,' said Sadie, glad Fi wasn't there to disagree. 'She's full of ideas.'

'Bet you're paying her peanuts.' James beamed as if he'd

paid Sadie a compliment. 'Bet you're taking the piss.' He turned to his brother. 'She looks the sort, doesn't she?'

'Anybody takes the piss out of our sister has us to deal with,' said the sour one.

A voice said loudly, 'No piss is being extracted, gents.' Fi emerged from the stockroom to stand shoulder to shoulder with Sadie. Her bulk was comforting; Fi gave off heat. 'Now, can I book you in? Maybe you want your bits waxed?'

'The lady seems to be implying that we don't scare her, James,' said Joe.

'Fat birds,' said James, 'are always mouthy.'

'True, true,' said Fi, unperturbed. 'We'll tell Cher you dropped by.'

They went. Slowly enough to signal that they were only going because they wanted to.

'Bye now!' called Fi cheerfully. She elbowed Sadie. 'They seem nice.'

'I feel as if they're watching us all the time.'

'I love saying this.' Fi drew herself up to her full height, and hoicked her bra strap so that her magnificent bosom fell into place. 'I told you so.' She relaxed. 'Employing Cher was a mistake.'

The mistake turned into the mews. She seemed to be shaking something off, shooing it away with a flapping of her hands. The something, it transpired, was Jez.

'The poor petal's trying to hold her hand.' Sadie was on

the side of romance after three years of avoiding it. Hero popped into her mind almost as regularly as Jack. She and Cher had more in common than she thought.

I feel conflicted too.

Despite their growing closeness, Sadie didn't know how she'd react if Hero tried to take her hand in public.

'Ooh, he's going for an arm around the shoulders now.' Fi winced. 'She's reacting like he's a mugger.'

As Cher blew in, all activity, tearing off her cropped denim jacket, Sadie said, 'Did you have a nice—'

'It was a burger.' Cher spun round. 'You've had a burger before. It was like that.'

'Oi!' Fi went up like a firework. 'That's your employer you're talking to, lady.'

'Sorry.' Cher didn't sound sorry. 'Don't call Jez my boy-friend, yeah?'

'Who called him that?' laughed Sadie.

'Talking of boyfriends,' said Fi to Sadie, 'my Cole reckons you and Hero are a good match.'

It was a positive step that Fi referred to Cole, the only good guy in a battalion of wrong 'uns, as hers, but 'my Cole's' nuggets of advice featured too heavily in Sakura conversation for Sadie's liking. He was quoted on politics, the weather, which 1970s light entertainment figure would be jailed next. 'Me and Hero, it's something or nothing. I'll leave the romance to you and Cher.'

'What romance?' Cher seemed to believe that if she simply denied it over and over the other women would disbelieve the evidence of their eyes. She and Jez were pulled together by an invisible thread that kept tightening. Lunch every day. A curry on Saturday night. A movie. They had all the makings of a romcom if it weren't for Cher's foul mouth and her insistence that nothing, but nothing, was going on.

'Don't start,' said Fi. 'I saw you this morning, standing at opposite ends of Mary's shop, as if you'd never met.'

'What does MOBuk stand for, anyway?' Cher's sleight of hand was clunkily obvious.

'Ooh yes, let's change the subject,' laughed Fi.

'Nobody knows,' said Sadie. 'Some obscure charity. Dogs, I reckon.'

'Mary's shop smells a bit.' Cher, who travelled in a fug of body lotion, hair product and perfume, wrinkled her nose. Her contouring had been hurried that morning; Sadie detected a line the colour of mud down either side of her nose as it wrinkled.

'That skirt, Cher . . .'

'*What?*' The word was lobbed like a grenade. 'It's longer than me other one.'

'But your other one,' said Sadie, 'is a belt.' It was time to be imperious. 'Get on with whatever work you're pretending to do, madam.'

Sullen, Cher muttered, 'Jez is just a bloke, yeah.'

The bloke who was just a bloke watched from the cobbles, confusion all over his face, before he disappeared into U-Turn.

Noel was at large.

'You on your ownio?' asked Sadie, bending to pick him up. The dog's cataracts were worsening, and he'd been snarling at his own reflection in the windows of Yummy Mummy.

It was late, midnight-ish. Sadie had said goodbye to Hero at his door, giggling, refusing his offer to walk her home. The few metres of courtyard and some deep breaths of good dirty London air would clear her head.

Hero fuzzed up her thinking. Overrode her checks and balances. Made her feel instead of reason.

Thoughts of Jack receded but did not disappear.

She remembered the weeks after his death when she'd scrabble for his face in her mind. Now she knew Jack would always be solid. Never become a ghost. Never really become an ex, despite the affair; death leaves so many loose ends.

Which made her relationship with Hero a mite crowded.

The mews was breezy and warm and alive. The cobbles massaged the soles of Sadie's feet through her pumps, like free reflexology, as she regarded the sky.

Even in the middle of one of the greatest cities on earth, stars poked through the pollution. So far away, and yet they spoke to Sadie.

When she had first arrived at Cherry Blossom Mews, Sadie had watched the blossoms fall from the tree she now stood under. She leaned against its slender, solid trunk, and held Noel to her chest, remembering.

Such grief. The beautiful blossoms drifting down on the damp air had felt like snow. She had been so cold. She had been chilled to the bone. She had, Sadie realised, with a guilty jolt, come a long way.

'Let's get you home,' whispered Sadie to the little dog. She regretted picking him up; this close his odour was overwhelming.

If you could bottle that, it would be as effective as mace.

Mary was surprised to see her companion in Sadie's arms. 'You naughty boy, Noel Lockridge!'

'Can I come in? Cup of tea, maybe?'

'I'm perfectly happy to make you a cup of tea,' said Mary, in her quiet, formal way, 'but you're really checking up on me, aren't you, Sadie?'

Honesty was the best policy with a beady-eyed old bird like Mary. 'Yes.'

A sigh. 'Come along, then.'

The tea was strong, served in a proper cup, with a plain and decent biscuit on the side. Noel got a saucer of the same, while Sadie excavated a spot to sit in the cluttered room. She watched Mary covertly as her friend, with an occasional grimace at some arthritic pain, settled herself in a winged armchair and took up a piece of tatty knitting that never seemed to grow.

'Noel must have slipped out,' said Sadie, with a hint of admiration. Noel wasn't built for slipping. 'You've moved the mirror that used to hang in the hall.'

'Little Miss Nosy,' murmured Mary, rooting through a bag of wool.

'That's me.' Sadie was always equable around Mary, recognising the acidic throwaways as self-defence. Tonight, she could have borne outright abuse; her entire body was warmed by Hero's embrace. She could feel his arms still, as if he'd branded her. 'Did you sell it?'

'I chopped it up for firewood.'

'In summer? It looked like an antique.'

'Not all antiques are valuable. I'm an antique.'

'You're priceless, Mary.' Slowly eating her own fat, Mary was selling off her inheritance piece by piece. 'How's business at MOBuk?'

'I sold a box of buttons yesterday.' Mary's needles flew. 'Please don't give me a lecture about pricing.'

Poor old MOBuk, whoever they are, make only a pittance from Mary.

'I wouldn't dream of lecturing you.'

Mary gave her a look over her wool.

They sat in a silence broken only by Noel's yippy dreams from the hearthrug. Sadie had an early start in the morning, but she was tethered to Mary's lumpy sofa by bonds stronger than her desire to yawn. Nobody got left behind on Sadie's watch.

Loneliness doesn't smell. It can't be tasted. Yet it makes itself known. Mary was a voyeur of the human race. She watched them, intrigued, sometimes aping their language and their mannerisms. Her isolation sat around her shoulders like a fur stole. At times she seemed proud of it, but Sadie wanted to wrench it away, pull Mary into the dance.

Sadie was lonely, too. Despite Fi. Despite the mews. Despite the new, thrilling, terrifying addition of Hero. She didn't give in, though. She didn't barricade herself away, like Mary.

At least I had a love to lose.

Mary, her feet not reaching the ground in her enormous armchair, tutted over a dropped stitch. She had never had a love to lose. There was not one photograph of a man. No ring on her bent fingers, no special name on her lips.

Sadie settled back on musty cushions. She could stay a while yet.

'Sorry! Sorry!' Sadie was late for the residents' meeting.

She tore off her newly purchased kimono jacket – 'New man, new clothes!' Fi had said – and dropped a pile of leaflets as she took her chair.

'You were supposed to hand them all out.' Cher was severe. 'I slogged me guts out printing them.'

'Yeah, I saw you,' said Fi. 'It took such perseverance to, like, click "Control" and "Print".'

After hours, Bob's Caff looked bigger. All the chairs were neatly stacked, the tables pushed back, the floor swept. The lino was so old and pitted that it never looked clean, but it had an air of order and professionalism completely lacking in Yummy Mummy across the street. Utilitarian. Plain. Mrs Bob, who'd relinquished that day's stained apron, was good at what she did.

Pity she gets no joy out of it.

'Sorry, Sadie.' Amber hunched her shoulders up to her ears. 'We started without you.'

'S'fine.' Amber had a habit of apologising for things that didn't need an apology. 'What have I missed?'

Fi was smirking. 'We volunteered you to do the whip-round for the window cleaner's wedding.'

'I always do the whip-rounds!' Sadie narrowed her eyes.

Hero, sitting shoulder to shoulder with Michael, said, 'Fi told us you'd be pleased.'

'It's his second marriage,' grumbled Sadie, making a note in the little pad she always took out at meetings, much to the others' amusement. 'He should refund us for the first present.' She was at sea. 'What do you buy a window cleaner?'

'A nice . . . um . . . sponge?' Amber drew a sponge in the air with her fingers.

'Very romantic,' said Fi.

'I'm sure he's good for sponges,' said Sadie.

'Quite a problem,' said Hero. 'What do you buy the window cleaner who has everything?'

Sadie knew he'd see her secretive little smile.

'Get him a gag,' said Cher, from where her chin slumped on her chest. Having fought to be included in the residents' get-togethers she now radiated boredom. 'His singing drives me mad.'

'I'm biased,' said Michael, as if he'd suddenly woken up, 'but why not get him a book?'

Sadie read between his lines.

'Books show you care,' Michael continued. 'Lovers bond over books.' He let out a fluttery breath, and added, to himself. 'Even if one of them doesn't realise what's going on.'

I do, I do.

Other people's feelings were tricky to navigate. Sadie wondered how to make it clear that she appreciated his thoughtfulness, but he'd caught her at the very moment her life had unexpectedly creaked open on a rusty hinge. Michael was a good man. A nice man. Sadie liked 'nice', considered it an underrated virtue in a world where most people strived to be kooky and unique.

But he's not my type.

Nor, truly, was Hero. She watched him as he patiently listened to one of Amber's baroque tales of bin misery.

He's too handsome for me.

Jack had been nice-looking: regular features, fine lashes, a good head of hair. Not noticeable, though. Not a stand-out person in any way. If she was honest – and Sadie tried to be, even when it hurt – Hero's unabashed, glowing sexual attractiveness made her nervous.

It made her want him; it also made her doubt that she deserved him. This was uncomfortable territory, terrain she should have left behind in her teens. Fi would deal with it in a few sentences, all of them peppered with swear words.

'What do you think, Sadie?' asked Amber suddenly.

'I think . . .' began Sadie.

'Sadie thinks she wasn't listening,' said Hero.

'Guilty!' Sadie laughed.

Amber almost – *almost* – showed irritation. 'The bins!' Her eyes flared. 'Isn't it time we bought nice co-ordinated ones?'

Mary got there first. 'I, for one, am not spending good money on fancy bins. A bin,' she declared, 'is a bin.'

Bob was gentler. 'Not everybody has your sense of style, Ambs.' He spread his arms wide. 'I ask you, do I look like a man who wants a designer bin?'

The laughter was collusive, good-natured. Bob's belly stuck out under his T-shirt like the promise of triplets.

'You look like a man who should be *in* a bloody bin,' said Mrs Bob, with not a glimmer of humour. She eyed Sadie as she said this, daring her to comment.

Sadie didn't take the bait.

She was reliving the day just gone.

No leaflets had been delivered. Not one. She'd had the best of intentions, working out a route that avoided schools or even nurseries.

Why, then, had her sandals carried her astray, to deposit her outside Lightfoot Road Primary School? The intoxication had taken hold, as surely as if she'd uncorked a bottle of Sauvignon. A bell had rung. A stampede had begun. Hundreds of sensible shoes on playground concrete.

She'd followed a little gang. There were four of them. An awkward number for female friendships, she had thought, discerning some jockeying for position around the lynchpin, the most popular girl, as they trailed behind a seemingly bored childminder.

The children dawdled and she'd had to slow her usual walking speed. Sadie had been terrified she'd draw attention to herself, but nobody had given her a second glance. Nobody suspected this mature woman of stalking schoolgirls. Her crime was so absurd that it went undetected.

Slowly, slowly, with a stop for lollies, the girls led her to a patch of dehydrated green. Like a spy in a bad film, Sadie settled herself on an adjacent bench, unseen by the childminder who only had eyes for her phone. London parks are shared by junkies and toddlers and meths drinkers. Sadie saw how the girls created a bubble for themselves, with sudden bursts of shrieking laughter and ardent huddles and abrupt bored splaying on the tinderbox grass.

About seven years old. About what Sadie thought of as Teddy's 'real' age. As if her daughter hadn't fallen prey to a big black full stop in her fourth year.

Sadie's Teddy was all theory.

A speech pattern, a way of shouting 'No! No! No!' to get the others' attention, reminded her of Teddy. Sharply. Like a punch to her stomach. The girl in question was dark, middle-eastern with a long plait of hair as thick as rope. Nothing like Sadie's girl, yet her voice restored the factory settings on Sadie's heart.

Now, with her neighbours chattering around her – the meeting had moved on to the controversial topic of discounts between the businesses – Sadie thought back to when she used to take Teddy to the park. It was like seeing a woman she once loved but no longer recognised.

'I need to bring up something very – *very* – sordid.' Mrs Bob rummaged in her bag. 'This!' With a flourish she held up a small box.

'Are they tablets?' Michael couldn't quite see.

'They're drugs.' Mrs Bob rolled the 'r'. 'I knew this would happen once About-Turn, or whatever it calls itself, got going. Medical paraphernalia strewn around. It'll be syringes next.'

'May I?' Hero, unruffled, his classy accent acting as anaesthetic on the residents, took the white box. 'These are hay fever tablets.' He handed them back. 'Not, so far as I know, addictive.'

Mrs Bob rearranged her face, ignoring Fi's cry of 'Careful everybody! You know how violent hay fever sufferers can get!'

The meeting staggered to a messy close. Mary dealt it a death blow by saying, 'I can't sit around listening to you lollygaggers all evening.'

'I have no idea what a lollygagger might be,' said Fi, folding her chair. 'But I agree with you, Mazzer.'

In the midst of the leave-takings and the snaffling of the last bun, Sadie sat staring at the ground. She could still hear that seven-year-old's voice in her head.

At the door, Hero looked around as if expecting her to be at his side. Amber stood close to him. Too close. Just a fraction. She called out to Sadie. 'You don't mind if I join you both for a coffee, do you?'

Sadie minded enough to make her fillings hurt, but she was only half in the room. The little girl's voice had triggered a memory so vivid that it unspooled in her mind's eye like a home movie.

'You two go,' she said, looking down, one foot already in the mud of memory that would claim her evening.

'Hey.' Hero crossed to her, bent down. 'What's up?'

'Go,' said Sadie. She lifted a shoulder in Amber's direction. 'She's waiting. Go on.'

Hero backed away, one eyebrow cocked. 'If I was to stand under your window later what would happen? Might you let down your hair so I can climb up?'

'Bit of a migraine, actually.' Sadie didn't know how he took that because she hurried past him and Amber, whose air of triumph rose from her like perfume.

Sadie's ruthless subconscious knew just how to nobble her.

Her monastic bedroom mutated into a different, equally dark room: the old sitting room in Suffolk. A mix of contemporary touches and the period bones of the house she had loved.

The curtains were drawn. A duvet lay on the sofa, stained and torn, as if it had been trampled.

On the floor, her head resting on the coffee table, Sadie wasn't sure what day it was. Had it been two days, or four, since the policemen visited? When had she crawled round to Tish's house?

The phone, resting in a sticky puddle on the carpet, squawked missed calls and messages. None from her sister. None from her parents.

The silence boomed. No doors slammed. No televisions chattered. No laughing. No shout of 'Mummy!'

A lesson was learned on Sadie's wine-drenched carpet: the world has teeth and is not reluctant to use them. She was a mass of bite marks.

It took a year to reach the door when the doorbell rang. Sadie seemed to be swimming upstream. On the doorstep was not the off-licence delivery man – her knight in shining armour – but her mother-in-law.

Merle was in black. Usually, she avoided that colour; too ageing, she said. Now she was a charcoal column in the centre of Sadie's sitting room. Clean. Fragrant. Holding a shiny handbag in gloved hands.

Merle's pointed court shoe set a bottle rolling. It came to a juddering halt against another one.

'You reek of sweat,' she said.

'I'm not well.'

A tut. 'I assume you're not coming to the funeral in this state.' Merle seemed to be looking down at Sadie from a great height, like a statue on a plinth. 'You look surprised. Yes, today's the day. I've been trying to get hold of you.' She gave the room an eloquent look. 'You're clearly too busy to take my calls.'

'It's today?' Sadie's mouth was as arid as her heart. Beyond the blacked-out windows, gears had been grinding and cogs whirring. A funeral had come together. 'I can't, Merle. I can't watch two coffins go into the ground.' She was hot. Cold. Brittle.

There was a momentary crack in Merle's disdain. 'What do you mean?'

'What do you think I mean?'

Am I shouting?

'My life's over. It's dead, with them.' Jack and Teddy must not be named; Sadie's swollen, drunken brain insisted on that voodoo. 'I can't,' she said. She may have said it a hundred times. Or perhaps she didn't say it at all.

'How can you drink at a time like this?' Merle seemed curious rather than angry. A dispassionate outsider asking a practical question. 'You, of all people. When it was your habit that killed them.' When there was no answer – devastation rarely finds a voice – Merle said, 'You stay here, Sadie. In the dirt, where you belong.' She turned her back and saw herself out. On the threshold she intercepted a courier and took a clinking plastic bag from him. 'Your goodies have arrived,' she said, and left.

Sadie had lain on the floor and stared at the ceiling. A word swam at her:

Clunch.

She and Jack had tested countless Farrow and Ball whites before deciding on Clunch for the ceiling. They'd laughed at the name.

Sadie sat up and vomited.

She had done nothing for their funeral. Only she knew Teddy's favourite hymn. Who would be there? Merle didn't have a number for Jack's best mate.

Sadie crawled towards the bag. All fingers and thumbs, she was feverish. Thank God they were screw-top bottles; a corkscrew was beyond her powers.

Before she blacked out she faced the fact that she had deserted her family in death. The last ritual of their lives was overseen by somebody else.

Three days later, shaking, choking down bile, she'd locked up the house. That carrier bag had contained Sadie's last drop of alcohol.

A train to London. A speedy decision on a near-derelict mews property.

Just once, Sadie went back to the house, now with a SOLD notice sprouting in the front garden. She had taken the bare essentials to populate her flat then closed the door, and embarked on a fresh start with what was left of her soul.

WEEK SEVEN

To The Bobs <bob@bobscaff.co.uk>, Amber <amber@yummymummymews.net.co.uk>, Hero <hsmith@u-turn.net>, Michael T. <qwertybookshop@hotmail.com>, Fiona J <filove@aol.com>, Cher Mogg <whatulookingatcher@gmail.co.uk>, Jez <jeremy.gray@u-turn.net>

From Sadie <sakuraspa@gmail.com>

Subject CHERRY BLOSSOM MEWS RESIDENTS' ASSOCIATION MEETING

Hi Guys,

By popular demand – no cake.

Date Wednesday 4.7.18
Time 6.30 p.m.
Location Sakura
Agenda Doing meetings properly!

I've already told Mary. (And Noel.)

Sadie x

One of the benefits of mews life was the constant supply of hot snacks.

The accident had cleaved Sadie's life into two distinct sections. Before and after. 'Before' had involved the odd lazy lie-in, but 'After' meant leaping up as soon as she awoke. Introspection led nowhere nice, so it was a bonus to have a caff two doors down.

Yawning, Bob apologised for yawning, and expertly cracked an egg into a pan. He knew Sadie's order. Sadie appreciated Bob; she felt almost maternal towards him, if that was the right word for her attitude towards a man two decades her senior.

She felt maternal towards many people. Those thwarted instincts flowed like a dammed river finding ruts to trickle down. When Jez appeared, sleep in his eyes and newspaper in his hand, she beckoned him over.

'Can you bear a bit of company, Jez?' Some people can't stomach conversation first thing. Jack had had no sense of humour until his third coffee.

Jez was a morning person, and allowed Sadie to squirrel details of his private life from him as they demolished their eggs. From a traveller family, Jez had opted out to live among the gorgers, as he called non-travellers.

'So, your form of rebellion was to get a house and a job?' Sadie smiled at Jez's topsy-turvy disobedience. 'Do you miss it?'

'Here, I do.' Jez put a hand over his heart. He was dinky, miniaturised. A sexy elf. 'But I've put down roots now. I love my job. It has meaning.' He looked at Sadie, properly looked. His eyes, she noticed, were almost black. 'We're all searching for meaning, aren't we?'

Ten years clean, his sobriety was central to Jez's life. 'Alcoholism is a monster,' he said, signalling for more toast. 'Turn your back on it and it pounces. You have to be aware all the time.'

'So I hear,' said Sadie.

'It's not just about avoiding booze. I have to avoid extremes, you know. Of emotion, of circumstance. I try to take the middle road.'

'Is love too extreme?'

Jez sat forward, buttered toast. 'Love, that's a biggie. I haven't had time. But when you meet somebody special . . .'

'Cher . . .' Sadie hesitated. She'd been about to use the usual language, say that Cher was a 'lovely girl'. She wasn't though. Cher was a nightmare. 'Maybe you see the same things in her that I do. Most of the time. The rest of the time—'

'—she's a rattlesnake! Guess I like rattlesnakes. What's the deal with you and my boss?'

'Deal?' Sadie attempted incomprehension.

'You a thing or what?' Jez didn't buy her innocence. 'He needs a bit of luck on the woman front.'

'Surely women fling themselves at him?' Sadie gave herself away; only a woman who found Hero dangerously attractive would think that.

'They do, yeah. But not the right ones. The ex-wife . . .' Jez exhaled and his wiggly fringe blew upwards. 'What a piece of work.'

'His son,' said Sadie, casually, thinking what a terrible private detective she'd make. 'His son lives a long way away.' This was the piece of Hero's jigsaw that didn't fit. The piece that made her worry she'd concocted a personality for him. That he'd disappoint her. 'How does he cope?' Sadie would do anything to see her own child for just one minute. The hopelessness of that desire floored her for a moment.

'Hero's strong.' Jez had nothing more than that.

A musky smell overrode the fried grease as Amber wafted in. A Chanel bracelet on a suntanned arm. Oversized sunglasses on an undersized nose. 'Isn't it divine in here? So *real*,' she said, to nobody in particular. She froze in front of Jez and Sadie. 'Stay still. What a tableau. Hang on.'

Out came the inevitable phone. She shot one, two, three, eleven pictures. Still she wasn't satisfied.

'Can we move now?' Sadie's tea was getting cold.

'It needs something more.' Amber concentrated fiercely on the six-inch screen.

'You mean we're not enough?' Jez was mock hurt, but Amber was too focused to get the joke.

A family was settling down at a corner table as Mrs Bob swiped a J-cloth across the formica. 'Menus.' She slapped down the laminated A4. 'Spam's off.'

'May I borrow your child?' Amber had the five-year-old by the arm before his parents could answer. Gap-toothed, freckled, apparently the little boy was the 'something more' Amber needed. 'I'm being sponsored by these lovely herbal tea people and I need some texture, you know?'

Nobody knew.

She manoeuvred the threesome into position, covering up the non-photogenic dirty plates, arranging the retro glassware to its best advantage. 'Got it!'

It was left to Sadie to return the boy to his parents.

'It's not easy,' said Amber ruefully, 'to make Bob's caff Insta-friendly.'

'That's why we like it,' said Jez.

'Want to see my latest?' Amber stroked her phone, speeding through her Instagram stories.

Amber larking around with an equally photogenic chum, both of them, for some reason, wearing feathered headdresses.

'We were in that horrid little park on the corner.'

'You've made it look like the garden of Eden,' said Sadie.

Amber laughed the girlish giggle she reserved for accepting compliments.

Through the hatch, a dispute arose.

'I said fried not scrambled, you stupid, stupid man!'

Amber pulled a face. 'Mrs Bob's off again.'

'My mistake, darling.' Bob could be seen bent over his hob, cracking eggs at warp speed.

'It always is!' Mrs Bob couldn't be derailed by submission. Her fury had to burn itself out. 'You're a dead weight around my neck and you always have been.' She slammed down a pile of plates as Sadie approached with her own tray of empties.

'Perhaps,' said Sadie in a low voice, 'you should appreciate your husband a little more.'

From his seat, Jez said, 'Listen, don't—'

'I lost my husband with no warning in the blink of an eye.' Sadie wanted to rescue Bob. 'Be grateful for what you have.'

Bob bent his head, plied his spatula.

Mrs Bob gaped. 'Mind your own business,' she managed. She seemed rigid with shock.

The atmosphere thickened. Sadie didn't feel heroic. She'd made things worse.

As she left, Bob called out, 'She loves me really!'

'Tell her,' screeched Mrs Bob, 'that she's barred for life!'

The sofa stood in the middle of the spa where the unhelpful couriers had dumped it, complaining all the while about 'that bloody cherry tree in the bleedin' way!'

'It's naff,' said Cher.

'It's horrible,' said Fi.

Sadie didn't like it either, but it was perfect. 'It's our nana sofa. They can't cope with that low-level funky furniture. This is comfy and easy to get out of.' She demonstrated.

'You old softie,' said Fi.

'Actually, that's brilliant,' said Cher, reluctantly. She tended to praise only her own ideas.

The first bottom to test drive the sofa was the top notch one that belonged to Hero.

When Sadie said she had 'tons to do', that she couldn't see Hero that night, he didn't question it. He was snowed under too, he said. They'd make up for it at the weekend, he said. He kissed her and held her tight and messed up her hair and told her she was the sexiest thing he'd seen since the last time he'd seen her.

Sex was a great distraction. Sex with Hero was not like sex with Jack. Sadie had assumed that sex with Jack was fabulous, but now she reached for compliments of a higher grade.

Experienced but not jaded. Tender. Strong. When Hero's body arched over Sadie's, tan limbs against her fluorescent whiteness, Sadie was in another land altogether.

Their togetherness took no effort.

Fi couldn't be gagged. After Hero left she said, with a swooning look she also used for Curly Wurlies, 'Bet he's brilliant at . . . you know . . . *it.* Cole's not bad, but bloody hell, Emanuel, my ex . . .' When she came out of her X-rated reverie, Fi said, 'Hero's a gent *and* a stud. He's the perfect person to kiss our Sleeping Beauty and bring her back to life.'

Mrs Bob was still seething.

'Life,' she yelled, 'means life, lady!'

Thrown out alongside Sadie, Fi fumed. 'She was just about to hand over me bap. Did you *have* to give her the hump?'

They had no option but to browse the falafel and quinoa specials at Amber's, as Sadie defended herself above the hubbub of entitled kiddies enjoying themselves. 'I had to defend him. She's so mean to poor Bob.'

'Poor Bob loves it.' Fi picked up a Health Bowl and looked genuinely sad that such a thing should exist. 'You shouldn't get in between couples. It never ends well.'

A woman browsing the plush unicorns, turned in alarm and said, 'Whatever's going on outside?'

Raised voices brought Amber and her customers to the doorway.

'It's that toothless wonder again,' said Fi.

'Protect the young ones!' said Amber breathlessly.

And unnecessarily, since the dishevelled man whirling on the cobbles was no threat to them. Like a sheepdog, Hero was herding him towards the gates.

'We've poured resources into your recovery,' he was saying.

Sadie stole a look at Amber, who was visibly quivering at the commanding timbre of Hero's voice.

'We'll always do our best for you, mate, but your choices matter. We can't allow you to shatter the peace. I'm drawing a line. We can help but only if you let us.'

Threat hung in the air. The man was clearly in agony, but a confused agony, as if he suspected Hero might be the cause of it. As suddenly as he had exploded, he deflated and went like an obedient sheep to the gates.

Hero pushed his hands through his hair. Took a deep breath. His eyes were troubled. He saw Sadie and strode across to her. Fi drew back, and pulled Amber with her.

'My mind's full of you,' he said to her in an urgent whisper. He put his hands on her shoulders. 'But what's on your mind?'

As promised, there was no home-made cake at the next residents' meeting, but Sadie knew better than to ignore food altogether. As the mewsites picked over the Quavers and cheese straws, she expanded on the agenda.

'Listen, *listen*! Why not do these meetings correctly? With a register and minutes and proper votes? We can gossip all we want after that.' She began to call names. 'Bob?'

'Here, miss!'

'Mrs Bob?'

'You're still barred.'

'Mary?'

'My dear, you're looking right at me.'

'Cher? Cher? Cher!'

'I'm not gonna say "here". It's stupid.'

Sadie gave up. She threw the clipboard over her shoulder and took the bowl of Quavers to her chest. 'Please yourselves,' she said, and they did.

'Tell me something, Mary.' Michael dislodged Noel's snout from the groin of his trousers; that dog had some very bad habits. 'What do the initials of your charity, MOBuk, stand for?'

'Must be in aid of animals.' Mrs Bob, who detested most humans, treated animals with respect. She smuggled Noel a cheese straw and he coughed it up on Sadie's white flooring.

'If you must know,' said Mary, erect in a Crimplene sundress that surely amplified the scorching heat that had the rest of the residents sitting back like sea lions. 'MOB stands for Mad Old Bat.'

Fi looked up from her phone. She was, Sadie could tell, sexting Cole; she liked to distract him when he was in Tesco. 'You serious? That must be the least politically correct mental health charity ever.'

'What gave you that idea it's a charity?' Mary was sucking a Werther's Original.

'The rubbish you sell,' said Cher.

'You've got "in aid of MOBuk" on the sign,' said Sadie.

'It looks like a charity shop,' said Bob, who was mopping his brow and his bald spot, one hanky for each.

'I'm the mad old bat referred to in the title,' said Mary.

'You keep the takings?' Mrs Bob was horrified.

'Oh dear.' When Michael was perturbed he pushed at his glasses with a forefinger. 'I suspect that's illegal.'

Applause broke out. Bob started it, on his feet, shouting 'Mary, you're a marvel!'

Amber joined in. Fi hugged Mary; Mary allowed this to happen.

'If you didn't exist,' said Hero, 'we wouldn't dare make you up!'

'Smile, Mary!' Amber aimed her phone in Mary's face, but the old lady put her hands up to her face. 'I'll make you famous!'

Mary's acerbic answer went unheard by Sadie, who whispered to Hero, 'Can she get into trouble for this?'

'Even if it's against the law,' Hero answered, 'that shop brings in about thruppence a week. It's hardly *Ocean's Eleven*, is it?'

A stranger's voice punctured the hubbub.

'Hello?' Eight earrings in one ear, spindly limbs in dungarees, the mixed-race woman was hesitant. She held up a key. 'I can't get this to work.'

Her name, she told them, was Grace. She was an artist – Mrs Bob sniffed, Michael beamed – and she had just leased the last empty space on Cherry Blossom Mews.

Following her like courtiers around a slender queen – this was the most interesting thing to happen at a meeting for many a year – the residents took it in turns to wrestle with the rusty old lock of number two, sandwiched between U-Turn and Yummy Mummy.

It was Bob who cajoled the door open.

'At least you're good for *something*,' said his wife.

Unmodernised, a blank and filthy rectangle, the property was untouched since the days when the mews were stables for a handsome house that stood with its back to them.

'The main house was badly damaged by fire in the seventies,' explained Fi, looking about her with undisguised disdain at the cobwebs and the mouse droppings. 'It was called India House.'

'They turned it into swanky flats,' said Cher. 'Our estate's built on land belonging to the old mansion, that's why we're called India Park.'

The history lesson was news to Sadie. Cherry Blossom Mews was one incongruent square in a patchwork left behind by a noble house.

Cher was more prosaic. She held out a manicured hand and wobbled the worm-eaten panelling. 'This place is falling to bits.'

Grace was silent. She turned in the centre of the room. 'I love it.' She hugged herself as if she was surrounded by gilt and riches.

No matter how much the others pointed out the defects – no proper bathroom, a loo fit for a museum, various eight-legged tenants in the rafters – Grace's smile only burned brighter.

I like you.

Sadie's reaction was immediate, never to be revoked. Grace was a free spirit. Not the social media version, the real deal.

'I'll clean it up a bit.' Grace had a low voice. She kept her eyes low, too; being the centre of attention seemed to tax her. 'Then I can get on with my work.'

The work spilled out of portfolios. Fi was uninterested. Mrs Bob prodded Bob to get home. Only Sadie and Hero hung about to see Grace's artworks.

She rubbed at the dimpled glass in the narrow windows so they could see better. 'I take old photographs and I colour them.' Grace held up an image of Queen Victoria. The unsmiling old boot had subtly pink cheeks, and the blue of her eyes glinted through her scowl. 'Then I add little somethings here and there.'

'She's holding a mobile phone,' laughed Hero.

Grace bit her lip, pleased. 'I'm building bridges. People from other times can seem like aliens but we're all alike really. This helps us relate. I hope.'

'Stands to reason,' said Hero. 'We can't be the first generation to have emotions.'

Grace grinned. 'You get it,' she said.

WEEK EIGHT

To	The Bobs <bob@bobscaff.co.uk>, Amber <amber@yummymummymews.net.co.uk>, Sadie <sakuraspa@gmail.com>, Hero <hero.smith@u-turn.net>, Fiona J <filove@aol.com>, Cher Mogg <whatulookingatcher@gmail.co.uk>, Grace Esparza <Gracetheartist@gmail.com>, Jez <jeremy.gray@uu-turn.net>
From	Michael T. <qwertybookshop@hotmail.com>
Subject	CHERRY BLOSSOM MEWS RESIDENTS' ASSOCIATION MEETING

Dear All

Why don't we have a book club instead of a residents' association? No? Oh well. Worth a try.

Date	Wednesday 11.7.18
Time	6.30 p.m.
Location	Qwerty Books
Agenda	New nameplate for mews

Mary and Noel will be a little late due to a vet's appointment. (Noel's, not Mary's . . .)

With all best wishes

Michael

'It's been a whole week,' said Sadie. 'Maybe she's forgotten.'

'Mrs Bob doesn't forget,' said Fi. She shielded Sadie as they made for the door of the caff. 'Hopefully she's forgiven you.'

She hadn't.

'OUT!' bawled Mrs Bob.

Waiting outside while Fi haggled with Mrs Bob about whether or not she was permitted to purchase a pasty for a barred personage, Sadie threw her energy into moving tubs of flowers around.

These were, in theory, communal tubs, but only Sadie ever tended them. Today she was glad of their neediness, pulling off dry leaves and nudging them into a prettier formation. The mind that Hero couldn't see into – he'd made this point jokingly at first, but in the past few days her preoccupation had made him sigh – needed to be busy, busy, busy.

Moving a large planter revealed a wriggling society of translucent insects. Beneath these beasties, Sadie discerned a foundation stone.

INDIA HOUSE MEWS
FINISHED THIS DAY 27TH OF NOVEMBER, 1882
BY H.T.L.

NOTHING WITHOUT LABOUR

The square stone's simplicity pleased Sadie. She snapped it with her phone. Its permanence was a reminder of how long small things can endure. The palatial house had burned, but this modest marker remained. Around it, the silly, straggly mews was enjoying a second life as silly, straggly homes and businesses.

'Sorry, babes.' Fi emerged from the tasty fug of Bob's with one paper bag. 'She says life means life.'

Sadie laughed, but it was hollow. Bob's Caff was a sanctuary, like her own spa. The services they offered were vastly different – holistic massage versus fried foods – but they were both necessary.

Fi pulled up a chair and watched Sadie lug the tubs around. Cher stood at the door of Sakura and watched, too. As if it was a spectator sport.

'No, please, whatever you do don't help.' Sadie's face was red with exertion.

'I'm on my lunch break,' Fi reminded her.

'Flower arranging ain't in my job description,' said Cher.

Help arrived. Grace's long thin arms were strong.

'Ta,' managed Sadie when they'd finished. 'I keep meaning to offer to help you decorate.'

'Decorate?' Grace seemed puzzled. 'My studio's perfect.'

She'd swept it. The peeling plaster and the rotting floor were, apparently, perfect.

'I hope I have somebody who sees only perfection when I'm that decrepit,' said Sadie.

'Listen to her!' Fi, mouth full, was exasperated. 'She's already got somebody like that but she keeps giving him the brush off.'

'I like your tattoo, Grace.' A change of subject was called for.

Grace put a hand to her long neck. A long leaf wound around it. 'Mary doesn't approve.' The two women, separated by sixty years, had formed a superglue bond. Sadie was no longer the only one checking in on Mary and coaxing her out of her eyrie.

'Excuse me!' Cher was indignant from the door of the spa. 'Do you two actually, like, *work* here or what?'

A week ago, Fi would have blown her sizeable gasket at such cheek, but relations were easing. 'Yessir,' she said amiably as she and Sadie trotted back.

'No Jez today?' asked Sadie casually as she washed her hands.

'Are you an actual policewoman?' Cher banged a drawer shut with her hip. 'Questions, questions, questions.'

Sadie homed in on her. 'You all right?'

'See? Another question.' Cher shrieked, 'Hello! Welcome to Sakura!' at a woman stepping tentatively over the threshold.

'Boyfriend trouble, eh?' Fi charged in where angels fear to tread.

'Jez isn't my boyfriend.' Cher took the customer's coat as if she was mugging her. 'He's not even my friend. He's married to that dumb job.'

Sadie rescued the client, sat her down, offered her ice-cold cucumber water, hoping she could ignore the extended rant Fi's comment had provoked.

'He didn't walk me home last night. He only rang me once yesterday evening. He forgot today was KFC day.' Cher ticked off Jez's offences on her fingers. 'I've done my hair completely different since the weekend and he hasn't even noticed.'

'You sound,' said Fi, 'a little high-maintenance, if you don't mind me saying.'

Cher did mind. Which only served to make Fi more adamant.

'You're a grown woman, Cher. Walk yourself home! It's two hundred yards away. You're carrying on like a clingy sixth-former.'

'At least I don't have a boring bloke like yours.' Cher unpacked a scented candle and slammed it onto the counter. 'Cole's a cardboard cutout.'

Sadie managed to manoeuvre her client into the treatment room but the argument could be heard through the door.

'My Cole's a saint and don't you have his name in your mouth, babes, or you'll have me to reckon with.'

Sadie turned up the tinkly music but Fi was in full flow.

'None of you know what he goes through, he—'

The rant stopped dead. Grateful for the silence, Sadie made her customer comfortable in the fragranced, dimly lit room.

Something rankled.

Why did Fi stop short?

Discretion about her man was a bad omen.

We all have our patterns.

Sadie's own dizzy routine had led her to drink, and to school gates.

Fi's had led her to A&E.

In the passenger seat, Mary fussed over her dog, swaddled like a newborn in her lap.

'What did the vet say about Noel's, um, *lumps*?' Sadie's car inched around the cherry tree as the gates clanged shut behind them. Relief emanated from her passenger, and

Sadie understood. The outside world was safely held at bay once again.

'He gave us ointment.'

Ointment is a conversation killer. 'Come on, we'll just catch the end of the meeting.' Sadie had an urge to see Hero. Drink him in. Remind herself of his flesh and blood solidity. She had been deep in the quicksands of memory all day; he could tug her out.

'Let me freshen up a little first.' Mary stumped off towards MOBuk.

Trying to hurry her would only result in those bunions working even more slowly. Upstairs in Mary's flat, Sadie went to flop in a chair that was no longer there and found herself on the rug.

The case of the disappearing antiques.

No point asking about it. Sadie would watch out for her friend and she would help if she could, but she would do Mary the favour of not quizzing her about her money worries.

'Thank you, Mary,' she said, as her friend bustled back into the sitting room, tucking a hanky up her sleeve, patting her hair, running the gamut of old lady displacement activity.

'Whatever for?' Mary rifled through a bowl of keys and coins.

'For never asking me about Hero. Everybody else watches us like hawks. Not you, though.'

'I never talk about romance.' Mary was curt, clipping shut her immense handbag. 'Thought I was in love once.'

'Really?' Sadie softened the surprise in her voice.

'It turned out to be dust.' Mary dangled Noel's lead. 'Ready?'

The meeting, frankly, was no longer important. 'Tell me about it.' Sadie lowered herself onto a sofa that belched dust. 'I had no idea, Mary.'

Mary seemed to consider her options. Looked from the door to Sadie and back again. She sat.

'Arthur was his name.' Mary blinked. Said it again. 'Arthur.'

'Nice name,' said Sadie, encouragingly.

'If you're going to listen, listen, but don't butt in with nonsense.'

'That's me told,' murmured Sadie, settling back.

Arthur had worked for Mary's father, the bewhiskered papa in a photograph on the piano. 'We were tea importers.' Started in 1837, the company was still a titanic business in the sixties, when Mary first laid eyes on Arthur.

'The past is a different world. Even in a big house like ours, only a couple of rooms were heated. Just one telephone, in the hall. It was difficult to arrange to meet. I was so . . .'

'Sheltered?'

'Imprisoned.' Mary leant down to fondle Noel's scabby ear as she talked of the innocent love affair. 'We were so naive. But I believed we shared something profound. He kissed me.' Mary's voice faded. 'Eight times.'

A flash of memory. Sadie's first date with Jack. Drunken sex, and sitting on his lap the next morning wearing just his shirt. 'You remember how it felt,' said Sadie.

'I do. I remember each one.' Mary put a finger to her lips. 'One hears about the swinging sixties but they didn't swing in our house. I was forbidden to have a young man. Arthur and I went for walks in the park with the original Noel. We dared to hold hands, terrified we'd be seen. He was ambitious. I liked that about him.'

It had been the young Arthur's dream to work his way up in Mary's family business. 'His goal was to run the head-quarters, far away in Assam, where the tea was harvested. Before he met me, London was a place he needed to escape from. His family exploited Arthur. He was the only one with a job, the only one bringing in money. He felt trapped by them. That was something we had in common.'

Sadie imagined a different Mary. A young bride in a hot climate, living a colonial life. 'How did you feel about making such a move?'

'I told him point blank it wasn't possible. The idea of leaving Mother and Father . . .' Mary grimaced. 'I lived in a dictatorship. It would never have been allowed. So, slowly, Arthur stopped talking about his dream.'

Inevitably, they were found out. 'I was sent away.' The

dictatorship flexed its muscles. 'A deal was struck. If Arthur and I could live apart for six months then Father would give us his blessing. A job for life for Arthur, a new house for us both. All very generous.'

'Except he didn't mean any of it.'

'Precisely.' Mary had been carted off to Scotland. 'I stayed with my great-aunt, who treated me like a fallen woman. I thought of Arthur incessantly. I remembered how he brushed my hand with his as we parted.' Watched night and day by her jailer aunt, Mary hid her most prized possession. 'We'd managed to steal away and have our portrait taken in a photographic studio. Just two copies were made. One for him and one for me.'

'Surely you managed to sneak in a phone call now and then?'

'You girls who stroll around with the world in your ear have no idea . . . Phone calls were public then. The only telephone Arthur had access to was the one in his office and all calls were logged. My aunt didn't possess a telephone. Arthur didn't even have my aunt's address.' Besides, she explained, they were obedient creatures, playing by her father's warped rules.

A hollered 'Hurry up you two!' came from the mews. Fi was impatient for them to join the meeting.

'We don't have to go.' Sadie wanted Mary to do her story justice now she'd finally opened up.

'We should show our faces.' Still obedient, it would seem, Mary stood with difficulty. 'Let's get to Qwerty.' She opened a glass-fronted cabinet, overflowing with gewgaws. 'This is Arthur.' She handed over a stiff rectangle of card.

Two young people. Younger than Sadie was now. Eyes bright. Mary was no beauty but the challenge in her face demanded attention. An awful dress, a shapeless hat – even then Mary had been impervious to fashion.

And Arthur. Thin, as if starved. Pale hair cropped close. An enigmatic face with strong thin features. Only his hands, balled at his sides, betrayed his anxiety.

They didn't look like a happy couple – how could they? – but they did look like a team. They looked *right*.

Mary was already on the stairs, stumping lopsidedly down, one hand on the banister.

'Six months was nothing for me,' she said over her shoulder, slightly out of breath. Even when the gruesome aunt confiscated the photograph, Mary hadn't wavered. She could feel Arthur's constancy.

'If your aunt took the photograph, how come you still have it?'

'That's Arthur's copy. He gave it to me.'

Sweet.

Sadie followed Mary out onto the mews.

'Father got to Arthur the way he got to everybody. Via his wallet.'

Sadie didn't want to hear this bit.

'Father offered Arthur his dream position. Head of production in Assam. But only if he relinquished *me*.'

'And?'

'And? What do you think, Sadie? Off Arthur went. Pausing only to send me the portrait with a scribbled message on the back.'

Sadie turned over the photograph.

Mary, I have been offered a chance to better myself. I cannot refuse. You'll find somebody else. I'm sorry. Arthur.

'Here.' Mary snatched the photograph. She tossed it into the bargain bin outside her shop. 'Best place for it.'

Sadie sat beside Mary as the residents debated whether or not they needed a new nameplate to replace the cheap and not particularly cheerful plastic rectangle now degraded by the sun and exhaust fumes.

Mary just threw the love of her life in the bin.

Sadie had thought of Mary as untouched, but the old lady was mangled out of shape by love. They both voted for a new nameplate.

Michael counted the raised arms and, for once, a motion was passed. 'Next week,' he said, 'we can all argue about whether it should be brass or chrome. Right. Any other business?'

'Actually, yes.' Mrs Bob studied her fingernails. 'In case Sadie's wondering, she's still banned.'

Amber pulled up her stool beside Sadie as Michael read out a council proposal for a change to local parking rules.

She smells delicious.

It was easy to get caught up in Amber's bludgeoning femininity.

'So, you and Hero?' Amber put her mouth so close to Sadie's ear that her breath warmed her neck. 'Hard to tell if anything's going on.'

'Going on?' Sadie didn't much like that way of describing her relationship with Hero.

'I mean, you're not his type, are you? No offence.'

'I might be offended if I knew what you meant.' Sadie couldn't tell if Amber was a kitten or a cobra.

'Well, after Zizzi, you'd expect him to go for . . .'

Somebody like you, Amber?

Sadie had lost one lover to a rival; lessons had been learned. 'It's early days.'

'I hope it works out.' Amber patted Sadie's hand, as if they were discussing a colonoscopy. 'I love that top. Smile for me, and I'll put you on my feed.' A flash of light. Another. Amber needed eight takes – each, so far as Sadie could tell, identical to the last; she was generally cross-eyed in snaps – before she was done.

'Ladies, if the photo shoot's finished?' said Michael. 'We need to move on.'

Hero smothered a laugh. When Sadie pursed her lips at him, he pouted his own and blew her a slow, silent kiss.

A tickle of tension knotted in Sadie's stomach. The pleasurable kind. She felt the need to cough, to cross her legs; Hero saw what his kiss had unleashed. His eyes, slanted with amusement, let her know.

Forgotten tunes of sexual attraction played in Sadie's ears, blotting out Michael's tirade about council tax. She was out of practice at flirting. Not that Hero complained; perhaps it was something you couldn't unlearn, like riding a bike.

Or perhaps he's easily pleased.

There was a third option. That Hero liked whatever Sadie did because it was Sadie doing it.

She couldn't rely on that option. The black cloud of Jack's betrayal was always there when she relaxed, raining steadily on her parade.

'U-Turn,' said Michael suddenly. 'I believe Amber has a complaint?'

'Not at all! I wanted to say how amazing I think it is, yeah? Like, Hero, you just help all those poor alcoholics and you save lives, and there's hardly any swearing and no bottles in the gutter or anything.'

'You're practically Gandhi, mate,' laughed Fi. She took a sly look at Amber. 'Gandhi with abs.'

Amber wasn't finished. Hero began to squirm – it was fun to watch, if you were Sadie – as she gushed on about 'enlightenment' and 'personal growth' and 'community oneness'.

Mrs Bob broke into the eulogy with, 'Some of them don't half *stink*, though.' She grudgingly agreed with Michael's diplomatic comment that their fears about U-Turn had turned out to be groundless, adding, 'I've still got my eye on you, Hero.'

'I wouldn't have it any other way,' said Hero.

'If it fitted my brand,' said Amber, simpering apologetically, 'I'd mention you on @ambermagiclondon but, sadly, lifestyle accounts and detox centres don't mix.'

'Lifestyle?' tutted Mary. 'We all have a lifestyle, surely?'

'Did everyone see my post about Sakura?' Amber bounced in her seat, waved her phone about. 'I raved to my followers about the amazing chakra rinse Fi gave me.'

Sadie sent a questioning look Fi's way.

Fi sent back a *Don't ask* look, as she declined the plate of biscuits Michael handed round.

They were Jammie Dodgers. Fi had never before turned down a Jammie Dodger. Fi would rise from her coffin to accept a Jammie Dodger.

The meeting disbanded. Fi raced out to meet Cole

tooting his horn on the street outside. Cher hurried away, nose in the air, without once looking at Jez.

Sadie felt Hero circling her. Their post-meeting tryst was more than tradition, it was habit. A good habit, in stark contrast with the bad ones that shaped her life.

Outside, Mrs Bob took a long, grateful drag on a cigarette.

'No Bob tonight?' asked Mary.

'Nah. In bed.'

Sadie couldn't resist. 'Recovering from another week of your insults?' She put her arm through Mary's.

Michael looked at Sadie, stricken. To Mrs Bob he said, 'How is he? Any change?'

'Don't talk about him like he's at death's door!' Mrs Bob ground the cigarette beneath her Primark pump. She was red in the face. Ready to blow.

Sadie's sarcasm turned to ashes in her mouth. 'Is Bob not well?' The silence that met her question was an articulate answer.

They all know.

'What's the matter with Bob?' she asked, more forcefully.

'Congestive heart failure,' said Mary. 'Poor Bob has chronic shortness of breath. Chest pains. His ankles are swollen.'

'He never stops going on about his bloody swollen ankles,' groaned Mrs Bob. 'I say to him, listen mate, you're not a foot model, what's it matter?'

'There's treatment, though?' Sadie loathed the irony of Bob's big heart letting him down. 'There's stuff they can do?' The 'they' in this instance were white-coated, clever doctors who would, surely, rush in and save the day.

Never one to shirk the heavy lifting, Mary said, 'The prognosis was a year.'

Sadie felt her free hand enclosed by Hero's. 'In that case,' she managed, 'let's all get together and make it the best year ev—'

'That prognosis was eighteen months ago.' Mary asked, 'Surely you've noticed how he gasps for breath?'

'I thought that was just a side effect of that airless kitchen.'

Hero said, grave, 'Now I come to think of it, Bob's always having a sit-down.'

Mrs Bob was the only person in the subdued little circle who seemed unaffected. 'He's always having a sit-down,' she repeated, 'because he's a lazy bugger. Bob exaggerates for the attention.'

The flippancy revolted Sadie, but her recriminations went unsaid.

They had skipped the coffee after the meeting and rushed straight to the part where they lay in bed together. Curled together in a post-coital brew of cosiness and sensuality, Sadie and Hero didn't need to speak. Their communication was perfect in this formless state, both of them high on the love they had just made.

It had to end.

'That boat.' Hero lifted Sadie's hand to point at the *Lady Sadie*. 'It's the only decorative thing in your entire flat.' He let her hand drop. 'Ah.' The sigh rippled through his whole body, and transferred to Sadie's warm torso pressed against his. 'It's Jack's. You only freeze like that when I mention him.'

'Don't. C'm'ere.' Sadie was holding on tight to the groggy oblivion, and pulled him back when he made to move.

She could tell Hero liked that. He settled back beside her, but the spell was broken. Sadie surfaced and said, 'So. Bo.'

'Bo,' repeated Hero, putting one hand behind his head. 'What do you want to know?'

She spat it out. 'Why'd you let him leave with Zizzi if she's so flaky?'

Hero shut his eyes. 'It's a long story.'

'I prefer a long story.' Sadie traced a figure of eight in his chest hair.

Hero grabbed her hand and kissed it. Playing with her fingers, he said, 'During the divorce I was adamant that Bo should stay with me in London so I could make sure he got three square meals a day and did boring things like actually go to school. But Zizzi wanted full custody. Then one day she told me, in a bored sort of voice, that Bo wasn't my son.' Hero waited for Sadie to lie back down when she started up in shock. 'She'd slept with two dickheads at a wrap party for some shitty reality show. She hadn't planned to own up, didn't see the point, but now that I was being mean, as she put it, she used the truth as ammunition. If I fought for custody, Zizzi would tell Bo I wasn't his real dad.'

'That's evil.'

'Clever, though. She used my love for Bo against me. I knew that hearing such a revelation when his world was already being capsized by our divorce would break his little heart. Zizzi's cruelty is always elegant.' Hero propped himself up on one elbow. He looked intently down at Sadie. His face seemed older. Still beautiful. Still poetic. Even with bed hair. 'My attitude to Bo didn't change. Not one iota. Babies are made in all sorts of ways. This is the story of my son. I held him when he was born. I held his hand crossing the road. It was me who taught him how to tie his shoelaces.'

'I bet he's brilliant at tying his shoelaces,' murmured Sadie.

'All I can do is keep the lines of communication open, be his dad, counteract the madness. Zizzi doesn't get in the way. Ironically, we're good at being divorced.'

'There's no simple fix for that kind of problem.' Sadie admired Hero for taking the long view, for putting Bo first. 'If you'd called her bluff, Bo might be lost in the madness of LA, but this way you're his legal guardian and a bona fide father figure.'

'Exactly. You get me, Sadie. It's good to be got.'

Their tender moment was demolished by the xylophone beat of Sadie's phone. 'Fi?' she said into the mobile. Then, 'Fi?' then, louder, 'For God's sake, Fi, you idiot!'

'Another pocket dial?' Hero pulled her back down into their nest.

They kissed. Sadie's head emptied and stayed pleasantly empty until they drew back from each other, sated. Again.

'Oh God, Bob,' she groaned.

'So insulting,' whispered Hero, 'when you say another man's name during sex.' He accepted the clout she gave him.

'Poor Bob,' said Sadie. She snuggled closer, seeking Hero's warmth to forget the overripe smell of death. 'Poor, poor Bob. Why do such terrible things happen to good people?'

'Because to the universe we're not good people. We're just atoms. We're blown about in the storms. Sometimes, though, we find something to cling on to and we make the mistake of thinking we're safe.' Hero tightened his grip. 'We're safe, though, Sadie. For tonight, we're safe.'

He fell asleep that way. It was tricky to wriggle out of his arms. For a while there, she'd believed him.

In such a small flat, there weren't many places to go. Daring herself, Sadie crept into the other bedroom. Teddy's room, as she foolishly called it. If she sat on the edge of the bed it was almost as if she was a mummy again, settling a child down to sleep.

The bedclothes were flat. The bed was empty.

Distraction was necessary; she'd learned all about triggers at rehab. About avoiding extremes of emotion, of policing her reaction to bad news. Bob's frailty had thrown her.

Distraction came in the form of Amber's Instagram feed. Sadie leafed through it, looking for the snap Amber had posted earlier. 'Eek!' The photograph was unflattering. 'Is my chin really that shape?' She checked out the hashtags; Amber was prolific with her hashtags.

#maturestyle #ageinggracefully #nevertoolate

How old does she think I am?

The narrowness of Teddy's bed fitted her needs. She was after simplicity. Hero, snoring gently across the hall, was the opposite of simplicity.

Sleep was coy; it wouldn't come no matter how much she called it. She turned to her phone again for diversion. Editing her photographs was surely dull enough to send her off.

A good one of Fi, mid-laugh.

A fuzzy one of Cher, mid-insult.

A close-up of the foundation stone she'd found in the mews.

A profile of Noel VI.

An off-kilter image of Hero, looking over his shoulder, one blue eye visible through his hair.

She sat up. She zoomed in on one of the images. Noticed what had been there all along.

There was no way she could sleep now. Sadie got up, accepting the inevitable long night of wakefulness. Just her, a mug of something and the changing light outside her kitchen window.

Come on! she urged the waking day. *Come on!*

WEEK NINE

To   The Bobs <bob@bobscaff.co.uk>, Michael T. <qwertybookshop@hotmail.com>, Sadie <sakuraspa@gmail.com, Hero <hero.smith@u-turn.net>, Fiona J <filove@aol.com>, Cher Mogg <whatulookingatcher@gmail.co.uk>, Grace Esparza <Gracetheartist@gmail.com>, Jez <jeremy.gray@u-turn.net>

From   Amber <amber@yummymummymews.net.co.uk>

Subject   CHERRY BLOSSOM MEWS RESIDENTS' ASSOCIATION MEETING

Hello!!!!!

We're having a gluten-free festival at Yummy Mummy so expect oodles of healthy goodies!

Date   Wednesday 18.7.18
Time   6.30 p.m.
Location   Yummy Mummy café & party emporium
Agenda   Positive things only please!!!!!

Somebody tell Mary! Oh and I know I'm being fussy but could we make sure darling little Noel sits outside this time? It took ages to clear up the pressie he left last time!!!!!

Amber xxxxxxxxxxxxx to infinity!

Seven a.m.

Sadie couldn't wait any longer. Her dressing gown flapping, she crossed the mews in bare feet. Skirting the tree, she laid a palm fleetingly on its trunk. For courage. A ring at a doorbell, a rap on a door.

By five past, she was in Mary's utilitarian kitchen, saying, 'You're the landlord, Mary. You own Cherry Blossom Mews.'

Mary, sleep in her eyes, wore a vest under her nightie. 'You're far too clever for your own good. Tea?'

'No. Sit down and look at me.' Sadie had to go in hard and fast. This was no dotty little old lady; this was Mary. 'The foundation stone I found in the mews told me everything. The motto carved into it – nothing without labour – is the translation of the words beneath the painting of your mother.'

'*Absque labore nihil*,' recited Mary, upright in a stern-backed chair, ignoring Noel's snuffly requests for breakfast.

'The name of our landlord's bank account: Christmas Properties.' Sadie poked Noel fondly with a bare toe and he licked it. 'That's a reference to Noel, and all the Noels over the years, isn't it?'

'Ten out of ten, you revolting nosy parker.'

'This means, I assume, that your family, the Lockridges, owned the big house that the mews backed onto? The one that burned down?' She realised another nugget. 'Plus the land that Cher's housing estate is built on?'

'We were wealthy,' said Mary, as if admitting to a venereal disease. 'We were powerful. We were, pardon my French, absolute shits.'

'Not you, Mary.'

'If you insist on the full story, I require tea.'

Tea was made. Currant buns were unearthed. Noel was placated with foul meat from a tin. They took their seats in the sitting room for story time.

Sadie noted another bright rectangle on the wallpaper where an oil used to hang.

'India House was a jail. My parents had successfully seen off the only love I ever knew by dangling money in front of Arthur, and after that they took no chances. Treated me like a valuable asset that must be protected. Mother complained constantly of vague ailments, tethering me to her side with tears and neediness. That, Sadie, was what she called love.'

Sadie imagined the younger Mary from the photograph, hat on head, handbag over arm, almost out of the house – *almost* – before her mother appeared, weeping, on the stairs. 'You can't fight emotional blackmail.'

'I'd had my chance to run and I didn't take it. Back in nineteen sixty, when I received the photograph from Arthur with its painful farewell, I evaded my aunt's beady eye and escaped to a neighbour who had a telephone. The only number I could think of to call was our local police station. They knew Arthur there, felt sorry for him, as he constantly bailed out his feckless family. I couldn't believe it was true, you see. I couldn't take it in that Arthur would really do that to me.'

They both sipped and munched. Mary needed time to gather herself; the shock of Arthur's betrayal was fresh, as if refrigerated for sixty years.

'The police chappie told me I could find Arthur in Assam. He was very cheerful, but I didn't see the joke myself.'

'That's when you accepted that Arthur really had left the country.'

'I closed my heart up in a vault, just like the one father kept his stocks and bonds in. Arthur had been *bought* with a new life that involved servants and status and all the things we both professed to hate.' Mary brushed crumbs from her lap. 'After Father died, it became clear he'd horribly mismanaged the company he'd inherited. It was all front. Mother was forced to sell up to pay crippling debts. We sold the orchards and the tennis courts, and in time high-rise flats sprouted from them. Mother achieved the impossible and became *more* possessive. We only heated a couple of rooms in the basement of India House. It was always dark down there. Mother had a seizure if the door-bell rang.'

There, plain to see, were the roots of Mary's fear of 'outside'. Her mother's phobia had been contagious.

'The house caught fire one night. The place went up like a haystack. Mother didn't survive.'

'I'm sorry.'

'She only lived half a life. It was a release.'

For her, Mary? Or for you?

'I should have burned with her. I fainted from smoke inhalation. Yet I woke on the pavement. A fireman carried me out and laid me on a pile of blankets. I remember blinking up at the sky made bright by the flames, and thinking that I felt safer than I had felt in years. I never did thank that brave man.'

Sadie thought, but didn't say, that he was likely dead by now.

'Noel the second was by my side. My little talisman.' Mary regarded the fire as an act of God, one that finally allowed her to turn her back on India House. 'It was uninsured, of course. So I moved into the empty mews.'

Sadie imagined those iron gates slamming shut, holding her in once again. 'How did you live?'

'Well, there was money from selling the ruins for those ghastly apartments to be built. That didn't go far, not with the family debts.' Mary existed frugally, enjoying, she said, the challenge. 'Luckily for me, much of the furniture was salvaged. I used to have it stored all around the mews, in the days when I lived here alone. When things got tight, I'd ship off another Chippendale to Sotheby's and I'd get by for another year or two.'

'You have no attachment to them at all?'

'They're *things*, Sadie. They represent money, and money is what Father used to tempt Arthur into betraying me. Father saw that Arthur was worn out by his dreadful family, always expecting him to support them when all they did was steal and fight. He offered Arthur a way out, and, well, you know what happened. So, no, I have no attachment to the evidence of my father's love of money.'

Outside, the mews was shaking itself awake. Radio 1 blared out of Bob's Caff. The awning outside Qwerty Books flapped. Jez swept the cobbles around U-Turn. The tree stretched out its arms.

'I have a manifesto, Sadie. Cherry Blossom Mews might look as if it came together willy-nilly but I handpicked each of you. I have made a family to replace the broken one God saw fit to give me, and to compensate me for the family I never got to have with Arthur.'

Sadie felt the room change around her. Felt her own shape shift. She was a daughter again. She was needed. 'Why charge so little rent?'

'Because money, my dear, bends people out of shape. The Bobs had already spent everything they had on private treatment for Bob's congestive heart failure. U-Turn are a charity, and that Hero will achieve great things.'

'I could have paid you more. I still can. Jack's life insurance is lying in the bank.'

'You're not listening. I don't want more money, my dear. I want *less* of it. When you turned up here, you needed the unconditional support only a parent gives, so I gave it to you.'

'Yes, you did.' Sadie didn't trust her voice to say more.

'Look at Michael. The world needs more books. Books are bandages. Books are friends. But the rent on the high street was way beyond his means. So here he is, thriving quietly, curating his Dorothy Ball collection, spreading book love without lying awake worrying about money. *Romance*, now that's a different problem for Michael.' Mary treated Sadie to an extra special look. 'That I can't help him with.'

'Amber probably has a trust fund with more noughts on the end than Noel's had hot dinners.'

'Noel's never had a hot dinner, Sadie, and Amber has no business sense whatsoever. No other landlord would allow her to set up on their premises, but she's welcome here *because* of that lack of business sense. Amber has no self-knowledge; I couldn't let her wander about *out there*.' Mary shuddered at the world beyond the gates. She was stern when she said, 'We're kind here, Sadie, and we look out for one another. You might have issues with Amber, some girlish jealousy going on, but in Cherry Blossom Mews we are good to one another.'

Sadie nodded. She felt admonished. And loved. That was a clever trick of Mary's. 'Your tone's prim, Mary, but your words are like sunshine. The mews is all about love, isn't it?'

'I distrust that word. Now off you go, get on with your day and let me find Noel's worming tablets.'

Sadie turned the book over in her hands, enjoying the aged feel of it.

The Lopsided Love Affair by Dorothy Ball. She read the strapline on the cover aloud: DOES SHE EVEN NOTICE HOW HE ADORES HER?

Feet on the stairs. Hero had stayed over again. Sadie bundled Dorothy into a drawer. Hero was already burdened with a dead rival, no need for him to know about Michael, too.

'Come here, you.' Hero was impolite. Grabbed her. Kissed her face. Sought out her mouth.

'Ow.' That big chunky watch his mother had given him always got caught in Sadie's short dark hair.

Untangling took some time. Hero laughed into her hair.

Sadie wished they could stay bound up like that. They communicated best when they didn't speak. She refused to dwell on what that might mean.

'Fi approaching,' murmured Hero. He turned her neatly around, arms still tight, so Sadie could see her friend on the cobbles, phone to her ear.

They pulled apart. 'Later?' asked Sadie.

'Definitely. I need to go to that big DIY warehouse by the tube station. Wanna come with?'

'Not even slightly,' laughed Sadie.

'It can't be all minibreaks and hotel rooms. I need a new hammer.'

'Well, when you put it like that . . .' Sadie was bluffing. She'd happily trail around the Tools section with Hero.

'Good.' Hero looked out at Fi as he stretched, sloughing off sleep and sex and *her.* 'I pity whoever's on the other end of that phone.' Fi was bellowing, jabbing her finger in the air.

'She claims she and Cole never fight but . . .'

'I overheard her shrieking at him the other day,' said Hero. 'There's trouble at t'mill.'

'Jesus, I hope not.' Fi's brand of man trouble was catastrophic. 'She's keeping it from me, which is bad news.'

'Because you're the nosiest woman on God's Earth?'

'Because when she's secretive it means something's badly wrong.'

Beyond the glass, Fi seemed to sense she was being watched and did an about-turn, detouring to Bob's.

'Should I tell the others about Mary?' asked Sadie, as she woke up the spa, putting out pitchers of water, straightening leaflets.

'No. It's her business, Sades.'

Sadie smiled. She liked being a Sades. Especially in his silly posh voice which she no longer thought was silly.

Not that I'll tell Hero that.

'You're right. You're always right.'

'You're damn lucky to have me,' said Hero as he left.

As Fi emerged from Bob's Caff, Sadie attempted to transmit her need, nay *longing*, for an Americano. Fi, her face black with fury, didn't notice. She was still spitting into her phone.

Through the open door of Bob's floated the terrible music of Mrs Bob's morning rant. Sadie heard only snatches before the door closed again, but she could see the woman throwing up her hands as if dealing with a wilful pet. Sadie had googled Bob's condition. The information was bleak. He could expect dyspnoea, a shortening of breath that felt like smothering; fluid in his lungs would mean his chronic cough would worsen; finally, Bob would grow confused, the low sodium levels in his blood affecting his brain.

It would take a miracle for Bob to see out the year. Sadie

pitied him for spending his last days with an unsympathetic monster.

'Yo,' said Sadie when Fi walked in and threw down her bag with venom. 'No bacon sarnie?'

'What are you, the food police?' Fi harrumphed into the stockroom, but not before Sadie noticed that her customary caramel latte had been replaced by what looked like a mint tea.

A mint tea.

Not a big deal in the grand scheme of things; gallons of the stuff are drunk every day. But Fi was a woman who ran on great vats of flavoured coffee. Sadie smelled a diet and the smell was easily as unpleasant as one of Noel's presents.

Fi and diets meant bad moods. It meant long-suffering sighs, and mid-morning hallucinations about Wotsits. Worst of all, it meant that Fi's equanimity had taken a blow, that her belief that she was mistress of her own body had been rocked.

Only a man could do that to Fi.

Sadie knew the techniques by now. The ex, Emanuel, had been a master. A comment here or there. A 'naughty, naughty!' when Fi contemplated an eclair. His gaze on a slender young thing's bottom for a shade too long.

If Cole, Fi's Mr Perfect, was using these tricks, Sakura was in for a rocky ride.

*

'What do I owe you?' Grace fished out a tatty purse from the patchwork sack she carried.

'Nah, it's free.' Cher waved her away, gliding back to reception on plain flat shoes she had slipped on in the loo first thing, replacing her ankle breakers. 'I'm not a professional, so . . .'

'But you're brilliant,' insisted Grace. She flexed her fingers. 'That was the best hand massage I've ever had.' She was waiting for a full-body sports massage; the third Sadie had given her, and entirely necessary. The lithe girl was a collection of knots, like tangled knitting; being an artist was evidently more stressful than Grace made it seem.

'You don't have to say that.' Cher's taut answer twanged.

Grace's face clouded, as she tried to work out how she could have offended Cher.

'Our Cher's a natural at massage,' Sadie waded in. 'But she needs training in how to take a compliment.'

'Want a tea or summink, Grace?' This was Cher's version of 'sorry', and Grace somehow spoke fluent Cher, because she unleashed her megawatt smile and the sticky moment was done with.

In the holy hush of the darkened treatment room, Grace let out ecstatic little exclamations as Sadie's firm, unforgiving fingers worked their magic. 'Decided where to hang the painting yet?' she murmured.

'It's at U-Turn. You should go in and see. Looks great.' The painting had been Grace's way of thanking Sadie and Hero for the hours they'd spent helping her knock together a makeshift live/work space. It was – Sadie gulped at the notion – the couple's first piece of communal property. Sadie had offloaded all her artwork three years earlier, each image hiding a dagger of memory to dig through her chest.

Her walls would remain bare until ... when? Sadie kneaded Grace's tortured back.

Until Jack and Teddy come home?

They had stood together, she and Hero, contemplating Grace's gift.

'Hang on!' Hero had homed in. The sunlit hills in the painting were misleading. 'It's made of trash!'

'What's it called?' Sadie had asked. Then, before Grace had time to reply, she'd laughed, '*The Relationship*?'

A small vein in Hero's temple had tightened.

Not only did Noel attend the residents' meeting despite Amber's plea, but he found an expensive cushion embroidered with the words PROSECCO O'CLOCK to lie on.

Hero bent down to stroke the unwholesome creature's ears. Jez squeezed a chair in next to Cher, who was doing her level best to hide how pleased she was to see him. Grace picked flakes of paint from her fingers as Amber set down a three-tiered cake plate on a coffee table she had bought from Mary for fifteen pence and was now selling for one hundred and fifty pounds after a speedy upcycle with matt grey emulsion.

'Fi, hun!' called Amber in the especially sugary voice that meant she was *really* irritated. 'We're waiting!'

Fi prowled the back of Yummy Mummy, among the floaty scarves and the distressed signs advising her to LIVE. LAUGH. LOVE. She paced like a tiger in a zoo. 'Who is she?' she said into her phone. 'Tell me the slag's name.'

'Um,' said Amber.

'Shall we start without her?' suggested Michael, with an eloquent look at Sadie.

They did. They got on with the register, and they ploughed through Amber's log of how many times Cher had parked her jeep in front of Yummy Mummy. All the while, Fi prowled and growled and enlarged on 'the slag's' personality. The Slag was not a nice person, apparently. Not at all.

'Fi,' said Sadie, when Cher finished a spirited, gobby defence of her jeep. 'Come on.' It was an appeal, woman to woman, and Fi gave in, jamming the phone into her overall pocket.

Her boiling anger. The absence of ease. It was painful déjà vu.

The absence of the Bobs was noted. A communal decision

was made not to worry about that; not yet. Bins were discussed. A broken cobble was tutted over. There was a heart-wrenching saga from Grace about a falling roof tile narrowly missing a stray cat's tail.

Michael took up her cause. 'I don't like making a fuss,' he said, 'but surely we can appeal to the landlord's better nature? Things can only get worse in a mews of this age. Maybe we could ask him how he'd feel if his own home was falling apart around him.'

Like a seasoned spy, Mary's face was deadpan. She ignored the discreet looks from Sadie.

Damn, you're good, old lady.

Mary neither nodded nor disagreed. She tended instead to Noel, who chose that moment to fart and distract the residents.

As they fanned the air and exclaimed and held their noses, as Cher sprayed the dog with her perfume, Sadie was mugged by memory.

This was happening a lot since Effie.

It might be a phrase the girl had used about her lover, Sadie's husband. A description of his eyes. An in-joke. The memory would suddenly blot out all other sound, and Sadie would be trapped.

Today's was the worst so far. Effie had said – and Sadie could hear the exact intonation, see the curve of the smile on the girl's face as she said it – 'He was so *cuddly* in bed, you know, wrapping us both up in the covers, holding me really tight.'

Sadie's memory had assumed she held the exclusive rights to that.

But no, Jack, you had to go and stain the only bit of you I have left.

He'd spilled dirt on their love. It would never be the same again, no matter how hard she scrubbed.

Then, as he sometimes did, Jack answered her.

How come you didn't notice I was having an affair?

That wasn't fair. Sadie didn't notice because she trusted him. She didn't notice because she was busy.

Jack didn't say anything.

Was I busy?

Too busy to notice her husband was making love to another woman.

'Which are the gluten-free muffins?' Grace leaned forward.

'Err, those ones,' said Amber. When Grace frowned at her vagueness, Amber said in a confidential tone, 'I mean, it's not like gluten's an actual thing, is it?'

Grace sat back.

Michael whispered to Sadie, 'Now all we do is wait for the court cases to begin.'

Sadie laughed. Hero took her hand. She wondered if it was a display of possessiveness for Michael's benefit; had he seen the Dorothy Balls stacking up in Sakura?

She decided against that, trusting Hero to be non-macho in such matters. *Like you trusted me*, said Jack, who was very chatty for a dead person. She let go of Hero's hand.

'I have an announcement.' Grace was awkward, standing then sitting again, her long limbs seeming to grow even longer as she tried to arrange herself on the chair. 'I'm having an exhibition of my work in the mews. My first ever,' she added, shyly. 'It was Mary's idea.'

'Brilliant!' said Sadie.

'Just what the mews needs!' said Michael.

'I'll help promote it!' Amber lit up. 'I'll create a hashtag and toggle it across all my platforms.'

'There'll be free booze, yeah?' asked Cher.

'I'll need a ton of new work, so this is an appeal for any old photographs you might have lying around. The older the better, and they must be black and white, so I can colour them.' She put her hands together, as if praying. 'I promise I'll take good care of them.'

'I've got loads of shitty old snaps,' said Cher.

'I might have a couple for you,' said Fi, whose emotional temperature had lowered.

Sadie had nothing to offer. Her own photographs were locked away.

The others, however, all promised to help out. Sadie felt Yummy Mummy close in around them as they pulled together. With a sudden peak of feeling, like a hot flush of the heart, Sadie longed to throw her arms around them all.

She saw Mary allow herself a small smile. Grace was the old lady's protégé; Sadie doubted that Grace was paying much at all for her studio space. Providing a safe berth for waifs and strays was commendable but risky – bankruptcy would spell disaster for the commune Mary had gathered under her wing. The breeze blowing around the cobbles had a chill undertone.

No matter how much the old dame distrusted the word, Mary was running her business on love. Love, however, doesn't pay the bills.

A clatter at the door. Mrs Bob was struggling with the handle. 'Sorry I'm late,' she said, the S word unnatural on her lips.

'Where's your old man?' Cher craned her neck.

'Hospital.' Mrs Bob shook her head testily at the blizzard of questions. 'Calm down,' she tutted. 'Just a little collapse. No need to get your tights in a twist.' She sat, crossed her legs. 'Any point me bringing up the stupid cherry tree again? I had to park out on the main road.'

'No point at all,' said Mary.

Time alone with Cher was rare. And a bit frightening.

Sadie, diligently filling in customer care forms – skin

type, allergies, favourite treatments – felt the girl's presence strongly.

There was an energy about Cher that cracked and popped, all the more hectic because it had nowhere to go. Receptionist duties didn't stretch her. She had the job at her fingertips, even if she declined to do much of it.

The unwillingness to get involved puzzled Sadie. She wondered if it was fear of failure, despite the T-Rex levels of touchiness. She would have liked to ask after Jez, to discover how the love affair that had seemed so promising was really going. She dared not; the T-Rex had sharp teeth.

Cher broke the silence. 'Your husband,' she said.

Sadie didn't respond.

'What was he like?'

'He was . . .' Sadie described him. In full. Not just the fuzzy-edged memories, but all the distinctly *noir* details.

'Shit,' said Cher.

'Quite.' Describing Jack's affair was cathartic. She felt cleansed, her anger redoubled.

'You must really, really want to punch him.'

'I really, really do.'

'I'd cut his balls off.'

When Sadie didn't answer, Cher elaborated: 'With blunt scissors.'

'Well,' said Sadie, awkwardly, but Cher wasn't finished.

'You can't, though. He's dead. Like, literally. You should forgive him.'

'Where is Cher and what have you done with her?' laughed Sadie.

'Seriously.' Cher padded around to face Sadie in her new flat shoes. Her hemline was on a nodding acquaintance with her knees. 'Forgiving him is best for *you*, not that slimy little scumbag. *I* don't forgive. Not a chance. I set me brothers on people. But you're not me. You might have divorced him or something if he'd lived, but whatever. You're free now. You have Hero.' Cher broke off to laugh. 'Your face! You really think we don't see how mad you are about him? Listen, do you think this Jack really loved you? Yeah? Good. It is what it fucking well is, babes. Put that in your back pocket and go slay.'

'That's the longest speech I've ever heard you make.'

Cher mooched back behind her counter. 'People talk too much.'

It would be wrong to hug the cherry tree.

Sadie knew that. She resisted the urge, in case a neighbour saw and diagnosed her as terminally strange. Instead, she circled it, nibbling her lunchtime sandwich, feeling its strength and its age and liking them both greatly.

The cherry tree spoke volumes about nature's tenacity. It flourished in the midst of London smog and fumes, year after year, its silvery bark peeling away and renewing.

She wasn't alone. A small creature was circling too.

'Don't you dare!' warned Sadie as Noel VI cocked a leg.

'Oh let him,' said Mary, swaying to a halt beside them. 'The tree doesn't mind.' She reached out and stroked its raspy surface. 'It's an old friend.'

Sadie said nothing. She finished her sandwich. Waited. A story was about to unfold.

'Arthur and I,' said Mary, in a small voice which somehow rose above the clamour of the lunchtime traffic. 'We kissed here, for the first time. He took down a sprig of blossom, fat as a pompom, and put it in my hair. I leaned back against this tree and he leaned over me and . . .' She closed her eyes.

Sadie almost felt it. The gentle kiss still disturbed the air decades later.

Flowers arrived. All three women circled the extravagant bouquet.

'No note,' said Fi suspiciously.

'They're from Hero.' Cher seemed sure.

Sadie found a card amongst the foliage. 'They're from Jez!'

Fi, deflated, went back to rearranging a pyramid of overpriced skin cream.

'Why?' Cher seemed angry. 'What do I do with them?'

'Put them in a vase?' suggested Sadie.

'That,' said Fi, 'is what normal humans would do, anyway.'

'I haven't even shagged him.' Cher was exasperated.

'Then it must be—' Sadie didn't risk it. Cher and love didn't mix.

When Hero showed his face – a slightly careworn face; Sadie could tell he'd had a tough morning – he raised his eyebrows at the supernova of roses and lilies and amaryllis. 'Somebody's given me a lot to live up to.'

'Nah. I don't need flowers. Just you.'

Hero's surprise at Sadie's sudden corniness made her feel sorry for him.

Do I really withhold that much?

'Listen.' Hero was earnest. 'We need to have a chat.'

'Okay . . .'

'Me and Fi are worried about you.'

The noise Sadie heard was of the stockroom door swinging shut behind the scarpering Fi.

I'll get you later, lady.

'Worried?' Sadie knew what was coming.

'This business of hanging around schools—'

She interrupted. 'I don't do it every day.'

'Most days,' said Hero. Gentle. Adamant. He moved closer. 'This is my area, Sades. Take my advice seriously. There are ways to deal with losing Teddy that won't do you harm. Your ongoing coping strategy—'

'Ongoing coping strategy? You're talking like a textbook, Hero.'

'You need to examine your behaviour if it makes you think, "I know I shouldn't be doing this but . . ." It can bring on shame, and shame can lead to a relapse of your drinking.'

'You're cheerful today.' Sadie reached out to primp the flowers.

'And you're evasive.'

'Maybe I am.' Sadie tried to swallow the next words but they found their way out into the ether. 'Or maybe my new boyfriend of five minutes doesn't have the right to boss me about like this.'

Hero swallowed. 'We've been together for more than five minutes. We've become – I thought – very close. It's not my intention to boss you about. It's my intention to help, but I do know that people can't always accept help.'

'People? I'm not people, Hero.' Sadie put her hands over her eyes, as if to escape the sight of herself messing up. 'Sorry. I'm spiky.' A tear dribbled through her fingers.

The ding of the bell above the door announced the arrival of Sadie's two forty-five appointment.

An arm around her, Hero steered her to the kitchenette. 'Better you have a little sob here than in front of your clients.'

Sadie leaned against him. 'It's hard, Hero. Something swells up inside me, like a bubble, and the only way to deal with it is to be around kids of Teddy's age.'

'You feel elated?'

'Yes.'

'And afterwards?'

'I feel empty.'

'Does that pattern sound familiar?'

It was the same loathsome circle as her drinking days. 'You're good at this.'

'So are you, if you'd only listen to your common sense.' Hero's arms went about her. They were just tight enough. 'Advise yourself like a best friend would. Like a lover would. A lover who's mad about you.' He laid his cheek against the top of her head.

'Would it be a deal-breaker?' Sadie felt him stiffen. She was poisoning a beautiful well. 'I mean, if I, if I . . .'

He held her at arm's length. An arm can feel very long at such a time. 'If you couldn't stop?'

'Part of recovery,' she said, 'is choosing nourishing relationships. You've said that a million times.'

'Are you telling me you won't try?'

'I'm not telling you anything. Just asking.'

'Here's a question for you, Sades. Are you going to visit a school today?'

'No.'

'That's good enough for me. One day at a time, as somebody once said.'

Hero left, the set of his shoulders telling Sadie that he was thinking hard. He seemed dejected, as if she had painstakingly extracted all the joy out of him.

Her client fidgeted.

'I'm sorry,' said Sadie. 'I have . . . um . . . something urgent, family business.' She was already out on the mews, pushing her arms into her thin jacket. 'Cher will reschedule you!'

Just one more time.

Sadie broke into a run. She recognised this hunger. She recognised the glib promise.

I want to mean it.

Surely that counted for something?

Appropriately for the last ever school run – *I swear!* – Sadie travelled further. This establishment was private, set behind high walls. The girls leaking out of an archway were made of the same ingredients as other schoolgirls but wore blazers that cost as much as couture.

A different brand of parent waited. Some sat in double-parked estate cars, others formed chattering knots. From the festive atmosphere Sadie deduced it was the last day of summer term. The high spirits were intoxicating.

Dangerous word, that.

She stood, eyes closed, as the girls surged past. Hugging each other goodbye. Whooping as they located their mothers.

Recharging like a battery, Sadie reassured herself that she was in charge of this situation. That she could stop. That she *should* stop. It was, she told herself, counterproductive.

All it does is pick the scab off an old wound.

Fate ensured her promise would be kept.

I can't do this next week even if I want to; term's over.

She would use the school holiday to detox. Sadie longed to tell Hero. To offer hope. To ask him, quietly, to stay.

Sadie opened her eyes. Strength suffused her. She could turn around and walk away.

A girl stopped in front of her, took off her straw boater, and said, 'Mummy?'

WEEK TEN

To The Bobs <bob@bobscaff.co.uk>, Michael T. <qwertybookshop@hotmail.com>, Sadie <sakuraspa@gmail.com, Fiona J <filove@aol.com>, Cher Mogg <whatulookingatcher@gmail.co.uk>, Grace Esparza <Gracetheartist@gmail.com>, Jez <jeremy.gray@u-turn.net>, Amber <amber@yummymummymews.net.co.uk>

From Hero <hero.smith@u-turn.net>

Subject CHERRY BLOSSOM MEWS RESIDENTS' ASSOCIATION MEETING

Dear Mewsites

This has been a turbulent week to say the least. Looking forward to seeing you all.

Date Wednesday 25.7.18
Time 6.30 p.m.
Location U-Turn therapy suite
Agenda Anything we feel like

Please make sure Mary knows about the meeting. And tell Noel he's guest of honour.

H x

Sadie didn't respond. She assumed she was hallucinating. In her drinking days she'd seen things that weren't there. Had stand-up arguments with invisible people.

Teddy, however, was real. She was too tall. She had a fringe. She was sobbing. 'Mummy,' she said, again and again, like a mantra. 'Mummy, Mummy, Mummy.'

Sadie said the unbelievable word. 'Teddy.' She crouched over the child, unable to believe the tightness of the little arms about her waist and the pressure of Teddy's head against her torso.

A woman hovered.

'Who are you?' Sadie said. Brusque, she backed away, dragging Teddy with her.

'I'm, um, I'm . . .' The figure in jeans and tee whose shabbiness looked expensive, backed away too. 'I'm Millie's mum.' She gestured to a gobsmacked little girl in the same uniform as Teddy. 'I normally take Teddy home,' the other woman said, holding out an ineffectual hand. 'Look, I should—'

'You should get away from us.' Sadie was electric.

'Teddy, darling, do you know this lady?'

Teddy lifted her head to say, 'She's my mummy.'

'Okay.' Uncertain, but evidently unwilling to take on the tigress, the woman's phone was already to her ear as she turned.

Elated, sick with it, Sadie's thoughts came clear and simple. Thudding one after the other.

She'll be taken away again.

They must sit in plain sight.

The stone bench in the shopping centre was broad, uncomfortable. Sadie had to stagger there with Teddy entwined about her like a koala.

'Let me look at you, baby.' Sadie extricated her – gently, feeling it to be a betrayal – and looked and looked and looked. She could look at Teddy for the rest of her life and never be bored.

'I knew you'd come back.' The tears had dried up. Teddy was happy. She was made of happiness. There was no jarring detail for her. She held on tight to her mother's hands, unaware that the feel of her chubby fingers, the sight of the felt-tip hearts scribbled on her palm, set off a chain reaction of emotion that could detonate the mall's soaring iron and glass ceiling.

She chattered while Sadie looked.

The voice hadn't changed. Still sounded like a cool stream threatening to burst its banks, but now went up and down wildly in register.

You've lost one of your front teeth.

'I knew you'd come back, Mummy. Granny was wrong. Did you come today because it's the last day of term? I have a huge long holiday now. Really ages. Now you're back can we go to Spain? To that place they throw tomatoes at each other? Oh. Look at these!'

One hand released. Sadie felt adrift.

'This is my keyring collection. I have eight. No keys. The fluffy one's my favourite. You smell the same. Where have you been?' Teddy didn't wait for an answer. 'Granny's got really strict. Tell her to let me go to sleepovers because I'm not a baby, Mummy. She says I look more like Daddy every day.'

The casualness of the mention winded Sadie.

'She's wrong. I look like you. I've got your nose. Daddy always said that.'

Sadie found something to say. 'Are you all right?'

Teddy shrugged. 'Yeah.' She smiled and suddenly she was a tiny Jack in a straw boater and a blazer. 'Granny'll have to admit she was wrong.'

The fuzziness of the new scenery firmed up a little. 'About what?' Conversational, amused. With bitter black tar running beneath.

'About you, silly! She said you'd forgotten me but I knew you wouldn't.' Teddy looked stern. The dimples disappeared. 'But where have you been, Mummy?'

'I've been ...'

Teddy stood up. The weather on her face changed yet again. 'Come on. I'll take you home.'

Home.

This bench was home. Anywhere with Teddy was home.

The small human took the new turn of events much better than the larger one. She led the way, limping, a pale scar zigzagging up her skinny leg. Sadie hung onto Teddy as if spies lurked at every corner, ready to snatch the girl away. The streets felt unreal, just a backdrop to an outrageous storyline. Lorries juddered past. A bus sank to let a wheelchair disembark. Life went on.

It should have been wonderful, but it was too strange to call it that. Teddy was alive. Sadie and her daughter had beaten death.

'Nearly there.' Teddy enjoyed being in charge. 'This is the best street for miles, Granny says so.'

I bet she does.

They were on hallowed ground. A conservation terrace of smug grandeur.

Sadie stopped, primal responses kicking in. Why was she walking *towards* danger? Shouldn't she flee with her child?

'Mummy,' complained Teddy, tugging at her. 'Come *on*. Granny's going to be amazeballed.'

They halted at three storeys of orderly prime real estate.

'Hang on a second, darling.' Sadie needed a second before Teddy stretched up to ring the bell.

This was what Sadie has smelled on the air. This was what the wind had promised. It was her own flesh and blood pushing out a message to her.

Come and get me, Mummy.

The room was a room to think beautiful thoughts in.

Every detail was considered, deliberate. The high windows – original, of course – were draped in heavy silks. A hand-painted mural of cherry blossom brought a hint of nature's pretty disorder to the formal arrangement of deep sofas. The carpet was so thick that Sadie might have been standing in snow.

Sadie's thoughts were not beautiful. She was dazed. She couldn't appreciate the views of the garden square beyond the Georgian windows. She needed to pull herself together.

The rest of her life hinged on the next few minutes.

There was just one detail in the room that was unsophisticated. A cardboard box covered in red crêpe paper, with a black slit in the side.

A school project. It almost broke Sadie, but she didn't have time to fall apart because the lady of the house appeared.

'Teddy's very upset.' The refined accent. The up-do worthy of a wedding. The level judgemental eyes.

'Me too,' said Sadie.

Teddy had divined that this conversation would be important, and her small face had collapsed when she was sent upstairs so it could take place without her. Her squeaky shout of 'Granny! Look who's here!' hadn't been met with the enthusiasm Teddy expected. Merle, pre-warned by Millie's mum, had greeted Sadie with cold formality.

Now, her hostess motioned for them both to sit. She was polite, steely. She was not rattled.

This rattled Sadie. She sat. Then she stood. She wasn't here for chit-chat. 'Where do we start, Merle?'

'There has been,' said Merle, pursing her lips, 'a misunderstanding.'

'That doesn't begin to cover it.'

Despite everything, vestiges of Sadie's old deference to her mother-in-law remained. Sadie still felt the need to police herself in Merle's presence, to not let herself down. Even when faced with the other woman's soul-scarring lies.

'We mustn't argue, Sadie. The child will hear.'

'*My* child.' It needed saying. 'Not *the* child. I last saw her on the fourth of October 2015. I thought she was dead.'

The words were so ridiculous there was no way to say them without sounding like a soap opera.

'Teddy was abandoned. I took her in.'

Sadie rocked on her feet. If she'd thought that Merle would crumble she was wrong; with her back against the wall, Merle merely doubled down.

'Drink?' Merle turned to a glittering array of bottles on a mahogany side table. She smiled, malicious like a cat.

That was how Merle had smiled over the Sunday lunch table on the day of the accident. They'd all been alive then, all the dear ones, each with a beating heart and a beavering brain. Sadie. Jack. Teddy. All at the fashionable Southwold restaurant at Merle's invitation.

'We must have wine,' Merle had murmured, taking an age to choose. Tasting. Conferring with the sommelier.

Sadie sat through it, toying with the cutlery, answering Teddy's questions about the menu. Four-year-olds tend to be baffled by French cuisine.

Merle doesn't get it. I'm not tempted by fine wines.

It's oblivion that alcoholics crave, not the act of drinking itself.

Merle had leaned down to Teddy. 'Oops! I shouldn't really encourage Mummy's little habit, should I? Mummy's not awfully nice when she's had a drinkie-poo, is she?'

'Mum, Teddy wouldn't know.'

It had seemed for a moment as if Jack were going to carry on, go into battle against his mother on Sadie's behalf for once.

But no.

Sadie heard him change the subject. Jack was skilled at diplomacy. Got it from his mother.

Perhaps if he knew how hard I work to hang on to my sobriety he'd be more protective.

The goading went on throughout three interminable

courses. Nothing major – no out and out accusation. Merle was patient, building a beach from grains of sand. Sand that cut Sadie's feet.

I won't let her get to me.

Sadie had repeated this to herself in the hall mirror as she put in her earrings. Small pearls. Anything less humdrum and Merle would comment, like she'd commented on Sadie's coat when they arrived: 'Did you borrow it from a younger chum?' She commented on Sadie's hair: 'Ooh, a touch of grey already?' She commented on *Teddy*'s hair: 'Needs a brush. You didn't take a swig of the cooking sherry, did you, Sadie?'

'Teddy's hair is untidy because she's four years old.' Sadie had refused to give Merle the satisfaction of losing her poise. 'Besides, Jack can lift a hairbrush.'

'Leave me out of it, ladies.' Jack held up his hands in mock surrender.

If he had lived, Sadie would have been up half the night berating him for that.

It's not some girly catfight! It's bullying!

Instead he'd died, and got away scot free.

Teddy had been bored at the table. Grumpy. Jack gulped down the vintage wine his mother had chosen. He'd cited 'things on my mind' when Sadie had asked, discreetly, what was the matter.

She knew now it was Effie on his mind.

The straw that broke the camel's back, the comment that made Sadie jump to her feet, was mild by Merle's standards.

'Look at Mummy,' she stage-whispered to Teddy, 'pretending to enjoy her glass of boring water.'

'Is this what you want, Merle?' Sadie upended the red wine over her own face. It splashed like blood on her neck. The fumes made her dizzy. A droplet on her lips reminded her of the wasteland she used to inhabit.

Jack's voice was the only sound in the shocked room as he jumped back from the red spray. 'Love, watch out!'

Sadie stalked from the gilded restaurant, her dress drenched. She wiped her mouth with distaste as she found the family Renault and tore off through the town.

Home. To regret her temper and await her little family.

She had assumed Jack would call a cab. After all, he'd been drinking solidly through lunch. Instead, he drove Merle's car, dropping her at her hotel before driving himself and Teddy home.

When the police arrived with sombre faces, Sadie's ears had begun to buzz at 'fatal collision'. They'd been taken aback by her screaming.

Like a cat held over water, Sadie freaked out. She wanted them to stop, get out, unsay it all. They had kept going, her whirring brain hearing only the odd word.

The odd word was enough. 'Husband'. 'Minor'. 'Deceased'. 'Dead on arrival'.

The taller officer told her he was a neighbour of her sister's. 'I can break the news to Tish, if you like. Get her to come round.'

'Yes, fine, please go.' Sadie had pushed at them.

There was never a moment when she felt like calling Merle. Her mother-in-law would say, 'Yes, you're right. This is your fault. If you had remained at the table and driven them home safely Jack and Teddy would still be here.'

That night, Sadie feared her mind was leaving the building. When Tish didn't show up, she grabbed her bag and crawled to her house.

The porch light came on as she staggered up the path.

Sanctuary.

Tish's face appeared. 'Don't come here with your grief,' she said, and slammed the door.

Sadie went home.

Home is the wrong term for what was just a stupid house, full of stupid furniture.

The doorbell was ignored. The nice lady next door came and went unacknowledged. Concerned friends tapped on the window until Sadie drew the curtains. Food left on the step went into the bin. There was no room inside Sadie for home-made lasagne, what with the grief.

And the booze.

She drank seamlessly. It was delivered – vodka, beer,

strange liqueurs – and she drank it all and ordered more.

Day bled into night. She ached. Mysterious bruises bloomed. One eye was bloodshot.

The discomfort was welcome. Sadie could almost believe she'd been in the crash with them.

Merle's materialisation had been worthy of a panto villain. One minute, Sadie was alone. Then – *pff!* – her immaculately dressed and coiffed mother-in-law was standing on the filthy rug and frowning down at her.

Today, they were both sober. Sadie stitched the story together with surprising speed. The shock was on hold. 'When you came round on the day of the funeral, at what point did you realise?'

'That you were drunk? The smell hit me in the hall.'

'No, not that.' Sadie ignored the insult. 'When did you realise I thought Teddy was dead?'

'Teddy needed you, Sadie. Her leg was smashed. Her father had died beside her. Where were you? Crawling inside a bottle.'

'You didn't answer my question.'

Merle crossed to the marble mantelpiece. Fussed with her hair in the enormous mirror. 'Drunks are so selfish.'

Clenching and unclenching her fists, Sadie refused to be derailed. 'You knew I thought Teddy had been killed. You used my drinking as camouflage to smuggle my own child out of my life.'

'You're an unfit mother.' Whiplash-fast, Merle turned. Her voice was a sibilant hiss. 'You fell apart the moment trouble arrived. That little girl needed stability and attention. I gave her all that.'

'You stole her.' Sadie took a step towards Merle.

Merle stood her ground. 'You gave her up when you collapsed under the weight of your vile addiction.'

They regarded each other without speaking. Sadie, exhausted by zigzagging emotions, saw that Merle was depleted too. She sat down heavily on velvet upholstery the colour of a blush. 'I assumed, when the police told me to prepare myself for bad news, when they used the word "fatal", that both my darlings were gone.'

'Drink addles the brain.'

'I started drinking *after* the police left. Don't you get it, Merle? That endless criticism was all pointless. I was sober throughout my marriage.'

'You certainly weren't the day of the funeral. What wife misses her own husband's burial? You were contemptible, a pile of self-pity on the floor.'

'That's all true. The fact remains that I'm Teddy's mother. You looked me in the eye and let me go on believing she was dead.'

'It was in the local paper, for heaven's sake. It was even on television that night. The car on its back like a turtle.' Merle was spirited in her own defence. 'While we're asking questions, why did you leave Jack to drive home that day? You were the designated driver, which is an excellent joke in itself.'

As if watching them both from a great height, Sadie saw the outlines of her life clearly.

'Yes, I took the car but the obvious thing for Jack to do was call a cab.' Sadie paused; Merle had handed her a blade and now she must use it. 'Jack knew he'd drunk too much to drive. The decision was his.'

'How dare you talk about my son like that.'

'How dare I?' Sadie let out a mutant, almost-laugh. 'I can talk about my husband if I please, Merle. We never did talk about him, did we?' The secret seared her lips. 'We never talked about how much Jack drank. How often.' Sadie hadn't felt able to comment, given her own track record. 'Jack wasn't an angel, Merle.' That was as far as she would go. Some vestige of empathy remained, even though Merle was no better than a swamp creature dressed up in designer labels. 'Full disclosure, Merle. Now.'

The older woman sat abruptly. The lines around her thin mouth deepened. Electricity seemed to crackle through her matchstick limbs. 'Very well,' she said, and her voice was hoarse, as if she'd already made her confession.

Sadie stood and leaned against the mantelpiece. Power was important to Merle; Sadie had always refused to play her games. For today, she would join in.

I won't take a seat until she's finished the whole sorry tale.

'I went to the hospital as soon as the police informed me about the accident, as any responsible adult would, I'm sure you'll agree.' Merle reached for a table lighter. Heavy stone, multi-faceted, she played with it as she spoke, passing it from one hand to another. A worry bead. 'Jack was dead. He never stood a chance. They said it was a momentary distraction behind the wheel. Worrying about his unhinged wife, possibly. Worrying about what manner of mess he'd find at home.'

A quick glance, then, to see how her daughter-in-law was taking this.

Sadie's face was a fixed mask.

'Teddy was in the operating room. There were forms to sign, but the child's next of kin was drinking herself unconscious so I did the necessary. Her leg, if you care to know, was shattered. Her femur – that's the thigh bone – was fractured badly. There was mention of amputation.' Another sly glance. 'Her big toenail was torn off. The doctors were wonderful. They placed long flexible nails inside the bone, holding it in place while it healed. Her body was . . .' Merle wavered. 'To see a small girl suffer like that changes one.'

Not enough to make you human.

'You could have come and got me, Merle.'

'I had plenty on my plate without nannying you! Teddy

needed me. I sat by her bed. You were not my priority. She was.'

'I thought she was . . .' Odd, now that Sadie's daughter was wonderfully, terrifyingly alive, she found it hard to say the word 'dead'.

'How was I know to know your sozzled ears had misheard the police officers?'

There was no benefit in pointing out, again, that she'd been stone cold sober at the time.

'The funeral was beautiful,' said Merle. 'So many people, all wanting to pay their respects to my dear son. But his wife . . .' Merle spread her hands, as if puzzled, one hand weighed down with the lighter, the other with diamonds. 'Nowhere to be seen. Imagine how I struggled to make excuses for you.'

One day I might laugh at that.

There was no doubt that Merle had trashed Sadie left, right and centre.

Merle carried on. 'I organised the coffin. The hearse. The church. The invitations. The catering. All from Teddy's bedside. I took three hours away from her to attend. I even attempted to get you to the service, if you remember.'

'If I remember!' That was the pivot of the tragedy. 'You could have put me right with one sentence. You could have lifted me out of my agony. Instead you let the misconception take root.' Sadie and Merle both quivered like cobras about to strike. 'You stole my daughter.'

'She's my life!' Merle brought the lighter down on the coffee table with a sharp crack. 'That child wants for nothing.'

'You stole her,' repeated Sadie.

'I stepped in. What could you possibly offer her?'

'If you weren't in the wrong, why run away?' Sadie took a step forward, feet sinking in carpet. 'I went to rehab days after the funeral, and when I came out I wanted to make amends. I flew up to Scotland but your house was cleared out.' Sadie remembered a FOR SALE sign sticking up like a flag of war. 'Your phone numbers were disconnected. I assumed you wanted nothing to do with me, now that all we had in common was gone. If I'm honest, I never wanted to see you again, either. I'd planned to tell you, once and for all, that I hadn't drunk during my marriage to your son, but I figured you wouldn't believe me, so I let go. Of that, of *you*.'

'I moved house to escape the memories.' Merle ignored the snort of disbelief. 'Teddy and I needed a fresh start. Her leg was healing fast, but there were endless hospital appointments. We talked often of Jack. And of you.'

Sadie noted she was an afterthought. 'Why London?'

'I wanted a diverting place for Teddy to grow up and—'

'No.' Sadie chopped the air with her hand. 'You chose London because it was the one place you could be sure you wouldn't bump into me. No bullshit, Merle, not now.' Sadie cut off the blustering before it got going. 'I used to bang on about hating London. You weren't to know that after the crash it drew me like a magnet. I wanted to un-exist. I wanted to be just another face in the crowd.'

'Paint my actions in lurid colours if you wish, but the truth is that everything I've done is for Teddy.'

'A child needs its mother.' Sadie would not let her voice quiver as she said, 'And a mother needs her child.'

Merle made a noise of derision. 'I've protected her from you.'

'You abused her.'

Merle's cheeks burst into flame. 'I devote my *life* to Teddy.'

'But she's not yours! She's my daughter and she's coming home with me, Merle.' This incendiary declaration had the unexpected effect of calming Merle. Sadie, however, felt panic creep through her.

I have no home fit for Teddy.

Sadie had created a childless realm above the spa.

'I have an idea.' Merle stood, a feline unfurling that belied her age. 'Why don't we ask Teddy what she wants?'

'Don't!' Sadie made to catch hold of her mother-in-law's arm, but a disgust of Merle's starved body stopped her. 'You can't ask a seven-year-old to make a decision like that, in front of us.'

'Scared she'll choose me?'

Merle's arrow hit home. What if Teddy opted for continuity, for the grandmother who doted on her?

Teddy thinks I couldn't be bothered to see her.

The stairs took a moment. Sadie felt Merle bolt after her but she had a few years on the woman.

'Teddy!'

A door opened. A bright little face peeped out of a colourful room. A built-in bunk and painted cupboards. Warm. Safe.

'What do you want to bring?' Sadie smiled, as if this was all fun and games. She recognised a small purple creature. 'Humphrey must come, of course.' She found a rucksack, pushed the plush elephant into it.

'Bring? Where?' Teddy's head shrunk into her shoulders.

It was cruel. Sadie knew that. 'Come on, darling. Nightie. Knickers.'

Teddy half-heartedly opened drawers, and her mother dipped her hands into cupboards like a cat burglar. One eye on the door, she expected Merle to suddenly appear, like Nosferatu in court shoes.

'This?' Sadie held up a pen with a daisy on the end. Felt tips were packed. A book. Glittery shoes. Teddy, sensing the urgency, her cheeks heating up, shoved this and that in with them.

'Am I coming back?'

Another question Sadie wasn't brave enough to answer. She grabbed Teddy, regretted it, released her, then took her hand again, more gently. Her panic might be contagious.

'Let's go and see Mummy's house,' she said.

At the bottom of the stairs stood Merle, looking up at the mother and child as they descended. She was talking, in the clickety-clack tone she used for dealing with staff. 'Of course, we must organise access now that you've surfaced.' She held out an arm gracefully as a cue. 'For now, however, I insist you leave. Alone.' Merle took one step and was in their path as they reached the bottom of the stairs. 'Darling Teddy needs her rest. This term's been very tiring for her.'

Teddy froze, eyes flicking between the two most important women in her little life.

With a smile, Merle went on. 'Please do as I say, Sadie, or I'll have no option but to call the police. Surely we don't need any more unpleasantness?'

Sadie didn't move.

She thinks she's in charge.

Juggling the rucksack, Sadie took out her phone. 'You're right, Merle. It's time we involved the authorities.' A doubt skipped across her brain. Had Merle committed a crime?

Merle's touch was dry, lizard-like. She lowered Sadie's hand. 'No am-dram please. Let's not drag the police into a family matter.'

'Teddy, run back up and fetch, um, your dressing gown.'

When Teddy – reluctant, suspicious – was out of earshot, Sadie whispered to her mother-in-law, 'You're not family.'

'I'm your only family,' gloated Merle.

'I see you, Merle. I see you clearly. I see how you can't stop, not even when your cruelty's discovered. Don't sugar-coat this; you put a knife to my relationship with my child. It wasn't about Teddy's safety. You know, deep down, that I was sober all those years. You might even accept that my relapse was understandable. You exploited the situation. Teddy's safe with me, but you need her as a buffer against loneliness. You're even prepared to use the insecurity you've caused to try and hang onto her. Teddy's my responsibility. Nobody's asking her any difficult questions today. She's leaving this house and she's coming home with her mother.'

Merle watched them go from the front step.

'This is the beginning, madam, not the end,' she called.

Teddy's fringe bugged Sadie. The girl was herself and yet not herself. Teeth rearranging themselves. That jagged line down her left leg.

'What do you mean this is my room?'

They were Teddy's first words since leaving Merle's house; her ebullience was replaced by a mulish introspection despite Sadie's attempts to kickstart the chit-chat again. She held on tight to her rucksack. 'My room's at Granny's.'

'This room's been waiting for you.' Sadie saw it through a seven-year-old's eyes. Austere. Anonymous. 'We'll soon make it nice.' Gently she took the bag. 'Where'll we put Humphrey?'

'On the bed.' Teddy forced the words from sewn-up lips.

Sadie fussed over the toy, sitting him just so, talking to him. 'Comfy, Humphrey?' When she began to pull out the other bits and pieces, Teddy grabbed the bag.

'Don't,' she said. 'They're mine.'

'Okey-doke.' Sadie hung back. She felt awkward.

With my own child.

'Some of this,' said Teddy, without looking at her, 'is secret.' She put her felt tips and a stack of white postcards under the plain white pillow. 'Not for you.'

After Teddy was tucked in, Hero came over to listen as Sadie stuttered out her news over the kitchen table. There were gaps, many of them, but enough details to horrify them both.

He agreed with her that, yes, this was a unique situation. Neither of them had heard of anything similar happening.

'Hero, is it a crime?' They had turned that one over and over.

'You need legal advice.'

'First, I need a patterned duvet cover and a telly and chicken nuggets and a shelf of books and a ton of sundresses and shorts.' She wondered, wildly, if she'd forgotten how to mother. 'I had to ask Teddy what time she normally goes to bed.'

Hero bowed out, whispering, at around ten. He leaned back in through the glass doors for one last kiss, then another last kiss, then he said, 'If you need me, switch your bedroom light on and off three times, and I'll dash right over.'

'Okay.' As he backed away, Sadie felt overwhelmed. She reached for him, found him, and kissed him. Properly.

'Well, now see what you've done,' he murmured. 'I don't want to go home.'

'Shoo,' she smiled. He backed away across the cobbles. She watched him. She smiled when he almost fell over the cherry tree.

Upstairs, she peeked in at Teddy, at the amazing gift this day had given her.

'Mummy.' The voice was drenched in sleep. 'Leave the landing light on. And my door open a bit. Not that much. Bit more. Bit more. That's it.'

Sadie breathed in the bath time smell. Gratitude flooded her, so deep it was a prayer. She leant down to kiss Teddy's forehead.

The girl baulked, dipping down into the bedclothes. 'I'm a bit old for that, Mummy.'

'At seven?' laughed Sadie. She saw a small white rectangle caught up in the covers, covered in writing. Teddy had used one of the blank cards.

My baby can write?

Sadie crept out.

The voice from the bed was tiny now, giving up the fight against sleep. 'Mummy, does Granny still love me?'

Night drifted through the flat, dragging Sadie along with it. She got out of bed, made hot milk, threw it down the sink.

A couple of the letters on the postcard had been back to front, but the words were spelled properly, and clearly set down. Sadie had time to make out one sentence only. It had leapt out at her, as if drawn in neon.

I wish I still lived with you.

Cross-legged on the floor, she stared at the *Lady Sadie*.

After all the pain of their separation, after all the longing Sadie had stoppered up inside her, Teddy wanted to go back to Merle.

And Sadie? She wanted the best for Teddy.

She needed a drink.

She needed more than that.

'Jack,' she said to the dark. 'I need you.'

WEEK ELEVEN

To Amber <amber@yummymummymews.net.co.uk>, Hero <hero.smith@u-turn.net>, Sadie <sakuraspa@gmail.com>, Michael T. <qwertybookshop@hotmail.com>, Fiona J <filove@aol.com>, Cher Mogg <whatulookingatcher@gmail.co.uk>, Jez <jeremy.gray@u-turn.net>, Grace Esparza <Gracetheartist@gmail.com>,

From The Bobs <bob@bobscaff.co.uk>

Subject CHERRY BLOSSOM MEWS RESIDENTS' ASSOCIATION MEETING

As we over-bought sausages there will be sausages available. Some may be slightly old.

Date Wednesday 1.8.18
Time 6.30 p.m.
Location Bob's Caff
Agenda Do not mention Bob's health

Was it possible the late Dorothy Ball had titled her novels with Sadie's life in mind?

One week into her second stab at motherhood, *Daughter of m'Lady* had been waiting for her when she opened up on Saturday. *Michael*, she thought fondly, conjuring up his baffled empathy when she'd introduced him to Teddy. He had formally shaken the girl's hand, and welcomed her to Cherry Blossom Mews. He was, Sadie concluded, a good man.

A good man headed for a fall. All the books in the world can't inspire love in a woman's heart. Sadie's heart was full to the brim with it, no room for one more.

The bookings spreadsheet was hectic. Sadie fished in her tunic pocket for a pen to jot down some notes and found instead a pencil-top eraser shaped like a corn on the cob.

Fingering the nubbly plastic as if it was a sacred talisman, Sadie looked up at the ceiling of Sakura. On the other side of that plaster, Teddy was curled up in front of rubbish TV, Humphrey clamped to her side.

New, unexpected anxieties had arrived by the truckload. Should Teddy spend so much time watching television? Should she be doing something more challenging? Should she be with her friends? Who are her friends? Sadie had only first names, and no numbers or addresses.

'Daydreaming, eh?' Mary's voice, cool and amused, brought Sadie back to the present.

'Where did you spring from?'

'From Treatment Room One,' said Mary, serving a side dish of sly triumph. 'I've had a facial.' She nodded her head of unkempt white hair at Cher. 'Your young assistant persuaded me, and now I'm a convert.'

Sadie, who had no idea that Mary and Cher had ever even spoken to one another, was happy to be blindsided.

'I did the facial.' Cher was brusque, confessional. Her eyes, outlined today with an emerald green that gave her a pantomime air, avoided Sadie's.

Before Sadie could pull on her boss's hat and point out that Cher wasn't trained or insured, Mary cut through the sudden atmosphere. 'I want to book five sessions, please. But only if Miss Mogg carries out my treatments.'

When Mary left, Cher said, 'Me and Mary have so much in common.'

'Like what?' Sadie couldn't imagine Mary in a Wonderbra.

'I inherited her family land, in a way. Orissa House, my block of flats, is built on it. She explained that Orissa's a tea-making bit of India. She must be loaded.'

'Mary's rich in love.' Sadie knew that would make Cher mime being sick, and laughed when it did. If only Cher could use her persuasion skills to make Mary come up with a modernised business plan. Before the mews collapsed, bankrupt, under the weight of good intentions.

Sadie envisaged herself fleeing, Teddy tucked under one arm, Mary under the other.

And Cher? And Fi?

Can I carry them too?

The Bobs were heavy. Amber – given the hungry way she looked at Hero, Sadie was tempted to leave her in the ruins.

Then there was Hero.

Does he need saving?

Having peeked behind the scenes, Sadie decided yes, somehow she'd need to slip Hero into her handbag when a fault line opened up in the cobbles.

'I still can't get it straight in my mind.' Cher unwrapped another stick of gum. She chewed all day, a pretty cow. 'How'd your mother-in-law manage to trick—'

Fi intervened, emerging from Treatment Room 2 smelling of lavender. 'None of your beeswax, Cher.'

'I don't mind talking about it.' Sadie appreciated the security blanket Fi flung over her, but discussing Merle's deception helped her come to terms with just how simple it had been to fool her. Merle had exploited Sadie's isolation. If she had spoken to one neighbour, picked up one local newspaper, or breached Tish's self-protective barrier, the plot would have foundered. 'But not right now, not in front of . . .' She lifted her eyebrows at a customer who followed in Fi's wake.

This glowing woman, fresh from Fi's care, was evangelical about her massage. 'I feel brand new,' she chirped. 'Take these. As a thank you.'

Fi accepted the box of chocolates. High-end. Tied up with a satin bow. When the woman was safely through the gates, she said, 'I'd rather have a tenner.'

'Open them.' There was lust in Sadie's voice. 'I'll take the nutty ones you don't like.'

'Have them all.' Fi put them down, and Cher undid the ribbon and dug in like a dingo. 'I'm not hungry.'

'Chocolate's not about hunger,' said Sadie through a caramel.

Cher pointed a shellacked nail. 'You're on a diet,' she whooped. 'You haven't had one of Bob's baps for ages.'

'Fi doesn't diet,' said Sadie. She was certain. Proud. They'd often discussed, over a second helping of pavlova, body fascism and the futility of weight loss regimes that end in tears. She paused. She'd been wrong about so much lately. 'You're not, are you?'

Saved, not by the bell, but by Teddy's sudden appearance, Fi didn't answer. Instead she bent over her goddaughter – a back-dated title both she and Teddy were happy with – and cuddled her. Cuddled her good and proper.

I'll have to go back to Merle's at some point.

In Sadie's mind, Merle's exquisite home had become a house of horrors, surrounded by a moat full of piranhas, but Teddy's hastily bought dungarees didn't quite fit. The girl needed her familiar bits and pieces.

'Look, Tedster,' said Fi. 'A box of chocs for you!'

Cher looked miffed.

Settled on the sofa with a can of Coke – contraband from her godmother – and a magazine, Teddy seemed content.

'Stop it,' said Fi, as she helped Sadie unpack a carton of essential oils.

'Stop what?'

'Watching the kid like a hawk. She's fine.'

'Pardon me for worrying about the daughter I thought was dead.' Sadie felt got at. 'How can she be fine? After all she's been through.'

'That's the past. From now on, everything's normal, yeah?' Fi lowered her head, gave Sadie a fierce, full-fat look. 'Not sort of normal, *properly* normal. You treat her like a case study and she'll act like one. She still sneaking into your bed?'

'Every night.' It was never mentioned. Never planned. Sadie knew now to expect a silent visitor, Humphrey beneath her arm, clambering in after lights out. There were no kisses. No drowsy cuddles. Teddy turned her cheek away, and squirmed out of reach if Sadie tried. So Sadie had stopped trying, and cherished the sweet moments when her daughter fell asleep, and turned towards her, and burrowed into her side.

'That kid's a better contraceptive than the pill.' Fi stood on the empty box and squashed it. They took turns at this satisfying chore. 'How's Hero with all this? Can't be easy sharing his new lady-love.'

'He's fine,' said Sadie. 'I think.' She was more concerned with how Teddy felt about sharing her mum. The little girl had asked tetchily, 'Why is that Hero man always hanging around? I don't like him. He's an idiot.'

'If this was a movie, Hero'd be swinging her round in soft-focus sunshine.' Fi gave the cardboard one last jubilant stomp. 'She'd be asking if he could be her daddy.'

'Life,' said Sadie, 'is nothing like the movies.'

'Except *Psycho*,' said Fi. 'Your mother-in-law's starring in her own version of that.' She lowered her voice. 'Anything new from the cops?'

The day after Teddy rose from the dead, Sadie had spent two hours at the local police station. Half expecting to be laughed out of the building, she had been led immediately to an over-warm room with plastic chairs and foul coffee to be interviewed by a young man with a very low centre of gravity. She wondered where such people were grown, the serious ones who always know what to do.

By the end of the day Merle had been arrested for Child Abduction under section 2 of the Child Abduction Act 1984.

'Her bail was met,' she told Fi. 'Merle's at home. They took her passport, and she has to call in to the police station once a week.' Even though she'd set it in motion, Sadie found it difficult to believe this state of affairs.

'She should crawl through the streets on her knees.' Fi was an advocate of rough justice. 'We should throw eggs at her. She should—'

'Okay, okay.' Sadie had fantasies too of Merle growing old and dotty in a cell. They didn't comfort her, even though her blood boiled with fury.

'Your favourite breakfast!' Sadie set down the painted tray – a new acquisition from MOBuk – on the equally new bedclothes. 'Eggy bread.'

As Teddy settled herself against her pillows, Sadie pootled around the small room. Bending to pick up discarded knickers, and opening a drawer to tuck in a vest, she found herself suffused with gratitude at being allowed to perform these small sacred tasks again.

'Sorry it's so messy.' Teddy's voice was grave, her eyes sombre beneath the harsh fringe that must surely grow out soon.

'That's all right, sweetie.' Sadie loved saying sweetie. She hadn't said it during the wasted years when her daughter was as good as dead. So she said it again, 'A little bit of mess never hurt anybody, sweetie.'

Teddy looked more puzzled than reassured.

Merle was obviously a stickler for tidiness.

'Look!' Sadie threw a pile of comics in the air. 'Who cares?'

Teddy giggled so hard that milk came out of her nose. It was like music. Sadie had a euphoric thought she had to immediately quash.

God, I'd love to tell Tish about all this.

'Do you want to come down to the spa with me?'

'Do I have to?'

Deflated, working hard not to show it, Sadie said, 'Of course not.'

I thought she enjoyed being in Sakura.

The little girl kept changing the goalposts. Sadie watched her as closely as a private detective, monitoring her mood, wondering if those written words still rang true; did she still wish she lived with Merle? 'Tell you what, I'll pop back up every hour and see what you're up to.'

A solemn nod. Teddy used to be so noisy. Bursting into tears. Laughing at Sadie's singing in the car. Scolding her and Jack when they fought.

She used to kiss me, too.

There had been no wet little smooches from Teddy since her resurrection.

'And Mummy,' said Teddy. 'I don't really like eggy bread anymore.'

*

The extensions, which had dripped from beneath Cher's real hair, were gone. Sadie approved. 'Your hair's lovely!'

'So it wasn't lovely before?'

Jez, hanging around, mostly just gazing at Cher, said, 'Take a compliment, hun. You look amazing.'

Mollified, but only slightly, Cher plumped up a white cushion with unnecessary force.

Sadie, writing up client notes at the reception desk, watched the lovers circle each other. The air glittered with desire. She felt like a voyeur. Her phone buzzed and she was grateful, but when she saw the caller ID she muted the sound. There would be no distraction there: it was Effie's umpteenth call.

She thinks she made a friend.

'We still on for after the residents' meeting?' Jez always lounged. He never stood up straight. Today he lounged against the pillar in the very middle of the spa that Sadie had been unable to knock down without endangering the ceiling. 'Drink somewhere. Bit of dinner.'

'When did we organise that?' Cher was snappy. Not playful snappy. Velociraptor snappy.

'Yester—' Jez saw the flaw in his strategy and corrected himself. 'Let's organise it now, hun.'

'Nah. Don't come to the meeting,' said Cher, without looking up.

'What? Why?'

Sadie felt for Jez, who seemed hurt by his girlfriend's vehemence.

'God!' Cher pronounced it *God-duh!* 'Do I have to explain every bloody little bloody thing? And don't surprise me by just turning up, either. You think it's cute but it's not.'

When Jez slunk away, Cher followed him, shouting, 'I want a night off now and then!' She rounded on Sadie. 'What you looking at?'

'I'm looking at you, Cher, and before you treat me like you treated poor Jez, remember I pay your wages.'

Cher's mouth became a hen's bum as she battled her instincts.

A small voice from the back of the spa lowered the temperature of the situation. 'Can I stay down here for a while?' asked Teddy.

A pad and coloured pens were sourced. Humphrey was ceremoniously seated on a cushion. Cher's anger dissipated as she laughed at the portraits Teddy drew.

'Your hair's really gorgeous,' said Teddy, with the air of a connoisseur. She took a crumpled postcard out of the pocket on the front of her dungarees, smoothed out its crumples with one small hand and then covered it as her mother approached.

'I have to go and give a nice lady a facial now.' Sadie stood over her daughter, a stretch of parched ground between them. Catching up with all the changes that had happened while they were apart made Sadie short of breath.

Tousling the hated fringe, Sadie assessed the child. 'Do you want something to eat? A smoothie? Are you, you know, okay, darling?' The worst thought of all assailed her. 'Are you bored?'

Fi took her by the shoulders and swivelled Sadie towards Treatment Room 1. 'There are worse things in life than being bored. Teddy's cool. She's with us. Get on with your work, mommy dearest. Sext your boyfriend or something.'

When Sadie lingered, Teddy took out the crumpled card.

That's the postcard she wrote to Merle.

It was Teddy's secret, not for Sadie's eyes, but Sadie felt she'd read enough to get the painful gist of it. Teddy reread it to herself, as she often did.

Dear Daddy

Me again.

i wish i still lived with you and Mummy in our old house now we live in a weerd flat. i have my own room. the wardrobe smells. i miss Granny. i miss you. i am a tiny bit worried that Mummy is in romantic love with a man. She keeps putting on lip gloss. he makes good fart noises but i won't let myself like him.

Don't worry i still love you the best.

love Teddy xxxxxxxxxxxx

Fi said, 'Oi, Teddy. Have you seen that fair round the corner? Want to go later?'

Teddy nodded so hard she burped.

'Thank you,' said Sadie. Fi had pledged her precious half-day off for babysitting duties, to free Sadie for an afternoon of sleep and sex.

'Greater love hath no man,' said Fi, 'than she lay down her how's-your-father for a friend.'

Sadie couldn't remember offering to walk Noel but Mary insisted it had happened. 'Off you trot,' she'd said, slamming MOBuk's door behind them, giving Sadie no time to suggest a chat.

Their chats centred on the topic Mary hated most: change. Cherry Blossom Mews was becoming an ongoing concern instead of a wacky commune. Sadie sympathised with Mary's reluctance to talk.

Just like Mary, I wish the mews could run on goodwill.

Noel VI was, on the whole, anti-walkies. He stopped to sniff the base of the bargain bin, and Sadie foraged through the tat inside it.

'Hello again,' she said to the black and white pair sitting stiffly in a photographer's studio. Mary and the double-crossing Arthur were still in love at that point, with no knowledge of the storms gathering above their tidy hair.

A snatch of dialogue drifted across the sun-warmed courtyard.

'You're going to be fine.'

Hero was talking to a woman over by the gates. His hands went to her shoulders. Sadie recognised the after-effects of a crying jag in the woman's red-rimmed eyes. Her self-possession was knitting itself back together.

He's so passionate.

Sadie imagined courage travelling through Hero's hands into the woman's body.

'That guy saves lives.' Grace was beside her, scratching Noel's head hard, the way he liked it. 'My dad's an addict. I know what it's like to live with alcoholism.'

'Me too,' said Sadie, before her lips pulled a zip across themselves. She revealed her own problems only to a very limited circle.

'Some people see past the alcoholism to the humanity. I wonder what he's saying to her?' Grace became caught up in the moving drama unfolding quietly a few feet away. She leaned on Sadie, reminding her of the way Noel liked to lean.

It felt as if Grace had been part of Cherry Blossom

furniture for far longer than a month; Mary's knack for adopting the right stray meant that Grace gave more to her new community than she got. She was everywhere at once, in her trademark dungarees with one tab hanging undone, nipping from caff to Yummy Mummy to spa, a cupcake in one hand, builder's brew in the other.

I'm not sure I'd radiate such happiness if I slept on a blow-up mattress and showered at the health centre.

The stranger composed herself, hugged Hero and turned away.

'Aw, look!' Grace nudged Sadie, but there was no need.

Sadie had seen Hero wipe his eye. Embarrassed. Quick. Darting a glance their way in case they saw it.

'If only men knew that's what we really want from them,' murmured Grace. 'Emotion.'

The clans were gathering for the weekly meeting.

Sadie stood, arms wrapped around herself, watching the mews through Sakura's wide glass frontage. Fi and Teddy were late. Only a little, but Sadie fretted as if they were lost at sea.

The sole of her foot was sore. A tiny pink hairbrush on the stairs had bit into her bare skin like a hedgehog.

Come on, you two!

Her imagination transformed the streets outside the gates into a bedlam of knife crime and muggings and—

Oh, here they are!

'Mummy!' called Teddy, one hand in Fi's and one in Cole's.

'Mummy!' echoed Fi, laughing, juggling the cheap and enormous stuffed toys they'd won.

'We got a bear or maybe it's a dog!' Teddy broke free and hurtled into Sadie, banging against her legs.

Sadie couldn't speak. Another homecoming. She was fit to topple with the weight of her emotional ballast.

Ever astute, Fi defused the moment before Teddy could register her mother's unwarranted relief. 'We went on all the rides, even the scary ones. Teddy's so brave!'

'Except for the Chair-O-Planes,' said Cole, laughing, his whole body heaving. 'Old Fi couldn't fit in the seat!'

'Yeah, the Chair-O-Planes man was horrid to her.' Teddy took up cudgels on her godmother's behalf.

Cole pulled Fi to him. 'What, Sadie? Don't look at me like that! I love my fatty bumbum, don't I, Fi?'

Fatty bumbum absorbed that, but Teddy answered for her. 'Fi isn't fat. She's round. She's perfect.'

They all smiled at Teddy's passion.

Perhaps it's only me Teddy's reserved with.

'Come on. The meeting's about to start.' Sadie held Teddy's hand tightly, as if the girl might blow away.

'Why didn't you visit me in hospital, Mummy?' Like paparazzi, seven-year-olds ask the bluntest questions.

'Because . . .' Sadie knew Teddy had no concept of what Merle had perpetrated.

Hero had suggested that Teddy might always be unwilling to face Merle's crimes, 'because she needs to love her granny'. Sadie had agreed that the truth was too rich a dish to serve a child.

'I was sick myself,' said Sadie. 'I didn't know you needed me, or I would've been there in a flash.'

'I know,' said Teddy. 'Granny was there all day and all night. She used to snore, like this, in the chair.'

Sadie laughed dutifully at the impression. This version of Merle didn't quite gel with the witch who had kidnapped her own flesh and blood.

'The doctors are so clever,' confided Teddy. 'Like, really clever. They put nails in my leg and hid them. My favourite was Doctor Batman.'

'Not his real name I hope.'

'*Her*, not him. Mummy?'

'Yes, darling?'

'I'm a bit too mature to hold hands all the time.'

'Sorry.' Sadie dropped Teddy's fingers.

'I might need another operation when I'm a teenager.' Teddy was blithe at the prospect.

Sadie was not.

They had reached Bob's Caff. The usual suspects milled about inside, each with a banger on a stick.

'Can I . . .' Sadie hesitated, shouting into Mrs Bob, who was replenishing the sausage fortress. 'I mean, I'm barred, but presumably I—'

'You're unbarred,' said Mrs Bob. 'I keep meaning to tell you, but I can't find the time 'cos my lazy bastard of a husband lies in bed all day and leaves me to do all the work.'

'So there's no improvement?'

'Did you read the agenda?' said Mrs Bob. 'I'm sick of talking about Bob. Bob this and Bob that. Michael came in to help with the lunch rush today.' She raised her voice so he could hear from where he sat quietly with his sausage. 'He was rubbish. Bloody rubbish.'

'I could help out. If you like.' Sadie readied herself for a verbal slap in the chops.

'Thank you,' said Mrs Bob, and she moved away to berate Amber for some minor transgression of caff law.

The register was taken.

Jez's absence was noted, as was Bob's. Nobody dared comment on either.

Bins were discussed.

Noel lay across Sadie's feet.

Cher pre-empted Sadie's call for a Good Samaritan to take minutes by asserting that nobody in their right mind would want to.

Michael raised his hand. 'The most important item on

today's agenda, surely, is to properly welcome our newest resident, Teddy McQueen.'

At the sound of her name, Teddy leaned so hard into Sadie's side she was almost inside her tunic with her.

'She's a bit shy.' Sadie laid a protective arm over her.

'Teddy,' said Michael, 'you're now a life member of the Cherry Blossom Mews Residents' Association. There are few benefits and many duties, but you'll find that there's always a snack, and you can doze off if it gets too boring.'

There were no questions. No probing. The mews grapevine had carried the miraculous story without any need for Sadie to explain over and over.

'To Teddy!' said Hero, and raised his mug.

'To Teddy!' they all roared, toasting her.

'Stop it,' she whispered. Her smile made a lie of her reluctance.

'She's so cute.' Amber homed in for a snap. 'Is that a Burberry skirt?'

'Hardly. I picked it up in a Tesco trolley dash,' said Sadie.

'Cool,' said Amber.

'Could you not . . .' Sadie gestured at Teddy, fidgeting, turning. 'I don't really want pictures of her on Instagram.'

'She has the looks to be a model,' said Amber, shocked at such maternal dereliction of duty.

Fi pushed the phone away. 'She. Is. Seven.'

Amber's puzzled face told Sadie that she couldn't fathom anybody, even a child, turning down the fleeting fame of Instagram.

The meeting disbanded, with nothing agreed on and no plans made.

Business as usual.

The residents' lack of skill at having meetings plus their persistence at holding them endeared them to Sadie.

That new nameplate will never happen.

'Hey, Hero Smith.' She yoked her arm through his. 'How d'you fancy dinner with two glamorous laydeez tonight?'

'You and your little Instagram model?' There was a moment before Hero said, 'Yes.'

Sadie examined that moment and didn't like it. Was it reluctance? Delicacy? A jangle of muttered comments from the others tore her attention towards the gates.

'Shit, the dreaded Mogg twins,' she breathed.

'What're they up to?' Mrs Bob wanted to know. Quite loudly.

Cher hurried towards her brothers. She was back in her stripper shoes, Sadie noted.

'I'm coming, I'm coming,' she squawked as a twin held up his wrist and angled his watch towards her. When their sister reached them they closed around her like security guards. Questions flew. Cher defended herself. The men bristled with temper, staring down any mews folk who dared to look over.

Mary would not be stared down. She stood, listing to one side, eyeing them as if they were zoo animals. 'This,' she said finally, 'is private property.'

'Calm down, Granny.'

'I'm not your Granny, thankfully.' Mary hobbled nearer. 'Cher's welcome here, but you are not.'

Hero was at Mary's side in less time than it took for Sadie to process the thought that somebody should have the old lady's back.

'Keep your knickers on,' said a twin. 'We're just collecting our baby sister. Wondering what it is that keeps her here so late.'

The arm he put around Cher was not so much protective as possessive. The gate was closed with sarcastic precision.

'I've got something for you, Teddy.' As they traipsed up the narrow stairs to Sadie's flat, Hero burrowed in the canvas bag over his shoulder.

'Barbie,' said Teddy, accepting the cellophane-fronted box. 'Thank you.'

Her manners were perfect.

Drilled into her by Merle.

'I didn't know what to get you.' Hero was nervous, Sadie realised. 'Hope you like it.'

He expressed surprise at the well-stocked kitchen cupboards. 'Usually it looks like a puritan's pantry,' he said, picking up and studying boxes and jars. Hero made Sadie's diminutive kitchen seem even smaller. He was big, healthy, *glowing.* It struck her again that this man had grown up in a house with its own bell tower, yet had transplanted himself to a damp flat in a crumbling, its-days-are-numbered mews.

Dinner done with, Teddy nodding off under the eaves, the sofa beckoned to Sadie and Hero. They sat close together, warming each other. His bulk buoyed her. It was so comfortable that she almost didn't want him to make his customary move – the hand on her waist, the lips on her neck.

Yet, when he didn't make his customary move, she wondered why.

Talk turned to Merle. Hero was a good sounding board, less prone to righteous rants than Fi. When Sadie mentioned her second thoughts about pressing charges, Fi had fumed that Merle was a witch, an eye for an eye, she needed to be punished, yada yada yada.

'There are pros and cons,' said Hero. 'On one hand, justice must be done. Merle almost destroyed your family, after all. On the other hand, a court case would be an enormous strain on you and Teddy at a time when you're focused on rebuilding.'

'How does Teddy seem to you? Is she settling down?'

'While you were making dinner she informed me she doesn't like Barbies.' Hero was amused, but Sadie sat up.

'Teddy *loves* Barbie!'

'Not anymore.' Hero stood up. Not with any real purpose, just to idle by the window. 'Teddy needs time. She seems to be her own person, even at seven. Take your foot off the pedal, Sades.'

And just like that, the pleasure of being understood evaporated.

Can't Hero and Fi see that I'm without a map, in a country I used to know well, wondering why the landscape has changed so drastically?

'You want to know what's really weird?' she said. 'I keep wanting to call Merle. That cow is the only one who really knows Teddy now, so I have questions and I—'

'Listen.' Hero blurted it. A stop sign. A warning. 'There's something I have to tell you. I put two and two together. About Effie and Jack. The surname gave it away. Her Steve was your Jack, wasn't he?'

Sadie went very still. She felt caught out, ashamed. 'Yes,' she said eventually. 'I really was going to tell—'

'Never mind that. Let's deal with what is, not what might have been.'

'Okay.' This Hero was not her Hero. This was the pragmatic Hero who took care of situations, cutting through trouble with a knife. 'I'm sorry.'

He ignored that. 'Effie's in a state because you won't pick up her calls. She's sensitive, you know.'

And I'm not?

'Effie slept with my husband, Hero. She's not my new best mate.'

'I might've helped,' said Hero. 'If you'd confided in me.'

'I just couldn't. Call it cowardice. Avoidance. Whatever. I'm sorry.'

'Without trust, nothing works properly.'

'I do trust you!'

'Good. Can I trust you?'

'I hope so.' Sadie was in a no-man's land between anger and repentance. 'Jesus, Hero, I don't need this.'

'And I do, I suppose?'

'I didn't mean . . .' Sadie closed her eyes. Sighed.

'What am I, Sadie?'

'You're you,' she smiled, aiming to lighten the tone. When he remained impassive, she said, 'You're my lover, Hero. My boyfriend. You know what you mean to me.'

'Actually, I don't. You leave me to guess. If I was your boyfriend, you'd be telling people about me, instead of making them wonder what's going on with us. Am I revenge? A sex toy to pass the time? A cosh to beat your dead husband with?'

'Where's all this coming from?'

'Here!' Hero shouted and thumped his chest. He turned away, breathing hard, head down.

Upstairs, a tiny bare foot sounded on the floorboards.

Shit.

'I should . . .' Sadie half stood.

Hero turned. He was calm. Leaden, even. 'You need to concentrate on Teddy now.'

'Can people *stop* telling me what I need to do with my own daughter!' Sadie's outrage surprised them both. Silenced them both.

The *trip trap* of Teddy on the stairs.

'I should go.' Hero picked up his bag, pushed his hand through his hair. He didn't look at Sadie.

'Yeah, go. Just *go*, Hero, and leave it all behind.'

Hero stopped. He said deliberately, 'If you have a problem with Jack, go to a psychic, Sadie. Don't take it out on me.'

Teddy was easily coaxed back to sleep with a story.

The sitting room seemed to bear the marks of the argument.

I want a drink.

Sadie wanted a drink badly enough for her skin to shrink around her bones.

But not badly enough to leave her daughter alone while she went in search of one.

Thank you, Teddy!

Sadie sank to the rug, preparing for a long night.

*

The knock on the door came at midnight.

Hero had only managed to stay away for four hours.

I'll make it up to him!

They'd start again. She'd been thinking about his mother's theory, that Hero looked after people but nobody looked after him.

I'll look after him.

She would involve him, value him. Sadie had pushed him to the margins and Hero was too good a man for such treatment.

'Darling!' she said, pulling the door open.

Merle held out a package. 'Teddy needs this,' she said, and walked away.

WEEK TWELVE

Dear Residents

I'm sure we all have better things to do but I am required to tell you that the next residents' meeting is at my flat this Wednesday, 8th August.

Kindly pass this note around.

Regards,

Mary

p.s. Please be quiet on the stairs as Noel dislikes loud noises.

p.p.s. I have three slices of fruit cake. First come first served.

Sadie recognised it from Merle's drawing room.

Whatever it was, it was home-made: a tall cardboard box, originally the packing for supermarket kitchen roll, now recovered with scarlet crêpe paper; a slit in one side had been painted black. It sat, untouched, for a week in Sadie's sitting room.

Merle was wrong: Teddy doesn't need it.

Apart from a surprised 'Oh!', Teddy hadn't mentioned the box, nor gone near it.

It had been a week of Teddy sleeping in Sadie's bed. There had been a bad dream or two, one change of soggy sheets, but no kisses.

'Mummy, do I *have* to come to the resi-thingy meeting?'

'You're a life member, sweetie.' Sadie swept Teddy up. It almost always changed the girl's thought processes. 'Let's check on Humphrey.'

The poor elephant had been drenched in a freak corn-flakes accident. He luxuriated on the kitchen radiator, only slightly shrunk after his adventure in the washing machine.

'Not dry yet. Hurry up, Humphrey,' scolded Teddy. She was in her uniform of jeans with a strawberry motif on the pockets and a drab T-shirt the colour of mud. They were her favourites; Sadie could not persuade her into the new, funky clothes she took pleasure in buying after avoiding shop windows for so long. 'Hero thinks he's so clever.' Teddy hopped to a new subject with no warning, as usual.

'Does he?' Sadie thought he was clever, too. Clever enough to avoid her since their pressure-cooker of a fight.

'But he doesn't even know I don't like Barbies. Everybody knows that.'

'Perhaps not everybody. Oh, sweetie, don't . . .' Sadie bit back the reproach as Teddy began to pull packets out of the fridge and drop them on the floor.

'What?' Teddy was agitated. A yoghurt hit the lino and splattered her feet. 'What, Mummy? What now?'

'Nothing, just . . . let me help you.' Teddy wanted cheese, it transpired. 'Here you go.' Sadie cleared up around her daughter's sandals.

When she'd first arrived, Teddy had the habits of a nun. Too tidy. Too prudent. Sadie, identifying Merle's oppressive influence, had encouraged her to be childish. If things went too far, if the childishness tipped over into naughtiness, Teddy was hypersensitive to censure.

'Sorry,' said Teddy, miserable.

'Stop saying sorry.' Sadie saw Teddy's face disintegrate. 'No, that wasn't a telling-off, sweetie. Honestly. I just mean . . .' She gave up and grabbed her little girl and swung her around.

It worked.

It was hard on Sadie's arms, but it worked.

The phone trilled.

Teddy returned to her cheese. 'Is it the police?'

Sadie said, 'Nope.' Another little fantasy shattered. How did Teddy know she talked to the police? 'It's Fi. Pocket-dialling yet again.'

'Let me hear.' Teddy listened, rapt, to the other-worldly noises.

Sadie wondered if Teddy had heard her latest call to Detective Inspector LaManna. He'd confirmed that yes, of course it was a provision of Mrs McQueen's bail that she stay away from both Sadie and Teddy. He would, he said, send 'somebody around to see her'. It could end in Merle's being taken back into custody.

Perhaps Merle was in a cell. Perhaps she was scolding a housekeeper in her home.

Best not to know.

Outside, in the August evening that fell like a velvet cloak over the shoulders of the mews, Fi was clambering into Cole's car.

'You're pocket-dialling!' yelled Teddy, as she and her mother skirted the cherry tree, making their way to MOBuk.

Sadie teased, 'After all the fuss you make about being included, you're not coming to our fascinating residents' meeting.'

Fi didn't answer. She was battling the seat belt, tutting, distracted.

'Kiss!' shouted Teddy.

That broke through Fi's preoccupations. She held out her cheek.

Sadie was glad Teddy still kissed somebody. She remembered the lonely nights when memories of those chubby arms around her neck could make her wail. Now, she had the real thing, her own little Tedster back in her orbit.

So why the reserve?

'Cole and me've got to be somewhere.' The line of Fi's jaw made it clear she wouldn't be taking questions. 'We're already late.'

'Off to the meeting?' Hero's voice behind Sadie made her swallow hard.

'Yeah. You?'

A nod. A smile. From a man who had thrown her on his bed and had his way with her.

I'd prefer out and out warfare to this neutral politeness.

He even said, 'After you,' at Mary's front door.

Teddy made sure to get between them as they climbed the stairs. When Amber arrived, dithering about where to sit, Sadie pursed her lips.

You're going to sit next to Hero – just get on with it!

Sure enough, Amber perched beside him, all bangles and layers and tousled hair. 'I hear you did the breakfast shift at

Bob's.' She laughed and leaned over to pat Sadie's knee, as if they were besties.

'I scrambled many eggs.'

Mrs Bob, setting down her handbag, said, 'And burned a lot of toast.'

'You're an *angel*, Sadie,' said Amber.

'I'm not the only one helping out.' Michael had taken on the apron after Sadie, and Mary had – very slowly – waitressed. 'Are you on the rota?'

'Is there a rota?' asked Amber vaguely, very much in the manner of somebody who didn't want to know.

'There is,' said Mrs Bob. She would accept no sympathy, offer no bulletins about Bob's condition, but she was very keen on slave labour. 'I'll put you down for the lunchtime rush tomorrow.'

'Um . . .'

Sadie saw how Amber caught Hero's eye and shared a moment with him. She forced herself not to care, a strategy that had never worked before and didn't work now.

'Can we get, like, started?' Cher was slumped in a low armchair, long skinny legs stretched out in a trip hazard. 'Where's Mary?'

'Here, here, I'm here.' Mary carried a tray of sickly fruit cake and banged it down on a small table. Her flat was thick with tables, a forest of turned mahogany legs. 'Must I do the register? It's such a bore.'

Traditions carry their own weight, so Mary gave in and reeled off their names. Noel VI, dozing at her feet, was particularly radioactive that evening. Mrs Bob produced a can of air freshener and sprayed a fog of synthetic lavender above them all.

'That drunk of yours, the one who shouts the place down,' she said, prodding Hero. 'He had a right go at me. Of course, Bob was upstairs, useless old fool, so I had to throw him out of the caff on my own. You promised there wouldn't be no trouble on the mews.'

Wearily, warily, Hero said he hadn't meant to mislead them. 'I meant we don't encourage people to visit when they're under the influence. For what it's worth, Trevor – that's his name – is banned from the centre, so if I see him I'll persuade him to go elsewhere. Mind you, legally, I can't really stop Trevor from entering the mews.'

'So, he's not your problem anymore, but he *is* mine?' Mrs Bob was puffed up with noble anger. 'Bleedin' charming.'

'All I can say is sorry,' said Hero.

He's sad.

Maybe it was because of Sadie. Maybe he was hurting the way she hurt. When her life calmed down, when Teddy was no longer a miracle, when Merle was dealt with, they might find each other again.

Maybe this is just a break.

Anybody who saw the hunger in Amber's feline eyes

would doubt that. Even Grace, so self-reliant and busy, busy, busy, let her eye linger on Hero. He was a prime piece of male real estate; he wouldn't remain on the market for long.

'This is boring,' mouthed Teddy.

Sadie slipped her a sweet, knowing the fruit cake was Teddy's idea of 'old people food'.

Jez raised his hand. 'Here's a suggestion. Why don't we install an intercom system? Then we can buzz people in after working hours instead of schlepping down to the gates?'

There was a murmur of approval.

Cher rolled her eyes. 'Fascinating,' she mocked.

Sadie saw how Cher side-eyed Jez, checking his response. He hadn't been to Sakura since the day Cher forbade him to attend last week's meeting.

'If you really try, maybe you can come up with something even more boring.' Cher kicked the leg of Jez's chair.

If this was a playground, you'd pull his hair.

Sadie was glad when Jez stuck out his tongue at his on/off lady-love. He didn't realise she'd saved him from a mauling by her brothers. A more evolved girl would be frank with Jez about her family, but Cher didn't trust love. Instead of honesty, she stage-managed scenarios to manipulate him. He deserved better.

And so did Hero. Sadie's conscience scraped its fingernails down a blackboard.

I should have told him about Jack and Effie straightaway.

'As an intercom would benefit the whole mews,' Michael was saying, 'why don't we ask Christmas Properties to contribute to the cost?'

Sadie didn't look at Mary. Mary didn't look at Sadie.

'Any other business?' asked Mary instead, obviously hopeful there was none.

'One other thing,' said Sadie, 'Sakura's expecting a big delivery tomorrow so I'll be putting out cones to save a space for the van.' When asked what was coming, she took a deep breath and said, 'A cooling RF microcurrent ultrasonic massage unit.'

'Always wanted one of those,' smiled Michael.

Amber hooted, her hand landing on Hero's thigh.

'So you went for it,' said Hero to Sadie. They'd discussed it many times; she'd admired his ability to withstand long soliloquies on spa tech. 'Good.'

'None of your beeswax,' said Teddy, aping her godmother.

'True,' said Hero mildly.

No need to protect your mummy any longer, sweetie.

Their little family unit was no longer under siege from love. Sadie stretched backwards, peeking out through Mary's lace curtains as Grace, with a catch in her voice, thanked them all for the old photographs they'd donated for her exhibition. 'Don't forget to look in on Saturday!'

Cole's car, Sadie saw, was still in situ. No longer in a

hurry, apparently. Sadie squinted. Through the ornate lace she saw that Fi had her face in her hands.

Laughing?

Odd how laughing and crying look so similar from a distance.

By the time she and Teddy reached the cobbles, the car had raced away, tyres squealing with outrage.

'Is it all right if I leave Teddy with you?' Sadie saw Cher's shoulders rise. 'Just for half an hour while I help Grace set up her exhibition.'

Looking down imperiously at Teddy, Cher said, 'Don't touch my shit, yeah?'

This wasn't the babysitter of Sadie's dreams, but single mothers can't be choosers. As Sadie left, with one stricken look back, she heard Cher say, 'Want to play receptionists?' and she relaxed a little.

'What if nobody comes?' fretted Grace, up a ladder, hooking a banner over a nail.

'Don't you worry, every single Mewsite will be here, or Mary will put them against a wall and shoot them.' Sadie laid out plastic glasses and stood fizzy wine in an ice bucket commandeered from Yummy Mummy. 'All the chatter and popping of corks will tempt folk in off the street.' She wanted to smooth out Grace's furrowed brow. The girl was strong but far from tough; she brought out the protectress in Sadie.

'Everyone's coming except Amber.' Grace hopped down from the ladder and wiped her hands on a rag.

'I hope she's got a good excuse.'

'She's off at some festival in the West Country. She took some pictures of my work before she went and promised to post them. It's to build my brand, or something like that.'

'My brand,' said Sadie, 'is being slightly too fat and lying down.'

'Mine,' said Grace, 'is being covered in paint.'

Noel wandered in.

'His brand,' said Sadie, holding her nose, 'is chemical warfare via his arse.'

Lunch in the flat was eclectic. Birds Eye potato waffles and Greek salad. One of Teddy's favourites married to one of Sadie's.

'Was it fun playing with Cher?'

'Yes.'

'I like Cher. Do you?'

'Yes.'

'Waffles okay?'

'Yes.'

Teddy gives me the answers I want.

The patina of 'good' behaviour was hard to chip away.

Every so often, there were flashes of prima donna naughtiness. Her daughter was on a see-saw, either too disciplined or too wild.

The red box that Merle delivered sat by the newly acquired television. When Sadie asked Teddy where it should go, Teddy hadn't responded. A clever child, it must have occurred to her that Merle had brought it to the house, but she'd asked no questions.

'Do you want to . . .' Sadie had Teddy's attention. 'Do you want to wear your new leggings to Grace's show?'

'Yeah!'

Sadie had been about to say, 'Do you want to see Granny?' but she'd swerved. That would be too toxic to countenance. They had to be normal.

Dear Daddy

Diffrent rules here. no rules!

Granny told me a big lie like hundreds of times. mummy didnt now where i was and Granny didnt tell her.

sometimes i forget it was a fib and i look at mummy and i dont like her because she forgot about me.

So am i not allowed to love Granny any more because of the big lie? you would know that kind of thing like you knew names of countries and how to spell ~~beleeve~~ ~~beleive~~ believe.

Sher swears. i like Sher.

i found your watch in a draw mummy gets sad if i talk about you

love Teddy xxxxxxxxxxxxxxxx

*

The still evening pressed like a roof on Cherry Blossom Mews.

People spilled out of Grace's studio onto the cobbles. Flirting. Laughing. Debating.

Sadie with Teddy beside her, greeted two or three Sakura clients in the crush. The outreach was working. A community was being built, person by person.

On shaky foundations?

Even as Sadie exulted at the success of Grace's opening night, she saw the risks in inviting in outsiders. Shark-like developers circled London's up-and-coming back streets, and they smelled bankruptcy like blood in the water.

'Can't see Mary,' said Sadie, on tip toes as they approached the buffet. Yes, there were wittily modernised old photographs tastefully displayed on the whitewashed walls, alongside the untouched originals, but woman cannot live by art alone.

I need a canapé.

'She's at home with Noel,' said Teddy, accepting a scotch egg with the respect it demanded. 'He's been doing funny poos.'

'Nice.' Sadie hadn't noticed Teddy leave the spa, never mind trot off to visit Mary. The girl had an inner life, much of it inaccessible to her mother. This was natural, obvious, *necessary*, but that didn't make it easier to contemplate.

So much of Sadie's time was spent wondering about Teddy. The hours she'd once spent withstanding her loss were now devoted to studying the little girl. The endless question swirled – *How has Merle's lie affected you?*

'I like booze,' announced Fi, suddenly at their side. 'But best of all, I like *free* booze. Cheers!'

She and Cole were welded together, already well acquainted with the free booze. Usually, Fi was discreet about alcohol around Sadie; not today, apparently.

'Nice leggings, kid.' Fi waved her glass in the direction of Teddy's sparkly legs. 'Very Studio 54. Isn't she lovely?' Fi asked Cole, as proud of Teddy as if she'd made her herself.

'She is.' Cole was awkward around Teddy, as if the child was an exam he had to pass. 'You're lovely,' he said, bending down and speaking slowly.

After a brief withering look for Cole's effort, Teddy said, 'Can't Fi be my auntie instead of my godmother, Mummy?'

'No.' Sadie was so sharp that both Teddy and Fi blinked.

She recalibrated her tone. 'Fi's much more than an auntie. We don't have much luck with aunts in our family.' Tish was going about her business elsewhere, the family ties so slack they trailed on the floor.

As Teddy and Fi browsed the nibbles, a question reared up at Sadie.

Does Tish know about Merle's deception?

It was unthinkable. But. It could be true. The unthinkable had come true just recently.

The smell of the cheap wine was nauseating, and seductive. Sadie moved outside in search of fresh air.

'Look,' said Teddy. 'It's Mary!'

Not in the flesh, but pinned down in time on a huge easel by the entrance. A 'sold' sticker on its frame, the modified portrait of Mary and the faithless Arthur was now in full, natural colour. Arthur sported headphones over his brilliantined hair, and Mary's stiff lace dress had been swapped for gym gear. It was a triumph. They looked real, alive, so much more relatable than the original displayed alongside.

It was as if Mary and Arthur had been trapped in amber, only to be freed by Grace's kind cleverness.

'I hope Mary approves.' Sadie knew the volatile woman could go either way.

Beside her, Michael was teary eyed. 'You must come and see what Grace has done with the pic of my grandfather.' He was choked with emotion. 'She's got rid of the old car he was in and put him in a Mini, like the one I drive now. It's as if he's come back to visit me.'

'Oh, Michael!' Sadie was moved by the way he owned his feelings so readily. They shared a small moment, the two of them, in the midst of the mob.

A voice she recognised cut through the clamour. 'I'm just saying . . .' Cole was tailing Fi. 'Slow down!'

Fidgety, hunted, Fi pushed past them. Whether Cole was talking about her stride or her drinking wasn't clear.

A hand took Sadie's. Not Teddy's, it was bigger. Grace was wide-eyed. 'There's a journalist here! He wants a few words. What do I do?'

'Give him a few words of course!' When Sadie squeezed the small brown hand in hers, it squeezed back. 'Go on. Fly.' Giving support made Sadie feel stronger.

Still no Hero.

Which didn't matter. At all.

A nudge in Sadie's side. Cher scowled, speaking low. 'Why the f— sorry, why am I jel of Jez?'

'Jel? Oh, *jealous*?' Sadie mulled it over. 'He's a nice-looking bloke. It's only natural for you to worry that he—'

'No, not jealous of him and other women.' Cher's facial expression tried to do justice to Sadie's misinterpretation. 'I'm jealous of *him*.' Cher snorted at the lunacy of it. 'Of his stupid little life. He's a mug but I'm jealous of him. I mean, everybody knows proper jobs are for idiots. We live on the top floor of that huge block.' Cher pointed up at her high-rise home. 'We look down on you lot like ants, everyone bustling around. Mugs, that's what you look like. All of you working hard to make somebody else rich. And Jez is the biggest mug of all! Nobody makes a mint working for a *charity*.'

Sadie recognised the first-at-the-trough doctrine of the Mogg twins. Family first, but with none of the Walton's overtones that phrase implies. It was pure selfishness. 'I respect Jez.'

Cher wriggled, uncomfortable. 'But you ain't scared of him.'

'Respect isn't about fear. It's about admiring the way somebody behaves. Jez looks after other people. He takes the hard road, even though there are easier, more lucrative roads.' It struck Sadie that Cher was brave. By taking a job at Sakura, she had stepped out of Orissa House and towards the light. 'Cher, are you scared of your brothers?'

A lightning flash of anger before Cher decided not to take offence. 'They love me,' she said.

'That's not what I asked.'

'You're too nosy, that's your problem.'

One of them.

The set of a man's shoulders brought Hero to mind. Only trouble at U-Turn could keep him away from a Cherry Blossom Mews extravaganza. Sadie hoped it wasn't the notorious Trevor. She wandered back to Grace's studio, where the artist posed beside her work, her smile a slash of teeth, her beautiful eyes nervous.

The crowd parted to let Bob through. He leaned heavily on Jez, making his way to a chair hastily set out by Michael. Skin the colour of bone, lips cracked, Bob was altered.

Fi managed to slip a cushion under him as he painfully lowered himself. Teddy stood behind her godmother, instinctively recognising sickness, and instinctively keeping space between it and herself.

'Our very own little Picasso!' rasped Bob.

His wife, wearing bright lipstick and almost unrecognisable without her pinny, said, 'You wouldn't know Picasso if he bit you on the arse.'

'She loves me really,' said Bob, with the last of his available breath. The Mewsites looked away, discreet, as he fought to fill his lungs.

'Making a show of me,' muttered Mrs Bob.

Teddy was growing bored. 'Where's Amber?' she asked her mother. 'I like her clothes.'

'At a festival,' said Fi. 'The type of thing where posh birds wander about in the mud in hundred quid wellies and pretend they're not taking drugs.'

'Amber's tweeting about Grace's show.' Sadie hoped she was using the right language when she added, 'Apparently, she has amazing reach.'

'This is as far as I want to reach.' Fi snaffled a glass from a passing tray.

Passing them, Noel was nose-to-the-floor, hunting

dropped titbits. He lifted his head as a raised voice rose above the good-natured hubbub.

'How dare you!'

Other – human – heads turned too. Sadie recognised the voice.

'You evil, evil girl! That is *my* property. My past!'

Sadie burrowed her way to a clearing where Mary stood, stamping her feet, shouting in a reedy wail that was equal parts anger and pain. The picture of her younger self was in her hands.

'How could you, Grace?'

Sadie and Fi took an arm each. Other residents circled them. One of Mary's kinked little arthritic hands went to her mouth, muffling her sobs and her protests. 'My privacy . . . Grace *stole* it . . .'

As the old lady lapsed into wordlessness, she sank against Sadie.

It was quiet. Or as quiet as London ever gets. The mews was empty, swept clean, a bin bag leaning against the tree. The last of the revellers gone.

Up in Mary's flat, the hysteria had run dry. Now there was only regret, and a resigned sadness.

'What they don't tell you about getting old,' said Mary, slumped on a lumpy sofa, 'is how close the past seems.'

Grace had been and gone, their misunderstanding ironed

out with tears and embraces. Mary had clean forgotten she'd consigned the picture of herself and Arthur to MOBuk's bargain bin. She had stemmed Grace's breathless apology with fluttering eyelids and an apology of her own.

Beneath the window, Teddy lay full length with Noel VI, both of them tuckered out.

'I've never stopped thinking about Arthur.' Mary turned a very proper monogrammed handkerchief over in her fingers. 'But recently I've thought of little else. It's as if he abandoned me only yesterday. How can grief feel so fresh? Surely, it should be stale by now.'

Sadie was only too aware of grief's little tricks.

'He went without a fight. That's what Arthur taught me – I'm not worth a fight. Oh, don't get me wrong, Father will have threatened him just as much as he will have tempted him, but surely Arthur could have stood firm long enough to tell me to my face he couldn't marry me. No, no, off he went on the first ship to India, to Assam.' She scowled, as another arrow hit home. 'Did he mean *any* of it? I used to daydream about our lives together if Arthur had stayed, but maybe he'd have left me anyway. Reverted to type, gone back to his dreadful family.'

'Every life is littered with "if onlies".' Sadie was up to her neck in them.

'Sometimes,' said Mary, her voice constricted, 'I wish I'd died in that fire.'

'And if you had?' Sadie sat up, stern. 'Where would we all be? Remember what you've built here, Mary. It matters.' Her voice caught. '*You* matter.' Arthur had been wrong; the old girl was worth fighting for. 'Cherry Blossom Mews is a family and that makes you its matriarch. Did you see how everybody rallied around Bob today? That depth of feeling doesn't happen by accident. We know we're lucky to have this mews, to be allowed to live here whether or not we can afford it. Grace. The addiction centre. Loopy old Amber, and bookworm Michael. I stitched my heart back together in the mews, and now Teddy is . . .' Sadie glanced at her daughter. Like a feral child, Teddy was asleep with her arms around Noel VI. 'Teddy is the future, and you're all helping her come to terms with her weird childhood.'

Quietly, Mary asked, 'How much does she know?'

'I'm not sure. One day I'll tell her about Merle's betrayal.'

'Such a fine line,' murmured Mary, 'between protecting and deceiving.'

The little girl stirred. She nuzzled the dog. 'Noel,' she murmured, sleepily. 'Noel,' she repeated. Teddy sat up. Scrambled backwards. 'Mummy!' she breathed.

Noel didn't move. His stout little legs were still. His barrel chest neither rose nor fell.

He'd gone peacefully, Sadie said, comforting her keening child.

Mary got down, slowly, knees cracking, to wrap a blanket around the dog.

He made barely a bump in the floor.

Mary patted his head. 'Good boy,' she said.

Bed was calling.

Sadie had put Mary in a vast four-poster bed that took up an entire room, pulled the covers up to her chin and promised her it would all be all right.

What would be all right, and whether it would actually end up that way, neither of them knew.

Now, back in her own flat, with Teddy finally asleep after much rocking and crying but no clinging – she had resisted Sadie's arms – Sadie realised she was exhausted.

Dog-tired.

She thought of the little shape in the boot of her car. The sad chore that awaited her tomorrow.

The window drew her, but Sadie resisted. Tonight she didn't want to see the splashes of moonlight on the cherry tree. Noel VI would no longer rub his rump on it. Arthur was gone, too, his kissing days done with. Sakura, a word that meant so much to Sadie, didn't only mean renewal. It was also a reminder of the fleeting nature of life.

A blossom can't last. It disintegrates. Perhaps such beauty can't sustain itself.

She looked in on Teddy, a treat she allowed herself each

night, the miracle renewing itself in the narrow bed, the pale sleeping face in the spilled lamplight.

Sadie tucked her in. She kissed her; her only opportunity to take such a liberty. A white shape caught her eye: a stack of virgin postcards on the floorboards.

With every sinew, every follicle, Sadie wanted a drink. She went to her bed and sat cross-legged on it, letting the darkness hide her shame and her struggle.

Teddy wants to go back to Merle.

Around her in the black were shapes. Books. Bags. *Stuff.* Since Teddy's return, Sadie had been accumulating possessions. The flat was humanised. A rug underfoot. A painting from MOBuk on the wall.

Even so, the flat was all wrong for a kid. Too small. Too lacking in comfort.

The darkness held memories, too: of her departure from rehab, six weeks after the funeral, when she'd sat rigidly like this with her phone in her hand.

She could remember the exact wording of the texts she'd sent. One to Merle, and one to Tish.

We've all suffered so much. Perhaps we can help each other recover?

Neither responded.

The advice from therapists had been to move on. It was that, they warned, or disintegrate. Everybody relapses, they said; the secret is to get up and carry on.

Sadie had wanted a drink then. She wanted one now.

Her own daughter, more priceless than rubies, went against nature and wanted to live apart from her mother. Sadie bent her feelings in two, forced herself to confront a future where that might happen.

Teddy would have continuity, security. I'd have access.

Most of all, the adult in charge would not be an alcoholic, with all the ugly potential that implied.

Her phone dinged.

A round robin text from Grace, thanking all her neighbours. A link to Amber's Instagram account opened up a painstakingly curated scene in a . . . was that a yurt?

Funky clothes. Casually sensational hair. Glitter on her cheekbones. Amber's static image ticked every green box of envy. Here with great mates! Love you guys! And a handsome boy or two! The gorgeous @GraceArtist3 has a STUNNING exhibition just starting! Get yourself along and buy up her amaaaaaazing work!!!!

On the edge of the shot, almost cut off but not quite, despite Amber's neurotic eye for detail, was a hand. Disembodied. Belonging to a man – it was a male hand, without doubt – it was little more than a flesh-coloured smear.

Wearing an antique watch with a blue face.

WEEK THIRTEEN

To Amber <amber@yummymummymews.net.co.uk>, Hero <hero.smith@u-turn.net>, Sadie <sakuraspa@gmail.com>, Michael T. <qwertybookshop@hotmail.com>, Fiona J <filove@aol.com>, The Bobs <bob@bobscaff.co.uk>, Jez <jeremy.gray@u-turn.net>, Grace Esparza <Gracetheartist@gmail.com>,

From Cher Mogg <whatulookingatcher@gmail.co.uk>

Subject CHERRY BLOSSOM MEWS RESIDENTS' ASSOCIATION MEETING

I know what you're going to say but shut it because I go to these meetings so it's only fair I get to be chairperson.

Date Wednesday 15.8.18
Time 6.30 p.m.
Location Sakura reception
Agenda Memorial for Noel

I'm warning you now that if you don't like Viennetta you better bring your own food.

I'll tell Mary because I don't trust none of you to do it.

Cher

A taxi purred in the mews.

Out stepped Hero, and a slender boy who seemed to radiate sunshine.

'So that's the famous Bo,' said Sadie.

'Ooh,' said Teddy.

Above her head, Sadie and Fi gave each other a look. They knew what that tone of voice meant. 'He's handsome, isn't he, sweetie?'

'He's mine,' whispered Teddy.

The famous Bo was slightly too tall for his limbs, a gangly Bambi in surfer shorts. His hair was a peroxide buzz cut, his teeth were California white, and his legs were brown. He carried a skateboard like a shield.

'Looks like his dad,' said Fi, with unconvincing nonchalance. They were all being nonchalant about Hero at Sakura. All pretending not to notice how he stayed away.

Except for Teddy, who wondered aloud why 'that idiot who got me that stupid Barbie' never came round any more.

Dating is like this.

It was one of the reasons Sadie had always been so bad at it, as if romance was a skill she had never acquired. A guy could be crazy about you one second, erasing your number the next. A whirligig of rejection; addicts should keep away from whirligigs.

Another Dorothy Ball had been added to the shelf. *A Portrait Can Lie* had amused Sadie with its topicality, and warmed her with the knowledge that there was one man in her life who still cared. Michael kept going, despite lack of encouragement. Sadie made an effort to be extra nice to him.

Out on the mews, he rushed out to help Hero with Bo's suitcases. There were enough for a visiting diva. Hero bobbed and chatted, paid off the cabbie, hugged his son, clapped Michael on the shoulder, all the while fizzing with repressed excitement.

I know how he feels.

Sadie had been wary of showing her elation to Teddy in the early days of their reunion. Embarrassing a child with too much emotion is a cardinal sin for parents.

We're not natural together, me and Teddy. Not yet.

Many times Sadie looked at Teddy's bowed head and wondered what went on in there.

The glimpse she'd been offered wasn't pretty.

I wish I still lived with you.

The welcome party for Bo was Grace's suggestion. The mews needed a get-together after the hullabaloo of the exhibition.

Bob's Caff wasn't the natural venue, but Mrs Bob insisted. When she insisted, people tended to listen, because if the insisting wasn't listened to, the shouting started.

From his throne on a plastic chair, Bob directed the catering. His wife, dashing in and out from the kitchen with foil-covered trays and jugs and plates, shrieked that she didn't need his advice, thank you very much.

'Business as usual,' said Michael, stealing something beige from under its foil cape.

'She . . .' Bob bent double, wheezing suddenly, his whole body empty of air.

The others took a communal step forward, then hesitated.

Bob straightened up. Face beetroot, he rebooted his breathing. 'She loves me really,' he whispered.

'For the last time' – Mrs Bob banged down a litre bottle of Russian cola – 'no, I bloody well do not.'

Hero looked good in an apron, helping out, prodding the golden boy child to do the same. Sadie accepted a burger from her ex-lover in a casual manner. Neither of them behaved as if they carried a braille map of each other's bodies.

There was a insouciance to the way Bo loped about in his brilliantly white clothes, head down. His manners were perfect, but they were throwaway. He was hard to read.

But doing well for a twelve-year-old who's meeting all these people at once.

'Say cheese!' Amber aimed her phone.

'I don't like cheese,' said Mrs Bob, who would no doubt be cropped out of the shot. She didn't fit Amber's brand; Sadie felt a rush of affection for the hair bollocked back with a sandwich-bag clip.

Within seconds the image was online. Nervously, Sadie sought out her own face. Amber had worked her magic, they all looked presentable. Surreptitiously, Sadie scrolled back through the preceding posts. Looking for that watch. For the owner of that watch.

Hero hadn't mentioned the festival to anybody. Amber, during her gushing about how sensational the bands were, how bright the stars, how, you know, *empowering* the whole shebang had been, didn't mention Hero.

Sadie had begun to think that perhaps another man owned an antique blue watch with a blue strap and *that* man rather than Hero had stood near Amber in a yurt. She knew why she tried to think that and she knew she was wrong. Amber had been poised, ready to swoop the moment a crack opened in Sadie's relationship.

I have to admire the woman's speed.

The skateboard Bo had carried was still with him, but at his feet. In two pieces.

'What happened?' asked Sadie. Teddy, her eyes eating up Bo, was agog.

'I wrecked it.' Bo's accent was familiar from movies,

a laid-back Cali-drawl. 'It was the best skateboard I ever had.'

'Are you getting a new one?'

'Nope. My dad says . . .' – here Bo affected a faultless English inflection – 'it's too expensive.'

Daring to speak, Teddy asked, 'Would it cost thousands of pounds?'

'Only three hundred,' said Bo.

'Only?!' said Sadie.

As Bo trailed away, the skateboard corpse in his arms, he called, 'Hey! Hero! Come on, old bean!'

'He doesn't call you dad?' Sadie's surprise shocked the question out of her; she rarely spoke directly to Hero these days. The only conversation worth the title had taken place when she'd reminded him that the hammer she'd help him choose at the DIY superstore was still in the boot of her car.

'It's uncool, apparently.'

Hero jogged after his son. Sadie mouthed 'Ouch' on his behalf; Hero took fathering seriously and saw so little of Bo.

He dearly wants Bo to call him dad.

Teddy tore away to greet Fi, who was motoring, head down, across the cobbles towards Sakura.

'Hey, the party's at Bob's,' laughed Sadie, catching up as Fi unlocked the spa. She gasped. 'Bloody hell, is that—'

'Shut up and yes.'

Fi turned her face this way and that in the large mirror along the spa's back wall. 'It looks worse than it is.' The concealer she dabbed on the black and blue bruise framing her right eye did little to calm it down.

Sadie swayed in the nervous, negative energy flowing from Fi. One wrong question and the woman would blow, taking Sakura with her. 'How did—'

'Door. Loose carpet.' Fi tutted. 'You know me. Clumsy as hell. Especially after a couple of shots.'

Teddy was fascinated and horrified. 'It looks like you were beaten up.'

'I know. Actually, here's a secret.' Fi made a joke of her half-closed eye. 'Cole bashed me.'

Teddy laughed at the ridiculous suggestion. She mimed Cole's punch. '*Bffff!*'

Sadie didn't laugh. Fi didn't catch her eye.

A shout from the door. It was Amber, fringes on her miniskirt, quirky boots on her feet, a scarf tied around her hair which would make Sadie look as if she should be sectioned, and fast.

'Delivery! Looks like your ultrasonic doodah has arrived.'

Hero was helping a grunting man manoeuvre a tall rectangular package around the tree.

'Careful!' Amber danced alongside them. 'Isn't he strong? Mind your back, Hero.'

It was like Christmas, Cher helping Sadie and Fi tear at the packaging.

'What's *that*?' Bo was back, having given his skateboard a decent burial somewhere.

'It's a cooling RF microcurrent ultrasonic massage unit,' said Teddy, amazing them all.

Amber bent down to her. 'Aren't you clever?' she cooed. She seldom spoke to the child. She held out one arm and pulled Bo to her side. He acquiesced rigidly. 'You two should be friends.'

'She's a baby,' said Bo, with twelve-year-old hauteur.

'Bo!' reprimanded Hero.

'She's a nice baby,' said Bo. 'But she's a baby.'

'I'm not a baby!' Teddy was affronted, as if accused of murder. 'I stopped being a baby ages ago.'

Amber looked lost, as if she'd started something she couldn't finish. She appealed to Hero. 'Daddy, help me out here.'

'Is he your daddy too, Amber?' Teddy was so surprised, she forgot to be insulted.

'No, he's my, um . . .' Apparently there was no name for what Hero was to Amber. 'I just meant he's Hero's daddy, so . . .'

'*Daddy*,' snorted Bo. 'So English.'

'Oi, matey,' said Hero. 'You're made of one hundred per cent English material, remember.'

'Matey!' Bo snorted again.

Hero looked around for a partner in his gentle outrage. His eyes met Sadie's. She managed to raise her eyebrows, as if she was a sympathetic fellow parent and not a former lover.

Sadie noticed how he made sure not to touch Amber in front of her. She appreciated his gallantry, even though she was stung by his speedy re-coupling.

He's trying to protect me.

'Who was that on the phone?' Fi, in dark glasses, was perturbed by Sadie's wan face. 'You look as if you've seen a ghost.' Her lips pursed. 'Let me guess. A ghost called Merle.'

'It was the police.' Sadie read her scribbled notes. 'I rang about withdrawing my statement.' She closed her eyes and held up a stern forefinger at Fi. 'Do. Not. Start. I have my reasons. I felt we needed to move on, that it might damage Teddy even more growing up thinking she got her granny into trouble. But apparently it's all out of my hands. The . . .' She checked her scrawl. 'The CPS are going ahead with a trial because it's in the public interest.'

Fi was so intrigued she took off her sunglasses. Her left eyelid was bulbous, peacock-hued. 'You mean Merle's such a vile old bat she's an actual danger to the actual public?'

'They didn't put it like that, but yes, it's too serious to ignore. They took into account the very young age of "the child", and apparently our three-year separation is a "period of consistent concealment".' The bald language, so precise and aloof, couldn't reflect the emotional damage, but it respected it. 'They also bore in mind the impact on the mother/daughter relationship, plus there's something called "deliberate harm" which relates to Merle telling Teddy I'd abandoned her, "thereby demonstrating intent to sever the relationship".'

'They understand,' murmured Fi.

'Jesus, Fi, have I done the right thing?'

'And now it's your turn to not start.' Fi flared up, the way only she could. 'This was a crime. Of the heart. Of the laws of the land. You're a victim, here, Sadie. That witch'll get what's coming to her.'

Sadie felt cold with nerves. There would be a trial. She realised that was what she wanted. *Needed*. It was recognition of a terrible wrong done to her.

'Teddy,' said Fi, 'must be kept as far away from this as possible. The poor little scrap won't know what to think. Will Merle get jail?'

'Up to seven years.'

Perhaps they were both thinking that Merle would be in her mid-eighties by the time she had served her sentence. There was no flippant comment to be made about that.

'Am I getting paid for this overtime?' Cher wanted to know. All three of Sakura's workforce had stayed late to acquaint themselves with the new ultrasonic facial massage unit.

'It looks like a petrol pump.' Fi circled the machine. An array of steely tools were connected to a central white plastic tower by hose-like arms.

'Hop on the bed, Cher.'

'No way.' Cher backed away. 'You'll electrocute me.'

Cajoled into lying down with the promise of a fiver, Cher became a convert. 'Ooh, it's mmm . . .' she said sleepily as Sadie passed a metal roller across her face.

Making notes, Fi watched Sadie get to grips with the new technology. 'Where's Teddy?'

'Out on the mews with Bo. Hero volunteered him for babysitting duties.'

'Things back to, well, not normal, you know what I mean, with you and our local Hero then?'

'We're cordial.'

'No tearing off each other's clothes and getting right down to it?'

'No, Fi, none of that. Concentrate.'

Cher complained, 'Yeah, concentrate. It's my face you're practising on.'

Sadie pressed a dial. The machine buzzed. Cher jumped. 'I hope Teddy's all right with Bo. He's only a kid himself,' Sadie said to nobody in particular.

'She's fine. The gates are shut for the night. You overthink everything,' Fi chided her.

'And you don't think enough.'

Fi ignored that. Her black eye was the elephant in the small white room. 'My go,' she said, taking the tools.

Cher and Sadie changed places, and Cher wandered off to check her phone. 'Jez is waiting to walk me home,' she said. 'Idiot.' Then she let out a guffaw. 'Look at this! It's brilliant!'

Somebody had set up a new Instagram account. @ambertragiclondon was a parody of @ambermagiclondon.

'They recreate Amber's posts, but with, like, a sarky description,' said Cher.

'Not so much sarcastic as realistic.' Sadie had to laugh. Beneath Amber's latest stage-managed view of the Party Emporium, the copycat had written: 'My shop!!! My haven!!! A new consignment of the most perfect silk scarves made by orphans in India with no rights, and sold here for ten times what they make in a year!!!'

'Bit mean,' said Fi.

'You're laughing though,' said Cher.

Sadie felt the same shiver of cruelty. Seeing Amber's affectations skewered so neatly was enjoyable.

She deserves it.

All is *not* fair in love and war; Amber pounced on the body of Sadie's love affair while it was still warm.

'I'm gonna comment.' Cher typed some encouragement. 'Dopey so-and-so probably doesn't even know it's happening.'

'When it comes to social media, Amber's anything but dopey,' said Fi.

She's also non-dopey around other people's boyfriends.

Still undecided about the morality of the parody account, Sadie was sandwiched between Fi's puritanism and Cher's glee.

While Fi went out to round up Teddy, Sadie darted upstairs to start the bath running. The pastel smell of Johnson's Baby Bath coiled around the tiny flat. Bath time was a sacred ritual, marking the beginning of the long bedtime folderol. After that Sadie would be alone, with no hope of a visit from Hero.

Teddy's presence helped with the loss of him. All the tiny chores were joys that studded Sadie's day.

And yet . . .

Nothing comes free. The spectre of Merle's prosecution glimmered darkly in the corners of the flat, nestled next to Jack's betrayal.

I miss him more than ever since Teddy came back.

Only Jack would understand her worries about Teddy. Only he could want to talk about her as much as Sadie did. Teddy was their great joint adventure. Solo parenting was tough.

Living with Teddy was still novel. It should be comfortable, like an old shoe, but instead Sadie second-guessed her instincts. Teddy's behaviour baffled her sometimes, and upset her often. They hadn't found their stride; perhaps they never would. Not all ruptures are repairable.

Sadie didn't see the latest postcard, hidden carefully beneath a copy of *Mary Poppins*.

Dear Daddy

Mummy rang up the police. Am i going to be arrested?

i miss nole he's a dog

There's a boy called Bo and his hair is the best

i wish you'd write back

love Teddy xxxxxxxxx

*

'Hello, this is Doctor Balakrishnan.'

The voice was brisk, harried. Sadie had found her on the website for the nearest hospital to her old home. 'I believe you treated my daughter a few years ago, and I'd like to ask you some questions, if that's okay?' Teddy's childish mishearing had stuck in Sadie's mind: Doctor Balakrishnan was obviously Doctor Batman.

The doctor remembered Teddy. 'Lovely kid,' she said, and then, without prompting, 'Her grandmother sat by her bed day and night. Wouldn't go home, no matter what we said. Some tragic element to the family history I can't quite recall.'

Sadie gathered herself as Doctor Balakrishnan looked up Teddy's data. Tales of Merle's self-sacrifice unsettled her.

Nobody is just a villain.

'Here we are. Yes, as I remember. Fractured Femur. Quite bad, but we patched her up nicely.' She told Sadie about the long flexible nails inserted to hold the bone in place while it healed. 'The nail was in place for four weeks, one for each year of her life. She started nursery school on crutches, I believe.'

That was an image to sear a mother's brain. Teddy had hobbled off to start school with no father and a mother who didn't want to see her.

'You know, of course, about the months of physical therapy. I didn't oversee that, but it says on her notes that she was very determined.'

Don't cry. Don't cry.

'Ah.'

Sadie didn't like that Ah.

'The cracked femur grew faster. That often happens. Your daughter has leg-length discrepancy.'

'That's why she limps?'

'I'm sorry, is the child with you now? In your care?'

'Yes.' The shame was not Sadie's, but somehow it found its way around her shoulders.

'There may be overgrowth. Are you still in the area?'

'No. London.'

'Get the ball rolling with her treatment options. She may need epiphysiodesis.'

After spelling out this alarming word, Doctor Batman had to fly.

The top of Bo's hair was ice blue.

'He did it while I was out,' Hero told Sadie, when they met in Qwerty. 'Looks like a pillock, but what can you do?'

'Bo looks great.' The boy had the best of both his parents. Embedded in the life of the mews, he was in and out of all the premises, a good luck charm. 'How's he coping without his skateboard?'

'Gradually coming to terms with his loss.'

Sadie liked Hero in this mood.

I miss *him in this mood.*

'Bet you cave in and buy him a new one.'

'No.' It was final. Hero meant it. 'Zizzi will, though. He's already whined on his Twitter about it, so no doubt a skateboard-shaped parcel will arrive any day now.' Hero looked down at a novel in his hands, a modern angst-ridden tale of love. 'And you? You're okay, aren't you? You and Teddy?'

She hadn't expected interest. 'Um, yeah. Good. Well, getting there.'

'There you are!' Amber banged on the bookshop window.

'What a great tableau! You and the books and the reflection on the glass!' She aimed her phone, shot, then bent her head to crop it, *improve* it.

Sadie knew she'd be excised by the time the snap turned up on Amber's Instagram account.

Amber mouthed and shouted until she managed to make Hero understand that she could give Bo lunch.

'Yeah, okay, if you like.'

He's embarrassed.

Amber did everything but hang a 'taken' sign around Hero's neck.

I know he's yours, Amber!

With one last selfie – the sudden look of extreme bliss was unnerving – Amber retreated.

Hero took up the conversation as if the interruption had never happened. 'Where's Teddy right now?'

'Hanging out at Grace's. She'll come home covered in ink.' There would be no telling-off. The serene atmosphere in the flat above Sakura was compensation for the losses and lies. 'She never cries, Hero. Ever.'

'Does that worry you?'

'Of course! She lost her daddy but she talks about him easily. Shouldn't that upset her?'

It upsets me.

'Children are resilient. They live in the moment. Whereas adults . . .'

Perhaps he hesitated because they were trespassing on the topic that had stunted their togetherness. Jack. 'We take longer.'

Sometimes we take forever.

Hovering, Michael got between them to slot a novel onto a shelf. ''Scuse me.' He lingered, a bespectacled gooseberry. 'I'm wondering if I should put aside a Dorothy Ball for Mrs Bob. Bob sleeps a lot of the time, so I've been taking her books to read in the evening.'

'Give her something about empathy,' said Sadie.

'Ooh,' winced Hero.

'I'm only being honest,' said Sadie. 'If I'd been allowed to nurse Jack, instead of losing him . . . let's just say I'd have treasured the time, made him comfortable, stored up memories, instead of nagging him all day.'

That was still true, despite the affair. Love is highly peculiar.

Michael pulled his pile of books to his chest. 'Where's *your* empathy?'

'I—' Sadie was thrown off guard, as if a mouse had roared.

'Mrs Bob isn't nagging Bob because she's in a mood, Sadie. She nags him because she's always nagged him.'

'Well, she—'

Michael wasn't finished. 'Everything's falling apart around Bob. His body. His business. Everyone treats him differently, fussing over him, speaking in whispers. He doesn't feel like he's dying when his wife has a go at him. He feels *normal.*

If Mrs Bob came over all sweetness and light, it'd be like admitting the end is nigh. She told me, over a cup of tea, that she'd like to shut the caff and run off to the seaside with Bob for his last few months, but Bob genuinely loves his life. He loves his grotty eatery and his cantankerous wife. How many people can say that about the choices they make?' He blinked, as if surprised by his own eloquence. 'It's obvious, Sadie, that Mrs Bob's doing this *for* Bob.'

Hero widened his eyes as Michael moved away.

'He's right.' Sadie gave a little cough. This was not the place to cry. 'There's no right or wrong way to grieve.' She felt mean, small-minded. 'All those massive emotions. Those stunted thoughts.'

It would have been good to talk about it, but Amber was back at the window, her arm around Bo, ruffling his hair, mouthing that it was time for lunch.

As the residents assembled at the spa, all eyes were on Mary. She had been all but invisible since last week's meeting. True, the mews smelled sweeter since Noel's demise, but he'd left a hole in his mistress's life.

Mary was composed, tidy, as she sat on the sofa. She was next to Bob, whose brushed hair and clean shirt seemed to be the result of great effort. For this week only, he had relinquished his role as the mews' object of pity. Sadie could tell this was a relief to him.

'Right, listen up.' Cher took charge. 'We're going to do this *properly*.'

Sadie smiled to herself: inside their rebel receptionist was a Thoroughly Decent Citizen trying to get out. The register was taken, with a sharp rebuke for Amber whose attention was on her phone.

'Actually,' said Cher, holding out her hand, the diamante talons curving, 'give it here. New rule. No mobiles at meetings.'

Amber handed over her phone as if she was in a remake of *Sophie's Choice*.

'First item on my agenda,' said Cher, 'is Bo's hair. Love it, mate.'

Bo blushed, turning his tan a muddy colour.

From beside Sadie on the white seating – she'd refused to sit on her mother's lap – Teddy agreed. 'It's so stunning,' she lisped.

'Second item.' Cher forged ahead. 'We are *not* discussing the bleedin' bins.'

'But—' Michael seemed crushed.

'No, Michael, shut it,' said Cher. 'Right.' Her voice softened. She turned to Mary. 'What do we do to remember Noel?'

Mary looked at the ceiling.

'I fancy a little statue,' Cher went on, 'in the middle of the mews.'

'How would we park?' Mrs Bob was horrified.

'Um, is a statue a *little* over the top?' wondered Michael.

Mary was impatient. 'It's preposterous.' Her voice wavered as she said, 'He was only a dog.'

Fi, wearing a different pair of sunglasses, suggested a wake. Grace offered to paint the late Noel 'doing what he loved best'.

'Farting?' suggested Fi.

'Going for walkies,' said Grace, trying not to laugh.

'No memorial,' insisted Mary.

'I agree,' said Mrs Bob. Her lipstick had bled past the outline of her thin lips. 'Can we *please* stop talking about death?'

Somebody brought up the intercom again. Grace asked about council tax. There was general disbelief at the utter cheek of foxes. Nobody mentioned the nameplate.

Sadie sat quietly, relishing Teddy's sticky, childish warmth against her side. She loved these meetings, she realised. The whimsical ideas. The little feuds. The awkward silences. The sudden bursts of laughter. The stories.

I'm not sure I believe Hero's tale of the fox who sat at the end of his bed.

It was life, in all its messy wonder. Her old life, keeping house for a man who was frequently away, had been sewn up and insular. *I was smug*, she thought, criticising her old self, the woman who'd thought she had it all.

If Sadie had been anchored by a community like this ragbag commune, Merle would never have got away with her crime. *I'd have known; somebody would have told me.* Nobody had looked out for her, not even Tish.

Some ties are thicker than blood. *Blood can be rather runny,* thought Sadie, *when it comes down to it.*

As they dispersed, Amber was reunited with her phone. She took a selfie, then another, then backed into Hero as she posed, who laughed. They were still laughing as they strolled out of the gates together, Bo loping behind.

He never used to laugh with Amber.

Sadie was sullen as she herded up Teddy and Mary, collecting the old lady's handbag and the child's Etch-A-Sketch. Hero used to laugh *at* Amber. At her pretensions and topsy-turvy values. As Sadie said her goodnights and put an arm through Mary's and took Teddy's hand, she wondered if posh people naturally gravitated towards each other when all was said and done. Like exotic birds flocking at twilight.

Without a dog to turn the circuit of the mews into a walkies, it felt vaguely absurd to stroll around the cobbles. Mary needed the exercise, Sadie insisted.

'We're like Jane Austen heroines,' she said. 'Taking a gentle turn about the grounds.'

'Jane Austen would have killed me off by now,' said Mary.

'She wouldn't dare.' Sadie had heard Mary's voice seldom in the past few days; Noel's death had knocked the stuffing out of her. Like all pets, he was more than just an animal.

For all his faults, Noel had been Mary's closest companion. He was a bridge to all the other Noels. A bridge, Sadie knew, to Arthur.

'Home, Mummy.' Teddy pulled her towards the spa.

'Let's walk Mary to her door first, sweetie.'

'No.' Teddy was whining. 'Her house is boring.'

A glance at Mary told Sadie that she hadn't heard. This in itself was worrying – Mary had the ears of a bat, normally – but she was grateful. 'Teddy, that's not—'

Sadie was talking to thin air. Teddy had bowled over to Bo, who was swigging from a can. He greeted her with a complicated handshake he'd taught her.

Let her go, Sadie counselled herself. The fragile balance they were finding must not be disturbed. *Plenty of time to be an authoritarian mum later.*

'I'm tired,' said Mary. She sounded frail.

Sadie wanted to shake her. *You can't be frail!* Matriarchs have to last forever. Instead, she said, tenderly, 'Of course you are. Let's get you home.'

A wry side-eye told Sadie that, tired or not, Mary wasn't quite ready to be patronised.

'Oi!' Cher was at their heels. 'Leftover Viennetta,' she said, sounding shocked that such a thing existed. 'You wannit?'

'Bring it up to Mary's and she can have it later.'

A pile of bills on a gateleg table was swept aside by Mary's pale hand. Space was found in the tiny icebox by a grumbling Cher.

'When did you do this kitchen, Mary?' called Cher from the draughty scullery at the back of the flat. 'When Queen Victoria was alive? Fancy a pot of tea?' Without waiting for an answer, she filled the resolutely non-electric kettle at the tap.

Keeping an eye on her daughter through the window, Sadie muttered, 'Who can this be?' when her phone buzzed. 'Fi, hi.'

Another pocket dial. Sadie tried to explain the concept to Mary, but she was uninterested. Her entire demeanour screamed, 'Leave me alone.'

Which meant she must not be left alone. Sadie wondered if Cher was of the same mind; she had left Jez scuffing the cobbles below in order to take tea with an inhospitable old woman.

The troublesome portrait was propped up amidst the mess on the mantelpiece. The original Noel was uncannily like Noel VI. As Cher noisily hunted down spoons, Sadie removed it as Mary settled herself in an easy chair.

Turning it over to tuck it away somewhere, Sadie paused. 'Hang on,' she said. 'Mary, the message on the back.' She held up the photograph, baffled. 'It's different.'

'How could it be?' Mary was querulous, searching her bag for her glasses. 'I know it by heart. It says "Mary, I have been offered a—"'

'No,' said Sadie. 'This message is *to* Arthur, and it's signed by *you*. Look!'

'Impossible.' Mary held out her hand. 'Impossible,' she repeated, but with less confidence as she put it down in her lap and took off her glasses. 'How can this be?'

'Who takes sugar?' bellowed Cher.

Sadie's mind leapfrogged. 'That isn't your writing, is it?'

'Of course not!' Mary read the words aloud. '"Dear Arthur, I regret to tell you that I love another. Please be a gentleman and do not approach me again. Regards, Mary."' She was scornful. 'I never wrote anything of the kind!'

'Mary. Think. Where's the copy Arthur gave you when you went to your aunt's?'

'Um, oh.' Mary frowned. 'You mean . . .'

'Not the one he *sent* to you to say goodbye. That was the one *you* originally gave *him*. Where's the one you took with you when you went to your aunt's, when you and Arthur were still engaged?'

'My aunt took it from me,' said Mary. 'She promised to return it when I left, but by then Arthur had sent me the copy with that horrid message on it so I never asked for it.' Mary caught up. 'This is the one she took from me, isn't it?'

Another shout from Cher. 'Where's the milk? Never mind. Found it!'

Sadie inched along the only possible explanation. 'Mary, your aunt took the photo Arthur gave you, and handed it over to your parents. They forged that message – "I love another" – and gave it to Arthur. He thought you'd abandoned him. *That's* why he took the job and left the country! He went all the way to Assam to get over you, not to escape you.'

Mary tried to stand and fell back. 'How could they?'

Sadie knelt in front of her. She took her hands. 'I'm so, so sorry.'

'We could have had a life.' Mary wept.

Sadie cried too. It was all such a waste.

A detail nagged as they sat quietly together.

Where did this copy of the photo come from?

It wasn't the one that Mary had tossed into the bargain bin; that portrait had Arthur's sad goodbye on the back. Presumably, this photo had remained in Arthur's possession.

How, then, did Grace get hold of it for her exhibition?

'Tea's up!' Cher stood in the doorway and lowered the tray. 'What happened?' She took in their stunned expressions. 'Did somebody die?' She laid down the tray. 'And what are you doing with my picture?'

'*Your* picture?' snapped Mary.

'I gave it to Grace. It's me great-uncle Arthur and some bird.' Cher looked from one shocked face to another. 'What? What have I said?'

WEEK FOURTEEN

To	Amber <amber@yummymummymews.net.co.uk>, Hero <hero.smith@u-turn.net>, Sadie <sakuraspa@gmail.com>, Cher Mogg <whatulookingatcher@gmail.co.uk>, Fiona J <filove@aol.com>, The Bobs <bob@bobscaff.co.uk>, Jez <jeremy.gray@u-turn.net>, Grace Esparza <Gracetheartist@gmail.com>
From	Michael T. <qwertybookshop@hotmail.com>
Subject	CHERRY BLOSSOM MEWS RESIDENTS' ASSOCIATION MEETING

Dear All,

After the shocking events at Sakura, let's use this residents' association meeting to come together and show support for Sadie, Fi and Cher.

Date	Wednesday 22.8.18
Time	6.30 p.m.
Location	Qwerty Books (outside if hot)
Agenda	Security

I will tell Mary personally.

With all best wishes,

Michael

Her pillow was too warm. Sadie turned it, savouring the cool underside against her cheek. The model yacht on her chest of drawers was a spiky silhouette in the moonlight. Jack's creation sat beside his daughter's creation, the crêpe-wrapped cardboard box.

Everybody has a deeper layer. Every story is a Russian doll of hidden stories. That evening's story, unravelled by Cher, had upended Mary's beliefs.

A sudden noise, like a finger jabbing between Sadie's shoulder blades, made her sit up. Londoners are accustomed to noise; it's their lullaby. Since Teddy came back, Sadie was more alert.

Is she having a nightmare?

A trot across the hall allayed her fears. Teddy was asleep in that abandoned, dropped-from-a-great-height way of seven-year-olds. Mouth slightly open. Hair crazy on the pillow. There'd been a rebellion at bedtime, when Teddy had crossly pointed out that 'Bo doesn't go to bed this early' as if a seven-year-old and a twelve-year-old enjoyed equal privileges.

'Night night,' whispered Sadie, just because she could,

just because there was somebody to whisper it to. Teddy no longer slept in her bed, and now Sadie longed to climb in beside her daughter. She wondered if children knew how much comfort they bring their parents when they snuggle up with them against the night, and concluded, as she slipped back to her own bed, that they probably had more important things to think about. Sweets, dogs, etcetera.

Punching the pillow, Sadie yearned for sleep. Her mind had other plans. It condemned her to replay again and again the scene in Mary's sitting room.

Cher had pointed to the photograph of Arthur and Mary in their stiff sixties pose. 'Is this the one that caused all the trouble at the exhibition? Grace didn't get this from the bargain bin. *I* gave it to her.'

Mary, peppery with nerves, quavered, 'Arthur is your great-uncle?'

Cher took a step back. Wary. 'Yeah,' she said slowly. 'What's this about? He didn't do nothing wrong. He was boring, Uncle Arthur, not the type to cause bother.'

After being reassured by Sadie that nobody was pointing the finger at the Moggs, Cher sat, poured the tea, handed it out, and told her tale.

Silent throughout, Mary didn't touch her tea.

'Uncle Arthur was the first person to move into the flats when they were put up. He was in the next block along from me and my folks. Number one Assam House.'

A tremor went through Mary. Arthur hadn't taken the job in India, if one even existed. He had migrated only across the road.

'He was hired as a caretaker, and he was good. Strict, you know. Never left his window, always looking out at the street.'

Mary's street.

The estate was built on Mary's family land, directly opposite the big old house where Mary lived with her parents.

'He loved that pokey flat.' Cher rattled along. To her, this story was only a musty piece of family lore. 'He'd sit at the window, with his newspaper and his stupid cat, all day long.' Her voice softened. 'A funny onion, my Uncle Arthur. That photograph was on his desk with all his little personal doodahs. It was there right until he went.'

Time for a question. As Mary's chin dropped to her chest, Sadie asked, 'When did he go, Cher?'

'Two weeks ago.'

Outside in the mews, Cher had keened, 'I upset Mary! Why'd you let me upset her?'

Jez had emerged from U-Turn to walk Cher home.

'But only to the corner, yeah, as usual?' Sadie heard her say as they were claimed by the street.

Now, Sadie fidgeted in her bed. Like the central

misunderstanding in Sadie's past, Mary and Arthur's separation had been engineered by malicious family members. It had relied on the victim's isolation to succeed.

I got a second chance. It was too late for Mary. Two weeks too late after a hiatus of decades.

Those noises again. Sadie chose to reimagine them as music. Inner-city music. She fell into a listless, dream-addled sleep.

Teddy found it exciting.

Sadie found it distressing.

Fi was beside herself, buttonholing the mild police officers who wrote down everything they said, demanding to know if they would 'catch the bastards'.

Sakura's doors stood open. A lightning-shaped crack ran through the glass. Police cars stood at odd angles around the cherry blossom tree.

There wasn't much missing. The officers pointed out that the register was untouched. 'They came shopping for one thing in particular.'

The ultrasonic massage unit had been walked out into the mews by the cocksure burglars. When asked, Sadie could recite to the penny how much it was worth. She had saved for it, daydreamed about it.

'I daresay you're insured?'

Sadie nodded.

The policeman shut his notepad. 'That's not really the point, though.'

A female officer, who seemed about ten years old to Sadie, pointed at U-Turn and said, 'Junkies don't make the best neighbours. We'll ask Mr Smith for his CCTV tapes. Could you give me the names of everybody who works here?' She scribbled, then stopped. 'Mogg, did you say?'

Cher had straightened up, walked around the counter. 'Got a problem with that?'

'Not at all.' The police officer's demeanour changed not a jot. 'Care to tell me where you were last night, Ms Mogg?'

'With my fella, Jez. Oh hang on, no. He walked me home, but he had a migraine, so I watched telly with my mum.'

'Thanks.'

With Cher out of the way, another officer murmured, 'Her mum has experience at giving alibis. Watches an awful lot of telly with her kids.'

Sadie was stung. 'Cher wouldn't do this to me.'

'Her brothers would.'

When the marks on the floor had been cleaned, and the glass repair company called, and the early clients' curiosity fed, Sadie battled the sensation that somebody had pawed her beneath her underwear.

Strangers had violated her home and taken what they wanted. It was violence of a kind.

Now that the excitement of crackling police radios

and the residents gathering in their dressing gowns had abated, Teddy was quiet. She stuck to Fi's side, eyes on the floor.

This mews in a dingy postcode could never be a fortress like Merle's house. When she'd moved in, Sadie had seen more than just a hinterland of streets around a tube station; she'd seen a community, where a sense of morality held sway.

Apparently, I got that wrong.

'Right, sweetie!' Sadie clapped her hands. 'Want to help me put back all these bottles that got knocked off the shelves?'

'Do I have to?' Teddy's mouth turned down.

'It'd be nice,' smiled Sadie.

'I don't want to, Mummy.'

'Off you pop, then. I'll come up in a while.'

Fi watched the child, still in her Peppa Pig nightdress, scoot up to the flat. 'Teddy *should* help, you know.'

'She's just a kid.' Sadie turned to her first client of the day and apologised that no, there would be no ultrasonic today but could she offer her a complimentary lifting and reviving facial instead?

The day kicked off, as normal as it could be, given the circumstances.

Cher helped. Sadie noticed. She was grateful when Cher threw on her denim jacket and said she was off to view a possible replacement unit they could hire until the insurance coughed up.

According to Fi, this was not so much helping as 'staying out of the bloody way'. Plaiting Teddy's hair in a lull between appointments, she mused, 'Notice Cher didn't seem as shocked as the rest of us?'

'I was too busy freaking out.' Sadie spotted a heaped plate tented with clingfilm on the low table. 'Brownies?'

'From Mrs Bob.' Fi wound a glittery scrunchie around Teddy's plait. 'Don't get too excited. They're last week's.'

'I should pop over to Mary . . .'

'You don't have the time. Back-to-back appointments from noon.'

It was only later that Sadie realised most of the residents had popped in. Michael had wrung his hands, wounded by this assault on their mews. Sadie intuited his feelings for her were bound up in his dismay, and treated him gently. When Bob turned up they diplomatically refused his offers to help with clearing up, but accepted gladly the bespoke toasted sandwiches crammed with their favourite fillings, that he offered. Mrs Bob collected him and asked for the plates back as if Sadie was hell bent on stealing them. Grace was close to tears, and Amber brought 'on-trend' wildflowers. When she noticed the scuffed floor and the scraped paintwork she saw a silver lining: 'You can redecorate and bring the place more up to date!'

Hero did not appear.

Sadie felt the lack of him. It was Hero she'd wanted to call the moment she felt a breeze blowing up from the shop that morning and stopped in her tracks.

Not Jack. I didn't want to call Jack.

Some primeval section of her brain had accepted that Jack was gone.

'Feeling any better?' asked Fi, as the Sakura workforce closed up for the day.

'A little.' Sadie gestured to the cards and flowers. 'Everybody's been so kind, it's buoyed me up.'

They pottered. Tidying. Sweeping.

'Bet they never catch them,' said Fi, wiping the mirror, inspecting the fading bruise on her eye. 'There's so much crime around here. The police were telling me that wherever you get drugs on the street you get opportunistic crime.'

Sadie felt Cher tense up.

'If you join the dots,' said Fi, 'the scumbags who sell the drugs are as responsible as the junkies who do the break-ins.'

Cher threw down a duster. 'What you trying to say?'

'I *am* saying that if your brothers sell that shit then they're to blame for what happens.'

'My brothers are businessmen!'

'Yeah. Right. What business would that be?' Fi never backed down. 'Funny business, maybe.'

'Enough.' Sadie pulled rank. 'Whatever goes on out there, in here we are kind to one another. Got it?'

They got it, but grudgingly.

Sadie popped upstairs to turn on the oven and look in on Teddy, who was absorbed in something behind the sofa.

'No, Mummy, don't look!' she yelled, covering up a small white rectangle.

Dear Daddy

Are you mummy's one troo love?

i really like my barbie i gave her a tattoo like fi oh you don't know fi!

love Teddy xxxx

ps Mummy neerly caught me writing this!!!

ps i can't remember do you like twiglets

Downstairs, peace had broken out. Fi and Cher's heads were close together, looking down at something. They hurriedly subdued their giggles.

Sadie hummed to herself. She knew exactly what they'd been laughing at.

They think I'd disapprove.

@ambertragiclondon was painfully precise and therefore hugely enjoyable.

If you weren't Amber.

Sadie had seen Amber's soft-focus scene of books and

candles, captioned, 'Quiet night in. #loveyourhome! #YummyMummy #simplethingsarebest'. Everything in shot was available at Amber's shop, and when Sadie added up the cost of these simple things it came to over four hundred pounds.

The parodist – evil or righteous, depending on your point of view – had posted a pine coffee table strewn with a TV remote, a gravy-smeared plate, and some droopy gerbera gasping their last. It was the second post of the day; Amber's earlier picture of manicured hands making the shape of a heart had been swiftly followed by @ambertragiclondon's nicotine-stained fingers giving a thumbs up. The hashtags were the same. #staypure #youdoyou

'Look who it is,' said Fi, pointing out at the mews. 'About bleedin' time.'

Hero approached, hands in the pockets of his worn jeans. Bo was in his wake, that deliberate two-paces-behind walk that pre-teens insist on to illustrate that yes, they're here but they have other really, really exciting things to do, actually.

Sadie put a hand to her hair, hating herself for caring how she looked around Hero. Like she hated herself for scouring Amber's social media posts for evidence of his presence.

'Thought I'd see how you were doing.' Hero hovered.

'We're doing fine.'

Fi elaborated as she pushed past him. 'We are *not* doing fine. We are mildly depressed and wondering why the world is so cruel.' She picked up speed; a car was tooting impatiently. 'Be nice to her, yeah?'

'I'm always nice to her,' called Hero to her back. He turned to Sadie. 'Aren't I?'

Sadie sensed Cher watching.

All she needs is a bucket of popcorn.

'Of course you are, Hero. Hi, Bo, I must tell Teddy you're – oh.'

Teddy was already there, having whizzed downstairs at superhero speed. 'Ooh, what's that?'

When Teddy pointed, Sadie realised that Bo held a new skateboard. 'You gave in?' She laughed at Hero.

'Not me. His mum.' Hero managed to express by use of his eyebrows that this was Not To Be Discussed. 'Show Teddy how to skate. Go *on*.' Hero gave Bo a gentle push when the boy prevaricated.

They watched their children rumble across the flat strip of concrete outside Bob's Caff.

'Bo's sweet to give Teddy so much time. That's a hefty gap at their age.' Sadie, arms crossed, enjoyed Hero's nearness. She feared if she uncrossed her arms she might grab him. And that would be wrong.

'Bo only pretends to be reluctant. Who wouldn't enjoy a little fan following you around all day?'

They wandered in a circle around the cherry tree. Like old times, if you can call three weeks ago old times.

'How's Bo settling in?'

'He says London's like a Hobbit town after LA's sunny boulevards: teeny tiny rooms, narrow roads. He complains about all the walking; he's used to jumping in the car. Before this year, he used to spend his summer month with me in Suffolk, so I've had to promise to take him to Carnaby Street and the London Eye and all that tourist guff.'

Teddy shrieked happily as Bo pulled her along. It was a lovely, melodic sound, and much too rare. 'Are you peeved about the skateboard?'

'I wish Zizzi would wait sometimes, or even say no. But I have to choose my battles, so I won't make a fuss about this.'

Sadie didn't feel she had the right to ask what the other battles might be about.

He told her anyway. 'Bo's been offered a modelling contract. Gucci, would you believe.'

'Holy shit!'

'Quite.'

'That's amazing.'

'Too amazing. Bo needs to study, grow up, get his heart broken before he starts making money.'

'Yeah . . .' Dazzled by the mention of Gucci, Sadie saw both sides.

'Zizzi's furious that I've put my foot down for once, but Bo's a tiny bit relieved beneath all the attitude. Making money for youngsters is dangerous, but it's twice as dangerous when you make it with your face.' He looked at Sadie. 'Because that's where your soul peeks out.'

'It won't make you popular with him.'

'Not my job to be popular. It's my job to bring him up. I hardly have to tell *you* about the trials of, um, unusual parenting.'

They had always gone effortlessly deep, but this conversation felt mildly forbidden. Amber might see them after all, if she cared to look up from her phone and out of her window. Instead of inducing guilt, it sent a frisson travelling through Sadie as she held Hero's gaze.

Is this how Effie felt when she was with Jack?

That was a cold shower of a thought, so much so that Sadie was grateful to see Mary making her slow, suddenly so much more elderly, way across Cherry Blossom Mews.

'I came to offer my sympathy,' said Mary. 'And to see how I can help.'

Cher shouted from inside the spa. 'You can help by letting me pour you a glass of wine while we wait for my stupid boyfriend, who's working late for his slave-driver of a boss.'

Hero held up his hands in defeat, refused the wine, made an excuse and left. Sadie did her best not to watch where he went as she called Teddy indoors, but one last look over her shoulder confirmed – *dammit* – he was headed for Yummy Mummy.

'No wine for you, boss lady, I know, I know.' Cher tutted as she handed a glass to Mary, already on the old-lady sofa. 'She's so *boring,* Mary.'

'Or sensible.' Mary asked about the break-in. Cher was silenced by this topic; Sadie tried not to read between those particular lines.

'You wanna chat about Uncle Arthur, dontcha?' Cher butted in.

Mary half smiled, grateful at having been rumbled. 'How did he live, Cher, dear? Was he happy?'

'No,' said Cher. No sugar coating there. 'Uncle Arthur wasted his life, that's what we always say. He never did nothing. Just sat in his chair, staring out of his window.'

From where she sat with Teddy on the floor, Sadie exchanged a look with Mary.

He was watching over his beloved.

True, Arthur's life was wasted in one way, as was Mary's, but for fifty-eight years he never strayed from its core truth.

Love.

The wine, gulped down, loosened Cher as she balanced on a white stool. 'He was *straight*, Uncle Arthur. Disapproved of me brothers. Used to say he was glad they didn't share a surname. My mum got the right hump.' She giggled as she remembered his Christmas tradition of returning the twins' presents to them. 'Said he didn't want nothing bought with dirty money.' She paused. 'He had dignity, you know?' It seemed to strike her for the first time. 'He wasn't swayed by money.' She brightened up to tell the Moggs' favourite Arthur anecdote.

Mary listened hard. Storing it all away for the cold nights ahead.

'Funny how Uncle Arthur never went out, and then the one time he did he almost got himself killed! That big house, the one that's flats now, went on fire one night.'

Mary stiffened.

'This was long before my time, but the whole place went up apparently, and Arthur was out of his armchair and across the road like a whippet. Me mum was crying, *her* mum was crying, all screaming at him to come back, but in he ran. They thought he was a goner but suddenly he burst out of the flames carrying some woman. He was a hero! Nobody ever knew, though, 'cos he just slinked back to his flat. The papers said it was a fireman, but it was Uncle Arthur all along.'

'I should . . . It's time I . . .' Mary tried to raise herself from the cushions and failed. Cher and Sadie helped her to the door. 'Come along, Noel,' she said. 'There's a good . . . oh.'

Jez turned up before anybody worked out what to say. He offered one arm to Mary and the other to Cher, and off they went. Slowly.

'Mummy, that was a really stupid story,' complained Teddy, gearing up for an evening of grousing.

'It had hidden meaning, sweetie.' Sadie jollied up her voice. 'Come on! Race you upstairs!'

The stupid story had told Mary she had been in the arms of her sweetheart one more time than she knew of.

Arthur saved her life.

The street that had divided them was too wide for Arthur to cross outside of an emergency. It wasn't just tarmac and paving; it was a social chasm. Mary's parents had gambled on their victims' personalities and won. They had won big. Arthur was too humble to present himself at their door after hearing that Mary was promised to another, and Mary was too dutiful to suspect them of lying.

The week crawled by, hot and sticky. Lollies were bought on an hourly basis at Sakura. A new fan was installed.

'Nothing from the boys in blue?' asked Fi as she plonked down her bag each morning.

'Nothing.'

'No confessions?' Fi would say this extra loud, and was usually rewarded with a slammed door from Cher.

'Shush, Fi.' Sadie's reprimand was absent-minded. The stash of postcards in her daughter's room was shrinking. Cards were being written.

To Merle.

But where did the cards go? She imagined Teddy ripping them up, pushing them into the kitchen bin. Or throwing them out of the window, hoping they'd reach their destination.

'That music's too loud!' Fi buttoned herself into her tunic.

'Someone got out of the wrong side of the memory foam mattress this morning.' Sadie knew the music was at the same low level as usual.

'It's the burglary. It's got me all jittery.'

'Oh I see. It's not the black eye that's got you jittery?' Sadie was sardonic as she sorted the post. 'Not whatever it is you're not telling me about Cole?'

'Nothing to tell.' Fi sanitised her hands viciously, as if they had done something wrong. 'You have a bad mind.'

'I have a good memory.' Sadie had been nervous about starting this conversation but it was finally off and running. 'Something's not right, Fi. We've seen this pattern before. What kind of a friend would I be if I didn't worry?'

'A nice quiet kind of friend.' Fi's attempt at keeping things light was further proof that something was up. 'Cole's the best thing that ever happened to me.'

'Even though he makes jibes about your weight?'

'Let's face it: he's not wrong. I could do with shifting a pound or two. Or ten.'

This was heresy. 'You're perfect, Fi. Every inch of you. No man should dare suggest otherwise Especially not one who . . .' Sadie abruptly ran out of steam.

'Who what?' Fi was no longer light. She was leaden. 'Go on, Poirot. A man who what?'

'Does *that*.' Sadie gestured to Fi's eye. 'You promised yourself – and me – you'd never let this happen again, that you'd read the signs and get out before it got ugly.'

'I don't need guidance from a woman who didn't even know her own husband was cheating on her.'

'That was below the belt.'

'True, though.'

Both women stood like statues. Pissed-off statues. Sadie caved first.

'I have work to do.'

The rumble of small wheels bumping over the cobbles announced Bo. Unasked, he had become Sakura's gopher. Cher sent him to the high street for milk, for custard creams, for copies of *heat*. Clients handed him coins to feed their meters. On OAP days, white-haired ladies slipped him fifty-pence pieces saying he reminded them of their grandsons and lamenting his dyed hair.

All of which was heaven for Teddy, who tailed Bo like a private eye. Sadie found herself waiting nervously for the duo's return from their errands, but that was a small price to pay for Teddy being amused while her mother toiled at the coalface of open pores and stiff necks.

There had been a gentle, exploratory chat about Merle; those postcards were never far from Sadie's mind. Yes, Teddy admitted, she did miss her. 'She's my granny and I love her but . . .'

Sadie had waited. Seven-year-olds' reasoning can be way ahead of their vocabulary.

'She was bad to keep me to herself.'

That was that. The verdict. Sadie had wondered if Teddy had absorbed the truth of their unusual situation and here was her answer.

Teddy knows what happened.

The girl faced it side-on; possibly she would not be able to confront it fully until she was older. Whenever that happened, Sadie vowed to hold her hand through it.

If she lets me.

The current Teddy wasn't big on handholding. She had a question for her mother though. 'Do you miss Daddy?'

'So much.' That was true. Not the whole truth, because children and grown-ass women alike can't cope with too much truth all at once.

Should I ever tell her about her beloved daddy's infidelity?

'Mummy, we'll see him again one day but I really, really don't like waiting.'

'I wish I'd been with you when you were in hospital, sweetie.'

'S'okay.'

Teddy's readily given absolution landed like a feather. 'I spoke to Doctor Batman. She told me you were ever so brave. What was the physical therapy like?'

'Fun,' said Teddy, unexpectedly. 'We got in the swimming pool and I had to walk about. Oh, and I had to squat, as if I was on the loo only there was no loo there. That's *hard*, Mummy.'

As Teddy chattered, Sadie felt something between them shift, as if her daughter had nudged imperceptibly closer.

Teddy interrupted herself to say, 'Can I go round to Avalon's? Now? Today?'

'Avalon?' Sadie recognised the name: a school friend. 'Where does Avalon live? Is she the one with the Corgi? I'll need a surname, so I can look up her mum's number.'

Your granny, out on bail, is unlikely to hand over her address book.

A squall gathered on Teddy's features. 'Avalon has a *cat*, not a dog.' She was contemptuous, as if Avalon's cat was common knowledge. 'She lives near the school. You can drive me there.'

'Well . . .'

Perhaps Teddy read the dozen questions in Sadie's eyes. Where exactly did this Avalon live? Even if Sadie could track down the family's number and withstand the questions about why Teddy no longer lived with her granny – *Yes, as you ask, I* am *the mother who abandoned her!* – was there time in the spa diary for her to deliver Teddy?

'Never mind.' It was bitter, in no way an absolution this time, as Teddy slunk off to find Bo.

'How long is this gonna carry on?' Cher was between Fi and Sadie as they made their way to Qwerty for the residents' meeting. 'This frostiness is doing my head in.'

'What's frostiness?' asked Teddy.

'It's when grown women act like teenagers.' Cher seemed to be enjoying the high moral ground she suddenly found herself on. 'Is that your Barbie?' She took Teddy's doll from her.

The doll that Teddy claimed to hate. Its make-up had been redone with unsteady felt tip, its coiffeur now a crop. Was that a tattoo on Barbie's arm? The poor cow was dressed in makeshift clothes made from a sanitary towel. The hated doll had been thoroughly, lovingly played with.

Hero wasn't 'stupid' in his choice of gift, after all.

At Qwerty, Michael tried to assert himself. 'Are we all here? No Bob?'

'He's lying in bed like the great lump that he is.' Mrs Bob was disapproving.

'Give him our love,' said Sadie. The chair was comfortable. The biscuits Michael provided were Bahlsen. Her Cherry Blossom crew was around her. Amber fiddled with her earrings. Grace had moved her chair to sit close to Mary. Michael studied his notes. Fi was in a staring contest with Teddy. Mrs Bob tapped her foot. Cher was trying to be annoyed with Jez who had sneaked an arm around her shoulder. Hero watched Bo do slow circles around the group on his skateboard, before motioning to him to sit down. Bo's put-upon sigh was melodramatic.

Sadie felt cared for, protected. Even more so when Michael, having taken the register – his adherence to procedure an obvious offering to Sadie – made a short speech.

'Sadie, I hope you know how deeply the break-in has affected all of us in the mews.' He waited for the murmured 'Yes's and 'So terrible's to die down. 'Later we'll discuss security measures, albeit a little late, but for now it needs saying that we're here for you and we'll do anything we can to help.'

Mrs Bob lifted her chin, looked down her long nose. 'There's been talk,' she said.

'We needn't bring that up now,' said Michael.

Mrs Bob ignored him. 'Some of us think your burglar was one of U-Turn's misfits.'

Hero and Jez looked at each other, resigned.

She went on. 'But some of us think it might be even closer to home.' The air thickened as she pointed at Cher. 'Your family has a finger in every pie, madam.'

Bracing herself, Sadie awaited an outburst, but Cher was

composed. And probably more dangerous that way. She only moved to shrug off Jez's hand on her shoulder.

'I really think—' began Michael.

'You really think,' said Mrs Bob, 'that everybody should be as polite as you, but I wasn't made that way. I call a spade a spade, and a Mogg a Mogg.'

'It's not the time or the place for this,' said Fi, earning a quick, grateful look from Cher.

'That's not what you said yesterday in my caff. And the rest of youse needn't pretend you're not thinking the exact same thing. Michael mentioned Cher's *connections*.' Michael hung his head. 'Amber, you weren't backwards in coming forward about the twins, no matter how demure you look now.'

'Hmm? What's that?' Amber remained engrossed in her phone.

Grace rarely spoke at meetings, but she spoke now. She was calm, kindly. 'It can't be U-Turn *and* Cher. Truth is, we have no idea who it was. Perhaps, with Bob on your mind, you're—'

'What's Bob got to do with this?' Mrs Bob was livid. 'You're a newcomer, love; you don't get to have an opinion.'

Sadie had had enough. 'We were all newcomers once. This is just a little mews and we all have our say. No, Mrs Bob,' she said, as her neighbour opened her mouth. 'It's my turn now. Cher's worked for me for three months, and she's given me no reason to distrust her. I can't say I know her all that well, because she's a reserved person, but from what I do know . . .' – Sadie looked at Cher's bowed head – 'she has ambition and character and is making her own way. She's not just a Mogg, she's Cher Mogg, and that means something.'

Michael said, with quiet determination, 'Let's take a step back. Cher's one of the family now and—'

Cher stood up and made for the door, tripping herself in her haste.

Half rising, Jez was paralysed with indecision. 'Should I . . . ?'

'Perhaps she needs a moment to herself,' said Amber.

Jez sat down heavily.

The meeting was stained; even the bins discussion grew heated. All agreed that the mews needed stronger security measures, but when Grace riffed on the topic of putting their case to the landlord, Sadie, mindful of Mary, stood and said, 'Jeez, guys, can we leave it there?'

There was no disagreement.

Helping Michael put away the chairs, Sadie asked softly, 'No Dorothy Ball this week?'

He went a deep maroon. 'Is there any point?' he muttered, and beetled away.

Sadie felt a tug at her sleeve. 'Mummy, come on.'

Teddy's impatience translated as *Bo's getting away.* 'Coming, sweetie.'

As they walked out, a wall of anger met them, hot enough to sear their eyebrows. Cher stood, hands on hips, letting rip.

'Why are you such a crap boyfriend? Why didn't you follow me out? Are you a real man or what?'

'Hey, hey!' Jez's hands were up as he backed away. 'Let's not do this here, yeah?'

'I'll do it wherever I want!' Cher turned to the other residents. 'What you all looking at?'

'You, you loony,' said Mrs Bob, hurrying away all the same.

Jez took a cautious step towards his irate girlfriend. 'I'm not a servant, Cher. You can't tell me what to do twenty-four seven.'

'Maybe you should look for someone else, then. Someone who doesn't mind always coming last with you.'

Sadie tugged at Teddy, who was transfixed. 'This is *great*,' said the child, running over to Bo, who had stilled his skateboard in order to watch the street theatre.

'Cher, don't.' Jez's voice was low and placating. 'Let's just enjoy our evening, love. We barely get any time together, what with my hours and your family.'

'Do *not* badmouth my folks!'

'I wasn't!' Jez's voice went girlishly high.

'My brothers'd never leave me high and dry like you just did!'

'They might if they treated you like a grown woman and not a toddler.'

Cher had nothing to lob back. Jez had hit home. They glared at each other and it was Cher who broke the silence with her usual pugnaciousness. 'Sadie!' she barked.

Sadie jumped.

'I need a date for tonight as my prince has turned back into a frog. Come on.' She turned. 'Italian. I'm paying.'

Jez stormed into U-Turn, bristling with frustration.

Heaving open one of the tall gates, Cher shouted, 'Get a move on, Sadie.'

Sadie turned to Fi, who understood the question in her eyes. 'Yeah, I'll sit with the tiddler and watch some godawful kiddy DVD. Off you pop.'

The cold war was over. 'Thank you,' said Sadie with great emphasis. Falling out with Fi had felt every shade of wrong; now she must figure out a way to use their rapprochement to see off Cole.

As the flirty waiter retreated and left Sadie and Cher to the breadsticks, Sadie was distracted by her surroundings. This had been a favoured haunt with Hero. She peeked with trepidation into the candlelit corners, afraid she might see him and Amber sharing garlic bread.

'Hmm,' she said during the pauses of Cher's machine-gun chatter, and, 'Uh-huh.'

'So I feel a bit guilty, like,' Cher was saying as Sadie sighed inwardly at the musak that reminded her of Hero. ''Cos he's probably lonely.'

She tuned back in. Asked Cher to repeat herself. Listened this time, and threw down her breadstick.

'Cher, get your coat,' she said.

Hero insisted on driving.

In the back sat Mary and Sadie, striped by passing street-lamps. Left at home with Teddy, Fi had requested live-action updates, in the manner of election night television coverage. Dutifully, Sadie texted.

Almost there!

In the front seat, Cher swivelled round. 'How'd we get this so mixed up?'

Sadie took Mary's hand between her own and rubbed it. It was cold. 'When Cher said at the restaurant that her uncle *is* lonely, I realised that Arthur's still alive.'

'That's it, there.' Cher pointed and Hero slowed down, turning into the car park of a low-built nursing home. 'I've only been once, with my mum. It's a bit smelly, to be honest.'

'No need to be *quite* so honest, Cher,' said Hero, as he leapt out to open the rear door.

A harried care worker didn't want to let them in. She

was kind, but firm. It was late, she said. 'We have early nights here.'

Cher pushed to the fore, saying through the crack in the door, 'He's my great-uncle.' She glanced at Mary, wilting in the night air. 'I have a present for him.'

We're in!

A dash over linoleum. Down wallpapered corridors. Mary quiet, the pressure of her arm on Sadie's barely there. Hero led the charge, having a discreet conversation with the care worker, professional to professional. She gaped at him.

'Seriously?' she said.

The woman rapped gently on a door. 'Arthur?'

The room was miniscule; the Moggs weren't spending much of their ill-gotten gains on their disapproving great-uncle. An old-fashioned wardrobe. An old-fashioned bed. Beside it, in pyjamas, sat an old-fashioned man. Arthur was transparent with age, his hair a coronet of white floss. His long fingers were fine, his eyes still bright.

Sadie stepped forward with Mary, propping her up. She could feel the sob trapped in Mary's body.

Arthur smiled. 'Oh look at this! It's my Mary, come at last!'

Hero slipped a plastic chair under Mary just before her legs gave way.

'Arthur,' she said. Then, in a different voice, one full of tenderness, *'Arthur.'*

'Don't you cry, girl,' said Arthur. 'Don't you look bonny?'

It was hard to text with trembling fingers.

They're reunited!!!

Mary held out her hand and Arthur took it.

Sadie found herself weeping as years of longing found an answer in this tiny gesture.

A voice at the door. Not unkind, but unwelcome all the same. A woman, evidently higher up the management ladder, had been fetched by the care worker. 'What's going on here?'

Arthur looked up. He beamed. 'Oh look at this!' He pointed to the supervisor, dropping Mary's hand. 'It's my Mary, come at last!'

WEEK FIFTEEN

To	Amber <amber@yummymummymews.net.co.uk>, Michael T. <qwertybookshop@hotmail.com, Sadie <sakuraspa@gmail.com>, Cher Mogg <whatulookingatcher@gmail.co.uk>, Fiona J <filove@aol.com>, The Bobs <bob@bobscaff.co.uk>, Jez <jeremy.gray@u-turn.net>, Grace Esparza <Gracetheartist@gmail.com>
From	Hero <hero.smith@u-turn.net>
Subject	CHERRY BLOSSOM MEWS RESIDENTS' ASSOCIATION MEETING

Dear Mewsites

Another week, another meeting.

Date	Wednesday 29.8.18
Time	6.30 p.m.
Location	U-Turn therapy suite
Agenda	Our top secret plan

Ensure Mary knows about the meeting. She HAS to attend.

H x

Sundays used to be so tricky.

There had been an unwanted lie-in, then hours of thumb twiddling as Sadie impatiently waited for the week to resurrect itself, for Monday to bustle in and give her things to do.

Now that Teddy was there, Sunday meant laundry, cooking, tidying, answering a thousand questions, some philosophical, others mathematical, one about why women don't have willies. Flying blind, Sadie vaulted these maternal hurdles, sometimes enjoying the pressure, sometimes wondering if she was doing it right.

A chunk of Teddy's childhood was missing, as lost to Sadie as the blackouts she used to suffer. There was no school-gate posse to ask if it was normal for Teddy to spend so much time in her room, to canvass on whether sugar was as bad as all the websites claimed, to check that they also found CBeebies mind-blowingly dull.

There was a stamped foot every now and again. Teddy, her face set, refusing to help clear up the spilled cereal she'd trodden into the new rug. Sadie dithered, then mopped it up herself. It was tough to scold a little girl who was missing her grandmother.

Did Teddy grieve properly for Jack?

For all Sadie knew, the tightly wound Merle repressed any signs of unhappiness.

All the while, the trial loomed, like a storm gathering on distant hills. In about six months, according to her police liaison officer, all the McQueen shit would hit the fan. Was it best to tell Teddy or keep her in the dark?

What if it gets in the papers?

An email to Teddy's school took an hour to compose. She explained their unique circumstances, and asked fearfully about fees. The child needed a GP, a dentist, possibly a therapist.

And love. Lots of that. Sadie walked on eggshells around her small, reserved daughter.

Discipline can come later.

Mary was chatty, retrieving Trebor mints from the glove compartment. 'I saw Hero and Amber zoom off in that silly little sports car of hers.' Her head full of Arthur, Mary didn't seem to notice Sadie's fingers tighten on the steering wheel. 'I hope that shortbread's all right on the back seat.' The Tupperware box was safely belted in. 'You're very good to do this,' Mary said.

'The rota must be obeyed!' A copy had been distributed by Cher, with dire warnings of consequences if it was not adhered to. Every evening, Mary was chauffeured to

Streamside Residential Village. Only Mrs Bob was excused from duty.

'Arthur slept through my visit yesterday.' Mary was in no way sorry for herself. 'Today we'll listen to music. He loves the old tunes.'

'Maybe you can dance.' Arthur was steady on his feet some days; on others he remained glued to his chair.

'My dancing days are done, my dear.'

'Rubbish.' Always respectful of Mary, Sadie admired her afresh for her no-nonsense attitude to Arthur's illness. Alzheimer's, the Streamside nurses had told her. Nothing to be done about it. 'And yes,' they'd answered her question gravely, 'it's progressive. Arthur will deteriorate.'

Fate had been particularly acerbic. It had let them believe they were separated by half the world when they'd lived on opposite sides of the same stretch of road, both of them yearning for the other. As a final flourish, fate had waved its soot-black wand over Arthur's brain just before they rediscovered each other.

Mary had no truck with such metaphor. Sadie asked, 'What's in the handbag of destiny today?'

'Those marshmallows Arthur seems to like, and a newspaper, oh, and a slice of something rather odd and organic that Amber gave me.'

Probably something she couldn't palm off to her customers.

The latest posting by @ambertragiclondon had been of Sainsbury's own brand biscuits on a paper plate. 'Let's hope Arthur has hipster taste buds.'

The burglary had left its mark.

'Teddy jumps at every noise in the night,' Sadie told Fi and Cher as they watched the little girl hitch a ride on Bo's skateboard beyond the repaired glass doors.

'What's the latest from da copz?' asked Fi.

'Nothing to report. They had high hopes for U-Turn's CCTV but it was on the blink.'

The liaison officer reported that U-Turn's General Manager had known that the CCTV was broken. It was an inescapable fact that the General Manager's girlfriend also knew the CCTV was broken.

Purely circumstantial evidence.

Sadie only half understood the phrase from TV thrillers. Cher was her friend.

Or something close to a friend.

When skateboarding was rained off, Teddy ran in, shaking her hair. Fi put her to work, handing out cucumber water.

'Do I have to?' she grumbled, holding the tray at an angle that alarmed them all. 'Why don't we have a housekeeper to do this, like at Granny's?'

'Ooh, excuse me, Your Majesty!' laughed Fi.

Sadie stepped in before the customers received the cucumber water on their laps. 'We do things for ourselves here.' She enfolded the seven-year-old in a cuddle, but Teddy dodged away, as if Sadie's touch disgusted her.

Possibly seeing Sadie's discouraged face, one of the customers said, 'Don't worry, they all do that.'

Later, with Teddy out of earshot, Fi reiterated the client's words.

Although she agreed, Sadie argued, in a whisper, that Teddy was different. 'Other kids haven't gone through her trauma.'

On the dot of six o'clock, Cole pulled into the mews.

'Don't start,' said Fi, without even looking at Sadie. 'I love him. Cole's different.'

'Like Emanuel was different? I seem to recall all the punching and the infidelity and the nicking tenners from you was a result of his awful childhood.'

'See?' sighed Fi as she swanned out. 'Starting.'

The rota pointed its finger at Hero.

He insisted on Bo coming with him, and Teddy insisted on going with Bo. Amber brought up the rear, insisting that somebody had to sit in the back with the kids and 'keep order'. Mary waved like the Queen as Hero drove slowly out through the gates.

'Give Arthur my love!' called Sadie.

'Look after Mary,' called Fi.

Before the accident, Teddy had hidden behind Sadie's legs; now she was inviting herself along on joyrides. It was right. It was part of growing up. Children were supposed to gain independence; parents were supposed to applaud their growing confidence.

But does she find leaving me easy because our bond is shattered?

Sometimes Sadie felt more like a babysitter than a mother. 'Fancy breaking your diet?'

Fi considered this. 'Yes, Satan,' she said. 'I do.'

They turned towards the caff, jumping out of the way as a besuited man careered out of its door.

Mrs Bob was on the warpath, snatching back his sandwich, yelling, 'Bugger off! If you don't like my customers then eat somewhere else.' She stood aside for Sadie and Fi. 'That joker said he didn't like the *clientele*.' The clientele in question sat with Jez by the window. A couple of dishevelled individuals, in dirty clothes and a patina of shame.

If they stick with the U-Turn programme, thought Sadie, *they'll soon sharpen up.*

'Not like you to defend the honour of Hero's people, Mrs Bob.'

Mrs Bob looked discomfited at being caught red-handed.

'He was a difficult customer, anyway. Asking about the nut content of everything. I told him there'll be one less nut when you shove off.'

Jez leaned back to ask Sadie, 'How's our top-secret mission going?'

Sadie winked. 'The package will arrive just before the residents' meeting. I hope we're doing the right thing.'

'Bit of a gamble, but so's life. How's my lady-love this morning? She gave me an earful over the phone. My breathing was annoying her.'

'She's quiet.' Cher had been subdued since the break-in. 'She cheered up a bit when I cocked up an appointment and she could tell me off.'

'That's my girl.'

They were a perfect match, Cher and Jez. He absorbed all her noise and bluster. He understood. He cared. Presumably, when they were alone, Cher repaid him with kindness.

Back at the spa, Cher held out a book. 'That not-so-secret admirer of yours has a twisted sense of humour.'

The latest Dorothy Ball was *Thief of Hearts*. Sadie took it, relieved that Michael was constant even if Hero had moved on with an ease that undermined their relationship.

'What's this?' Sadie picked up a plastic bag and peered inside.

'That's from me.' Cher's eyelashes fluttered when she was

uncomfortable. 'Sort of like a present for the spa. 'Cos of the name.'

The plastic cherry blossom was cheap, gaudy. Sadie looked at it uncertainly. It was the opposite of the Sakura ethos. Everything within the spa was organic, *real*. 'Um,' she said.

'Yeah, it's shit,' sighed Cher. 'Give it here. I'll chuck it.'

'No, no, it'll come in handy.' Sadie put the plastic branch in a drawer beneath the reception counter. 'It's lovely. Thank you.'

I'll throw it out when nobody's looking.

Almost to herself, Cher wondered, 'What would you do if somebody close to you . . .' She sighed. 'If they, like, betrayed you?'

I already know the answer to that.

Jack had been closer to Sadie than her own skin. She was about to answer that she'd fall apart, but she hesitated.

I wobbled, but I didn't fall apart.

'Why do you ask?' she laughed. 'Jez been up to no good? Or are you planning to betray me?'

Cher didn't laugh.

Her answer suddenly felt important.

'I don't find it easy to do right by people,' said Cher, eventually. 'I can't always see the difference between right and wrong.' When she looked at Sadie, her eyes glittered with tears. 'I'm like one of those feral children, raised in the wild.'

'Don't say th—'

'Why can't I be nice to Jez?' Cher asked urgently, balling her fingers into a fist. 'He's lovely to me.'

'What's brought this on?' Sadie put down the book and moved nearer. She wanted to take Cher in her arms, but that felt like a step too far. It would scare her, like the feral child she identified as.

'Seeing Mary.' Cher pushed at her face with her hands. 'She's so kind to Uncle Arthur. All those years . . . we never took no notice of him. We never appreciated him. When he started going doolally we just stuck him in a home. Love is a language my family don't speak.'

A bang on the window. Jez waved as he passed. 'Laters, gorgeous!'

'Don't push your luck!' yelled Cher, then turning to Sadie, she said, 'See? Why can't I just be nice?'

'Let's do something nice right now for somebody, for no reason at all.'

'I know!' Cher perked up. 'Let's buy Fi a Magnum.'

A Magnum was procured. Fi declared herself delighted. Cher sought out @ambertragiclondon and held the latest funny but cruel post up for them all to read. They laughed and ate and all was harmonious.

The alarm bell sounding in Sadie's mind was the only bum note.

Why did Cher mention betrayal?

*

The bland but welcoming room at U-Turn was filling up for their usual Wednesday meeting. Amber's strapless lace dress was almost bride-like, in stark contrast with Grace's top-to-toe khaki. Sadie sat across from them both, alongside Mary, who was blowing her nose with vigour. 'Where are the youngsters?' she asked.

'Somewhere,' said Sadie, vaguely.

No Bob; this was customary, but still they all commented on it, and asked the stony-faced Mrs Bob how he was.

'He's dying, that's how he is,' she silenced the well-wishers.

Grace had a suggestion as soon as the register was dispensed with. 'Fairy lights,' she said, her face shining. 'We should have some in the mews. They make everything better!'

Amber was animated. 'The soft light's so good for selfies!'

'Bit girly,' said Michael, holding his hands over his head and saying 'Sorry! Sorry!' when every female present gave him the evil eye.

'Brilliant idea,' said Hero. 'It'll soften our edges. Who'll volunteer?'

Predictably, everybody found their fingernails fascinating. Except Grace. 'I'll do it!'

Recovering, Michael had a question. 'What's the latest on Arthur?'

For a moment Mary looked affronted. Unlearning a lifetime's habit of keeping herself to herself was a challenge.

'He's cheerful and in good health. The dementia creeps along. He needs help with bathing and visiting the loo, and some days he shows no interest in eating, so he needs assistance with that. I could have him for ten years, I could have him for months. There's much uncertainty.' She turned to Mrs Bob. 'You've been going through all this for so long, my dear. You're very brave.'

Mrs Bob sucked her lips into a thin line.

Mary cleared her throat. 'Emotional thank you's aren't my forte. I haven't had much call for them. But thank you, all of you, for driving me to and from Streamside.' She made another small *ahem*, then said, 'I beg you, somebody jump in with some news. I *cannot* cry in front of you all.'

'I have news!' Sadie flung up her hand. 'The stolen machinery's been returned.' She savoured the Mexican wave of astonishment. 'I know! I couldn't believe my ears when Cher told me.'

'Cher was first in, was she?' Mrs Bob loaded her comment with insinuation.

Sadie pretended to miss the double meaning. 'We can put the whole thing behind us.'

'I wonder why the criminals had an attack of conscience?' Michael looked to the others. 'Has anybody heard of this happening before?'

Silence. The jury was out on Cher's innocence, but for now a change of subject was needed. Sadie stood up. 'Anyway, never mind all that and sod the bins.' She saw Michael, dejected, tuck away a large manila folder. 'Something very special is happening on the mews today.'

Mary blinked, aware that everybody was looking at her, not at Sadie. 'Are you up to something?'

'You bet.' Sadie shouted. 'Teddy! Bo! Bring him in!'

They *burst* in. The Cairn terrier at their heels leapt at laps and skidded on the varnished boards.

'Meet Noel the seventh,' hollered Sadie.

Doubts jostled as Mary watched the canine jumping bean. Choosing a dog is so personal.

Will Mary feel insulted?

The secret meeting, held behind Mary's cardiganed back, had been so pleased with itself, so *sure*. Now that the imaginary dog was noisy flesh and blood and had already torn Amber's fishnets, the residents watched Mary for her reaction.

'This is ridiculous,' she grumbled.

'*Arf!*' said Noel VII.

'And quite possibly the nicest thing anyone's ever done for me.'

The residents relaxed. Until they heard the 'but'.

'But I can't possibly look after a dog. I'm a thousand years old. Noel the sixth wore me out, and this new Noel is a puppy, plus there's Arthur to consider.'

'We're ahead of you, Mazzer.'

Michael said, 'Noel isn't *your* dog.'

Mrs Bob chucked the dog under his chin. 'He's Cherry Blossom's dog, aren't you, Noellie?'

Amber took a snap of him. 'We'll take turns walking him.'

Noel jumped up onto Mary's knees. The tweedy skirt met with his approval. He settled down.

'All *you* have to do,' said Sadie, 'is love him.'

They dispersed in a gossipy trickle, as they always did. Bo, first on the rota for walkies, rolled his eyes as he took the lead and allowed Noel VII to drag him out into the night.

Hero bore down on Sadie and her daughter. 'Can I have a minute?' He was shifty, awkward. 'There's something you need to hear, and it's best it comes from me.'

His closeness was disconcerting. His assumption was insulting. 'For God's sake, Hero, I already know about you and Amber. Your private life's your own.'

He shut his eyes for a second as if counting to ten. 'Just for once, Sadie, will you simply do what I ask? It won't take long.' Hero leaned in. 'It's important.'

Cher came down to the main doors of Orissa House in a fluffy pink dressing gown. Novelty slippers on her feet. A scowl on her face. 'You? What d'you want?'

Sadie's hands were deep in the pockets of her jacket. She knew that Cher knew why she was there and she waited.

Cher stepped outside, onto the pavement. Gum. Cigarette ends. Takeaway cartons. Even though the night was warm, she pulled her fleecy dressing gown tight around herself.

'I came to tell you,' said Sadie, 'that Hero fixed the CCTV at U-Turn.'

Cher tried to look bored.

'So the camera that points into the mews and catches the front of Sakura was working this morning at three a.m.'

'So?'

'So it filmed you trundling the ultrasonic massage unit through Cherry Blossom Mews and into the spa.'

'You should have listened to the others' – Cher turned her back, nonchalant – 'when they told you not to trust a Mogg.' Over her shoulder, she said, 'Right. That's me sacked then. Take my advice: don't tell the police, or my brothers'll make you wish you'd never been born.'

'That's all I get?' Sadie's breath was knocked out of her. 'A threat? Not even the smallest apology?'

'Why bother?' Cher was framed by the scarred, heavy door of her block. 'It's window dressing. Bottom line, your mates were proved right and you can't employ me any longer. End of.'

'I trusted you, Cher. Doesn't that mean something?'

Cher's mouth worked as if she was trying to chew

something hard and obnoxious. Softly, as if sharing a secret, she said, 'It means everything.'

Triggered by the suffering on Cher's face, Sadie's arms went out.

Cher fell into the embrace. She spoke wildly, her nose running onto Sadie's shoulder. 'I didn't grow up like you. I grew up in Wonderland, with everything upside down and the wrong way round. Stealing's good. Lying's clever. Winning's all that matters. If there's a knock on the door, grab your baseball bat. I'm a soldier not a daughter. The family reputation protected me but Sadie!' Cher pulled back and she shook her boss. 'Where's the shield to protect me against your disgust? You taught me about being human and then meeting Jez blew my mind. But I'm not right inside. There's something dirty in me. Jez can't be around crims. He's an addict. He could relapse. He built his life with his two hands, not his fists.' Her mouth widened into an 'O' of sympathy. 'Look at you, you silly moo, you're crying for me!'

Sadie wiped her face with the back of her hand. 'We can fix this.'

'I don't want to.' Cher stepped back. 'I need my family. Tell Jez he's off the hook.'

'I'll tell him no such thing!' Sadie's mind raced. How could she save somebody who didn't want to save themselves?

She's like me on one of my binges.

'When my brothers say they love me,' said Cher, backing away in her slippers and pushing at the stiff door of Orissa House, 'they mean they own me.' As if she had pebbles in her mouth, she pushed out the words. 'I love you, you know, boss lady.'

The door slammed.

WEEK SIXTEEN

To	Michael T. <qwertybookshop@hotmail.com>, Hero <hero.smith@u-turn.net>, Fiona J <filove@aol.com>, The Bobs <bob@bobscaff.co.uk>, Jez <jeremy.gray@u-turn.net>, Grace Esparza <Gracetheartist@gmail.com>, Sadie <sakuraspa@gmail.com>
From	Amber <amber@yummymummymews.net.co.uk>
Subject	CHERRY BLOSSOM MEWS RESIDENTS' ASSOCIATION MEETING

Hello!!!!!

It's my five-year anniversary on Instagram so please come dressed up so I can post a pic of us all looking AMAZING!

Date	Wednesday 5.9.18
Time	6.30 p.m.
Location	Yummy Mummy café & party emporium
Agenda	Unicorns and glitter and rainbows!

Please let Mary know! And about the dressing up!!!

Oodles of hugs

Amber

Hi all! Sorry to text at the eleventh hour but this is urgent – tonight's meeting at Amber's is CANCELLED! Sadie x

The first day without Cher, Sakura's computer rebelled and the fridge broke down, condemning the clients to tepid cucumber water. Nanas reacted to news of Cher's absence as if there'd been a death in the family. Fi managed to weave an 'I told you so' into every conversation.

'I've been on the phone *all day*,' grumbled Sadie, holding up a finger for Jez to wait as she answered its insistent trill once again. 'Hi, thanks for getting back to me.' Not a prospective customer or somebody asking if she'd been mis-sold PPI, it was the Children's Orthopaedic department at St Mary's Hospital. 'I need to make an appointment for my daughter . . . Amelia McQueen . . . fourth of November, 2011 . . . She had a pin put in her leg for a serious fracture three years ago and I'm worried that her limp's getting worse.'

Jez hung about patiently and asked sympathetic questions

when Sadie put the phone down, but she knew why he was there. 'Cher still not picking up?'

'If you see her, tell her I want to talk.'

'She's a very confused woman.'

'I could help, if she'd let me.'

The ripples of Cher's departure reached Teddy. 'When's she coming back?'

'Not sure.' A maternal white lie for a child who'd already lost too many people.

The window cleaner was outraged, asking where 'the sexy girl' was. '*She* always has enough cash to pay me,' he huffed, as Sadie emptied the till and still came up short.

'Keep your knickers on.' Riding to the rescue, Fi rummaged in her bag for her purse. 'I got cash out of a hole-in-the-wall this morning, babes, I'll lend it to you.'

Sadie held out her hand, relieved.

'I must have been mistaken.' Fi's purse was empty. 'Sorry.'

Sadie forgot about the window cleaner's plight. 'You don't make mistakes like that,' she said. 'History's repeating itself.'

'Cole would never nick from my purse.' Fi dusted an imaginary fleck of dust from her tunic. 'You must be superfit by now, all the jumping to conclusions you do.'

With Cher AWOL there was never a moment to take Fi aside and deliver the pep talk Sadie had rehearsed. It was time for Fi to go cold turkey, to dropkick Cole into the same patch of scrub where her other bad lads had ended up. Fi had escaped before – she'd been, she claimed, crazy in love with Emanuel – and she could do it again.

Opening and closing drawers, searching for Sellotape, Sadie came upon the shoddy plastic cherry blossom lying against a roll of cotton wool.

Its artificiality rendered it wrong, but it looked as if it fitted in if you squinted. Like Cher. She had almost fitted in, too. Sadie slammed the drawer shut.

'Mummy!' called Teddy, skipping in from the mews. 'Was Daddy your one true love?'

'Yes,' said Sadie. Immediately. With conviction. The truth was more nuanced, but seven-year-olds don't need nuance, they need certainty. 'Mummy's busy, darling, so . . .'

Teddy went on. 'I asked Mary if you can have more than one true love and she said you only need one. Fi! Will you play with me and Barbie?' She brandished the punked-up doll.

'Maybe later, babes.' Fi never ignored her goddaughter; even this refusal was accompanied by a quick squeeze. 'I've got boring grown-up chores to do.'

'Now!' Teddy clapped her hands.

'Like I said, Teddy.' Fi was patient. 'Give me a while and then we'll—'

Teddy threw the doll. It struck Fi in the face.

Teddy hurled her anger into the shocked silence. 'You're horrible!'

Sadie pursed her lips, summoning calm in order to send her daughter away to think about what she'd said.

Fi took a different tack. 'You could have knocked my eye out, Teddy! You're a very, very rude girl.'

'You're rude!' shrieked Teddy. 'Play with me! Now!'

'Don't talk to me like that, madam,' said Fi, with heat. 'I'm your friend, not your servant.'

Teddy burst into tears. Confused, self-hating tears; Sadie recognised them as she'd often shed them.

As the child thumped up the stairs, Sadie turned on Fi. 'There's no need to talk to her like that! We're supposed to say she did a rude thing, not that *she's* rude.'

'She threw the sodding Barbie at my face!' Fi rubbed the red patch on her cheek. 'I didn't have time to check the nearest childcare manual.'

'You know what she's been through. Any bad behaviour is just acting out.'

Fi's chin went up. A bad sign. 'Teddy's running the show. She's a kid, Sadie, not a piece of china. You can tell her off without breaking her.'

'Don't you get it? My daughter's already broken.'

Upstairs, Teddy was a sobbing hump in her bed.

'Fi hates me,' she stammered through a barrage of snot. Then, haughty, albeit still snotty, 'And I hate her.'

'Nobody hates anybody in this house,' said Sadie. 'I'll make you a smoothie.'

As the blender – newly bought, a symbol of the McQueens' rebirth – whirred, Sadie's attention drifted to the sitting room, to where she'd moved the cardboard box, all wrapped in red paper, to a new home by the television.

The box seemed to pound, its colour deepening. Sadie approached it, a small truth dawning. Bending, she peeked into the jagged slit.

'Fi!' called Sadie, flying down the stairs with the box.

Fi was arch after their spat. '*What* is that?'

'It's a postbox.' It was so obvious. 'It's a bloody postbox!' Sadie pulled open the top and an avalanche of cards poured out onto the shiny spa floor.

'Should we . . .' Fi was undecided. 'Even kids are entitled to their privacy.'

'If there was a court of parents' rights,' said Sadie, 'the judge would rule in our favour. These cards can give us an insight into her feelings.'

With respect and full-to-bursting hearts, they dipped into the heap and took one each. They frowned as they deciphered the childish writing.

'This is too much.' Fi laid her card face down. 'She wrote this when she thought you'd abandoned her.'

'Read it to me. Please.' Sadie steeled herself to wade through the arc of her daughter's loneliness and confusion.

'"Dear Mummy and Daddy,"' Fi swallowed, and Sadie found herself loving her all the more for her marshmallowy tenderness. '"Please watch me when I fall asleep 'cos that's when I miss you worst."'

'Listen to this, Fi. "Dear Mummy and Daddy, when I get married to Justin Bieber I won't have my mummy and daddy there which is not fair and mean of God."'

Along with the fear and the grief, the ungrammatical scraps told a story. Using the improvement in Teddy's writing and spelling to guide them, plus the big dates like birthdays and Christmas, they built a rough timeline.

'She's getting stronger,' whispered Sadie.

'She bloody is, the little belter!'

There were mentions of helping Granny cope, of making Granny laugh. There was a desire to 'talk to Granny about you, Mummy and Daddy' which went unheeded.

The love never wavered. For Sadie. For Jack. For Merle. It glittered in every line.

'Look.' Fi pointed at a card in the snaking line they'd made. 'This is addressed to just "Daddy". That's the point where you found her.' Fi paused. Crumpled up her mouth before she could quote from the card. 'She says you're back and you've had a haircut, and she tells Jack she'll look after you for him.'

'All this time,' said Sadie, 'I thought I've been looking after *her*.'

The next card that leapt to her hand contained the sentence that had dogged Sadie since she first read it.

Reading it in context, with the rest of the postcard, knocked the wind out of Sadie.

I thought you were talking to Merle, darling.

Sadie's life folded over and in on itself. She'd been so wrong.

Dear Daddy

Me again.

I wish I still lived with you and Mummy in our old house now we live in a weerd flat. I have my own room. the wardrobe smells. I miss Granny. I miss you. I am a tiny bit worried that Mummy is in romantic love with a man. She keeps putting on lip gloss. he makes good fart noises but I won't let myself like him.

Don't worry I still love you the best.

love Teddy xxxxxxxxxxxx

'You okay?' Fi bent to look at Sadie's face.

'I'm good.' Sadie wiped her eyes, stood up shakily. 'Tell you what though: Teddy talks far more openly to Jack than she does to me.'

'What I don't understand,' said Fi, slowly, 'is why Merle brought all these round. I mean, that was . . .' Fi looked confused. '*Nice* of her.'

'Letting Teddy write these cards was nice, too. Emotionally astute. Empathetic, even.' Sadie found this evidence of Merle's humanity troubling. 'She loves her, Fi. Merle really loves her granddaughter.'

A door opening upstairs set them scrabbling to put away the cards.

Bursting through the door, Teddy sprinted to Fi. 'I'm sorry.'

Fi put her hand beneath Teddy's chin and raised her face. 'We're good, kiddo. We always will be.'

The phone rang and rang. A bored looking woman waited to pay for her head massage. A postman loitered, holding a package.

Sadie scampered to the desk. She cut off the phone call, gave the woman the wrong change, and signed for the parcel with her left hand.

'Can I help you?' She raised her head to the next in line.

'You really need a new receptionist,' said Hero.

'Is this your new hobby? Stating the bleedin' obvious? Oh, and good morning. Sorry. My manners fell off about an hour ago.'

'Can Bo help?' Even Hero didn't seem sure of his offer. They both watched Bo clamber up onto the recycling bin.

'I need a pro,' said Sadie.

I need Cher.

Every workplace is a family.

'If only she wasn't a lying kleptomaniac,' said Sadie.

'You miss her.' Hero fiddled with the edge of a pamphlet on non-surgical facelifts. 'Despite what she did.'

'That seems to be my karma.'

'Missing people? How's it working out for you?' There was a challenge in Hero's comment. A criticism, too, of how Jack's gooseberry ghost had forced them apart.

'It's working out fine, Hero,' she said. 'And you're fine. We're all fine, so happy endings all round.'

'How do you know I'm fine?'

Bo crashing into the bin distracted them, and saved Sadie from responding.

'Ouch,' said Hero as his son picked himself up and dusted himself down.

'Bo's interesting,' said Sadie. The boy had a watchful, slightly resentful air that hinted at darker depths. She saw how Hero watched him. Warily. As if watching an exotic animal that he wasn't entirely sure how to care for. 'You're a hugger, Hero. Why don't you hug Bo more?'

'Good question. You get to the heart of things, don't you?'

'Yup.'

They regarded each other. Sadie's brain raced. She might read a lot into that look if she chose to.

'Bo lives in a fragile ecosystem over there in la-la land,' said Hero. 'Zizzi moves guys in and out. As the years pass, they get closer in age to him.' Hero sighed. 'The kid needs continuity and stability. He needs a parent, not a mate.'

'A cuddle every now and then won't hurt.'

'My training taught me to go carefully.'

'Oh, Hero, nobody trains you to be a dad!'

'I should get on.'

He got on, and Sadie watched him walk away. She liked watching him walk; he was good at it.

A client, dripping with trendy must-haves, her style laid-back and expensive, asked, 'Can I hire you to do an at-home massage? I have a friend who needs some TLC.'

'What a lovely idea.' Sadie asked for the friend's name and address.

'It's very handy for you,' smiled the woman. 'She lives right over there. Above Yummy Mummy.'

Lugging a folding massage table across the cobbles, Sadie turned down Grace's offer of help. 'You're busy enough as it is.'

Up a ladder, knocking hooks into crumbling brick, Grace was garlanded with fairy lights. She had already wound a string of bulbs around the trunk of the cherry blossom tree. 'We'll soon be looking all Mediterranean,' she promised.

Mrs Bob, who didn't offer to help but who did laugh at Sadie's struggles, said, 'Don't make Amber too relaxed. She's hosting the residents' meeting in a couple of hours.'

'I'm sure she'll be up to the arduous task of setting out chairs and biccies,' huffed Sadie.

Bo raced up to her. 'Dad told me not to take no for an answer,' he said, taking the table from her. The blue in his hair was fading. The blue in his eyes was as bright as ever. 'Allow me, *madame*.' He bowed.

Sadie laughed. 'Thank you, kind sir.' She liked the otherness of Bo. His surf-tinged accent. His loose American vibe.

Amber's living quarters, above the colourful, rose-scented shop were painted dark chalky colours Sadie recognised from magazine peeks into stars' homes. Moody. Sensual. Rooms unfolded, filled with charming clutter. All carefully set out, very far from Mary's hoarded mess.

'Amber? It's Sadie. You shouldn't leave your door open.'

Peacock feathers in a luminescent vase. Vast old mirrors. An art deco armchair.

And everywhere pictures of the owner. Softly lit. Laughing with friends.

Sadie felt less feminine, less desirable with every step she took into Amber's silk and velvet cave. She sent Bo off, and imagined Hero carrying Amber through this temple to the senses. She imagined him comparing it to the austerity of her own home.

'Amber?' She would do her duty, give her neighbour an excellent massage, then get the hell out and maybe give tonight's meeting a miss.

A little bit of Amber goes a long way.

A parlour, the curtains drawn, the darkness studded with tea lights, was at the back of the flat.

On a carefully ripped Chesterfield sofa sat Amber. Her legs folded beneath her, she was wrapped in a rug. She rocked back and forth.

'Hi,' said Sadie.

There was something off. Sadie felt a prickle of unease.

Amber didn't look at her. Her phone was right up to her eyes. She stabbed a finger at it. 'Look at this bitch! Doesn't she *eat*?'

Sadie caught a glimpse of a social media feed.

'And her! She's vile, everybody knows that, but she's with *him*, and he's loaded and he's mad about her and he has a house in Monte Carlo.' Amber looked directly at Sadie. Melted mascara made a raccoon of her. Her nose was red. She had been crying. Or drinking. Perhaps both. She shrieked suddenly. 'Monte fucking Carlo!'

'Amber, why don't we—'

'What's the time?' Frantic, Amber interrupted her. 'Shit! I have to post, Sadie. I have to post. I have to post.'

This phrase spilled out of her bitten lips over and over as she dropped the rug and ran to the mirror over the fireplace. She scrabbled at her face, pushing blusher over her cheeks, rubbing balm into her lips, so hard that Sadie winced.

'Amber, let's sit down and take a minute.'

'I don't have a minute!' roared Amber. 'I have to post.'

A forcefield of mania surrounded her. Sadie dropped her massage table, but Amber didn't register the noise. 'Listen—'

'How do I look?' Amber turned a ruined face to Sadie. There was lipstick on her nose. 'Here goes.'

A transformation took place. The craziness retreated. Amber's features softened. Her lips curved with wry sweetness. She held her phone high and, head back, lost herself in its electronic eye.

Flash. Flash. Flash.

'Hmm.' Amber flicked through the images. 'No. No. Christ, no. Maybe. Maybe.' Up went the phone again. More starbursts of light. Amber eerily carefree.

Sadie had no idea that Amber's photographs went through such violent birthing pangs. She jumped when Amber seemed to notice her. She addressed Sadie with a hiss.

'Do you know how many followers @marthaprecious has? *Do you?*' Amber poked a violent finger at Sadie's collarbone.

'Who is she?' stuttered Sadie.

'*Who is she?*' Amber was outraged. 'She's who I should be. Sixty thousand followers. Two thousand likes for a picture of a dog with a hat on. Brand ambassador for Adora scented candles. Adora are *so* me, that's a travesty of justice.' She was off, skittering around the room, viewing her surroundings through the lens. 'Maybe here, in front of the bookshelf.'

Again, the metamorphosis. Eyes creased into merriment, as if Sadie had just told a brilliant joke. Again, the checking and cursing. 'No. No. Shit.'

'Sit, please. I'm here to give you a lovely soothing massage.' Sadie couldn't imagine massaging those jumping limbs.

'I can't run a stupid fucking café all my life!' yelled Amber, as if Sadie had insisted she do just that. She was off again, circling in her bare feet. Snapping constantly, unaware that her make-up was grotesque. 'There's always somebody prettier, newer, younger.' She glared at Sadie, suddenly stock still. 'I need to matter.'

'You do matter.' Sadie tried to break through. 'We all matter, Amber. We don't have to be young or pretty or—'

'Bullshit!' screamed Amber. 'Look!' She held up the phone.

Sadie saw a cute thumbnail of Amber. Head on one side. Tasselled scarf around her hair. 'You look lovely.'

'I look old!' Something gave way in Amber. She fell to her knees.

Taking advantage of the fact that Amber's energy was taken up by her sobs, Sadie manoeuvred her to the sofa. 'Here. Put your head in my lap. If I do say so myself, my head massages are famed all over the world. Well, all over the mews.'

The sobs slowed. Tears dried on Amber's face. She quietened, and Sadie began to murmur as she worked her fingers in Amber's hair.

'That's better. Everything's all right. We'll get through this together. You're good, Amber.' Sadie explored Amber's skull, roaming over its bumps and dips and leaving warmth in her wake. 'Your poor old brain, it works so hard. Your head deserves a bit of attention, doesn't it?' Sadie tenderly touched the scars behind the ears, where Amber's skin had been lifted. She moved to Amber's face, and delicately worked on the altered nose, the cheeks plumped with filler.

Sadie lifted one of Amber's arms. She kneaded it through the filmy sleeve. 'Such strength. All your muscles,' she murmured, 'all your limbs, all of them healthy and strong.' She was calming herself as much as Amber, reminding them both that bodies are not just there to be looked at, and certainly not to be judged. 'Your body looks after you, doesn't it? And now we're repaying the compliment.'

There was a sense of Amber floating back to her after a turbulent storm out at sea. Madness to imagine that Sadie could undo a lifetime of conditioning with one quiet interlude, but it was a start. Amber judged herself only on her beauty. Furthermore, she was using the bonkers standards of the internet, standards that made Kardashians lie down and weep.

'That feels so good.' Amber was almost asleep as Sadie eased herself out from under her and moved down to work on Amber's legs.

'Thank you, legs,' said Sadie, feeling slightly ludicrous. 'Thank you, feet. You keep us rooted.'

'Thank you, feet,' murmured Amber. Then, like a rifle shot ruining a sunny day, she said, 'Must do a post on my feet.'

'Ssh.'

'Where's my phone?' Amber half rose.

Gently, Sadie pressed her back among the cushions. 'Not now. We're busy. Sink back, Amber. Give yourself up to me.'

Amber didn't quibble.

Sadie worked on every inch of Amber. Sending kindness into her body like a vitamin shot. She felt Amber unclench. She felt her limbs lengthen, her spirit uncoil.

The massage helped Sadie, too. All the effort she put in came back to her. She was sharing her energy. Sharing her strength. Amber needed positivity; the real thing, not filtered perfection.

'Bed,' Sadie said firmly, when she'd finished.

Amber leaned on Sadie.

She's so thin.

Amber verged on frail, as if she'd been ill. 'In you go.' Sadie tucked the vintage coverlet in. 'You need a good night's rest. I'll cancel the meeting.'

'My phone,' whispered Amber, like a naughty child asking for chocolate. 'Please.'

'Take one night off.'

'I have to see what @ambertragiclondon's been saying about me.' Amber sat up, nerves jangling again.

'Ignore that rubbish.' Sadie, matron-like, pinned Amber in place. 'It doesn't matter.'

'It's all that matters on the internet.' Amber gave up. She fell back. 'Thank you,' she said.

'My pleasure.' Sadie waited until Amber fell asleep and then crept out of the flat.

@ambertragiclondon *had* posted. It didn't make Sadie laugh.

Typing a hurried text to the mewsites about that evening's meeting, Sadie examined her feelings about Amber. She'd always found the woman's shallowness off-putting, but if she was honest – not easy, but doable – it was Amber's closeness to Hero that had turned Sadie against her.

That was beneath me.

Amber needed help. Amber thought she needed to be envied, but she needed to be loved.

Just like everybody else.

Sadie liked to entertain the notion that she'd been drawn to London in order to find Teddy, but the truth felt simpler.

I was drawn here because of everybody in Cherry Blossom Mews.

They needed each other, each and every one of them.

'Mummy.' Teddy had crept up behind her.

Sadie jumped. 'Darling!'

'Did I scare you?'

'A bit.' Sadie wanted to hold her daughter to her, but she didn't quite dare. Teddy was still opaque, partly hidden from view. She recalled her advice to Hero, and applied it to herself. 'Come here.'

The hug was short; Teddy wriggled. It was, however, sublime.

'Can I watch half an hour of something?'

'If you jump into your nightie first, sweetie.' Sadie hauled out her laptop, but the accounts spreadsheet couldn't hold her attention. She wondered, instead, about all that Teddy had left behind at Merle's.

The walled garden. The playroom. The candy-striped blinds that matched the duvet on Teddy's custom-built bed.

The postcards Teddy wrote were all about feelings.

Not one reference to things. This messy mews, on a fly-blown high street, had all Teddy needed. It was clear, as sudden and as welcome as a rainbow after a summer downpour.

This flat has all Teddy needs because it has me.

Sadie turned and saw Teddy sprawled on the sofa, TV already blaring the garish colours of kids' programming. 'Nightie first!'

'No,' glowered Teddy.

'We had a deal.' Sadie kept her tone light. 'Go on, Teddy. Nightie, please.'

'You're just being annoying,' said Teddy, as if Sadie was a dim-witted servant. 'Shut up, Mummy.'

Sadie counted to ten. Or tried to. She only got to five. Still light, but firm with it, she picked up the remote control, and the gaudy screen died.

Teddy was shocked to her core. 'Mummy!'

'That was a very rude thing to say.'

'Put the telly on!'

'Get up those stairs and put your nightie on *right this minute*, Miss Teddy McQueen.'

'You're horrid,' squealed Teddy, scooting out of the room.

Secretly, Sadie agreed with her. Sometimes mums have to be horrid.

A man, an unexpected figure, was out on the mews. Sadie hurried down to intercept him as he executed a long slow circuit of the cherry tree.

It was so good to see him that Sadie could only say his name. 'Bob!'

'Me again, like a bad penny.' Bob motioned to the pup on the end of a lead. 'I'm doing my bit for Mary. He's a bonny little mutt.'

Thin and hungry-looking, Bob was like a bad etching of his true self, with dark scratchy lines beneath his eyes. She wouldn't ask how he was; it was plain to see, and surely he was tired of answering that question.

In the window over the caff, a curtain dropped. Mrs Bob was keeping an eye.

He probably refused her help.

'I've had a tough day, Bob. Will you walk me, as well as Noel?'

He didn't demur when she slotted her arm through his. They were in a joint fantasy, that they were just two folk out for a stroll, when they both knew that Bob was discreetly leaning on Sadie.

'I miss fresh air.' Bob chopped the sentence into manageable parts.

'You can sense autumn coming on the breeze.' The same breeze that had spirited Teddy home.

'Soon be time for Teddy to go back to school.' The words staggered out of Bob's mouth. They paused for a moment, both of them pretending they were letting Noel VII sniff the tree roots.

'I'm nervous,' admitted Sadie. The McQueens' strange story would be the talk of the school gates.

'Teddy'll be fine. She's such a funny little kid. Asked the wife if she believed everybody only got one true love the other day. You can imagine what my missus said. "*Still waiting for mine.*"' They began their slow progress again. 'Maybe it's you we should be worried about?'

It struck Sadie that Bob might not see Christmas. 'She hates me right now.'

'I hated my mum,' said Bob. 'The same way I hate the

wife. That is to say, I hate her as much as I love her, which is an awful lot. That's families for you.' Bob's face lost what little colour it had, but he blinked away Sadie's mew of concern. 'Sadie, you will look out for my poor lady when I'm gone, won't you?' He shook his head – it took some effort – when she tried to pooh-pooh him. 'Please. We both know she'll be alone soon, and she's bad at asking for help.'

'We'll all help, Bob. It won't be easy. I don't know if you've noticed, but she's a bit spiky.'

'She is!' Bob's laugh was a sandpaper wheeze. 'I'll hang on as long as I can. I aim to see that place finished.' He nodded at a tall house opposite the mews, scaffolding hugging it tight. Now in the throes of redevelopment, it had been four floors of miserable bedsits. 'I've lain in bed watching them take it apart, and I want to . . . to . . .'

Sadie powered down until Bob could speak again.

'I want to see it all spick and span and nice again.'

Because Bob didn't want to hear any nonsense about how he'd be around a lot longer than that, Sadie held back from saying so. 'I hope you get to see it, Bob.'

They stood and looked at the house. It floated in the darkness, half done, untidy.

'What's that?' Sadie saw a diamond flash of light on the third floor.

'Just headlights glancing off glass.'

There's no glass in those windows.

Sadie knew what it was. 'Come on, Bob. You've worn out poor Noel. Let's get him home.'

Sadie had a call to make.

After Sadie found the number and had the conversation, she drifted to the kitchen. Toast was made, and crunched without being tasted. By this time tomorrow, there would be a seismic shift in the mews.

Super alert since the break-in, Sadie took fright at a noise in the hall until she recognised the skittery tread of her daughter. Teddy tiptoed into the sitting room, then emerged a moment later and was back up the stairs in a trice.

Sadie wiped her mouth, and stood, arms folded, contemplating the postbox.

She decided against it. Any further correspondence was between Teddy and Jack.

Dear Daddy

guess what? We're getting back to normal! Mummy just called me Miss Teddy McQueen for the very first time since i came home.

Whats a troma? Mummy said i have one

love teddy xxxxxxx

WEEK SEVENTEEN

Dear Residents

Blah blah blah MOBuk Wednesday 12th September 6.30 p.m. blah blah blah biscuits blah blah blah no agenda because we always ignore it blah blah blah

Regards,

Mary (and Noel VII)

It was too early to go knocking on a neighbour's door, but this couldn't wait.

When Hero undid all the locks made necessary by the postcode, his eyes were sleep-small. The grit of irritation in his voice as he said, 'Yeah? What is it, Sadie?' brought home to her that she didn't have the free pass she once had.

There was a time when he'd have yanked me through the door and kissed my face off.

'I need to speak to Bo.'

'Bo?' Hero was incredulous. 'Look, it's early, why not—'

'Now,' said Sadie.

The sofa was dwarfed by Hero and his son, both of them long in the limb and given to sprawling. Hero, in his boxers, placed a protective arm along the back of the sofa. Bo rubbed sleep out of his eyes.

Hero's face grew more and more stony. Bo didn't once lift his eyes as Sadie unwrapped her tale and lay it in front of them.

'The name of the security firm refurbishing the house

opposite,' she was saying, 'was on a banner tied to the scaffolding. I found them on the internet, called, explained, and they were amazingly helpful.'

Digital footage from the CCTV camera Sadie had spotted in the windowless house hit her inbox within minutes. Labelled '18.8.18', it made for compelling viewing.

'The camera's trained on the front path of the house, but it also catches Cherry Blossom's gates.'

'And . . . ?' Hero frowned.

Bo said nothing.

'And,' said Sadie, 'it filmed the thieves leaving the mews.'

'The Mogg brothers, right?'

'Dead right.' The twins, black and white and jerky, were seen loading the bulky ultrasonic unit into the back of a small van. 'But no Cher. The person helping them was you, Bo.'

'Nah.' Bo shook his head.

'You're mistaken, Sadie,' said Hero. 'This is serious, you shouldn't—'

Bushed after a sleepless night, Sadie handed him a printout. 'That's Bo,' she said. No triumph, only disappointment and a jaded acceptance of the bomb she'd detonated. 'Bo has access to your keys. Possibly, Cher wasn't involved at all.'

Silence fell. Eventually, Hero said, 'Bo, mate, what've you got to say?'

'You should have bought me a skateboard,' mumbled Bo.

'But your mum sent you the money for that.' A visible jolt went through Hero. 'Or did she? You mean, this was to buy a *skateboard*?'

'I need my skateboard.' Bo was almost inaudible. 'You don't understand. I can't live without it, man.'

Sadie assumed Hero was thinking what she was thinking: Bo wasn't accustomed to waiting for what he wanted.

'I couldn't get hold of Mom. She's in the desert with some shaman. So I went on Instagram, said my board was broke, but I could tell from the comment Mum left that it's her dumb assistant running her account while she's away. *You* wouldn't give me the cash.'

Hero nobly ignored this classic teen counter-argument.

'I mean, jeez!' Bo warmed up, believing his justification. 'I never see my dad and he denies me this one little thing!'

'Three hundred pounds is a lot of money.'

'Crap, Hero,' sneered Bo. 'Your folks live in a frickin' *palace*.'

Hero said only, '*Our* folks, Bo.'

'I know from cop shows that businesses always have insurance. Sadie isn't *poor* or anything, so I thought it'd be a win/win if I took her new gear and sold it. I could buy a skateboard and Sadie could get something even nicer with the payout.'

'How do you know I'm not "poor or anything"?' said Sadie. 'That's a hell of an assumption, Bo.'

'I don't know, I just . . .' Bo didn't have an answer. 'Sorry,' he said.

That doesn't sound like a tactical apology.

Although Sadie's pre-teens were far behind her, she could recall its muddy thought processes. She was appalled by Bo in roughly the same measure as she felt sorry for him. The boy was so accustomed to instant gratification that he had stepped unthinkingly over a glaring red line. Bo was at a crossroad.

He needs his dad more than ever right now.

Bo explained in fits and starts. It hadn't been difficult to work out who to approach. 'Those guys, the twins, they're always hanging around. Plus, you told me not to go near them, so . . .' They had already groomed Bo, asked about his accent, asked if he needed any 'pills or sniff or anything'.

'And you said?' A muscle in Hero's jaw ticked.

'I told them I'm a vegan,' laughed Bo. 'I don't do drugs, okay? When I needed to get money, I told the twins about this amazing new equipment, that I could open the gates, and they were, like, yeah, cool. It was exciting.' Bo saw how badly that went down and sighed. 'Sorry, but it was. Like a movie. Opening up in the dark. It was awesome, the way they broke into the spa, and then they handed me three hundred pounds in cash. It was simple.'

The ultrasonic massage unit would fetch three times that, even on the black market.

They screwed you too, Bo.

'I felt good. Like a boss. Until the next day, when I saw Sadie.' Bo looked directly at her from under his wilting hair. 'You were, like, so sad.'

'I felt violated.'

'It wasn't funny anymore,' said Bo. 'That's why I tried to help, you know? You were unhappy and it wasn't like TV.'

Hero sat forward, elbows on knees, head in hands. 'Was Cher involved at all?'

'Jeez, yeah,' said Bo. 'She's *tough*.'

Sadie's heart, which she thought couldn't wilt any further, managed to droop some more.

'Cher found out about it. Said she'd chop my balls off and feed them to me.'

'Wait, she wasn't involved in the actual robbery?' Sadie's heart – exhausted by all this wilting and drooping – rallied.

'No! She was furious. She spotted the stolen equipment in the twins' . . . what's it called? A lock-up.'

A deal had been brokered by Cher, whereby the twins returned the machine and Bo gave the brothers his skateboard. 'They weren't happy about it,' said Bo, which sounded to Sadie like a magnificent understatement. 'Cher told me I had one day to put things right or she'd snitch on me. Gave me a real talking to. Said she didn't want to ruin my relationship with Hero. Said she wished she had family like that, who looked out for her in the right way.'

Bo nodded at Sadie. 'She went on about *you*. Yakking about how you try so hard to make things right for everybody else, that you don't deserve this and that kinda thing.' Bo sat back, depleted by his soliloquy. 'Said she'd stab me if I told anybody about her part in it and now I guess she will.'

'Cher sacrificed her job for you, Bo,' said Sadie. 'Well, for you and your dad. She's not going to stab you.'

Hero was dour, spent, all his energy drained out through his toes. 'There have to be consequences for this, Bo.'

'Just use the proper words! It's not *consequences*, it's punishment.' Bo sprang up. 'It's cool, Hero, I'll pack. Just send me home and you needn't bother with me ever again. If I was some perfect kid this might work, but nobody expects you to look after a little shit who isn't even your real son.'

Hero watched him slouch out of the room. His mouth hung open in shock.

'He knows,' said Sadie, horrified.

'Should I go to him?' asked Hero, dazed.

'Shit, yes!' Hero was overthinking. Sadie recognised the caution, the winding of crime scene tape around each emotional milestone.

I've been doing that and it doesn't work.

'Hero, do you really need to ask? Run after him.'

Hero spoke as if he hadn't heard. 'Bo needs space to calm down. I need to digest this.' He was changed, older, saying under his breath, 'He knows . . .'

'I should . . .' Sadie stood up. She'd unleashed a typhoon in Hero's home.

'Why would Zizzi tell him? I can't fathom it.'

'Seriously?' Sadie sat again, thinking, *Men!* 'It's very, very fathom-able. Revenge! You divorced her, Hero. You told Zizzi, in black and white legalese, that you didn't want her. She lashed out, and she's not emotionally mature enough to protect Bo from the fall-out. Telling Bo he's not your biological child was her selfish way of hurting *you*.' She hesitated, straying onto swampy ground. 'People do strange things when they feel undervalued. Or when they're madly jealous.' She swallowed. 'I should know. I'd never normally laugh at something like @ambertragiclondon, but I joined in with the sniggering.'

'Why?' asked Hero. 'It's bullying, pure and simple.'

Full disclosure.

'Because I was madly, crazily jealous.' Sadie steeled herself and jumped in at the freezing deep end. 'You and Amber, getting together, it curdled my blood.' She pushed on, past his rolled eyes. 'It was so *soon*, Hero. I spotted you in her festival Instagram story and I flipped. Don't get me wrong, I'm not asking for details, okay? You have no obligation to tell me what it really is, how far you've gone, whether it's serious, whatever. It's cool. It's my problem not yours; you can do what you want – you're a free agent – but I thought we had, well, *something*, not something you could name perhaps, but *something*, so when you immediately found someone else . . .' She distilled it down to its essence. 'Like I said, I was jealous.'

'Is it my go now?' Waiting for her to nod, Hero seemed balanced between anger and amusement. 'There's stuff you don't know.'

'And I don't want to know it.'

'Well, tough,' said Hero. 'Amber's an addict. Like you and me. Only not to alcohol. She's addicted to social media.'

'Oh, come off it.'

'It's a real thing, Sadie.' Hero seemed disappointed in her. Again.

Sadie remembered how Amber had babbled the day before, rocking, crying. 'Sorry. That was flippant.'

'She's a classic case. There's been an American study carried out on the Five-Factor Personality Model.' Hero counted them off on his fingers. 'Neuroticism. Extraversion . . .' He seemed to hear himself, and stopped. 'I'll stick to layman's terms. Amber needs the constant validation of likes and retweets and comments. Needs them like you and I used to need that shot of booze. The study concluded that breaking the social media habit may actually be tougher than giving up drinking.'

'If that's the case, we're headed for an epidemic.'

'I'm starting to see sufferers at U-Turn. One guy sets his alarm so he can wake up every two hours to check Twitter.'

'My Twitter feed's full of cats wearing scarves,' said Sadie.

'Yours is normal,' said Hero. 'Amber's isn't. Her online presence is her life.' He described how Amber subsisted on the thin gruel doled out by the internet. How her core group of real friends had fallen away, tired of having to 'look happy' for an audience they would never meet. 'She travels in a pack of similar-minded people, all of them hollowed out by their need for attention from strangers. Amber seeks out attractive people, as if that's the most important criteria for a mate. She snaps, snaps, snaps, then sits up till the small hours curating her account and liking other accounts and seething at people's stats. Even though she fabricates ninety per cent of the so-called fun on her posts, she believes everyone else's. Amber thinks the whole world's having a ball except her.'

'They're probably doing the same thing. Obsessing, comparing themselves.'

'Exactly. Didn't you notice Amber's lights staying on all night?'

I was too busy looking over at yours.

'I assumed she was partying with funky emerging pop stars.'

'Amber goes to parties, but she doesn't let her hair down. She's too busy feeling worthless, insubstantial, frantically chasing the next Instagrammable moment.'

'In other words, the opposite of what she projects.'

'Nobody's as happy as Amber's Instagram feed. It's not possible. I've been trying to help . . .' Hero scratched his head. Scowled. Stood up abruptly. 'I should go to my boy,' he said.

Cher slotted into place behind the reception desk. 'That's better,' she said. There was a softness to her, as if she'd shed a skin. 'I missed this place.' As if to atone for such mush, she added, 'I didn't miss *you*, Fi.'

'Yes, you did,' said Fi. 'I have a little speech.'

'God, please no speeches.' Cher grimaced.

'Sorry, love, you've got no choice.'

The row of nanas on their soft seating nudged each other. 'I love a speech, me,' said one.

'I misjudged you,' said Fi. 'I was wrong and I'm sorry. Welcome back.'

Cher blinked, waggled her head. She had no idea how to deal with a sincere apology. 'Can we just get back to normal?'

'Excellent idea.' Sadie was all a-bustle. 'Email my last client and tell her she left her phone here, and then get onto the suppliers about the new paper towels.'

'Will do, boss lady.' Cher scribbled notes on her new pad. She had never before written anything down.

You've pulled your hair back.

It suited her, but Sadie knew that wasn't why. This was turbocharged professional Cher. She wasn't going to waste her second chance. The skirt was – *crikey!* – calf length, and the fake tan was toned down from satsuma to peach. Sadie kept her voice low as she asked, 'Cher, why didn't you tell me the truth when I accused you?'

'When you grow up with my surname you know better than to argue with people's opinion of you.' Cher jerked one shoulder, as if that was neither here nor there. 'Besides, I made a deal with Bo.'

'As simple as that?'

'Some things are,' said Cher. She turned to face a new arrival. 'Good morning!' She took him in. 'Oh.'

'Yes, *oh*.' Jez's hands were on his hips. 'When were you going to tell me you're back at work?'

'You know now, dontcha?'

Jez's nostrils flared. His dark coils of hair were more Romany than ever. 'You're a useless girlfriend.' He rounded the desk and took her in his arms.

Sadie blushed witnessing what was not just a kiss, but a full-on snog.

Cher staggered backwards when he let her go.

'See you at six,' said Jez over his shoulder.

'Yeah,' said Cher faintly.

The nanas cheered.

Cherry Blossom Mews looked the same to the untrained eye. Sadie's eye was trained; she knew what was going on behind all the flowerboxes.

Over at U-Turn, Bo came and sheepishly went. She was due to sit with him and Hero soon to discuss his crime's 'consequences'. Mary went in and out, like a weathervane, chauffeured daily to and from Streamside. MOBuk was neglected, its tetchy WE'RE CLOSED! sign constantly in the window. Bob was a rumour only; that walk with Noel VII was the last time he'd been spotted in the wild. Sadie made good her promise to help out in the caff whenever she could, and she watched Mrs Bob turn gradually to stone as Bob's end drew nearer and nearer.

And then there was Amber. A gaggle of stylish gal pals were running the Yummy Mummy. Badly. They were helpless in the face of the many-levered coffee machine. Amber herself was a ghost at her bedroom window. Her Instagram lay neglected, like a house after war.

Sadie looked over at Yummy Mummy as she downed a hasty cuppa between clients. The fairy lights that followed the curve of its windows were just so many blind eyes. Grace's hard work had been for nothing: the bulbs that covered the mews sputtered on at dusk, then sputtered off again. Behind Sadie, Fi, who had declared a weight loss of five pounds, sidestepped the biscuits and said, 'Let's see what @ambertragiclondon's been up to.'

'Nah.' Sadie shook herself, as if seeing off a swarm of flies. 'Let's not.'

Grace sidled in, biting her lip. Somebody rather small

stood behind her. 'We had a bit of an accident,' she said gingerly.

Teddy stepped out from behind Grace. There was gold dust in her hair, sprinkled over her nose like costly freckles, and lodged beneath her fingernails.

'The tin was on a high shelf and Teddy was reaching for some paintbrushes, and, well, you see the result.'

'I like it.' Sadie tapped the tip of her daughter's nose and Teddy relaxed. The child still expected to be ticked off for daft mishaps, *à la Merle*. 'You're my golden girl.'

'See?' Grace squatted down to Teddy's level with a smoothness that Sadie's thigh muscles envied. 'Told you your mum'd be cool.'

I'm a cool mum.

Sadie was done with mourning their suburban family-friendly lifestyle, and made peace with the fact that she and Teddy were an inner-city team. The little girl was already more independent, more confident; living opposite U-Turn would teach her compassion, and living near the Moggs' estate would teach her vigilance.

'Teddy says she's going to visit her granny.' Grace said this breezily, so that Teddy wouldn't perceive the loaded information she was passing to Sadie.

'Ooh, did she?' This was news to Sadie.

Teddy wrinkled her barely-there nose. 'I won't if you don't want me to, Mummy.'

'I'll make the arrangements, sweetie.' *She's trying to protect my feelings.* 'You do what's right for *you*, Teddy. Never tone down your emotions for somebody else.'

'Okay.' Teddy accepted this life lesson with nonchalance, skedaddling off to her room.

Her room was mayhem. Naked dolls akimbo on a slag-heap of juice packets, comics, drawing pads. Splayed books everywhere. Sadie no longer compared it to Merle's exquisite townhouse.

What's right for me is right for Teddy.

The nanas had dispersed in a cloud of scented oil. Cher had stepped into her heels and tottered off with Jez. Fi hadn't said goodbye as she left, too busy on a call, saying over and over, 'What's her name? I said, What. Is. Her. Name?'

Tired, Sadie was ready to shut down and decamp upstairs where somebody awaited her, a small somebody who would raise hell about getting in the bath, then raise hell about getting out of it.

'Knock knock,' said Hero, loitering outside. He looked about, noticed the dimmed lights, the spa being closed down for the night. 'Don't worry, it'll wait.'

'No, come in.' Sadie saw how his shoulders sloped. He was burdened.

And I still care.

Feelings are not faucets; Sadie couldn't turn off her

tenderness. 'Pull up an uncomfortable chair. Can I offer you an organic mint tea?'

'I can say this to you, and only you.' Hero winced. 'I'd kill for a scotch right now.'

'Ooh, dangerous.'

'Don't worry. I'm not about to slip off the wagon.' Hero paced. 'I just checked on Amber.'

'I've been looking in on her,' said Sadie. 'I gave her a head massage yesterday. I feel bad about laughing at @ambertragiclondon.'

'If I'm honest,' said Hero, wincing, 'I feel bad about making you feel bad.'

They both smiled at their readiness to feel bad.

'Hero, while we're clearing the air, laying our cards on the table and . . . that's all the metaphors I can think of for the moment, isn't there something you could tell me?'

Hero said nothing. Until, eventually he said, 'Like what?'

'If you're saying it's none of my business, then I accept that.' Sadie was disappointed; she had squared her shoulders to hear the Ballad of Hero and Amber, but he wasn't going to put her out of her misery. She knew it had started at the festival, but she didn't know *how.* 'One thing, though. How the hell have you managed not to pop up in Amber's Instagram or Twitter or whatever?' When he looked blank, she said, 'I thought you'd at least let my bed get cold before you hurtled off to Cornwall to jump in another.'

Hero's face was empty. 'Do you remember me telling you about that conference I had to go to?'

'No. Hang on, yes.' Sadie struggled with the title. 'Something about sustainable health in, um . . .'

'Building a Sustainable Community Health Care Model in an Age of Uncertainty. So, you *were* listening. When was that conference?'

Sadie tried to think, but got nowhere.

'It was the weekend of the eleventh of August. Right after we parted ways. And where was it?'

'Cornwall,' said Sadie, in a small voice.

'Amber called me, suggested I swing by the festival. I had a couple of hours to kill, so I went along. I spent most of my time setting up props and marshalling people to throw glitter in the air for Amber's Instagram story. I left when I discovered that, despite being in Cornwall, the festival had no pasties available as it was a clean-eating event.' Hero frowned. 'That's it. Nothing more. What made you think otherwise?'

'That arm, *your* arm, with your watch on it, that was a signal.' Sadie ignored his impatient snort. 'Amber pores over every tiny aspect of her images. She made sure I saw it by tagging me. It was even *more* effective than if she had posted a full-on pic of you.'

'Sure you're not reading too much into Amber's behaviour?'

'Have you ever met a woman, Hero?'

'Amber's a mate, somebody to hang out with. She doesn't have designs on me.'

'Jesus, Hero, men are so dense.'

'Is this imaginary fling with Amber the reason why you've been weird with me?'

'You've been weird with me, too.'

Hero looked for a moment as if he was happy to launch into a game of You Started It, but he said, 'Why would I go for Amber, anyway? I was licking my wounds. I was . . .'

'You were what?' Sadie needed to know.

'I was off women,' said Hero. 'I met one I really liked but she wasn't very nice to me.' He held up his hands backing away. 'But, as you say, we don't owe each other explanations. It is what it is, Sadie.'

'But it's not what it was,' she murmured to herself as he walked away. 'And not what it could be.'

'Here's our little supermodel.' Cher presented a different-looking Teddy, one with her shiny hair woven into a plaited coronet.

'Cher's a genius.' Teddy twirled, showing off her new hairdo. 'But she wouldn't let me put lipstick on.'

'Plenty of time for that when you're older.' Sadie mouthed a thank-you over Teddy's head as she manoeuvred her into a jacket. The weather was on the turn. The year was moving on. 'I don't imagine Granny'll be pleased if you turn up in lipstick.'

'Where's the present?' Teddy looked anxiously around.

She'd chosen the bead bracelet from Yummy Mummy, and wrapped it in tissue the colour of hyacinths.

'Here, sweetie, don't panic.' Sadie needed to take her own advice as she double-checked with Fi and Cher that they could cope without her.

'Go!' ordered Fi. 'I think you're mad, but go.'

The Family Liaison Officer hadn't put it like that, but the request for Teddy to visit the woman accused of kidnapping her had been met with polite confusion. Sadie had pushed; Teddy needed to see her grandmother.

'Hang on!' Cher dashed over. 'Teddy doesn't need red lippy, but you do, Mummy.'

Sadie pouted and Cher drew her a more self-confident mouth, whispering, 'Can't have you facing that old witch looking all pale and nervous.'

'The power of red lipstick.' Sadie noticed something. 'Cher, you're not wearing any today.'

'Nah.'

'You can, you know, if you want to.' Sadie's success at toning down Cher was a hollow victory. 'You can express yourself. Don't conform for the sake of it.' The true Cher was a magnificent creature, bold and decent and prepared to sacrifice everything to do the right thing.

'I *am* expressing meself. This is me.' Cher laughed, and pushed Sadie gently on her way. 'I'm not a pair of high heels and a miniskirt, boss lady. I'm *me*.'

Outside, Hero lounged against Sadie's car. 'Let me run Teddy to her grandmother's,' he said.

Taken aback by the offer, Sadie was more brusque than thankful. 'No, honestly, you don't have to.'

'Who said I had to?' Hero was amused. 'Just because we don't make sense in . . .' – he glanced down at Teddy and her ever-open ears – 'in *that* way, doesn't mean we can't be friends.'

'Can Bo come?' asked Teddy, hopeful. She knew nothing about his fall from grace.

'If you want him to, then yes.'

As Bo, avoiding eye contact with Sadie as if it might prove fatal, sidled to the car, Sadie reeled off a list of instructions. 'And don't drop Teddy off unless the supervising officer's already in the house. Check for yourself; don't take Merle's word for it. And—'

'Mummy!' interrupted Teddy. 'Shush!'

'Yeah,' said Hero. 'Shush.'

Dear Daddy,

i am going to see granny

i made things go wrong and now i will put it right

love teddy xxxxx

*

The hours lagged. Sadie regretted her decision.

What if Merle takes her away again?

Hero had confirmed that the supervising officer had not only been present, but seemed like a no-nonsense guy.

What if Merle has a gun?

That was ridiculous enough to put an end to the what-ifs. Sadie reapplied herself to her work, to the grateful body warming under her touch.

At the end of play, Grace wandered in. 'It'll be a quiet meeting tonight. Amber's mate told me Amber's too poorly to attend, and Mary's been out of the mews all day.'

'But,' said Sadie, a tiny alarm bell beginning to jangle, 'the meeting's at Mary's.'

'Mary never goes out if she can help it.' Grace put her hand to her mouth. 'I was on the rota to drive her to Streamside today, but she told me not to bother.'

'She never misses seeing Arthur.' Feeling the need to tidy the mews, pop all the inhabitants back into their usual positions, Sadie started with the closest to hand. She took off her tunic. 'Let me look in on Amber. I might be able to persuade her to show her face.'

'Leave me alone, please,' keened Amber from her bed. Phones, an iPad, a laptop, lay shipwrecked in the sheets.

'It won't be the same without you.' Sadie privately thought that Amber added little to the meetings, but each resident was part of the warp and weft of Cherry Blossom Mews.

'Look at me!' Amber didn't find anger comfortable; her little-girl voice cracked. 'I can't let people see me like this.'

She looked wretched. Pale, pimply, and as creased as her bed. 'We all know what you look like by now, Amber.'

'I need a day or two.' Amber switched on a lamp against the encroaching dusk. 'Tell them I have a cold.'

'You sure?' Sadie was reluctant to leave.

'I'm sure. Thank you,' she said, raising her voice as Sadie turned away, 'for coming in the other day. You were kind.'

'No.' Sadie said it firmly; there could be no going back. 'I felt guilty. Because I enjoyed @ambertragiclondon's posts, Amber.'

Amber raised her head. She was shocked. Hurt. 'You bitch,' she said.

'I *am* a bitch,' agreed Sadie, her back against the wall, literally and figuratively. 'I'm jealous of you, Amber.'

'Yeah, right. Look at my wonderful life. No wonder you're jealous of me.' She vibrated with scorn.

'But you tried to . . .' Sadie lost confidence in her hypothesis. 'I *thought* you tried to make me jealous by including Hero in one of your photos.'

'Hero?' Amber sat up. Planted her feet on the floor. She seemed to be evaluating her next words. 'Yeah, well, maybe I did.' She pushed her toe into the rug. 'Sorry,' she said.

'Me too.'

The atmosphere in the room lifted, as if a window had been opened and the cherry blossom had filled it with scent.

All activity, Amber groped about beneath the bed, coming up with a buckled shoe. 'I should get dressed if I'm going to show my face at the meeting.'

Sadie helped. Ran and got her make-up bag. Pinned Amber's hair up.

Are we becoming friends?

'You look beautiful.' When Amber turned to the mirror on a chest of drawers, Sadie took her shoulders and made her face her. 'You don't need the mirror to tell you that. Life's about meaning and connection. It doesn't have to look good to matter.'

'So you laugh while I get bullied and I get a lecture into the bargain?'

Nope. Me and Amber are not friend material.

They joined the others at MOBuk, which was filling up with residents, thanks to Grace's spare key. Mrs Bob did a double take at Amber's less than impeccable appearance, but a quelling look from Sadie kept her quiet. There was no Bob, but the chair beside his wife was left unoccupied, as if he might change his mind and stroll in.

No Mary.

Sadie bit back on her anxiety. Mary was a grown woman who didn't have to sign out when she decided to go somewhere.

But she hates leaving the mews.

Amber sat beside Hero, dropping with a defiant *So there!* on her features for Sadie.

On the floor, Bo was cross legged, ostentatiously bored. Michael cleaned his glasses with a cloth; when his eyes met Sadie's they creased in greeting.

No Dorothy Ball book for a fortnight.

Sadie's other admirer had also moved on.

Cher's admirer was firmly at her side. Jez sat so close to his girlfriend that they could have worn the same clothes.

Grace pulled a chair across the pitted boards, and said, 'Is anybody going to admit how worried we are about Mary?'

Michael crossed his legs. 'What can we do? We can hardly report her missing. She's a free agent.'

'Mary's not helpless,' Hero reminded them. 'She can take care of herself. It's only because this is out of character that we're concerned.'

Cher put up her hand. 'Sorry, but bullshit. I say we get out on the streets now and look for her. She didn't go to see Uncle Arthur today. That's not normal.'

It was terrible timing, but Sadie had to leave.

I can't let Teddy stay with Merle for one second longer than agreed.

'For what it's worth,' she said, as she gathered her bag and fished out her keys. 'I agree with Cher. We need to do something.'

*

Teddy was quiet in the passenger seat as they headed home.

'So, was it fun?'

'Hmm.'

'Was Granny in a good mood?'

'Hmm.'

Sadie surrendered. Teddy was marooned in the middle of her mother and her grandmother, with fealty to both sides.

No good pestering her for answers she doesn't want to give.

The phone's tinny cry was a relief. Fi's name came up on the screen in the dashboard.

'Hi there!' said Sadie, with a glance at Teddy to see if she was interested.

Muffled noises floated from the speakers. Watery, incomprehensible.

'Another pocket dial.' Sadie, turning right at a notoriously difficult junction, said to Teddy, 'Switch it off, sweetie.'

'No, it's funny.' Teddy sat forward. 'I can hear Fi's voice. She's doing funny moans.'

Oh God.

The sounds of Fi having passionate sex filled the car. Too late, Sadie berated herself for not fixing the mechanical glitch that made it impossible to drop the call from the steering wheel. 'Um, let's not listen, eh?' Sadie turned the wheel jerkily at an orgasmic howl. 'Turn it off, Teddy!'

A man in a white van told Sadie what he thought of her through the open window. It wasn't a compliment.

Naive Teddy turned up the volume. 'I heard a word,' she said. 'Fi said "Help".'

A scream, clear and terrible, filled the car.

'Mummy?' Teddy turned to Sadie in panic. Expecting an answer, as all seven-year-olds do, from the nearest adult.

The audio was indeed X-rated. But not because it was sexual.

This is the sound of Fi being beaten.

Sadie did a U-turn that brought them face to face with the man in the van once again. 'Oh, bugger off!' she shouted, as Fi's muffled shouts for help ripped through the car.

Cole's flat was ten minutes away. Ten minutes of a hellish soundtrack: Fi winded by punches; Fi crashing against furniture; Fi whimpering like a dog.

'Come *on*, Mummy!' Teddy rode shotgun, urging on the Saab. 'We have to rescue her.'

Unarmed, with no superpowers to speak of, Sadie tried not to think of what they'd do when they reached the neat new build.

When they got there, it was tranquil. Lamplight showed through the blinds. Sadie wasn't fooled. She hammered on the door, adrenaline making her eyes bulge. Teddy, told firmly to stay in the car, watched.

Cole was irritated by Sadie's accusatory tone. 'She's not here. What's this about?'

'Come on Cole, I can hear—' As Sadie turned to the

car, sounds of violence drifting out of its open window, she stopped short. 'It's still going on,' she murmured.

'What is?' Cole tilted his head to listen. 'Is that . . . ?'

Sadie's thoughts scrambled. 'If Fi's not here, where is she?'

As if bewitched, Cole didn't seem able to move, let alone think. Sadie left him there, and tore back to the car. Teddy was shouting, bouncing on her seat as Sadie did up her seat belt, all action, with no idea where to go or what to do.

'Darling, *what*?' she said eventually as they pulled away.

'I said,' said Teddy, 'I saw a funny name on Fi's phone today, and she swore at it.'

'Think, Teddy. What was the name?'

As the little face screwed up, thinking hard, Sadie slowed the car. She knew what Teddy was about to say.

'Emanuel!'

Sadie put her foot down and they left Cole's cul-de-sac behind.

'You are brilliant, Teddy. *Brilliant!*'

They say people get the faces they deserve; Emanuel had the home he deserved.

A mildewed terrace hacked into squats, it brought back memories for Sadie. Grim ones, of standing outside and waiting for Fi to surface. Black and blue.

Once grand, the house had a raised ground floor approached by a set of wide stone steps. The front door stood open; nobody cared enough to close it.

Slowing as she passed, Sadie spotted Emanuel's car parked at the corner. *That* was where his money went. His time, his love. A sporty number in electric blue, it was a bird of paradise in the drab street.

Sadie slowed to a halt, and yanked at the handbrake. The indistinct sounds leaking out of the speakers had changed. No longer a cacophony of violence, it was more like a radio play on a fuzzy channel.

There was only one voice. Deep. Male. Petulant.

'Why'd you make me do this stuff? . . . You deserve it . . . You push and you push and you make me crazy . . .'

Muting the soliloquy, Sadie said, 'Stay here, sweetie.'

'Not fair!' Teddy was appalled. 'I want to save Fi from the horrible man.'

'Listen to me.' Sadie called on the voice all mothers keep in their back pocket. The no-nonsense one. The this-is-serious one. 'Stay in the car.'

Up the front steps. Into the hallway. Sadie froze at the sound of heavy feet banging down from a floor above.

It was a stranger, who paid no heed to the pale woman flattened against the wall.

Sadie stole up the stairs. She knew that Emanuel had one grubby room at the front of the house. She peeked around the curve of the bannisters. The quiet landing gave no clue to the abuse unfolding behind the closed door.

She felt her physical weakness keenly. She was no match for Emanuel. She had no weapon.

And if I did have a weapon? I wouldn't know what to do with it!

She did, however, have a brain. Sadie darted back out onto the street on feathery feet.

'Shush, Teddy. Stay where you are.'

Her jumping-bean daughter twisted around to see what her mother was up to at the boot.

'There you are!' After all her complaining, Sadie was delighted to see the large hammer Hero had neglected to pick up nestled in among the usual car boot debris. She took it up. It was heavy. She swung it. She summoned her nerve. She lowered it again.

Fi needs me.

Sadie stalked to the end of the street. She swung the hammer across her body and brought it down on the passenger window of the Nissan GT-R.

'*Mummy!*' Teddy's gleeful, shocked shout was drowned out by the loud mosquito screech of the car alarm.

Swiftly, Sadie dropped the hammer and darted across the road. She was standing in the shadow of the steps to the front door when she heard a window above her fly open.

'My fucking car!'

Seconds later, Emanuel flew out of the house and down the steps.

Sadie emerged from the shadows and raced up into the house.

It felt like a long time for Teddy, watching and waiting to see her mother emerge, but it was a couple of minutes at most. Minutes that Emanuel spent pacing around his ruined pride and joy, striking his forehead, grabbing passers-by to ask – none too politely – if they'd seen anything.

Pirouetting with frustration, he saw two figures at his front door.

'Hey!' His bellow was a booming bass note.

'Come on, Fi.' Sadie helped her friend manage the first step. 'You can do it.'

Fi shook. With tears. With fear. The right side of her face was swollen. 'He's coming,' she whispered.

'My car!' Emanuel bounded up the steps, two at a time. 'That was you, you stupid whore. Why don't you go home, Sadie, and mind your business?'

'Fi is my business.' She knew all about this man. How he was always angry, how he used it for fuel. Fi had told Sadie that Emanuel was most dangerous when he smiled.

He smiled now. His face was smooth, handsome. He raised his hand slowly, enjoying the women's instinctive shift backwards. Slowly, he placed his finger on the tip of Sadie's nose. 'Don't stick this in where it's not wanted.'

'Don't touch me.'

'This is between her and me. She likes it, you know. Just 'cos you ain't getting any action don't come between a man and his woman.'

'You're boring and wrong, Emanuel.' Sadie saw him bristle at that. She didn't want to rile him; she just wanted to get out of his orbit.

Out of punching range.

'One of your neighbours,' she carried on, 'called the police as soon as your alarm went off. I saw her do it. Any second now there'll be blue lights everywhere so why not just—'

'As if they care about a car alarm on this street.' He was amused; suddenly Sadie felt like an out-of-touch minor royal.

Fi held her head up with difficulty. She whistled slightly; a front tooth was missing. Blood caked on her lip. 'It's done, Manny. I'm going.' She said it again. 'It's done.'

Emanuel's whole body jerked with rage. He bared his teeth and pulled back his hand, palm open.

A child's voice, high and indignant, shocked him into a statue, hand held high, ready to slap.

'Don't you dare!' Teddy was, as instructed, still in the car, but she leaned out of the window as far as she could. 'That's my godmother!'

The rip in the fabric of Emanuel's concentration was

enough for the women to wriggle through. They pushed past, hurrying awkwardly down the steps like Siamese twins, speeding up as they neared the car.

Right on cue, a siren began to keen.

A different Emanuel chased them as Sadie fumbled with the car door.

'Fi, Fi, you love me, baby,' said this less cocksure version of him. 'You know you love me.'

Sadie hurried to the driver's side. 'Teddy,' she hissed. 'Sit!' She hit the window button, but not before Teddy had her say.

'If you want a girlfriend be nice and buy her flowers, yeah?'

'Bitches!' Emanuel thumped the roof of the car.

'And don't swear!' roared Teddy as they sped away.

At the far end of the road, the police car sped by, en route to some other incident. The metallic tick of the indicator drowned out Emanuel's car alarm. Teddy turned round in the front seat and held out her hand to Fi.

In a cubicle insulated by a thin curtain, the tired trio waited for a doctor.

'Poor Cole,' said Sadie. 'I've been having some very bad thoughts about him.'

'The affair almost destroyed him.' Fi's words fluted through the gap in her teeth. 'He should have left me. You two should have let me get what was coming to me.'

'I'm not listening to talk like that.' Sadie would have liked to shake Fi, but most of her hurt. 'Emanuel knows how to push your buttons. His stupid ego couldn't allow you to walk away from him. How long have you been seeing him?'

'Too long.' Fi closed her eyes, exhausted. 'I've been lying to you. Creeping off to see him. I couldn't break free. It was all the same, other women and drugs and fists. Cole begged me to stop. I told him to forget me. He said he couldn't.' Her mouth turned down. 'He will after this.'

Just as Sadie found time to fret that this wasn't a fit conversation for childish ears, Teddy offered her verdict.

'I can't believe,' she said gravely, 'that that man was your boyfriend. He's the worst man I ever met in my life.'

'Mine, too.' Fi shifted and the paper sheet beneath her crackled. 'I'm addicted to toxic men.'

'Addictions can be beaten,' said Sadie. 'This I know for a fact.'

There was no argument; Fi was staying the night with Sadie and Teddy. As they helped her out of the car, Sadie remembered.

'Mary!'

As if summoned by the thought, Hero emerged from U-Turn. 'Nothing yet,' he said. Coming nearer, he whispered, 'I've just called the police.'

More police.

Before Sadie could explain about Fi's battered face, a taxi pulled up outside Cherry Blossom Mews.

'It's Mary!' Sadie found herself shouting. 'Mary's back!' Other residents heard and came out, wearing PJs and naked faces. Cher, pulling a woolly around her, emerged from Sakura.

'That old bat's gonna get a piece of my mind.' Mrs Bob was enraged.

'Tomorrow, eh?' said Sadie, her arm around Fi.

Michael wore a proper dressing gown, with a collar and a belt. Without glasses, his eyes were small and vulnerable. 'Who's that with Mary?'

The cabbie who had helped Mary to disembark was now lending his arm to another passenger. Arthur wobbled a little on the pavement, and Mary steadied him.

Noel leapt from the taxi and whipped around the tree, while the neighbours tried to make sense of what they were seeing.

'He's here for good.' Mary led Arthur through the scrum. He was scrubbed and pink and wearing brand new clothes that hung on his slight frame. 'Why should he stay in a home when I can look after him?'

The dubious glance that Sadie exchanged with Hero skated over Mary's head. Arthur was in a world of his own, uninterested, vaguely confused by the fuss.

'Oh.' Arthur paused.

Mary paused too. 'What is it, Arthur?'

'This tree . . .' The old man reached out a hand latticed with blue veins. 'It's our tree.'

Sadie took off. She was inside Sakura in a nano-second, rifling through a drawer. She flew back down, to where Mary stood looking into Arthur's face with a desperate hopefulness.

'Here.' Sadie gently tucked the plastic cherry blossom behind Mary's ear.

Cher beamed.

'Mary,' said Arthur. He said it with wonder.

He kissed her.

'Let's get you indoors,' said Mary, her voice shaky. As she passed Sadie, she paused and whispered, 'I seem to have contracted the terrible mental illness called love. Tell me, dear, is there an antidote?'

Sadie smiled. 'It's incurable.'

WEEK EIGHTEEN

To	Michael T. <qwertybookshop@hotmail.com>, Hero <hero.smith@u-turn.net>, Fiona J <filove@aol.com>, The Bobs <bob@bobscaff.co.uk>, Jez <jeremy.gray@u-turn.net>, Grace Esparza <Gracetheartist@gmail.com>, Amber <amber@yummymummymews.net.co.uk>
From	Sadie <sakuraspa@gmail.com>
Subject	CHERRY BLOSSOM MEWS RESIDENTS' ASSOCIATION MEETING

Hi!

This is Teddy. Bo is helping me use my mums email because she wonnt let me have my own. I am in charge of this meeting because of feminnism. You have to come so do not make stupid excuses on the day.

Date Wednesday 19.9.18
Time 6.30 p.m.
Location Sakura reception
Agenda A MISTERY!

Yours sinserely

Teddy McQueen

It was the book that made her do it.

Sadie picked it up from the doormat. She'd missed Dorothy Ball more than she cared to admit. With a grateful surge of feeling towards Michael, she held it to her chest, whispering the title: *Come Home to Me.*

Without giving herself time to reconsider, Sadie snatched up the spa landline and dialled.

'Hi, it's me.' Sadie realised she'd have to announce herself. 'It's Sadie.'

A short silence, then Tish said, 'Hello, stranger.'

'Just calling to see how things are.'

'Oh, you know, the usual.' Tish seemed at a loss.

May as well plunge right in.

'Tish, there's something you should know. This is going to sound crazy, but I swear it's true. Merle has been keeping Teddy from me.' Sadie abridged the saga, knowing it lost something by being rushed. 'Can you imagine,' she ended, 'how I felt when Teddy suddenly appeared?'

Tish said, 'Answer me honestly. Are you drunk?'

'What? No. I just told you, Tish. I had a relapse after the accident, but I've been sober since then.'

Tish made a sceptical sound. 'Look, this isn't really my business but—'

'Not your business?' Sadie felt that like a slap to her face.

'Let me finish.' Sadie could imagine Tish, in her neutrally decorated kitchen, the phone to her ear. Tetchy. 'Merle did her best for that child. I mean, come on, it's hardly bloody kidnapping. That's one hell of an accusation.'

'That's what the police call it.'

'She told me you found a man. How's that working out? Not so heartbroken you couldn't get a bloke, obviously.'

'She told you?' Sadie felt sick. 'You talk to Merle? Tish, you knew?'

'I knew you had buggered off and left her to bring up your child, yes.'

'You actually believed that? What, you didn't try and help, didn't try to reunite us? I thought Teddy was *dead*, Tish! And all the while you sat back and enjoyed the spectacle!'

'You didn't think she was dead.'

'I did. Merle knew and she let me go on thinking it.'

'Merle wouldn't do that.' Tish didn't sound sure.

'She would and she did.'

A weary sigh travelled from Suffolk to Sadie's ear. 'Why is it always a drama with you?'

Sadie hung up.

*

They all agreed the past week had been tough.

The residents were now jointly responsible not only for Noel, but for Arthur.

A powwow was convened in the caff. Pouring tea from the big enamel pot, Sadie felt as if the right-hand side of her was missing, lopped off. It was Teddy's first day at school, and Sadie veered between wild optimism and even wilder pessimism.

'Sorry, what?' She asked Grace to repeat herself.

'I was saying that Mary's flat isn't the best place to care for an invalid.'

'You can say that again.' Mrs Bob had opened the caff especially for this huddle. It had been dark for two days, since Bob was taken into the hospice. 'It's a mess. The bathroom!' She pulled a face. 'Keeping Arthur clean'll be a problem.'

'Don't talk about him like he's a pet.' Cher bridled. 'He's my uncle.'

'I'm sure Mrs Bob didn't mean any disrespect.' Michael was looking natty in a red jumper that brought out the blue of his eyes.

'I can talk for myself, thank you.' Mrs Bob eyed Cher. 'You weren't this bothered about Arthur when you left him to rot in Streamside, were you, miss?'

Hero cut in. 'Let's concentrate on Mary and Arthur. You looked in on them this morning, Sadie?'

'I did.' She'd scrubbed the kitchen floor, changed the bedclothes, taken Arthur's pyjamas away to launder. She'd witnessed Mary's geisha-like devotion to Arthur's comfort. He was fed, watered, entertained. His thinning white hair was brushed. His hand was held. 'Mary adores him.'

'It's heartbreaking.' Amber was once more swathed in denim and feathers and chunky African jewellery. 'He can't adore her back.'

'I'm not so sure.' Grace saw the bright side. 'He recognises Mary, even though he never remembers our names without prompting. He's forgotten all the time they spent apart, but maybe that's a blessing.'

'They're not on the same page,' said Fi. 'Mary goes along with the fantasy, but she carries the weight of it all.' Fi could smile again – the tooth had been replaced – but she rarely did so.

Sadie agreed. 'Poor Mary knows the truth, that Arthur's sick, that they've both been lonely for decades.'

'It would make things easier,' said Mrs Bob, 'if Mary accepted help.' Mrs Bob was almost translucent, subsisting on cigarettes and gumption as Bob faded in a clean hospice bed. 'The old gal's a nightmare.'

Nobody disagreed. Mary wouldn't hear of moving Arthur downstairs, wouldn't hear of carrying a personal alarm, wouldn't hear of allowing a social worker to visit.

Hero defended her. 'Hard to change the habit of a lifetime and stop being ferociously proud in your eighties, eh?'

'I'll clean the bathroom later,' promised Grace. 'This time I won't let her shoo me away.'

Other offers were made. Michael volunteered to fill Mary's fridge, and Cher and Jez would sit with Arthur for an hour or two to give her a breather.

Jez wondered what Mary's title was. 'Is she his girlfriend? That feels wrong.'

'His partner?' offered Hero.

'She's his beloved,' said Sadie, and that settled the matter.

Michael tipped back his chair and hollered, 'Hey! Bo! Where are those toasties?'

Through the hatch, they could all see – and enjoy – Bo dashing around the kitchen. He dropped things. He burnt his hand. His quiff wilted in the steam. 'Coming!' he called, shakily.

The 'consequences' were in place. Bo had stood, trembling, in front of Sadie awaiting his sentence. She'd warned him that it was tough, that he'd have to be strong, before telling him that he was now the official Cherry Blossom Mews gopher. 'This is a community. Hurt one of us, you hurt all of us, so now you can make amends to everyone. Whatever's asked of you, you'll do, whether it's cleaning Grace's brushes, waiting tables in the caff, or entertaining the kids in Amber's party emporium.

You'll read to Arthur and you'll stack shelves with Michael. Got it?'

He got it. Bo threw himself into every chore, relieved that he wasn't in handcuffs. Neighbours reported that he was of very little actual use, but the poetic justice was satisfying.

The toasties arrived. They were charred around the edges, and nobody got what they ordered, but they were eaten all the same.

'Teddy!' Sadie had called softly, then less softly, then she'd shouted, and now she was annoyed. 'Come on! It's a long drive.'

'She's probably choosing what to wear,' said Fi. 'You know what Teddy's like once she gets in front of a mirror. If she didn't have a uniform for school she'd miss the first lesson.'

The new term had started smoothly; Teddy had the aplomb of a presidential candidate as she crossed the school yard. Her life change was already yesterday's news; Sadie would be forever grateful to the mother who'd run off with the PE teacher and moved her off the school gates' front page.

'Where you going?' Cher leaned over the reception desk, greedy for detail. 'Another hospital appointment?'

'No, we don't have to go back for a fortnight.' Sadie upped her volume again. 'Teddy!' She turned her wrist to look at Jack's watch. Retrieved from its drawer, the gold timepiece weighed down her hand. It spoke of more than seconds and minutes and hours; it spoke of choices made. 'We're off on a family visit.' Sadie pointed to the bowl that sat on the desk. 'This should be full of sweets, Cher.'

'It was,' said Cher. 'Until a certain somebody guzzled the lot.'

'Guilty as charged!' Fi held up her hand. 'Sorry not sorry. You show me a person who can eat just one Smartie and I'll show you a person you can't trust.'

The diet was over. Emanuel was once again in the dustbin of history. Cole had declared himself ready and willing to paper over the cracks, but had dolefully backed off when his offer was rebuffed. Fi had admitted to him, and to herself, that Cole was an experiment. She had tried to love a mild man, and found it impossible. She was, she had vowed, 'off men'.

'Is it our go with Bo tomorrow?' Cher cackled like a witch. 'I have some *lovely* jobs lined up for him.'

'Apparently,' said Sadie, 'he went straight to bed after his last afternoon here. He was babbling about wiping down massage tables and making old ladies' tea just the way they like it.'

'Poor little sod.' Fi cocked her head. 'I shouldn't feel sorry for him. Little bugger burgled us.' She shrugged. 'Can't help it, though. There's something sad about Bo, and God knows he's paying for his crime. Mrs Patton sent her tea back four times.'

'He's working through issues,' said Sadie.

'Bollocks,' snapped Cher. 'You mean he's got a lousy mum who's a bit of a slut and a dad who isn't really his dad. Bo's handsome and his folks are loaded but the poor kid needs attention. He's worse off than the snotty-nosed little boys who hang around our flats.'

'*We* see that Hero loves him,' said Sadie. 'But Bo struggles with it. He thinks Hero can't really love him, because he's not his birth dad.'

'What gets my goat,' said Fi, whose goat was often got, 'is that Hero won't get stuck in and just shower Bo with love. I mean, what's he waiting for?'

Sadie shouted again. 'Ted— Oh!' She jumped. Her daughter was standing behind her. 'There you are.'

'Are we there yet, Mummy?'

'I didn't realise children actually say that in real life.'

'I'm bored.'

'I'll put the radio on.'

'It's just people talking.'

'You'll find most of life is that, sweetie. Want a mint?'

'I'm sick of mints.'

Sadie had forgotten how draining it can be to drive long distances with a trainee human.

And how blissful.

She enjoyed knowing that other road users might peek in as they passed, and see just another mother and child.

Nothing to see here, move along.

Sadie wanted to shout, 'We are normal!' out of the car window, but shouting that would prove the opposite, so instead she said, 'I hope Mary's okay today. Arthur needs—'

'Mummy, you worry about everything,' said Teddy. 'Stop it.'

'Sorry, can't. And for your information we *are* nearly there.'

Teddy was reluctant at first. She stood by the wall, watching doubtfully as Sadie tidied the grave.

'So, Daddy's under there?'

'Well, his spirit is free, but yes, he's under the flowers.'

'Can I walk on him?'

'He won't mind.'

Teddy knelt down and brushed mud from the stone. 'I don't like it here,' she said.

'I thought it might help.' Sadie pushed a strand of hair behind Teddy's ear. 'Sometimes it's hard, isn't it, without Daddy?'

Teddy looked mulish. Her eyes flickered all over the grave. She ignored the question, saying instead, 'You should put daisies on it, Mummy. He likes daisies.'

That heartbreaking present tense. Or maybe 'that *correct* present tense'.

After all, we're here right now, and so is Jack.

Wherever they went, he trotted alongside. Death is powerful, but it can't evict someone who's lived in your heart for years.

They worked together, mother and daughter, at the little plot.

'Sweetie, run to that tap over there and fill this jug so we can water the new flowers.'

Just as she'd used to do, Sadie used Teddy's absence to discuss adult concerns with Jack.

'Are you still pissed off with me for trashing your grave? That was the worst row of our marriage. I never dreamed we'd fight over another woman. Not us.'

Over at the tap, Teddy dropped the jug and started again, water splashing everywhere like tears.

'Listen, we don't have long before Bugalugs is back. She and I are getting older, Jack. We're turning into people you might not even recognise. Even though that pierces my heart, it's right that life goes on. It has to, because I have a daughter to bring up, a daughter who likes ketchup on her mash, just like you did.'

Teddy carried the jug carefully, keeping to the path.

'Maybe you'd have told me about Effie. Hell, maybe you'd have left me for her. I choose to believe you would have been sorry and I would have forgiven you. That we'd still be together. But we're not together, are we, Jack? Hanging on to you, raging about your infidelity, cost me something that might have been a little bit marvellous. I won't let that happen again, my darling. If I do end my days alone it won't be because I'm pining for you.'

A stone angel caught Teddy's attention. She paused to examine it.

'What I'm saying, in the roundabout way that used to drive you crazy, is that you may rest in peace, Jack McQueen. You can float about the stars, doing your own beautiful thing without me trying to hook you back down to my level, or have a go at you posthumously.'

As Teddy made a diversion around the edges of the cemetery, Sadie put into words an uncomfortable truth that had been tapping at her shoulder.

'Something had changed, hadn't it?'

Their early passionate incarnations had slowly, imperceptibly become partners in a parenting enterprise who had sex when they remembered to.

'I know you well enough to be sure that your affair wasn't just about sex. I like to think I wouldn't have ever been unfaithful, but I do understand how you went in search of lightness and romance and *touch*.' Sadie checked that Teddy was still meandering. She laid her hand on the headstone. It was warm. 'I made a saint of you, Jack. The truth is . . .

you're a man. Just a man. My man, and a wonderful man in many ways. I'm setting you free, darling.' A tear fell and stained the stone. Sadie was setting herself free, too.

'Oh, Mummy, don't cry.' Teddy, with unlikely speed, was beside her. She put a finger up to Sadie's face to catch another tear.

It felt like one of the stone angels had come to life and touched her with magical tenderness. Sadie pulled her daughter to her, quite roughly, and said into her hair, which smelled of shampoo, 'We're all right, aren't we, sweetie?'

'We're great, Mummy.' Teddy seemed surprised by the question. 'We're amazing.'

Sadie let her go, laughed, wiped her own face. 'Fancy a magical mystery tour?'

All seven-year-olds fancy *that*.

Teddy wasn't quite so pleased with being told to stay put when they pulled up before a house unusual enough to be in one of her story books. She leaned sideways to see the top of the bell tower, and called, 'Don't be long,' as the front door opened for her mother.

After a moment, her mum came into view again, this time down the side of the house. Just visible through an archway, Sadie strode purposefully across a lawn. Teddy saw a slight figure rise up out of a slatted chair.

How she would have loved to hear what they were saying.

The two women were emotional, Teddy could tell. The smaller lady looked pretty, with the swingy hair Teddy aspired to.

Swingy Hair put her hands to her face. There was a lot of head shaking, a lot of gesticulation.

'Oh!' Teddy hadn't expected that. They hugged, a really warm cuddle, the sort that Teddy was now getting at bed-time after going so long without.

Then something else unexpected happened. Her mother unclipped something from her wrist. It glinted in the half-hearted sunshine that was all September had left after a blazing summer.

'Daddy's watch!' whispered Teddy, as Swingy Hair took it.

Another hug. Then her mum hurried away, head down, and was hidden by the house, before emerging again on the step.

As they tore out of the drive, Teddy kept her questions to herself. This felt like one of those subjects she would only understand when she was older.

'Got to get back in time for the residents' meeting,' said her mum.

'Yeah.' Teddy buckled up. Bo would be there.

The drive back to London didn't wear Sadie out. It energised her.

I'm on the way somewhere.

Sadie had opened a cage in her heart and let the poor, starved bird that lived there fly away.

Giving Jack's watch to his lover had closed a poisonous circle. Effie looked even younger than Sadie remembered. She was a fair, slight thing, staggering when Sadie revealed their strange connection.

'I don't hold a grudge,' Sadie had said.

Effie had said she was sorry.

Sadie had not believed her. Nobody in love can be truly sorry about it. Handing over the watch, she let it do the talking. Effie now had a memento; she could wear something every day that had been close to Jack's skin.

And I'm free of guilt, of anger, of fidelity to a dead man.

'Effie,' she'd said as she took her leave. 'Remember to get on with your life.'

Sadie tapped the steering wheel. 'Almost there.' The lights were taking too long. They were just two right turns away from the mews. She felt it pull, calling her back.

Calling me home.

'Hurry up, Teddy.' In her bedroom, Sadie zipped up her jeans and slipped her feet into a fresh pair of shoes.

'Post this for me, Mummy.' Teddy threw a postcard onto the landing.

Teddy knows I know about the post box.

'Okay,' she said slowly, wondering what else her daughter knew. She read the card.

Dear Daddy,
i have a plan! It is perfect! nothing can go wrong!
love teddy xxxxxx

Amusement at her daughter having a plan turned to puzzlement at the strange noises coming from outside.

Garbled shouts. What Mary would call a kerfuffle. Sadie went down and joined the knot of Mewsites looking towards U-Turn.

The door banged open, and Trevor, U-Turn's resident bad guy, barrelled out. 'I'll have him!' he shouted.

Others spilled out too. Hero, red in the face, with Bo behind him. A couple of regulars, fired up and bouncing on their feet.

Lastly, Jez, his arms outstretched, Jesus-like. He got in the middle of what were obviously two factions, Trevor vs the rest. 'Let's all stay calm, yeah?'

Cher scuttled to Sadie's side. 'Isn't he sexy?' She nudged Sadie, hard. 'Hero won't let him hit anyone but I reckon my Jez could take Trevor like *that*.' She clicked her fingers.

As if he held a box of lightning, Hero leaned down hard on his anger. 'Go home, Trevor.'

'That little toerag of yours pushed me.' Trevor pointed at Bo.

Cher shouted, 'He's twelve, mate! Pick on someone your own size.'

Mrs Bob, back from the hospice and still in her coat, shouted too. Perhaps it was a relief to have somebody to vent at. 'Gerroffoutofit!' When Michael put a protective arm around her, she shook it off.

'I didn't push him,' wailed Bo, humiliated, hiding behind Hero.

'I know you didn't.' Hero put his head down. If he'd been a bull he'd have snorted. 'We don't fix problems with our fists at U-Turn, Trevor, so do yourself and everybody else a favour and leave now.'

'Fucking do-gooder,' leered Trevor.

'Language!' shouted Teddy from the door of Sakura.

Jez, arms up, approached the troublemaker. He might have succeeded in herding Trevor out of the mews if Bo hadn't chosen that moment to turn and walk towards Teddy.

Like a dog after a hare, Trevor bolted after Bo.

'Hey!' Jez leapt after him, his fingertips grazing the man's collar.

Acting on pure instinct, Sadie shoved Fi out of her way to grab Teddy, but before she could reach her, Hero slammed into Trevor and toppled him.

Alive with ugly energy, Trevor lashed out with his fists.

Hero, holding him down, absorbed a jab or two, but there could be no doubting who had the upper hand. Those muscles, so discreet beneath his linen shirt, did their job, as did his anger.

'Never,' he roared, 'go near my son again!' Hero put one hand on Trevor's neck, and pulled the other one back in a shaking fist.

'Hey, Hero, no.' Jez stood over them, his face bloodless. 'Think, mate.'

Hero was thinking hard. Sadie had seen his jaw work like that before, but she'd never seen the vein in his temple twitch like mercury. She held Teddy tight.

If Hero hits that idiot it's the end of U-Turn.

She had thrown away her right to intercede but she had to say, 'Hero, don't,' her voice wobbling.

'Get off me, man,' gasped Trevor.

Hero's clenched hand was back and ready to pump. All at once, he let go, dropped back, staggered away.

The cause of all the trouble, no longer a threat, sloped off out through the gates.

Of the two, Hero seemed the most shaken. Sadie knew why he stood there, head down and silent, as the Mewsites crowded around him, patting him on the back, congratulating him.

He's let himself down.

Hero worked with lives disfigured by violence. He was a strong man who never wanted to resort to brutality.

'Don't,' he said, irritated, when his neighbours tried to shake the hand that had just uncurled.

Bo urgently pushed his way through. He cleaved to Hero as if they were magnetised. Arms around Hero, he squeezed, hard, his cheek pressed into his chest.

Hero teetered, then stood firm, arms automatically folding around Bo.

It was a private moment. Sadie looked away. She heard the whisper, though, in Bo's uneven London/Los Angeles accent.

'You really do love me, Dad. You really do!'

Sakura buzzed with high good humour as the residents pulled the furniture around and sat themselves down; they had seen off a baddie, like a small town in an old western. Hero might reject their admiration but their eyes followed him anyway.

He really was their hero.

There was the usual greed in Amber's expression as she watched him. The phone was still in her small paw, and she looked at it just as often.

Rome wasn't built in a day, and neither is recovery; Sadie had vowed to help Amber in any way she could. Hero had suggested that the first and best way to help was by keeping that vow to herself, at least for the time being.

A fuss was made of Mary, and an even greater fuss was made of Arthur, who shuffled in on her arm. He beamed, happy to be there, wherever *there* was. They had all noticed that the smile never faltered so long as Mary was within touching distance. It was only when she ambled out of his orbit that his cloudy hazel eyes fluttered in panic.

They were made comfortable, like visiting monarchs, as Sadie marshalled the food.

'Seriously?' Fi held up a platter of squashed pastry parcels.

'They looked nicer in the shop.' Sadie rearranged them. It didn't help.

The people pleasers present made nice noises. 'Ooh, yummy!' said Grace, and Michael took two.

'Look like somebody sat on them,' said Cher from Jez's lap.

'Special offer, were they?' Mrs Bob made a sign of the cross over the dismal little *amuse-bouches*. 'My Bob could knock up better than that with one hand tied behind his back.'

A shudder ran around the room, grounding them all after their adrenaline rush.

Mrs Bob had just complimented Bob.

He must be near the end.

The ground felt shaky beneath Sadie's feet. It was so

fragile, this family that had grown around her. They couldn't afford to lose any one of them.

'Can I help?' Hero came up behind her as she poured boiling water into a large brown teapot that was out of place in Sakura's white-out.

'You've extricated yourself from Bo, then?' Sadie had seen how the boy clung to Hero in the corner, talking, crying. Emotions had been sparked inside Bo that the boy seemed to have no idea how to handle.

'Yeah.' Hero looked over at Bo, now being hugged by Grace, with what looked like regret. As if he missed the feel of Bo so close to him. He drew nearer to Sadie, his lowered voice creating an intimate space that excited Sadie and made her sad, with its echoes of what might have been. 'Bo never cries.'

'Not in front of you, maybe.' Sadie stirred the tea leaves.

'He wants to stay.' Hero was incredulous, repeating it to Sadie as if it was a dream he'd had.

'That's wonderful.' Sadie ached at the profundity of Bo's change of heart.

'For good. Like, forever. He wants to live with me.' Hero swallowed. 'And be my son.'

'He *is* your son,' smiled Sadie. 'That's not just down to DNA, is it?'

'All the years of worrying and the sleepless nights and trying to contain Zizzi and insisting on his schooling and jumping through all her hoops just to have him here for a few weeks every summer – none of them proved I loved him.' Hero smiled. 'But I knock one shouty arsehole to the floor and Bo gets it. He sees, at last, that I love him. Full stop.' Hero seemed to hear himself, and took a step backwards. 'You don't need this, me rambling on.'

'No, I don't,' said Sadie. 'I like it, though.'

When Hero looked at her like that, he charged the moment with meaning. When he spoke, however, focus shifted back to Bo, and not their own two-left-feet dance.

'Bo just told me that he's known I'm not his biological dad since *before* the divorce. Zizzi just let it slip out one day.'

'The more I hear about that woman the less I want to meet her. How can life-changing information just slip out?'

'Zizzi's wired strangely.'

'Hang on.' Sadie made dark connections. 'That means that when she blackmailed you into letting her take Bo halfway across the world . . .'

'Yeah. She knew he already knew.'

'She's evil.'

'If I'd insisted on honesty there and then, I might have been able to bring Bo up here.'

'You weren't to know. You couldn't run the risk of devastating him.'

'There was another reason I didn't insist on honesty. A less noble one.'

Arranging cups on a tray – white cups on a white tray, naturally – Sadie said, 'You couldn't bear the thought of him thinking differently about you, of him not seeing you as his dad.'

'That's my deepest darkest secret.' Hero dropped his chin to stare into Sadie's eyes. 'How'd you know I felt like that?'

'Because that's how I felt with Teddy. We missed so much time together, and she'd been fed such a whopper of a lie about me, I found myself doubting our bond could survive it.' The pressure of tears behind her eyes surprised Sadie. She coughed them away. 'Turns out that kids see everything in broad strokes. I was wrapping her up in cotton wool when all Teddy needed was for me to tell her off. Like a proper mum.'

'We're lucky,' said Hero with feeling. He took the tray. 'In some ways.'

The time had passed to turn such moments into something more. Sadie recognised her feelings. She looked them straight in the face. They all came under the heading of 'love', and she'd met them before. She'd also met 'goodbye' before, and she read that word in Hero's bittersweet expression.

He helped with the tea. He did her bidding. As if a sweet friendship shorn of all sensuality was her consolation prize.

Everyone took a cup. Everyone refused a pastry. Arthur

was content. Mrs Bob was in another world, a grey one we all must visit some time. Grace and Bo were locked into a game of Hangman, which, judging by the snorts of laughter, was filthy.

Somebody was missing.

There he is.

Out on the cobbles, Michael led Noel around, while the hairy little princeling decided where to 'perform'. He saw Sadie was watching, and waved his pooper-scooper.

World weary, Teddy stood with her notes in her hand, all ready to stage her coup of the residents' meeting. 'Mummy,' she said, with a roll of her eyes, 'please get Michael in.'

'Yessir.' Sadie tripped over to the gates, where Noel was midway through the elaborate, bottom-shaking dance that meant he had found the chosen spot. 'Michael,' she began.

He turned to her. His clear eyes, his neat hair, his spruce jumper all conspired to make Sadie veer off course. Instead of summoning him inside, she said, 'I've been thinking about our mutual friend.'

'Who's that?' Michael tried to ignore the huffing and straining at ground level.

'Dorothy Ball.'

He went a painterly pink. 'Oh dear, am I rumbled?'

'Completely.' Sadie looked down. 'Oh, you'd better . . .'

Noel had excelled himself. Sadie looked away as Michael

wielded the pooper scooper. She turned back at the noise of the plastic bag hitting the bin. 'The thing is, Michael' – she said it out loud and it sounded like poetry – 'I'm in love.'

'Me too! It's so wonderful to bond over books.' His shoulders shot up as he recited a couple of titles. '*Daughter of m'Lady*! *Thief of Hearts*!'

Sadie panicked, terrified that her gentle rejection was turning into a declaration. 'Books are magical but they can't change the way you feel about somebody.'

'Surely you can't expect a bookseller to agree?' Michael was playful. He moved nearer.

Sadie braced herself for an embrace in full view of the captive audience in the glass box of Sakura.

'Love's so hard to pin down.' Michael's mouth went to her cheek. Moved to her ear. In a hot whisper he said, 'Sometimes I wonder if my gaydar is broken. I mean, is Hero even gay?'

Sadie froze. 'Michael,' she said slowly, putting her arm through his, 'some wires have been crossed.'

Michael went a much deeper shade of pink as he heard her out. 'He wanted the books for *you*? I helped Hero pick them out and he sent them to you?' He creased up. Giggling so hard he could only squeeze out the words. 'You thought *I* was wooing you?' He had to lean on her.

'I don't have a gaydar *at all*. I just assumed you were straight.'

'And dying of love for you!'

'Yes, okay, it's not *that* hilarious, Michael.'

'Sorry.' Michael put his finger to his lips. He looked contrite. 'I'm laughing now but I'll cry later. I really like that man.'

'But he has a son. And an ex-wife. How did you think . . . ?'

Michael looked as if he pitied her. 'You innocent kitten,' he said.

Sadie reassessed many givens. Kicked herself. Only metaphorically, but later she planned to do it literally. It wasn't only Michael who'd listened when she waxed lyrical about Dorothy.

Hero heard me.

He had always heard her. Even during their estrangement, the books kept coming:

Admired from Afar.

You Should be Mine.

Rivals in Love.

Hero was referring to Jack as his rival; I thought Michael was jealous of Hero.

As they stumbled back, the fairy lights came on. The residents held their communal breath, then let out a delighted 'Aww!' as the lights stayed on. The old mews was softened, flattered. Its flaws were invisible, only its charm remaining, as it glowed in the late September dusk.

At its heart, the cherry blossom tree glimmered like a good deed in a naughty world.

The meeting had to be got through. Sadie would tune out. Use the time to compose the right words to confess her feelings to Hero. To iron out the wrinkles of miscommunication and start afresh.

Even as she crept to her place, Sadie knew she wouldn't have the nerve. She'd have to sleep on it. More than once.

A shifty voice hissed in her ear.

When I was your friend, I helped you speak up.

Sadie reminded alcohol that it had never ever been her friend.

'About time.' Teddy gave her mother a reproving look.

I can't tune out – my girl deserves to be listened to.

'Greetings!' said her girl, pleased with herself. She frowned, looking out over the mews. 'What are *they* doing here?'

Looking in through the curled iron fronds of the gate were the Mogg twins.

'Shit.' Cher sprang up from Jez's lap.

They were shouting.

'Cher!'

'Time to get yourself home, love!'

'There's nothing to keep you here!'

'This stupid job's a joke, darlin'!'

The tone mixed love and menace. The Moggs had come to reclaim their own.

The holiday atmosphere created by the lights dimmed, hardened.

'Cher,' said Sadie, 'do you want to go?'

'No.' Cher took off, in her flat shoes and her jeans that fitted rather than strangled and her shiny ponytail.

'Wait, love.' Jez stood up, too.

'I can fight me own battles.' Cher seemed insulted.

'I know you can.' Jez held out his hand. 'I want to watch you do it.'

Fingers entwined, they approached the twins. Snatches of a conversation carried on through the closed gates, drifting back to Sakura.

The Moggs cajoled with the faux politeness they reserved for maximum intimidation. When the 'Come home, Mum's waiting' tactic didn't work, they pivoted to threats.

'If you don't come with us right now,' said one, 'you'll regret it when you do get home.'

'You know what he means,' the other added.

'I'm not coming home at all,' said Cher.

Sadie swallowed. Made a mental inventory of her clean bedding.

Teddy'll have to sleep in with me.

'Don't be dumb, where'll you go?'

Cher bit her lip. It had been spur-of-the-moment.

Her little shoulders are so narrow.

Sadie wanted to sweep her up.

'She's coming to me.' Jez turned to Cher. 'Aren't you?'

'Yeah, I am. Goodnight, boys.' She stalked back towards the spa, towards Michael's thumbs up and Mary's blown kiss.

Jez, still hanging onto her hand, turned around and walked backwards, addressing the stone faces of the twins. 'She'll make you proud,' he said. 'If you let her.'

'You're free, my darling!' Mary had laboured to her feet.

'That was *brave*,' said Grace.

'Can we shut up and get on with the meeting?' Cher tapped her foot, waiting for Jez to sit so she could reattach herself to his lap.

Outside, one figure remained at the gates. A twin lingered after his brother stalked off. 'Be happy, sis.'

He means it.

Sadie watched Cher try to assimilate such simple kindness. The road to freedom would be potholed, but they'd witnessed a turning point in Cher's life.

She's more like her Uncle Arthur than she knows.

'Everybody calm down.' Teddy wrested the spotlight back. 'I have an aj . . . an ajjy . . . Mum, what *is* that word?'

'Agenda, sweetie.'

Nobody laughed; Teddy had a whiff of Stalin about her. 'Yeah, *that*,' she said. 'First, Mum wanted me to mention Bob and to say we hope the hospice is looking after him.'

'Him again!' Mrs Bob threw up her hands in despair. 'I told you,' she waved a finger at nobody in particular, 'not to bring this up. Bob's doing *fine*. He has a lovely room, nicer than mine, with nurses running in and out, and calling him Bobby, and holding up water for him to sip, and he can see the garden, and he's going in and out of consciousness, and let me tell you that I did *not* sign up for this when we got married. He's leaving me with the caff and all our debts and he's not even worried, just lying there happy as Larry on the morphine, so thanks very much – not – for asking but Bob is fine.'

'As Bob's not here,' ventured Sadie, practising courage for when she cornered Hero at some point in the future, 'I'll say it for him. Mrs Bob, you love him really.'

'I do,' said Mrs Bob. 'I really do. I love that man and I have no idea . . .' – her voice gave in – 'what I'll do without him.'

Another intermission. Mrs Bob allowed herself to be held. She even let the others say inane but comforting things. Some of them cried with her.

Sadie wiped her eyes as they all coughed and composed themselves. Dying is hard work, for everybody involved.

How come I didn't notice how thin Mrs Bob is getting?

'Get on with it.' Mrs Bob blew her nose.

Teddy was ready. 'No register. No minutes. No bins. No nothing. My mummy has something important to say, so *listen*.'

In the day's emotional to and fro, Sadie had almost forgotten the main business of the meeting. She swivelled in her chair. 'Mary,' she said, and that lady fixed her with a shrewd eye, 'we all know you dislike being given advice.'

'In that case, don't give me any,' said Mary.

Arthur tittered, patted her hand.

'Families, however,' said Sadie, 'step over the lines we draw in the sand. We're your family and please don't scoff, because that's the word you used to describe the mews to me. Yes, Mary, I've told everyone your secret.'

Nods all round.

Grace spoke up. 'We know you're Christmas Holdings, our mysterious landlord.'

Fi was enjoying herself. 'You're busted, old lady.'

'Now I know,' said Mrs Bob, 'why our rent went down when Bob fell ill.'

'And I know how I was able to afford such an amazing studio space,' said Grace.

The room seemed to swell as each of them added to the pot.

'Nobody else would take a chance on U-Turn without a huge deposit.'

'Other landlords just laughed at Yummy Mummy because I doodled all over my business plan.'

Sadie went last. 'You gave me somewhere to recover

while I built a business.' She winked at Fi. 'Not to mention bringing me friends for life.'

'But now,' said Hero, 'those days are gone.'

'Cherry Blossom Mews,' said Amber, 'can't stagger on much longer.'

'Time we all got real,' said Mrs Bob.

'Time,' said Sadie, 'we paid more rent.'

Mary closed her eyes. Shook her head 'No'.

'It makes sense,' said Grace. Of all of them, she had the biggest mountain to climb. Grace was practically penniless; the others had given her permission to opt out of the rent rise. She hadn't moaned. She hadn't groaned. She'd found a part-time job. 'We want to pay you back, Mary,' she said.

Another 'No' from Mary. Loud enough and adamant enough to cloud Arthur's brow. He turned to her, concerned.

'Mary, my love?' he quavered.

She patted his hand. The touch quelled his fears. To the others, she said, 'I'm the one paying back. I'm paying Arthur back for the years he sat at his window, watching over me, even though he thought I'd rejected him. He saved me from the flames and didn't even wait to be thanked. Nothing I do can repair the loss of those years, but I owe Arthur. I always pay my debts.'

'Look at it this way,' said Sadie. 'The mews will falter if it keeps running at a loss. Then we'll all be out on our ears, *and* paying astronomical rents to some faceless landlord.'

'We'd much rather,' said Grace, 'pay somebody we love!'

Hero took up the baton. 'We'll see our money making a difference to the mews, plus we'll see you move down to the ground floor and modernise your living space to make things easier for Arthur.'

'Perhaps,' said Amber, blithely leaping into a topic Sadie was afraid to broach, 'you can hire some professional help to look after dear old Arthur.' She put her head on one side, as if Arthur was one of the fluffy animals she sold at Yummy Mummy. 'Bless him,' she added, in case he hadn't been sufficiently patronised.

Arthur wasn't listening. 'Mary?' he said, still anxious.

'Mary?' Sadie echoed him. The plan could only work if Mary accepted their help. This was love at work. Nobody had been coerced, but all had dug deep. Sadie had offered to run the properties, collect rents and arrange repairs. It would be, she suspected, a full-time job on top of her existing full-time job, but love is can-do and she refused to look too hard at the practicalities.

Soon enough, the caff would be re-let. Mrs Bob had intimated she'd like to stay on in the flat above; despite Sadie's certainty that she'd be the most demanding and least cooperative of the tenants, this was good news.

'Will you let us do this, Mary?' she asked. 'For all our sakes?'

'One for all,' said Michael. 'And all for one!'

Mary looked at Arthur. 'This,' she said, 'is the man who rushed into a fire to save me. His packaging lets him down these days, but he's still my Arthur. He deserves the best.' Mary nodded. 'Thank you all very much.'

'There,' said Fi, as everybody relaxed. 'That wasn't so hard, was it, Mazzer?'

'Shush.' Teddy was stern again. They shushed.

Sadie crinkled her brows. This should be the bit where they hugged and went home.

'I have a serious complaint to make.'

'Here we go,' said Mrs Bob.

'Why hasn't anybody in Cherry Blossom Mews noticed that Hero and my mum should be boyfriend and girlfriend?'

'Oooooh dear,' whispered Fi, delighted.

Sadie went red. Rather, she went right through red and found another colour altogether. She felt her nose sweat.

She didn't look at Hero.

Hero didn't look at her.

Everybody else looked from her to Hero and back again. This was spectator sport at its best.

Teddy went on. 'It's obvious that they like each other in, you know, *that* way.' She pulled a disgusted face. 'They keep ignoring it and pretending to be friends when they're dying to . . .' Teddy forced out the word. '*Kiss*. My daddy's great but he's not here so Mum should be getting me a new one, just like she *should* be getting me an iPad.' She paused here for a hard stare. 'Maybe Hero hates me and stays away because I was a bit rude to him when I got here. I made it all go wrong so now I'm putting it right. I do have an excuse, by the way. I didn't want a new dad, then. I wanted me and mum to be together all the time, but I've realised she takes a lot of looking after, so now I want a stand-in daddy, a nice one, who loves my mum and might love me when he gets to know me better.'

There was shocked laughter. Fi was crying, or maybe she had something in her eye.

'I don't hate you, Teddy,' said Hero. He was biting his lip. He seemed excited.

Catching her breath seemed beyond Sadie.

'Stand up, both of you.' Teddy clapped her hands when this command didn't meet with immediate obedience. 'Up!'

They stood, he on one side of Sakura, Sadie on the other.

'I've done loads of research. I used to think everybody got one true love but now I think maybe we get as many as we need. So, let's vote,' said Teddy. 'Put your hand up if you think Hero and my mum are each other's true love.'

Every hand went up. Fi put up both her hands. Bo held up Noel and waved his paws. Arthur put up his hand and asked, 'What's this about?' Mrs Bob blew her nose with her free hand. Amber tried very, very hard to look pleased. Michael seemed to be fighting a surfeit of some emotion, but he stood up and shouted, 'Well? Kiss, you idiots!'

They did as they were told. They kissed in front of everybody. Sadie would remember that kiss forever. It was tender, relieved, with a promise of fire.

A forest fire.

She clung to him like a new bride as the Mewsites hooted, clapped and marvelled, all of them lit by the starry splendour of fairy lights.

'I want you,' said Hero into her hair, so only Sadie could hear. 'I want you so badly, Sadie, and I never stopped.'

'I love you,' she said. Easily. Just like that. She felt his arms tighten.

'I love you too,' he said. 'More,' he laughed. 'Forever. Thank God you came home to me, just like Dorothy Ball suggested.'

She wanted him body and soul. At that particular moment, if she was honest, mainly body. That hunger could be satisfied when they were alone. The need for him, for the way he spoke, for the way he encouraged her, the care he took with her and Teddy, were a feast to enjoy at leisure.

Teddy slipped away from the riot. She had a task to do. A little card fluttered through the slit in the red box.

Dear Daddy

My plan worked. don't be sad. Mummys new boyfriend isn't you but he'll do. i will always love you because everyone only gets one daddy. When you really love people you want them to be. OK so i know this card will make you smile.

i will never stop writing

love Teddy xxxxxxx

ps You would LAUGH YOUR HED OFF if you knew his name.

EPILOGUE

To	Amber <amber@yummymummymews.net.co.uk>, Michael T. <qwertybookshop@hotmail.com>, Cher Mogg <whatulookingatcher@gmail.co.uk>, Hero <hero.smith@u-turn.net>,Fiona J <filove@aol.com>, The Bobs <bob@bobscaff.co.uk>, Jez <jeremy.gray@u-turn.net>, Grace Esparza <Graceth eartist@gmail.com>, Elaine Warnes <ew@snackeryeats.co.uk>
From	Sadie <sakuraspa@gmail.com>
Subject	CHERRY BLOSSOM MEWS RESIDENTS' ASSOCIATION MEETING

Minutes Cherry Blossom Mews Residents' Association Meeting 18/9/19

Hi Guys!

Date	Wednesday 25.9.19
Time	6.30 p.m.
Location	Sakura
Agenda	New tenant

Please make sure Mary knows.

Sadie x

p.s. Read the damn minutes for once – I've been doing them for a WHOLE YEAR and nobody ever bothers to read them!

CHERRY BLOSSOM MEWS RESIDENTS' ASSOCIATION

BOARD MEETING MINUTES

18/9/19

Present: Amber, Grace, Fi, Cher, Mary, Arthur, Mrs Bob, Teddy, Hero, Sadie, Jez, Michael, Elaine.

Proceedings: Meeting called to order at 6.42 p.m. by Chair, Grace.

- Sadie suggested that everybody try and keep this meeting about business for once, and not lapse into gossip, especially as it was the first meeting attended by new resident, Elaine.
- Everybody welcomed Elaine.
- Mrs Bob said she didn't like Elaine's refurbishment of the caff. Mrs Bob said she didn't like the new name and asked what is a snackery anyway?

- Mary warned Mrs Bob to mind her manners.
- Sadie reiterated that residents' meetings are serious and business-based. She brought up the bins.
- Fi blew a raspberry.
- Everybody laughed.
- Teddy fell off her chair.
- Everybody laughed harder.
- Michael said he had a new Dorothy Ball book for Hero and Sadie. Sadie said could he please give it to them outside the meeting as they needed to decide once and for all about the bins.
- Michael ignored her and handed over a copy of *A Year of Bliss* by Dorothy Ball.
- Hero said he wouldn't call it bliss.
- Hero ducked, even though Sadie was only lifting her hand to push back her fringe.
- Grace announced the date of her next exhibition, and confirmed that she had sold all but two of the works from her second annual summer show.
- Amber told Grace she, like, really liked her hair.
- Cher announced that she had finished her Level 4 course in Advanced Aesthetics.
- Everyone clapped.
- Cher asked for a pay rise.
- Sadie said they could discuss that later.

- Cher said that she and Jez needed the money to do up the flat above MOBuk.
- Sadie repeated that they would discuss it later.
- Mary asked if everybody remembered how Cher used to dress.
- Cher said, 'Do not embarrass me, old lady.'
- Fi suggested they all have a glass of champagne to celebrate the wicked witch of the west going to prison.
- Teddy reminded Fi 'That's my granny' and announced she would be visiting regularly.
- Hero reminded Fi that he and his wife were alcoholics, but said they could stretch to Coca-Cola.
- Fi and Cher handed out drinks.
- Sadie suggested they get back to business.
- Arthur sang a song.
- Grace asked how many times Arthur had recognised Mary that week.
- Mary consulted her notepad. 'Four times.' She added that she lived for those moments.
- Amber asked when Arthur and Mary were going to get married.
- Mary said they would continue to live in sin, as she felt the phrase had a ring to it.
- Sadie said she was going to give up about the bins.

- Almost everybody said 'Good'.
- Sadie was within her rights to go off in a huff but she didn't.
- Sadie said, 'It's one year tomorrow since we lost Bob.'
- Mrs Bob interrupted to say they hadn't lost Bob, he wasn't a keyring.
- Sadie apologised.
- Amber invited them all to the Yummy Mummy for a vegan extravaganza in memory of Bob.
- After a vote, residents decided against the vegan extravaganza in favour of bacon baps at Mrs Bob's flat.
- Amber conceded that would probably be nicer.
- Grace asked Mrs Bob what her real name was.
- Mrs Bob said, 'Mrs Bob is my real name, you cheeky cow.'
- Even though Sadie had expressly asked her not to bring up personal topics during meetings, Fi asked when was Teddy's next appointment for her overgrown leg treatment.
- Sadie told them there were only two treatments to go and that Teddy was responding well.
- Teddy showed them how well she was responding by pirouetting.
- Arthur sang another song. Quite a long one.

- Sadie said, 'It meant the world to me that I could be there for Teddy this time around, that we faced it together.'
- Teddy said, 'Mum, you tell Fi off for being personal at meetings and now you're doing it.'
- Amber noted that Fi had lost weight.
- Fi denied this.
- Fi reported she had eaten a five pack of Kit-Kats that afternoon.
- Fi reaffirmed that she is 'off men'.
- Amber said the guy who laid the new floor tiles in Yummy Mummy was asking about Fi.
- Fi said, 'Give him my number.'
- Sadie asked if they were all following Amber's new Instagram.
- Arthur asked what an Instagram was.
- Amber showed everyone her new Instagram, consisting of make-up free selfies; part of a campaign to highlight mental health awareness.
- Amber winked at Sadie.
- Sadie winked back.
- Noelle broke wind.
- Mary reported that the last of Noelle's puppies had gone to a good home. There followed various reminiscences of the day they realised Noel was not only a girl dog but a pregnant girl dog.

Blame was once again laid at Sadie's door for allowing Noel/Noelle to consort with a dubious labradoodle during his/her daily walk, resulting in strange puppies.

- Hero played the meeting a Viber video from Bo, telling everyone he missed them and he couldn't wait to get back home to the mews.
- Hero admitted he was still coming to terms with his son's rainbow striped Mohican.
- Arthur blew a kiss at the screen and said, 'Bo.'
- Teddy said she missed her brother.
- Fi said could they please get a sodding move on.
- Sadie thought that each time they all got together like this she appreciated them all anew.
- Sadie thought that they were her friends and her family; possibly they were 'framily'?
- Sadie looked at Hero because she could look at him forever and not get bored.
- After a moment, Hero looked at Sadie, because he always knows when she is looking at him.
- Sadie thought how she had got used to the idea of being loved by him, how her new normal was wonderful, how she still got annoyed at him when he left his mug in the sink instead of the dishwasher but luckily she would still rather tear his clothes off than bicker.

- Sadie thought the Mewsites would never let her hear the end of it if they knew her soppy inner feelings, but it was probably safe to write them down as NOBODY EVER READS THE MINUTES.

Acknowledgements

I'm hugely grateful to some wise friends for their advice on legal matters touched on in this book: Alison Last Anderson, Michael Anderson and Elizabeth Dean.

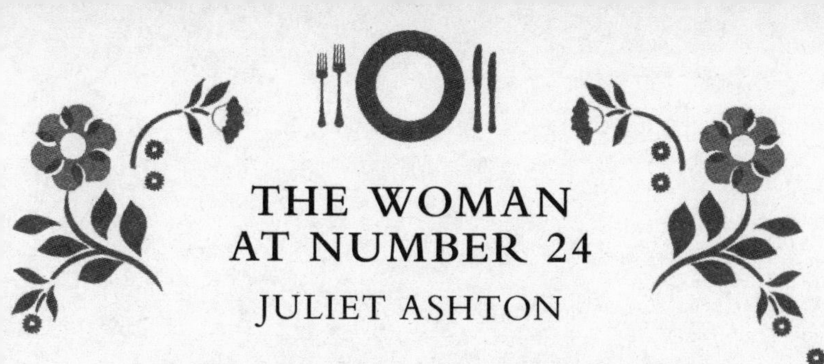

THE WOMAN AT NUMBER 24

JULIET ASHTON

Welcome to number 24, a Georgian villa in West London that is home to five separate families and five very different lives.

Up in the eaves, Sarah finds that recovering from a nasty divorce is even more heartbreaking when your ex-husband lives one floor beneath you with his new wife. Their happiness floats up through the floorboards, taunting her. A child psychologist, Sarah has picked up great sadness from the little girl, Una, who lives with her careworn mother three floors below, but is Sarah emotionally equipped to reach out?

Spring brings a new couple to number 24. Jane and Tom's zest for life revives the flagging house, and Sarah can't deny the instant attraction to handsome Tom. Having seen at first-hand what infidelity does to people, she'll never act on it… but the air fizzes with potential.

The sunshine doesn't reach every corner of number 24, however. Elderly Mavis, tucked away in the basement, has kept the world at bay for decades. She's about to find out that she can't hide forever…

Love, rivalry and secrets … all under one roof.

AVAILABLE NOW IN
PAPERBACK AND EBOOK